Treasured
by
Thursday

Also by Catherine Bybee

Contemporary Romance

Weekday Brides Series

Wife by Wednesday
Married by Monday
Fiancé by Friday
Single by Saturday
Taken by Tuesday
Seduced by Sunday

Not Quite Series

Not Quite Dating
Not Quite Mine
Not Quite Enough
Not Quite Forever

Paranormal Romance

MacCoinnich Time Travels

Binding Vows
Silent Vows
Redeeming Vows
Highland Shifter
Highland Protector

The Ritter Werewolves Series

Before the Moon Rises
Embracing the Wolf

Novellas

Soul Mate
Possessive

Erotica

Kilt Worthy
Kilt-A-Licious

CATHERINE BYBEE

Treasured by Thursday

BOOK SEVEN IN THE
WEEKDAY BRIDES SERIES

Published by Montlake Romance, Seattle

www.apub.com

Amazon, the Amazon logo, and Montlake Romance are trademarks of Amazon.com, Inc., or its affiliates.

ISBN-13: 9781477828045
ISBN-10: 1477828044

Cover design by Crystal Posey

Printed in the United States of America

This one is for Tiffany Snow.
New friends that get you are just as cherished
as old friends that know you!

Chapter One

Hunter Blackwell focused on his target and meandered through the crowd, turning heads of several women in his wake. It had been a long time. And although he seldom asked old friends for favors, he marched toward one now without a backward glance. If the rumors were true, half of his problems could be solved in a few short days.

Without any concern for the discussion he might be interrupting, Hunter moved behind his old friend, made sure those that could see him did, and lifted his chin.

The conversation died as the man in front of him turned and tilted his head.

A smile spread over Blake Harrison's face. "Blackwell."

"Your Grace."

Blake shot a laugh in the air and extended his hand.

Hunter accepted the man-hug and let a shiver of satisfaction wash over him as Blake Harrison apologized to his audience for the interruption, and then offered Hunter his complete attention.

"My God, man . . . how long has it been? Eight years, nine?"

"Texas," Hunter reminded his friend. "I believe you were marrying your wife for the third time."

Blake stared beyond him for a moment and let a memory take hold. "That had to be the craziest wedding to date." The notion of marrying the same woman, repeatedly, was ludicrous. The fact that Blake and his wife never divorced yet proceeded to remarry every year was certifiable. In some circles, the running theory was Blake's *player ways* had never changed, and he needed to reaffirm his vows annually to keep his wife happy.

Those who knew the duke, however, knew nothing could be further from the truth. Blake and Samantha Harrison had a marriage meant for the big screen. Young girls would pine over it, and happy bachelors would run.

"Married life is agreeing with you." Hunter might have come off as if making conversation, but his old friend did indeed appear to have a glow around his eyes and a few extra healthy-looking pounds a man might acquire from a settled life.

"I will let Sam know you approve."

He laughed. Chances were Sam wouldn't remember Hunter. They'd met at said wedding, where she had been busy renewing her vows—again.

Hunter nodded toward the back of the massive hall, where the crowd celebrating the retirement of a fellow entrepreneur turned philanthropist thinned. "Do you have a minute?"

Blake narrowed his dark brows and lifted a hand for Hunter to lead the way.

They wound around a dozen colleagues, old friends, and even older enemies before they found a quiet corner where it would be obvious they were having a private conversation. With any luck, they wouldn't be interrupted.

"You're a man on a mission," Blake said without judgment.

"Aren't I always?" Hunter had spent that last decade of his life with one goal in mind. Win. Didn't matter what he was doing, what business venture he'd taken on . . . what investment to dive into . . . his goal was to win.

"I've already given you the investment advice I have to offer."

"This isn't about an investment." *Well, not really.* "I despise skirting around the issues."

Blake grinned. "Then don't. You don't have to put on airs with me."

One of the qualities Hunter liked most about his old friend. "Certain circles tell me that your wife has her own business."

Blake kept his smile, but the way his eyes narrowed told Hunter he was walking close to an edge.

"She does."

"I believe she can assist me."

"Looking to remove your eligibility status, Blackwell?"

A slight weight lifted from his chest. Seemed his sources were right. "The Forbes list made my life more difficult than you can imagine."

"I don't know about that. I have a vivid imagination."

Hunter knew how vivid Blake's imagination could be. "Can she help?"

Blake reached to the inside pocket of his jacket and removed a single card from the back of his own business cards. He tapped the small paper on the edge of his hand and cocked his head. "You have to understand . . . I have nothing to do with Alliance. I can't guarantee Sam and her girls will accept you as a client."

"Accept me?"

Blake let his smile reach his eyes again. "My wife is meticulous when screening clients. If any of the women in her employ find a reason to dismiss you, you have to be willing to walk away."

Hunter thought of his goals, offered an innocent smile. "Women love me."

"Which works well when finding a date, not the same when searching for a wife. Fair warning, Blackwell: if they pass you over, I won't step in on your behalf."

Blake offered him Samantha's business card.

Taking his time, he took it and tucked it away without a glance. "I'm not worried."

Blake chuckled. "I know you, Blackwell . . . and I know my wife. Not only should you be worried, you might want to find plan B to whatever problems you have."

"I'm not the same kid I once was."

"None of us are. I just hope you've learned to take rejection better than your earlier years. I seem to remember you using your fist on occasion to get your point across."

"I think we were both guilty of that."

Blake considered his observation. "You were caught."

"You were the son of a duke. Rather untouchable, if I recall."

"True. Sam rejects violence of any kind."

"Amazing things happen when you can fix your problems with diplomacy and money. You grow up and stop fighting."

Blake shook his head. "We still fight, just not with our fists."

Hunter flexed his fingers and motioned toward the host bar. "How about a drink?"

"I'm so embarrassed."

"It's perfectly normal."

Gabi Masini glanced at her British friend, then to the smashed-up back end of her Lexus. She swore the person backing out of the other parking space signaled for her to go.

When the man in the other car smacked into her—or maybe she backed into him—they both emerged from their cars. Only the fifty-something *I've eaten too many doughnuts* man was waving his fist and screaming at her in a language she didn't recognize. Considering Gabi was fluent in three and working her way through a fourth, she still didn't comprehend the man. Anger, however, didn't require a language to understand.

It didn't take long for the private sensors on the car to notify the security team. That team happened to be close by, and Gabi's shame was witnessed by Gwen and her husband, Neil.

Neil walked past the cars, shoved himself between the irate driver and Gabi, and spoke in a low tone.

"Accidents happen," Gwen said while placing an arm around her.

"This is the second one in a month."

Gabi didn't want to consider the two that elevated her car insurance shortly after she'd relocated to Southern California.

"You lived on an island that only provided golf carts for years."

"I've been in California for eighteen months."

Gwen sucked in a breath and didn't comment.

"I'm the worst driver ever."

"Don't be absurd. There *has* to be others worse than you."

Where are they?

Neil walked toward them, his face as stern as the tight grip of control he always wore. He reached out a hand, palm up.

Gabi knew, instinctively, what he wanted. The keys dangling in her fingers rattled as she handed them over.

"I'm sorry."

Neil lifted one eyebrow before turning his gaze to his wife. "Drive her home. I'll be there shortly."

Gwen turned on her perfectly polished pedicure and started walking away.

Gabi had no choice but to follow. "Wait." She moved back to the car and pulled twice on the back door before the metal relented and let her in. She removed the mail and a handful of groceries she'd been in the shopping center acquiring and hauled them to Gwen's waiting car.

For several miles, Gabi pleaded her case, to which Gwen listened but didn't comment.

"I'm an awful driver," Gabi finally relented.

Gwen cautiously maneuvered onto an off-ramp and headed down the familiar Tarzana street where Gabi lived. "I'm going to have to agree with you. Four accidents in less than two years is above average."

"Maybe I should move back to New York. No one owns a car in New York."

"And when was the last time you lived in that city?" Gwen asked.

"I was a teenager. I barely graduated before Val was pulling my mother and me out of the city and onto the island." Her brother, Valentino Masini, owned and operated a resort on a private island in the Keys where golf carts shuttled guests. Gabi had lived on the island, sheltered, taken care of, up until eighteen months before her fourth car accident. With Val moving on with his life, a wife and an island to keep his attention, Gabi took control of hers and moved to the other side of the country, where not driving a real car wasn't an option. Public transportation in Southern California was difficult at best, unworkable at all other times. Nerves got the best of Gabi her first few months in the state. Then she seemed to do better. Only the last month she had a hard time keeping from playing bumper cars with others on the road . . . or in parking lots.

"Chances are you'd simply replace one worry with another if you moved back to New York."

Yeah . . . Gwen was right. Not to mention California was where her job was . . . where she'd found her backbone again. She couldn't abandon the state because she failed to stay within the lines of her side of the road. "Maybe I should take lessons?"

Gwen pulled into the driveway. "Or maybe we should hire you a driver."

"Oh, that's silly."

Gwen twisted the key and cut the engine before glancing over her shoulder.

Gabi squirmed in the passenger seat. "Every sixteen-year-old acne-faced kid learns how to drive. I think I have more on them."

Gwen, channeling her husband, who often said so much by not saying anything at all, silently pushed out of the car and walked up the short path to the front door.

A series of numbers on a keypad let her in. From there she moved to another monitor system that alerted the team that the resident of the house had breached the walls. Gabi set her bags on the kitchen counter, dropped the mail onto the table.

She moved about the room, depositing groceries where they belonged. "Was it hard for you to adjust to driving on the right side of the road when you moved here?"

Gwen told her about her adjustments to driving in the States, which apparently weren't nearly as difficult as Gabi's.

By the time Neil arrived, Gabi had exhausted her excuses for being a poor driver and conceded that something had to change before someone got hurt.

Then Neil delivered a series of facts that took some of her control away . . . at least temporarily.

"Your car is in for repairs, your insurance company has suspended your ability to hold them accountable until an investigation has taken place."

"Can they do that?" Gabi asked.

"They can and have. Renting a car without insurance isn't possible."

"Seems a bit extreme," Gwen said.

Neil stood silent for a moment. "The man she hit *this time* is a lawyer and had a call into Gabriella's insurance company before the tow managed to pull into the shop."

"Oh, no."

"Oh, yes." Neil removed his wallet and found a business card. "Here is the company Blake uses. I've already spoken with our contact there, they need thirty minutes' notice and they will drive you wherever you need to go."

Gabi pulled a long strand of her dark brown hair over her shoulder and glanced at the card. "That must be terribly expensive."

"It's this or a lawsuit. A taxi is another option, but in light of the majority of work and contacts you have, a private driver might prove best," Neil encouraged.

"How can I convince the insurance company to reinstate my coverage?" Because Gabi knew once her car was fixed, she still wouldn't be able to drive it without insurance.

"I have a call in for that answer. In the meantime, use the service."

Gwen placed a kiss to each side of Gabi's face before following her husband out the door.

Before Neil and Gwen turned the corner of the quiet street, Gabi's phone was ringing.

The name on the display had her sucking in a breath for support. Word traveled fast. She lifted the phone, closed her eyes, and pressed the answer button. "It wasn't my fault."

"What?" Samantha Harrison, otherwise known as Gabi's boss and new friend, didn't laugh or lay the blame on her.

"I thought he motioned for me to back up. I'm much better than when I first arrived."

"What are you talking about?"

Gabi sucked in her bottom lip. "You, ah . . . you don't know?"

"If I knew, I wouldn't pretend otherwise. What isn't your fault?"

"Minor fender-bender in the parking lot. No one was hurt."

Gabi thought she heard Sam groan. "And it wasn't your fault?"

She waved a hand in the air, as if Sam could see. "No. Of course not. So if you're not calling about the accident, what can I do for you?" Her thinly veiled attempt to change the subject as quickly as possible was met with a tiny laugh.

"I have a client I need you to crunch some numbers on."

Numbers . . . she could do that. Gabi was a savant with numbers. "Give me a name and the access code to your file and I'm on it."

Gabi jotted down the name and code. Hunter Blackwell. J836AY9

"Numbers is all you need from me?"

"No. Actually . . . I need more than a bottom-line portfolio report. Mr. Blackwell is an old friend of Blake's, so I'm giving him an extra chance. Based on what I've already learned, I would have encouraged him to look elsewhere for the future Mrs. Blackwell."

If there was one thing Gabi had discovered about her boss, the woman scrutinized every client, both male and female, with a high-powered microscope. She looked beyond any tabloid fodder and water-cooler gossip to determine the truth behind the persona. Nearly every male client searching for a bride had a driving reason for doing so, and sometimes they weren't forthcoming with their backgrounds. Sam always found the skeletons, displayed them for her clients to see, then determined their worthiness based on their reaction to the facts. Most high-powered men willing to part with over seven figures for a bride hated having their dirty parts displayed. They especially didn't like a woman advertising it.

If at any time during the initial meeting with Sam or now Gabi, they felt the slightest bit threatened, the meeting ended, and the ability to do business with the client dissolved.

"What has you dismissing him so quickly?"

"The few bits of information about the man available have recently been laced with an assault charge. The charges were dropped long before the case could see a judge. Then there was an accusation that Mr. Blackwell had been found with three women in the back of his limo after a fundraiser in Dallas."

"Since when do we listen to the gossip magazines?"

"We don't," Sam defended. "But one of the girls was allegedly seventeen. I'm digging into that now. But if this guy likes underage girls, I'm not setting him up with anyone."

Warning bells rang inside Gabi's head. "How soon will we know the facts?"

"I have a few people working on it now. In the meantime, I need his numbers crunched."

The warning bell rang a second time.

"Sounds like a risk."

"He is. But my head isn't in this right now with Jordan back in the hospital. I know I'm distracted and wouldn't want my personal life to interfere with my business."

"Oh, Sam . . . I'm sorry. I hadn't heard." Samantha's sister Jordan had lost her ability to really live much of a life years before. As a young woman, Jordan attempted to take her life and ended up having a massive stroke, leaving her severely compromised. Gabi didn't know all the details, but she did know that Samantha and Blake cared for the now thirty-year-old woman out of their home. A twenty-four-hour private nurse still couldn't keep away some of the decay and issues being stuck in a wheelchair without all her faculties created.

Since Gabi had moved to California, Jordan had been admitted to the hospital at least half a dozen times.

"So you'll take care of Blackwell?"

"Consider it done. Do you want me to meet with him?"

"Would you?"

"Don't be silly. Once the files from your contacts are uploaded in the system, I'll contact Mr. Blackwell for a meeting."

Sam sighed into the phone. "Perfect. And if you're not happy with him . . . with anything . . . feel free to dismiss him as a client. I trust your judgment."

Gabi hesitated. "But he's Blake's friend."

"Blake knew him and his brother in high school. They kept in touch the first couple of years in college, but they'd never been terribly close. Blake offered some advice over the years, but that's it. He made it perfectly clear that our decision wouldn't come between them."

Some of the tension inside Gabi's shoulders eased. "Do you want me to tell you of my decision before I tell the client?"

"No need. I've got too much going on. Listen, Jordan's cardiologist is on the other line. I've got to go."

"Go. Call if you need anything."

"I will." Without any more, Sam hung up.

Gabi prepared a cup of strong tea and moved into the home office. She sat at a desk that held three massive screens. She opened up the main computer, moved to the interface that linked to Sam's. Within a couple of minutes, she'd opened Hunter Blackwell's file.

She skimmed over the contact and personal profile information. It didn't matter to Gabi if the man was six two or four eleven. She could care less if he'd been married before or if he had children. All Gabi focused on was the numbers.

Really big numbers.

Hunter Blackwell recently made the Forbes list of eligible billionaires and was quickly referred to as high risk for making the list of "Billionaires and Their Outrageous Scandals" that Forbes would post at the end of the year.

Before jumping into the numbers, Gabi cross-referenced the media hype to determine why Blackwell was on Forbes's radar.

Hours later, her head still buzzing with the caffeinated tea, Gabi heard the grandfather clock sounding once. A crusty plate sat on her otherwise clean desk; three tea bags were now drying beside an empty cup.

She printed out the files she needed and noted the automated change in code to the Blackwell file before switching off her computers.

Gabi tapped the edges of the papers together and leaned back in her chair.

Her body screamed with the hours of inactivity as she stood and walked out of the office.

"Well, Mr. Blackwell. You better be an exceptional man in person or you're going to have to plead to your latest Bambi to marry you and not take you for all you're worth."

Chapter Two

Gabi shoved her nerves into submission and channeled Samantha as she sat in the coffee shop. The site of client meetings never changed. The Starbucks sat in the center of town and had a constant flow of patrons. The location was safe and easily found. Alliance didn't have an office outside of the room in Gabi's Tarzana residence. There were five mainframe computers scattered over the States, but Tarzana was the main house. Inviting a client for a formal meeting in an official office wasn't part of the program.

While Gabi had accepted a few male clients over the past year and a half, she'd yet to meet one as wealthy, and apparently difficult, as the one she was meeting today.

Knowing that 70 percent of her decision was already made, Gabi felt her palms itch. As much as she liked to think her unwelcomed fear of unknown men was controlled . . . it wasn't. Days like this made her realized the magnitude of her fraudulent life.

To make matters worse, Gabi forgot to download a picture of Hunter Blackwell before she left home. She was reduced to searching for images on the Internet, of which there were very few. Very few, very hidden, or very old. How he managed to stay relatively incognito while making the Forbes list was impressive.

If Sam wasn't at that moment in the hospital with her sister, Gabi would have made a quick call to get a lock on the basics of Hunter Blackwell's face.

She gave up on her search and glanced at her phone for the fourth time before tucking it into her purse. Ten minutes.

Her heart sped.

One slow breath followed by a meditative exhale had her pulse slowing.

She watched those entering the coffee shop. A family with two young boys harping for something filled with chocolate, who hung on their mother's legs. A half dozen college students huddled around a group table with laptops and cell phones plugged into the outlets available. Some of them had notepads while others sat quietly with their ears filled with music, lessons . . . or any number of things.

Gabi sipped her tea and glanced at the door every time it opened. Asian couple . . . not Blackwell. Two teenage girls. A pot-bellied sixtysomething in shorts and flip-flops . . . definitely not Blackwell.

Then came two suits . . . men wearing business attire, one slightly taller than the other. They spoke in low tones and moved through the line. At no time did they look around the room.

Gabi glanced at her watch.

Five minutes.

Tapping her fingers, she forced another deep breath. Then the door opened, someone beyond the panes of glass held the door open for a flustered woman pushing a stroller. "Thank you," the woman said to the man beside her.

For one brief moment, Gabi passed over the family as just that.

Then the woman with the infant pushed away and left him.

Gabi's heart raced.

Crisp and polished, Hunter Blackwell emerged. He stood an easy six four . . . maybe even taller. His suit made the other men in the room look as if they were wearing flannel. A firm-cut jaw with what looked like a scar under his left ear. Not that it took away from the man's appearance. "Dangerously handsome" had been used in a few tabloids she'd read, and they were spot-on. His full head of light brown hair and gray eyes scanned the room. They passed over her once and quickly returned.

Gabi felt her bottom lip curling in and forced the nervous habit away.

With her hand wound in a tight knot in her lap, she watched his slow descent.

Samantha's tutelage ran through her like a tape. Another mantra, one easier to remember, came from her sister-in-law, Meg . . . *fake it till you make it.*

Gabi held Mr. Blackwell's immediate future in her hands. She had something he wanted, and that empowered her.

At least it should.

"Mr. Blackwell." Gabi didn't bother standing . . . a slightly intimidating tactic Samantha had taught her.

"Miss Masini." His smooth voice was an octave below most.

She felt her heart speeding for entirely different reasons.

"Please, sit." Gabi indicated the chair beside her and forced a smile.

Hunter Blackwell unbuttoned his jacket and took a seat.

"I took the liberty of ordering you coffee," she told him.

Gabi glanced at the barista behind the counter and returned her eyes to the man in front of her.

"And if I don't care for coffee?"

So that's how this was going to be. Gabi felt her pulse slow . . . slightly. "A temp . . . I believe her name was Natalie, said you drank three cups, black, every morning before you took your first call. You appear to be a man who cuts the fluff, Mr. Blackwell."

He smiled, showing a divot in his chin.

"Coffee it is then."

Gabi signaled the barista.

For a brief moment, they spoke of the traffic, the warm day.

Once the employee left the coffee on the table, Mr. Blackwell took his obligatory sip and settled into his chair.

"So how do we proceed?"

Gabi glanced at her watch . . . set her internal timer.

"I'm in the business of matching people, Mr. Blackwell. No one slips through our proven system."

His left eye twitched. "I'm listening."

Whether Hunter Blackwell knew it or not . . . that was his only warning. "Have you ever been arrested?"

"Yes," he answered without hesitation.

"Care to elaborate?"

He shook his head. "I assume Blake's wife found all she needed in *that* file."

She had. The man had been arrested, released, and charges dropped a minimum of four times. Two in the last few years, two more before he was eighteen. The man knew Gabi had done her research, so she moved on.

"Have you ever hit a woman?"

"No." His answer was quick and difficult to dispute.

"Ever wanted to?"

He paused. "I saw a woman leave her child in a hot car once . . . the thought occurred to me. Other than that, no."

Gabi couldn't confirm his claim . . . couldn't deny it, either.

"Have you ever *harmed* a woman?" The question was her own. Gabi had a second set of questions that weren't a part of Sam's list.

"According to many . . . I have. But if you're referring to physically . . . no. I hold no responsibility to women claiming to love what they don't know."

So the tabloids were right about the player inside the billionaire.

The arrogant man didn't even appear to care that he'd broken hearts in the attempt to have a good time. Gabi wondered how many women fell for his devastating smile and natural charm.

Pushing past his exterior, it was time for Gabi to fire questions. "I need the name of your closest friend."

He shrugged. "I don't have a close friend."

Not the answer she expected. The tug at Gabi's heart threatened to kill the interview. "Everyone has a friend."

"I have enemies, Miss Masini . . . people who want a piece of me. I don't think of anyone as a close friend. Not someone I confide in."

A shadow passed over his gray eyes.

She shook off the feeling of déjà vu and continued.

"Who is your biggest enemy?"

He laughed. Tossed his head back and caught the attention of the coffee shop. "I've been told since I was a child that *I* would be my greatest enemy."

"So that's your answer?"

Hunter Blackwell's jaw twitched. "My enemies are too many to count. I'm sure your research has taught you that, too."

It had, which told Gabi that Hunter Blackwell's future bride would be in danger regardless of the disposition of the husband.

"Why are you looking for a wife, Mr. Blackwell?"

He held his chin high, narrowed his gaze on hers. "As I explained to Mrs. Harrison, the Forbes list of eligible bachelors has made my life a maze of insanity. I need a year to escape the chaos and refocus. Removing my eligibility status will clear my head of dating and temporary relationships. Sounds trivial, but the amount of women claiming I've slept with them and promised a ring has tripled in the last year. It's tiring, Miss Masini."

He did look a little fatigued, but that wasn't the answer she was looking for.

"Are you sure there's nothing else?"

He shook his head.

Too bad.

Gabi pushed her tea aside and gathered her purse from the floor. She looked at her watch . . . four minutes had passed since Hunter Blackwell sat down. She was one minute under her limit. "Thank you for considering Alliance, Mr. Blackwell. But at this time we're going to have to pass on any future contractual relationship."

She stood.

He was up and in front of her in a second. "Excuse me?"

"We're going to pass."

He shook his head. "Why?"

Instead of laying out all her cards, she started with the easiest. "I asked you for one name . . . someone you considered a friend . . . nothing. I asked you for an enemy . . . again your answer was nothing. I've sat across from politicians who are more forthcoming than you. Honesty is something Alliance holds sacred. Without it, two parties entering marriage can have devastating results. I wouldn't allow my sister to marry you, Mr. Blackwell, let alone a client."

She started to walk away, felt his hand on her elbow.

Without thought, she flinched, pulled away, and placed a foot between them.

Mr. Blackwell dropped her arm immediately. "I can send a list of potential enemies within the hour. As for friends . . . I can call Blake Harrison an old acquaintance, but can't say I've spent any time with the man in over a decade."

"I'm sorry."

He moved in front of her. "I need a wife," he said under his breath.

She swallowed her fear and took a closer step. "Then I suggest you ask your latest conquest for the privilege. Alliance isn't going to help you."

Gabi pushed around him, headed for the door.

"This isn't over."

She glanced over her shoulder, noticed more than one set of eyes watching them. "I'm afraid it is." With one last look at a man who on the surface was a woman's dream, she shoved through the swinging glass doors and out of the building.

She climbed into the back of the waiting car and noticed the darkened gaze of one ticked-off billionaire following her as they drove away.

Holy shit.

Hunter's eyes fell on the slim butt and long legs in a tight-fitting skirt as Gabriella Masini marched across the street toward a waiting car. A driver jumped out and opened her door. Without realizing his own actions, he followed the car with his eyes as his future sped away.

That did not just happen.

He'd walked in expecting an entirely different outcome.

If there was one thing Hunter was not accustomed to, it was losing.

A dry gust of hot wind propelled him to his car. Unlike Miss Masini, he liked to drive himself. Well, when he was in LA, in any event.

Once he was settled behind the steering wheel, he pressed the phone command. Instead of calling his office, he phoned his private investigator.

"If it isn't Mr. Blackwell," the man on the line answered with an edge of superiority.

"I need you to look someone up for me."

"You sound pissed."

"I'm not calling to chat, Remington. Do you have a pen?"

"I'm ready."

"Gabriella Masini. This is acquisitions and mergers," Hunter said.

"Someone is out for blood."

Hunter called Remington when he wanted dirt. Acquiring every possible piece of information on a conquest was paramount for success, and something he did with every person he did business with. He hadn't felt the need with Samantha Harrison's employee. A mistake he made with Miss Masini that he wouldn't make twice. Hunter knew that Blake's wife wasn't running his show, so he felt no remorse in digging into one of the duchess's employees now. Any woman with the flawless skin, smooth speech, and legs that shot to her luscious breasts had to have dirt. No one had ever turned their back, dismissing him, after five minutes of conversation.

She obviously didn't know who she was dealing with.

"I want every possible spec on this one, Remington, and I want it by morning."

Remington blew out a breath. "That's not much time, Deep Pockets."

"I want something by the morning. I'll keep you on the payroll so long as the information continues to come in."

"You're the boss."

Well at least someone recognizes that.

Chapter Three

Maybe the lack of a car thing wouldn't be so bad. Yoga in front of a TV was just as effective . . . right?

Gabi leaned into a warrior two, reached for the ceiling, and really hoped those who monitored the house system weren't watching her fold onto herself.

Not that she looked bad in her tight-knit workout clothing. She was in the best shape of her life. Strange how tragedy and road-blocks in life resulted in two options . . . they killed you or made you stronger.

She reminded herself that life without a car was yet one more roadblock. A detour that wouldn't knock her down.

She realized, too late, that the instructor on the DVD had already moved on to the next pose, and Gabi took a deep breath and tried to think of something other than the fact that she didn't have a car in the driveway.

What if she needed emergency ice cream? She was a woman, and there were times emergency ice cream was in order.

Gabi leaned past her reverse warrior and grabbed a pen from the coffee table. Without a piece of paper, she wrote "ice cream" on her hand in an effort to remember to place an extra half gallon in her shopping cart on her next trip to the store.

When the doorbell rang, she lost her concentration completely and gave up on DVD yoga. She clicked off the set and reached for a towel.

The bell buzzed again and Gabi pulled the door open in a rush.

All she saw was a lush bouquet of tropical flowers that reminded her of Florida.

The man peeking behind the stems paused when he saw her. His eyes ran down her frame and slowly made their way back up.

He had to be in his early forties . . . much older than a floral delivery boy. At least in her experience.

"Can I help you?"

"I-I am looking for a Gabriella Masini." The rough quality of the man's voice suggested a pack-a-day habit . . . maybe more.

"That's me."

"Well," he said, his eyes took her in again. "These are for you."

Gabi quickly felt too underdressed to encourage a delivery man into her house. Not to mention the suggestive way he was looking at her.

"Wait here," she said as she slid the door shut and retrieved a five-dollar bill from her purse. She returned and handed him the money. "Sorry. I needed to grab a tip."

The man smiled, and some of his edge faded. "No problem." He thrust the flowers into her hands and then pulled a tiny notebook from his back pocket. "Just need you to sign."

"OK." She hoisted the massive bouquet in her left hand and signed with her right.

"Have a good day, Miss Masini."

"Thank you."

The man took a final look before returning to his car in the drive.

She closed the front door with a hip and moved to the hall table. The explosion of color and fragrant buds were a nice addition to the room. She should grace her home with fresh flowers more often, she mused. Then she found a folded card tucked into the blooms.

For a moment, she thought maybe they were from her brother . . . maybe Meg.

Only the flowers weren't from her family.

The card said simply: *You don't have a sister.* And it was signed *HB*.

It took Gabi three reads before she realized who had sent the flowers.

Then she remembered her parting words to Hunter Blackwell. *I wouldn't let my sister marry you, Mr. Blackwell, let alone a client.*

She chuckled and sniffed the flowers. "Flowers won't work, Mr. Blackwell."

The man had unethical, untrustworthy, and underhanded written all over him . . . but he had superb taste in flowers.

———

"That's one sexy kitten you've found there, Blackwell."

Chatting with Remington was right up there with a root canal.

"Cut to the chase." Hunter gripped the phone to his car as he stood facing the corner office window, where he was met with a crisp view of LA.

"She is living at the address I found."

Sending flowers was the perfect way of confirming someone's address.

"Great, what else?"

"Like I told you earlier, the driver is from a service. Your sex kitten doesn't have a car in the drive and no windows into the garage. Much as I wanted to nose around, that house is wired like Fort Knox."

"Wired?"

"Cameras everywhere. A sophisticated alarm system at the door. It's impressive."

Hunter leaned against the massive pane of glass that separated him from a forty-story drop. "And what is Miss Masini afraid of?"

"That's what I wanted to know. Then I found a hidden fact . . ."

Hunter's jaw twitched. Remington paused for drama. "I'm waiting."

"Miss Masini isn't Miss Masini. She's Mrs. Picano."

"She's married?" *That*, Hunter didn't expect. Equally annoying, his gut twisted.

"Widowed."

Hunter sat on that for a minute. "Let me guess, she married some old shit who died?" The woman marrying some rich sugar daddy for money, just like Alliance claimed to support, made more sense.

"Nope. A young shit, and from a few old tabloids I found, they were all lovey-dovey and kissy-wissy." Remington added a few sound effects over the line.

"Do you know how he died?"

"Now this is where it gets interesting. Are you sitting down?"

"You're pissing me off, Remington. Out with it."

"Gunshot wounds . . . as in many."

"Law enforcement? Military?"

"Nope! Owned a winery from what I can tell. Details around his death are very tight. I might need a little more persuading to break some of these walls."

Hunter might as well slash his wrists now for all the bleeding Remington was going to take for this one.

Three hours later, and a whole lot lighter in the wallet, Hunter had the one piece of information he needed to force Miss Masini to bend to his will. Just in case it wasn't enough, he was sending

Remington to Florida. Leech had better come back with his weight in gold.

The phone on his desk buzzed. His secretary's line lit up.

"Yes, Tiffany?"

"I have your weekend schedule and reminders."

Hunter glanced at his watch. It was after five. "Come in."

Tiffany Stone was a curvy redhead in her late twenties. She was attractive but frankly, not Hunter's taste. Didn't matter to him that some in the office thought he was screwing her, he knew he wasn't. She typed like Clark Kent, kept meticulous notes, and never let him miss an important meeting. Sleeping with his secretary was a cliché he refused to fall into. He had his share of scorned women out there making his life difficult who knew nothing about him. A good secretary simply knew too much.

She took the seat across from his desk and tapped on a tablet. "You have lunch with Senator Fillmore at Providence tomorrow at one. The Ricker's fundraiser is at Patina at seven." She glanced over her tablet, which he knew was linking to his phone as she spoke with him. "Patina is at the Disney Concert Hall."

"I know where Patina is."

She continued without pause, "Your tux is cleaned and they confirmed delivery to your home at two today. Will I need to order a car?"

Hunter shook his head.

"Sunday is quiet, but don't forget you're in New York next Friday for the board meeting."

Like he'd ever forget that.

"Nothing tonight?" He could have sworn there was something planned.

Tiffany lifted one brow and offered a smile. "Not unless it's a date I know nothing about."

A date . . . a date?

Aww hell.

Tiffany rolled her eyes before setting her tablet on her lap. "Who am I sending flowers to?"

He was all kinds of asshole. "I have it."

She stood to leave.

He stopped her. "And Tiffany?"

She turned.

"I want you to jot this name down."

He waited for her to lift her notepad.

"Gabriella Masini." He paused. "Until I tell you otherwise, let her calls come through regardless of who I'm in with."

She lifted her gaze. "Anyone?"

"Anyone."

———

He didn't duck . . . he should have ducked.

What a shit day.

Hunter had stopped Shannon's second hit by bobbing to the right, the third hit by grasping her fist that came from the left.

She'd been fire in bed, if not a little demanding, but the real fight came when he told her it was over.

It was so much easier to send the flowers and say "It was fun." Or some such sentiment.

He was trying to be a better man . . . damn it. He just didn't know where to find him. Breaking it off in person was the better man . . . right?

Hunter tossed his keys on the hall table, dumped his phone and wallet in the same collection bowl.

"Mr. Blackwell."

Hunter removed his overcoat, handed it to his aging valet.

The man took the coat, stared at what Hunter knew was a bruise forming on his chin. "Don't ask."

"Of course not."

The man was itching to ask, but didn't. "I need whiskey."

"In your office?"

"Yes."

Andrew had been in Hunter's employ for over five years. In his midsixties, the man took care of his home and had the added fun of serving Hunter when he was in LA. The opinionated help was sometimes a pain, but Hunter trusted the man. And there were very few that fell into that category.

The light in his office turned on with the motion of him walking into the room.

He walked around his glass-top desk, turned on his computer. A remote opened the blinds, where he managed a stunning view from his Westwood penthouse. On a clear day he could see the ocean, tonight the lights of the city entertained his brain. It wasn't as spectacular as New York . . . but it worked.

The soft shuffle of Andrew's feet announced his arrival.

The crystal snifter held a generous portion of amber liquid. "No ice?"

Andrew reached out his other hand. A bag held the missing ice.

Hunter chuckled, took the ice, and winced when it touched his face. When the older man didn't immediately leave, he said, "I'm no longer expecting Miss Shannon's company."

Andrew lifted his chin in understanding. "Right hook?"

"She deserved one shot, I suppose."

"Shall I contact the front desk?"

Aww, one of the many reasons he enjoyed having the man in his employ. "Please. And while you're at it, add the name Gabriella Masini."

Now Andrew gazed at the floor and offered a shake of his head. "It's not what you think."

"I'm not at liberty to think."

Hunter huffed out a short laugh. "Yeah, right."

Andrew started to turn. "Anything else?"

He hesitated. "Any calls today?"

The grin on Andrew's face fell. "No. I'm sorry."

Hunter returned his gaze out the window and dropped the bag of ice on his desk. The whiskey added a nice slow burn down his throat.

Halfway through his drink he sat down at his computer and turned it on. The reminders for his weekend were blinking on his calendar, a gift from Tiffany so he wouldn't forget. He reached for the phone to call the desk for a driver and stopped himself. He removed a small notebook from his pocket and found the information about Miss Masini's service.

The phone was answered on the second ring. "First Class Services. How can I help you?"

"I'd like to schedule a ride."

"I can certainly help you with that, Mr. . . . ?"

"Blackwell."

The pleasant male even-toned voice on the line asked a rapid fire of questions. "Have you used our service before?"

"No. You come recommended."

"We do enjoy hearing that. When and where will you need a car?"

"This Saturday, six p.m. from the Wilshire to the Disney Concert Hall."

He heard the clattering of fingers on a keyboard and waited for a brief second before continuing. "Has Miss Masini ordered her car this weekend?" He was taking a gamble that she'd have weekend plans. According to the conversation Hunter had had with Blake,

the women in his wife's employ spent quite a bit of time fraterniz-
ing with the rich and famous on the weekends. Since the event he
was scheduled to attend was filled with an equal number of rich and
famous attendees, he crossed his fingers that the beautiful Italian
woman would be in attendance.

"I believe she has . . . shall I check on that reservation while I'm
in the system?"

A satisfied smile lifted the corners of Hunter's lips. "Please."

"One moment."

He sipped his whiskey and waited.

"Her standard car is scheduled for six as well, Mr. Blackwell.
Since your destinations are the same, shall I have one driver attend
to you both?"

Bingo!

"Please. I was supposed to meet her there, so let's order a stretch
and pick me up first."

"Not a problem, Mr. Blackwell. This will go on your card?"

"Of course."

Hunter gave the necessary information and hung up.

At least something in his day was moving in the right direction.

Chapter Four

Gabi grasped her clutch, checked to make sure her ticket for the event was inside, and turned off the light in her bedroom before walking down the stairs.

Her foot no sooner found the ground floor than the doorbell rang.

She peeked through the view in the door, noticed a driver, and proceeded to set the alarm.

"Perfect timing," she said as she exited the house.

"How are you this evening, Miss Masini?"

"I'm well, Charles. You?"

Gabi didn't think she'd be on a first-name basis with a personal driver in her life, and yet here she was walking up to the limousine . . . "I didn't request a limo." She hesitated and Charles opened the back door with a smile.

"It's all taken care of, Miss Masini."

Gabi grinned, assuming Sam had made sure she arrived at the Ricker's fundraiser in fashion. They were supposed to go together, but that was before her sister became ill.

She slid into the back, lifted her dress to mind the hem and keep it from becoming caught in the door.

It wasn't until the door closed that Gabi realized she wasn't alone. She tried to control the gasp and instant elevation in her heart rate.

She failed.

He loomed from the other side of the limo. One arm rested on the back of the seat, the other held a drink. His face was hidden in the shadows, but she knew who he was.

The need to escape and a swarm of unwanted memories paralyzed her.

"Miss Masini."

She couldn't find her voice. Why was Hunter Blackwell in the back of her car?

"Or should I say Mrs. Picano?"

The blood rushed from her face and her hands shook. Very few people knew of her brief marriage. The fact that the billionaire sitting across from her did shouldn't be a surprise.

The car started to move, prompting her to reach for the door.

"Jumping from a moving car is a bit extreme," he said.

She closed her eyes, sucked in a slow breath. "What are you doing here, Mr. Blackwell?"

"Attempting to have a private conversation with you, Mrs. Picano."

"Don't call me that!" She felt some of her fight returning.

He leaned forward and she saw his face. Clean shaven, dangerously handsome. "You look like you need a drink." He set his glass down and reached for the decanter at his side.

"No, thank you."

Her words had no effect. Fine, let the man pour a drink . . . at this rate he'd be wearing it before they left the car.

CATHERINE BYBEE

Amber liquid and ice filled the crystal glass. She took it to avoid him moving closer, then promptly placed it on the secure shelf at her side.

He raised an eyebrow and sat back.

"I have a proposition for you, Miss Masini."

"No." Such a powerful word, yet the man smiled.

"You haven't heard it yet."

"Any man who believes flowers and unwelcome visits in limousines are going to change my mind is obviously not listening to my words. *No*, Mr. Blackwell. Whatever you want, the answer is *no*."

"You might reconsider once we arrive at the Disney Hall. You see, I don't accept the word no. I need a wife, and I've chosen you."

Gabi felt the tension leave her system when she laughed. "You're delusional."

Her smile faded when his emerged and he sat back as if he'd just signed a million-dollar deal.

"Your late husband had a hefty life insurance policy."

She swallowed. Every time he mentioned Alonzo's name . . . or alluded to him, her stomach twisted and her palms itched. She decided the best action was none. Gabi listened.

"The insurance policy made you a relatively wealthy woman."

Lot he knew . . . anything that showed up after Alonzo's death went to charity.

"Insurance companies despise paying out. The clauses they place inside policies are designed to keep the beneficiaries penniless. Only Mr. Picano's paid out. Do you know what happens when insurance companies learn that they paid over a million dollars on a policy that was fraudulently obtained?"

What is he talking about? He was goading her . . . trying to get a reaction, she decided.

Gabi refused and concentrated on keeping her hands loose in her lap.

"You're a beautiful woman, but I don't think you'd survive wearing orange long-term."

"I have done nothing illegal."

"You cashed the check after violating the terms of the policy."

It was impossible to sit still. Gabi leaned forward. "You don't know what you're talking about."

"I hate to disappoint you, but I do. You signed the papers and removed your husband from life support. A direct violation to the terms of the insurance policy. One might speculate that you wanted your husband dead for the money."

"You don't . . . you're wrong." Only she knew most of what he said was true. The insurance policy, she wasn't sure about. So much happened during that volatile time in her life, she hadn't paid attention to most of the papers she'd signed and couldn't verify anything Blackwell was saying. Not that it mattered, she'd fight a fraud charge. Come up with the funds to repay the insurance company if it came to it.

"Then there is the offshore account to consider."

She jerked her attention his way. The desire to slap the smirk off his face was palpable. "What account?"

"Yours."

"I don't have—"

"Mrs. Picano most certainly does have an account." He reached into his pocket and removed a folded paper before handing it over.

She couldn't read the language, not completely, but understood a few key words. The money was in euros, there were several zeros, and her name was listed. Instead of telling the man she knew nothing about the account, she soaked in the name of the bank and the account number and returned the paper.

"Do I have your attention now, Gabriella?"

"You're a bastard."

"True. But I'm not the one who will find herself in prison for either insurance fraud or tax evasion."

The numbers that swam in her head were worthy of several years in a state penitentiary. She could fight it . . . probably win . . . eventually. But wouldn't it be easier to fix her *so-called* crimes if she was free?

"What do you want?"

"A wife . . . you."

"Why me?" She wasn't smiling now.

"Because you and I have a lot in common."

"We have nothing in common," she spat.

"I'm in need of a wife, and you need a husband who can financially fix your criminal background."

"Even if I had a criminal background, I wouldn't need a husband to fix it for me."

He grinned. "Becoming Mrs. Blackwell will start the process of distancing yourself from Mr. Picano's name. My lawyers understand the need to quietly remove problems. By my estimates, it will take eighteen months, give or take, to remove the threat of prison being on your resume."

"Let me guess," she said. "Eighteen months is the duration of time you need a wife?"

"Beautiful and smart."

"Condescending and a bastard."

He laughed, lifted his glass, and drank. "Touché."

———

Hunter remembered his first trip to Vegas . . . the lights, the women, the whiskey . . . the game. He'd walked up to an exclusive poker table, laid fifty thousand down, and proceeded to bluff. He collected over four hundred thousand dollars from one game on the premise of intimidation.

Wearing his poker face, he proceeded to bluff again.

Good thing the back of the limousine had poor lighting or Miss Masini would have seen his reaction to her face when he mentioned her late husband. There was so much more to her story than what he'd been given, and even if she walked away, called his bluff, he would find those answers.

Thankfully, Gabriella didn't take his threats by rolling over. She fought, which delighted him. So few people in the world spoke to him the way she did.

He was a bastard. One that always won . . . eventually.

"How much time do I have to decide?" she asked.

"The fundraiser will go on for several hours."

"You can't be serious." She was outraged, once again.

He relented, slightly. "I expect contracts on my desk in the morning."

"Impossible." She shook her head.

"Nothing is impossible."

The car started to slow, announcing their arrival.

"Blackmail is such an ugly practice."

The limo stopped and she reached for the door.

He moved forward, caught her ice-cold hand. "So is prison."

Their eyes locked, both of their jaws set in tight control.

Charles opened the door and extended a hand.

Hunter quickly followed her, ignored her flinch when he placed a hand to the small of her back to escort her inside. To her credit, she didn't take a swing. Though from the way she held her purse, she certainly wanted to.

The cameras flashed as they walked the red carpet. A bottleneck of celebrities blocked their quick entrance, and Gabriella was forced to turn to the cameras.

He leaned forward, was awarded the floral scent of her skin. "Smile, darling," he whispered.

She turned toward him, and he was grateful that looks couldn't actually kill. She mumbled something in a language he didn't understand and painted on a debutante smile. The expression didn't meet her eyes, but she twisted to the flash of cameras and sucked in a deep breath.

Why Hunter was so mindful of her every move baffled him. This was an acquisition . . . nothing more, nothing less. Yet he was pleased to see more color in her face.

Hunter kept close to her side so there was no question as to whom she was with. The sooner he established contact with his personal life and the public, the better. He heard his name in the flash of media and purposely pushed closer to Gabriella. "Keep moving," he suggested.

"And where would you suggest I run?" Her words were pure venom, her smile coy for the camera.

God, she was stunning. Her long, sleek hair was pulled up, with trails running down her neck. Her strong jaw with clenched teeth told him she would bite if he moved too close. Olive skin spoke of her Italian heritage; her guarded, expressive eyes hid so much from those around them. Yet he knew the daggers she tossed, felt them hit their mark every time she glanced his way.

The line moved, and he gifted his hand with the small of her back.

This time, her flinch was barely palpable. He reminded himself to keep his hand on the fabric of her dress as much as he could . . . all evening.

His eyes traveled to the sway of her firm hips. The thick material of her gown kept him from seeing what she wore underneath.

Attraction in this game would be lethal, not to mention useless. The woman hated him, and rightly so.

He was a bastard.

The worst kind.

Yet he plowed forward, his goal in mind.

The line released its hold on them, and they spilled into the hall of the famous restaurant. Hunter gave their names to the attendant and kept hold of his charge.

"I'm not here with you," she hissed through the crush of people.

He grinned. "You are now."

———

Escaping Hunter Blackwell was akin to running from rain during a hurricane. It didn't matter where she went, what she said . . . he was always there.

She accepted sparkling water and lime, sipped the beverage, and allowed Mr. Blackwell to introduce her for over an hour before she couldn't stomach any more.

She excused herself to the ladies' room, knew he was close behind, but detoured when she rounded the corner through a staff door. After pleading with an attractive young waiter, he helped her back into the main dining hall through another door, and she slid out of the venue.

Before long she was tucked back inside the limousine on her way back home.

The moment she arrived at her doorstep, she set her alarms, shut off all the downstairs lights, and retreated to her office.

Hunter Blackwell's cell phone information was in his file. Instead of making him chase her, which she innately knew he would, she drafted a text before he could knock on her door.

Contracts require time to construct. I will contact you in the morning.

Within two minutes, his brief reply read, Until then.

It took some time, but she managed to find the offshore account Blackwell told her about.

How stupid of Alonzo to set up passwords associated with his birthday. Everyone knew not to do that.

Then again, the man was dead . . . his stupidity eventually killed him.

Over five million euros infused the account.

Worse, someone was depositing and removing money from the account one thousand at a time.

Mr. Alonzo Picano and Mrs. Gabriella Picano . . . the account held a name she briefly claimed.

She wanted nothing to do with the blood money but knew sending it to a charity, any charity, might suggest she was scared and running. Maybe even prove that she was using the account and evading taxes in her own country.

Like every time she backed out of an online account, Gabi shifted the sequence of numbers and changed the passwords. She moved to a second computer and started an international search of her name. And that of Gabriella Picano.

A name she never claimed publicly.

She typed slowly, feeling her hands shake as she reached the *O* in Picano, and paused.

A cold sweat started at the nape of her neck and down the back of her evening gown . . . a gown she'd yet to change, even hours after the fundraiser.

When she hit *enter*, she released a long-suffering breath.

He's dead, Gabi, she told herself. *He can't hurt you now.*

Chapter Five

She was screwed. Before falling into a fitful sleep, she'd found a second account under Gabi Picano, one smack in the thick of Colombia. This one had a steady stream of money coming and going. The infusion of funds correlated with the withdrawals of the larger offshore account, which led her to believe that they were tied. Whoever was playing with one account was playing with the other.

Gabi woke with the intention of dragging Samantha into her troubles, only to find a message on her cell phone telling her to take care of any and all Alliance needs. Jordan had been transferred to the ICU and everything Alliance had to wait.

When she lifted the phone to call her brother, she stopped herself. Val had fished her out of hot water once before. A mess she made by trusting the wrong person. If blowing off Blackwell and landing in prison would only affect her, she might consider taking her chances.

But it wouldn't.

Alonzo had taught her that she could do nothing without it affecting everyone around her. Her trust in him nearly got her sister-in-law killed.

Instead of pulling in others to shovel her out of her past, Gabi decided it was time to dig herself out.

She brought up the boilerplate contracts Alliance used and started to modify them.

Two hours later she contacted the Alliance attorney and sent her an e-mail. Before Gabi could shower, Lori Cumberland called. "What in the world is this?" she asked in disbelief.

"It's a contract."

"A contract someone will actually sign?"

"Did I add something that's illegal?" Gabi was fairly certain that every clause that had ever been placed in an Alliance contract was legal. She decided a few other *conditions* needed to be in writing.

"Not illegal . . . just . . . wow. Am I reading this right? This is between you and Hunter Blackwell?"

The thought of marriage made her shudder. "That's correct."

"The zillionaire Hunter Blackwell?"

"Not sure about the zillion . . . but yes. I need to know if the conditions I added can be held up in court."

To render a lawyer speechless left a certain smile on Gabi's face.

"He'd be stupid to sign this."

"Or desperate."

Lori paused. "Does Sam know about this?"

"Her sister is really ill, Lori. She asked that I handle the Blackwell account."

"I don't think that means you have to marry the man. From what I hear, he's an ass."

Gabi smiled for the first time in hours. "An ass that will have me handing it to him if he violates our contract. Is it legal?"

"I need to modify a few words, but yeah. Wow."

"Glad you approve."

Lori sighed. "Approve? I'm impressed. I didn't consider you the shrewd one. Make sure I'm invited to the wedding."

Gabi doubted a ceremony was forthcoming. "I need to get these to Blackwell before noon. Can you modify and send them back?"

"I hope you know what you're doing."

"Me, too," she muttered before hanging up.

The tight black dress stopped above her knees, her black stockings had beads up the back that turned heads when she passed. Tall and slender had always been a gift to Gabi, she used it now by adding an extra four inches with her stilettos. Her hair was slicked back in a simple knot.

With her back straight, Gabi walked up to the ground floor security, expecting her first delay.

When she mentioned her name, they waved her through and escorted her to a bank of elevators. She stepped in and ignored the looks around her.

Blackwell Enterprises held the entire top floor of the building, making the reception space larger than the ground floor of Gabi's home.

She commanded attention as she walked to the desk. The receptionist offered a brilliant smile.

"Miss Masini for Mr. Blackwell."

The smile stayed and the twentysomething model-perfect woman blinked. "Right away, Miss Masini. I'll call Tiffany."

Gabi ignored the roll of tension down her spine. Walking into the office had been *too* easy.

She turned away from the desk, hoping to hide her nerves. The entire way into the city, she questioned her decision. Then again, Blackwell would probably shred her contract.

The quick, steady click of heels slowed as they approached. "Miss Masini?"

Gabi turned and couldn't help but smile.

"I'm Tiffany, Mr. Blackwell's personal secretary."

The introduction instantly had Gabi envisioning a very personal position between Hunter and the lovely woman beside her. She was luscious, beautiful, and appeared too innocent to be hooked up with the likes of Hunter. Gabi felt an instant desire to shelter the younger woman from the evil man.

"Hello, Tiffany," Gabi managed.

"Mr. Blackwell is expecting you." Tiffany turned back into the thick of the office and led the way.

Gabi lifted her chin and ignored the glances as she walked through. The sheer amount of attention her presence created as she rounded the corner made it clear that Hunter didn't often have personal calls to his place of work.

Somehow, that pleased her.

Tiffany stepped through a set of doors that opened to a large reception space complete with couches and magazines . . . and a desk that would engulf the one Gabi had at home.

Tiffany approached a set of sleek double doors and knocked. Without waiting, she opened one and stepped aside.

Gabi knew her practiced smile left, briefly . . . then she squared her shoulders and walked in.

Hunter stood behind a black desk that held a computer, a phone, and a pen. Behind him was a wall of windows overlooking the city. The space was completely masculine down to the leather couches, the simple art . . . the bar on the far end of the office.

Their eyes met . . . locked, and he stared.

There was a spark behind his gray eyes that screamed of his success by her walking in his door.

He'd won and he knew it.

"That will be all, Tiffany. Let me know when Ben arrives."

"Yes, Mr. Blackwell." Tiffany closed the door behind her.

He made a slow path around his desk. "I assume you had no trouble with security getting up here."

Gabi approached, set her purse in one of the empty chairs. "The ease of my entrance smacks of arrogance."

"Yet here you are."

Could she hate the man any more?

Keep your enemies close.

Instead of debating with him, she removed the contracts from her purse and slid them across his desk. "I took the liberty of adding a few conditions . . . in light of our *personal* situations."

He didn't bother a glance at the papers. "I'm sure we can work out whatever you might have come up with."

So arrogant.

"You're going to find your condescending words to be a mistake, Mr. Blackwell."

"Hunter, Gabi . . . my name is Hunter."

She wasn't sure what shook her more, the fact that he'd instantly put them on a personal level by the use of his first name, or the fact that he'd used her nickname.

"I despise you," she muttered.

He lifted a hand, indicated the chair at her side. "A fact that we will both recognize and speak of freely . . . when we're alone. In public, I expect a reserved wife who accepts a casual touch and even a smile."

"What kind of touch?" She hated asking.

"I won't maul you."

She sat across from him, comfortable with the desk separating them.

The despicable man was a stranger . . . he unbuttoned his suit jacket and sat before sliding his chair closer to his desk. He'd yet to look at the contracts.

"Why are you really doing this?"

"I've already told you—"

"*Beggianate!*"

"Excuse me?"

Gabi took delight in her ability to speak a language he couldn't. "I don't believe you. Your explanation is trivial at best. It's one of the many reasons Alliance rejected your application."

He lifted one brow. "Yet here you are . . . contract in hand."

She closed her eyes, sucked in a breath, and calmed her nerves. When she opened them again, Gabi found him watching her.

A wave of something resembling concern passed over his eyes before he said, "As soon as the contracts are signed, and we're married, I have a team of lawyers and investigators ready to move on your case."

"And if they find me guilty?" she asked.

That left a smirk on his face. "They'll find a way to exonerate you."

Such an ass.

"It doesn't bother you to believe you're marrying a woman with a history of killing a wealthy husband and collecting after his death?"

He smiled for the first time since she entered his office. "You're stunning in black." His eyes swept her frame before returning to her face. "But I don't think you're a black widow."

It was her turn to grin. "Mating before killing isn't necessary."

He laughed when she was hoping to intimidate.

I need to work on that.

Before he could comment, the phone on his desk buzzed.

Hunter lifted the receiver, listened. "Let him in."

Gabi stayed seated as Hunter introduced one of his lawyers.

Ben Lipton was a personal attorney who'd been given enough information to know that Gabi wasn't in Hunter's life because of a romantic relationship.

He shook her hand and took the contracts to the opposite side of the room to read.

"Can I get you something to drink, Gabi?"

Hearing her name from Hunter's lips wouldn't sit well for some time. "Tea."

He buzzed Tiffany, placed her request.

The silence in the office was broken by the door opening and the tea setting being placed on the table.

Tiffany glanced between the three of them and left in silence.

Mr. Lipton would occasionally lift an eyebrow, glance Gabi's way, then return to the contract.

When the man finally finished, he evened out the pages and stacked them on the table. "Have you read this?" he asked Hunter.

"That's why I have you."

Mr. Lipton was in his fifties . . . his salt-and-pepper hair and starch-filled suit would label him as sophisticated. He had kind blue eyes, but if he was in business with Hunter, Gabi believed he couldn't be trusted.

"Then let me spread before you Miss Masini's terms."

"I'm listening."

Gabi sat back and heard her words spoken through Hunter's lawyer.

"Your contract is for eighteen months. At which time divorce proceedings will begin without contesting from either side or the entire contract is forfeited and no money will exchange hands." All that was standard.

"The agreement is for twenty-four million, one million for each month of marriage, and one million for every estimated month it will take for the divorce to be final."

Gabi met Hunter's eyes. The amount was triple the normal contract.

He didn't bat an eye.

"Continue."

"As your wife, she insists on a *new* residence, one in keeping with *your* current lifestyle with no possibilities of a previous woman having ever been in attendance."

There was a smirk . . . maybe even a little admiration behind his eyes.

"Continue."

"If the marriage lasts eighteen months, she wants five years in the home you purchase before selling and splitting the profits. If the home loses money, you will pay the difference."

There was no doubt now . . . he was smiling.

"Continue."

Ben shook his head.

"Any extramarital affair going public . . . assumed or proven, will cost one million per affair."

That made him pause. "Really, Gabi?"

"I hate being made a fool."

He shook his head, rolled his fingers in the air. "Continue."

"In the event of any criminal charges being brought against Miss Masini, your marriage will continue until she has been freed of all charges, to which all funds will continue as promised. All legal expenses to exonerate Miss Masini will be paid for by you."

Hunter tilted his head. "Touché."

She grinned, feeling more confident with every word the lawyer spoke.

Ben tuned the page and continued to paraphrase. "In the event of any domestic violence, Miss Masini has the right to terminate the marriage and will obtain one hundred million dollars. Said funds will be placed in an account on the first day of marriage and held in trust until the completion of the contract."

Hunter's smile fell, and for the first time since walking into the office, Gabi felt exposed.

"I'll never hurt you," he said softly.

I've heard that before.

Staring directly at Hunter, she said, "Please continue, Mr. Lipton."

"In the event of Miss Masini bearing your child, half of your net worth will be placed in a trust for your child. The marriage can be terminated at any time after a pregnancy is determined, and the home you purchase will be free to live in until your son or daughter reaches eighteen or graduates from high school."

Hunter frowned.

"That's an expensive child."

She leaned forward, made sure he understood her words.

"The only way a child would be conceived between us would be through force. I'm assuring my safety, *Hunter.*"

It was his turn to hold her eyes with his own. "Anything else, Ben?"

"Standard stuff . . . if you both agree to early divorce, the original payout is applied."

Hunter twisted his phone toward her. "Get your attorney on the phone . . . I have a couple of conditions of my own."

Two hours later, Gabi agreed that if she were to have an affair, the settlement would be half of the expected twenty-four million. The home would be sold within one year of divorce, and any child not his would keep her maiden name and be entitled to half of the final settlement.

By the time Mr. Lipton left Hunter's office, the hour closed in on three.

Gabi's back ached from sitting in the office chair, the view from Hunter's office forever burned in her brain.

They discussed marriage in terms she never thought possible.

There was a day in her life that love and devotion were once a part of *till death do us part.* She knew better now.

There were many examples of "good marriages" around her . . .

but she couldn't help but question. What didn't she know . . . what was happening behind the scenes that no one spoke of?

It made her sick . . . the questioning . . . the wondering.

The memories.

"We missed lunch," Hunter said when they were alone.

The agreement was made . . . the contracts sat in front of them, waiting for their signatures.

"I don't think I can eat," she muttered.

He was silent until she met his gaze.

For the first time since they'd met, Hunter Blackwell's shoulders slid . . . and his eyes softened. His next words were quietly spoken. "I've never laid a violent hand to a woman, Gabi. You will not be my first."

The image of Alonzo smiling as the needle slid into her vein came from nowhere. He hadn't forced anything on her, either.

"That's little comfort."

Hunter stood and approached as if to a frightened animal.

Hadn't she gotten past that? The fear stage and on to the fight?

Before he could say anything, she swiped the contracts from his side of the desk, grasped a pen, and signed her name.

Tomorrow she would begin the task of removing her name from anything and everything Alonzo Picano.

Today . . . or at least until she signed her name to a marriage agreement, she would simply be Gabriella Masini.

Soon-to-be wife of Hunter Blackwell.

The blackmailed wife of a ruthless billionaire, the widow of a soul burning in hell.

Chapter Six

Twenty-four hours after she signed the agreement, he called to ask her ring size.

The contract was signed and recorded on the third day . . . on the fourth, a Thursday, they stood in the private quarters of a justice of the peace and exchanged meaningless vows.

Hunter didn't bother attempting a kiss, and the judge didn't ask for it.

He'd done it.

Marriage within two weeks of the initial onset of his unsolvable problem.

He turned to the pale stranger beside him as he walked out of the courthouse and felt every ruthless cell in his body.

"I honestly wish it didn't have to be this way," he said almost to himself.

"Excuse me?" Gabi asked.

"Nothing." He motioned her to the waiting limo and took her to her Tarzana home.

They wouldn't reside in the same house until Gabi agreed to a home.

Having little choice, Hunter walked behind Gabi as she approached her front door.

Like Remington had said, the home had an advanced security system, which Gabi disengaged the moment she stepped into the house.

The light furnishings were in direct contrast to anything Hunter owned. The pale green sofa and floral pillows were subtle and calming.

He watched in fascination as Gabi dropped her purse on the hall table. The table housed the flowers he'd sent. There must have been a look of surprise on his face.

"It's not the flowers' fault you're an ass," Gabi explained.

She stepped through the home, leaving him to close the door behind him.

He immediately noticed a light on the security panel light up. That's when he noticed the camera under a dome by the front door. There were other cameras and motion detectors. "Why is this house so heavily monitored?" he asked as he followed her into a kitchen.

Gabi moved about the space, filled a kettle, and placed it on the stove. For some reason, Hunter didn't see her as a domestic woman, yet walking around the kitchen, she seemed more relaxed than during the drive to and from the courthouse.

"The house belongs to Samantha," Gabi explained. "Since she married Blake, the house has been occupied by her staff."

"Women?"

Gabi nodded.

Blake was a good man, he mused. Still, the surveillance felt like more than just a safety measure for a single woman living alone. He couldn't help but wonder if maybe the security had something to do with Gabi's past.

He walked around the small dining area, looked out the back

window to the modest backyard. Even there he noticed cameras in the eaves of the house. "Who monitors the system?" he asked.

"Why do you care?"

He let the curtain to the backyard drop and turned to find Gabi watching him, her arms crossed over her chest.

"You don't have to be hostile, Gabi. It's a simple question."

She relented, pushed away from the counter, and opened one of the cupboards. "Blake has a security team."

"Of course."

She set a tea bag inside her cup, kept her back to him. The simple black pantsuit was stylish and not at all what Hunter thought she'd wear for their court appearance. Not that he thought she'd wear anything resembling a wedding dress, but black?

It was fitting, he supposed. Her hair, once again, was in a tight knot, making him wonder how long it was and when he might have the opportunity to see it loose.

"When are you going to tell me the real reason you needed to get married in such a hurry?" She removed the kettle from the stove and started to pour.

He wasn't expecting the question and had no intention of answering it. She'd find out eventually, but he wasn't prepared to tell her now.

"About the time you reveal the reasons behind all your conditions in our contract."

She stopped pouring and held perfectly still. "That will never happen," she told him.

"Then I'll just have to find out on my own."

She glanced over her shoulder and scowled. "Why bother? You have what you want. We're married and will stay that way for the duration of the contract."

He lifted his chin. "Eighteen months is a long time to keep secrets."

Gabi set the kettle down and placed both hands on the counter. "Where do we go from here?" she asked, changing the subject.

He glanced at his watch and then removed a folded paper from the inside pocket in his suit. "I have a meeting in New York tomorrow. I'll be leaving in a few hours."

She sighed, as if relieved, and twisted around to face him.

"I expect you to begin the search for the home today. If you don't find something suitable in a week, I'll find one."

"Why the hurry?"

"We're married, Gabi. No one will believe it's for real if you're living here and I'm somewhere else in the same city." He handed her the paper, watched her unfold it. "Phone numbers, addresses. We should be able to keep a lid on our marriage until I return. If something leaks, call me."

"I'm not one of your employees," she told him.

He wanted to contradict her, decided against it. "Please."

She turned the paper toward him, pointed at a number. "What's this?"

"The code to the parking structure in my building." He tapped his fingers on the counter. "What do you drive?" he asked.

She shook her head. "My car is in the shop."

"I'll have one of mine brought here for you."

Was that a grimace? "My insurance was canceled."

"Your . . . what?" he asked.

"My auto insurance. It's a long story."

Hunter looked at the time. "A long story will have to wait. I'll fix it, bring you a car."

Gabi rolled her eyes. "Do you fix everything with money?"

Yeah, he did. "And wives." *Was that a smile?* "I've got to go."

She turned away and picked up her cup. "I'd wish you a safe trip, but if your plane goes down, all my worries are over."

It was his turn to smile.

"Judy?"

Rick called her name from the open door of his office.

"Yeah?"

"Can you come here?"

She pushed away from her drafting desk and the project she was working on outside of the office. The desire to move up the architectural ladder was crying out.

The familiar wall of monitors and equipment that Rick surveyed filled an entire wall. There were a dozen homes, plenty of coming and going . . . lots of conversations that they most often didn't listen in on.

Judy slid her arms around the broad shoulders of her husband's back. He reached up and kissed one of her hands before clicking into his computer and bringing up one of the houses.

The image of Gabi standing over the sink in the kitchen of the Tarzana home looked innocent enough, then Judy realized the shake of her shoulders. She was crying, which cut Judy to see. "Oh, no. I thought she was doing better." Judy looked away, feeling like she was invading the other woman's personal space.

"I did, too. Russell told me she had a visitor, so I searched the video."

Rick cued the images, turned up the volume.

"Who is that?" Judy asked when a tall man walked in behind Gabi. His business suit told her he had money. He looked directly into one of the cameras and frowned.

"I'm not sure." Rick pointed at the kitchen feed. "Notice how Gabi is ignoring him."

"She's upset."

"Pissed, listen to her voice."

Why do you care?

"Wow. She's spitting venom at the man," Judy said.

"Keep listening," Rick told her.

It didn't take long for Judy to realize that the man was a client for Alliance, then Gabi laid into him. *You have what you want. We're married and will stay that way for the duration of the contract.*

The strange man stared at her and said, *Eighteen months is a long time to keep secrets.*

"Oh, my God." Judy sucked in a breath. "Did he just say what I think he said?"

Rick turned in his chair and lifted both eyebrows. "He sure did." He pointed back to the live feed and zoomed in.

There, sitting on Gabi's left ring finger, was a rock the size of Judy's thumb. "She didn't."

"I think she did," Rick said.

Judy turned from the monitors and headed for her office to retrieve her purse.

"Where are you going?" Rick asked, following her.

"To talk to her. She's obviously upset. My guess is no one knows what's going on. If Meg and Val knew, Meg would have called me." Meg was Judy's best friend and Gabi's sister-in-law.

"I'll take you."

Judy pushed her hand on Rick's thick chest. "No. She's still not completely comfortable with men. I'll go."

"I guess it's pizza for me tonight," he said with a grin.

"Save some for me, Green Eyes."

He kissed her and patted her butt as she walked out the door.

The doorbell buzzed several times before Gabi moved from the kitchen counter to answer it. She shouldn't have been surprised to see Judy's face behind the peephole, but she was.

Running her fingers under her eyes, Gabi knew it was useless. She'd been weeping since Hunter left, the reality of what she'd done set in.

She opened the door and tried to smile.

Judy's face filled with sympathy, and her first words brought fresh tears to Gabi's eyes. "Oh, hon . . . what happened?"

Judy pushed inside, kicked the door closed, and dropped her purse on the floor.

Gabi accepted the other woman's hug and cried. "I-I got married."

They stood in the hall for a couple of minutes, Judy tried to soothe her over with soft words. Who would have thought a woman a good five years younger would be the one comforting her?

"C'mon." Judy led them into the living room where they sat on the couch. "Start at the beginning."

The thought of letting it all out, every detail, was tempting. But what would be the point? Judy was a direct link to her brother, and if Val found out that Hunter had blackmailed her into marriage, she'd have to contend with his wrath instead of focusing on clearing her name.

"His name is Hunter Blackwell," Gabi told Judy.

"An Alliance client?"

"Yes."

"If he's a client, how is it *you* married him?" Judy asked.

Gabi shook the truth from her tongue. "He needed a wife, fast."

"Why?"

"I'm not entirely sure." There was no way around that truth. Gabi knew that fact shook Judy. "But he's a friend of Blake's."

Judy seemed to like that piece of information. "Did Sam approve?"

Gabi shook her head. "Jordan's really sick. She asked me to deal with Blackwell."

"Deal with . . . not marry."

The image of the justice of the peace asking her if she'd take him as her husband shot into her head. "He made me an offer I couldn't refuse."

"I don't think—"

"Twenty-four million."

Judy stared, open-mouthed. "Oh."

"Yeah . . . oh!"

They were silent for a minute, before Judy asked, "So if you wanted the deal . . . why are you so upset?"

Half the truth came out. "Memories."

Judy grasped both Gabi's hands and held them in her lap. "I'm sorry."

"Me, too."

She thought she'd loved Alonzo when he convinced her to elope. The memory was clouded, where the image of Hunter vowing to be her husband was fresh in her head.

Judy ran her thumb over the ring on Gabi's finger. "This is crazy," she said.

Gabi really hadn't noticed. She twisted the ring on her finger now . . . realized the size of the thing that very moment. "It is, isn't it?"

"It's got to be at least five carats."

"I don't know."

The tears were drying up, the memories of Alonzo with them.

"So what now? Are you moving in with him?"

Gabi focused on her hand, lifted it high to really look at the ring. "No . . . I need to find a house."

"What?"

Gabi dropped her hand, offered a grin. "I told him I wouldn't live in his house, that he needed to buy us a new one."

Judy let out a laugh. "Seriously?"

"Yeah. I figured that would give us some time to get to know each other before we're living under the same roof."

"So let me get this right . . . he's giving you twenty-four million . . . a house . . . and a ring that belongs in a safe and not on a hand?"

Gabi smiled, thought of the other ridiculous stipulations she'd added to their contracts. "I told you the offer was too good to pass up."

"Wow. Have you figured out how you're going to tell your brother?"

"No. Please . . . don't tell Meg yet. I . . . I need a few days to figure this out."

"OK. Your secret is safe with me."

Someone knocked on the front door, ending their conversation.

Gabi didn't recognize the person on the other side, but felt safe opening the door with Judy standing behind her. "Yes?"

The young boy, barely old enough to drink legally in a bar, stood at the door, a set of keys in his hand. "Mrs. Blackwell?"

The name didn't register. "I'm sorry?"

The kid looked beyond her to Judy. "Are you Mrs. Blackwell?"

Judy nudged Gabi from behind.

"No, ah . . . that's me." Gabi pointed at her chest.

He held out his hand, handed her a set of keys. "Mr. Blackwell told me to deliver this to you."

Gabi and Judy stepped out onto the porch and glanced in the driveway.

Judy started to giggle. "Does he know you suck at driving?"

Gabi would have been hurt if it wasn't true. "We didn't discuss it."

The kid walked to a waiting town car and jumped into the passenger seat while Gabi rounded in front of the matte white Aston Martin. She opened the door, found an envelope on the dash with her name on it.

Inside was temporary proof of insurance for Gabriella Blackwell.

Chapter Seven

Hunter walked away from the executive board meeting with more questions than answers. Someone in his company . . . or maybe several someones . . . were embezzling funds allocated for the charities Blackwell Enterprises supported. The numbers they reported to the IRS and the dollars removed from their accounts were off.

The accountants in New York were working overtime to find the leak and clog it. The last thing Hunter needed was an IRS claim that he was reporting thousands of dollars more in charity write-offs a year than were being paid.

Travis O'Riley walked beside Hunter as they left the board meeting, his feet moving twice as fast to keep up with Hunter's pace.

"That was ugly," Travis said as they walked down the hall.

"Ugly is what it will be when I find out who is stealing my money."

He marched past his New York secretary and into his office. The bicoastal business housed very different parts of his company. New York was all about international mergers and acquisitions, where LA was dedicated to domestic and new companies. His smaller London office kept the tax man in Europe happy, but the bulk of Hunter's investments were in the US.

"How long are you going to be in New York," Travis asked as the door to the office closed behind them.

"I'm flying out Sunday."

Travis tucked into an office chair, leaned back. "You really should consider a partner."

"Let me guess . . . you?"

Travis was one of the three executives that ran things when Hunter was away. None of them held more power than the other, none of them could take his place.

"Only with a massive raise," Travis joked.

"Let's start with a bonus if you find out who's behind the skim off the charity funds." If there was one thing Hunter had learned long ago, it was to offer money and people stepped up.

Travis leaned back, changed the subject. "How's the Adams oil acquisition going?"

"Merger . . . and the LA division is on it."

Travis nodded. "You really think pipelines are the way to go?"

Hunter moved to the window behind his desk and looked over the Manhattan landscape. The view really was spectacular. "I *know* pipelines are the future. Oil is useless sitting in one state, and with the conditions of the Middle East . . . we are ripe for a new oil rush in this country."

"I hope you know what you're doing."

He did.

"I'm out." Travis stood abruptly, moved to the door. "You know where I am if you need me."

Hunter lifted a hand. "I'm serious about the charity issue."

Travis lifted his chin. "I'm on it."

When he was alone, Hunter glanced at his watch. He'd been a married man for twenty-four hours. Married. The decision, like many in his life, had been impulsive. A quick fix to a problem bubbling in the near future. And like every impulsive decision he'd ever made, an expensive one.

He'd agreed to a million dollars per every extramarital affair. What the hell was he thinking? The desire to be celibate for eighteen months was right up there with cutting off his dick. What had Gabi said . . . "I don't like being made a fool."

What did that mean? And what about all the other stipulations she'd added to the contract. It was obvious that someone had hurt his wife. The question was who . . . and how bad?

He removed his cell phone from his pocket and decided a call to Remington was in order.

It rang three times before the man picked up. "Hey, Boss."

"Where are you?" From the sound in the background, a party, including a live band, was in full swing. Not what Hunter was paying for.

"Miami. This town is hopping."

He cringed. "I'm not paying you to party."

"Yeah, you are."

Hunter wanted to yell, but kept his cool. "What do you have?"

Remington muffled his next words, obviously speaking to someone else. "Who knew nurses liked to party?"

"Excuse me?"

The sound on the phone muffled and then quieted. "Looks like your little sex kitten was admitted to the hospital the same time her husband bit the dust."

"Why?"

"Don't know. She didn't die, and the HIPPA laws have the files shut. Crazy how when you die, those files are open wide. Not so much when you're alive."

"So you're partying with the nurses."

Remington started to laugh. "My job sucks, Blackwell. Might need a raise."

"Bloodsucking bastard."

Remington laughed. "I'll be in touch."

The real estate agent drove her to the sixth multimillion-dollar home in Bel Air.

Gabi had added the stipulation in the contract as a delay tactic; the house hunt, however, was actually really fun. She limited the budget to under ten million, which was a challenge in light of the fact that she wanted a half an acre of property.

Each property had a redeeming quality, and something that wasn't desirable. A view was nice . . . a swimming pool? Yeah, she missed her brother's island resort. She missed the ocean, but the image of it would sometimes make her break out in an unwelcome sweat. Alonzo took that from her . . . the love of the ocean. He took a hell of a lot more, but she refused to think about those things.

The outside space of one home was too narrow, the next, close to nothing.

The kitchens were large, but not something she saw herself cooking in. It was like those who lived in the houses didn't cook . . . or if they did, it was a microwave experience.

Her cell phone rang as she was walking around the back of one of the houses on a side of a steep hill. She didn't recognize the number but answered it anyway.

"Hello?"

"Gabi." His voice was actually soothing on the phone.

"Blackwell."

He laughed. "Asking you to call me Hunter is too much of a chore?"

"I haven't decided." She paused, then said, "I take it your plane didn't go down."

"No such luck," he laughed. "My pilot is one of the best."

"Your very own pilot? I should have guessed."

"Yes, you should have," he said.

"Why are you calling?" She moved away from the real estate agent, who hovered close by.

"I'd like to have dinner with you. I'll be back in town tomorrow afternoon."

She closed her eyes and pushed away the desire to tell him no. She'd not agreed to a simple date since Alonzo. There had been plenty of opportunities since moving to LA, but the desire to be alone with a man never manifested.

Truth was, she didn't want to now, but Hunter *was* her husband.

For a little while, at least.

"Fine," she mumbled. "We do have a lot to discuss."

"We do," he agreed.

"I'm looking at houses," she offered when he went silent.

"Find anything?"

She sighed. "Not really. I asked to see property that could be turned quickly. There's not as much out there as I'd hoped."

"Who is the agent?"

She told him and continued, "Beverly Hills is too congested. Hollywood is too . . ."

"Hollywood," he finished her sentence.

She found herself smiling. "Yeah. I'm looking in Bel Air."

"Close to the freeway . . . easy drive to the city."

Gabi found herself frowning. "I'm not trying to make this easy on you."

He laughed. "I'm sure you're not."

"I'd like to see the house before you make an offer," he told her.

"Don't trust me?" she asked.

"I don't know you well enough to trust you, Gabi."

That, she could agree with. "Fine. I'll give you a list when I see you tomorrow."

"Five?" he asked.

"Fine."

"See you then," he said.

"Not if your pilot crashes your jet."

Hunter laughed and hung up.

———

Gabi sat across from a stranger.

He wore a thin turtleneck sweater, something she wouldn't think was attractive on a sale rack, but on Hunter, it demanded her attention.

They'd walked into the posh restaurant, one she'd never been in before, and they were escorted to a quiet table in the back.

The host knew Hunter by name and offered a gracious smile Gabi's way.

She'd dreaded this dinner since he'd called the day before. Now they sat across from each other without words.

How this was going to work for eighteen months, she had no idea. "I'm not a very good actress," she finally said.

"I'm not following you."

"One of the qualities we search for with our female clients is their ability to pretend to be something they're not." She leaned forward and whispered, "Happily married."

"Ahh."

"Men seem better at the task of pretending they love someone to get what they want."

63

"That would be the secret class given in the locker room in tenth grade."

Gabi found a slight smile on her lips. "I suppose we were given lessons on how to ward off unwanted hands at that time."

"Lucky for some of us, not all of you girls took that lesson."

"I'll bet your list of conquests is long."

He sat back, smug. "What about your list?"

That was comical. "You're assuming I have one."

"All right . . . let's assume you don't. Why not?"

She wasn't expecting the question and had no way of answering it without revealing certain truths she wasn't prepared to share with this man . . . now . . . perhaps ever. "That's really none of your business."

"You'll learn that everything about you is *now* my business."

"You'll learn that a wife is not an employee you can boss around."

She saw his jaw tighten, knew there was something he wanted to say that he held back.

"Talking with you is right up there with walking through a minefield without a bulletproof jacket," he told her. "Is it so terrible that I'd like to know a little more about my wife than what I hear from my private investigator?"

"A private investigator? Why am I not surprised?"

"Because you're a smart woman."

She was about to reply when the waiter arrived and told them the specials. Hunter ordered a cocktail and Gabi ordered tea.

"Wouldn't a glass of wine help you relax?" he asked.

"I'm a smart woman," she told him. "Letting my guard down around you isn't the intelligent move to make."

"He must have done a number on you," he said.

"This isn't going to work," she whispered under her breath and reached for her purse.

Hunter placed his hand over hers. "Please. Let's start over. I'm really not that awful of a man."

"You blackmailed me into marrying you."

He pursed his lips, the motion almost comical. "Well . . . other than that. You didn't really leave me a choice."

What would be the point of running? They needed to move out of the *kick each other* stage, and Gabi needed to have a stiffer back whenever her past came up.

She lifted her hand away from his and set it in her lap. "One of the reasons these marriages work is the two clients actually like each other. We've established that isn't us."

"Speak for yourself," he said.

"Oh, please."

"You stood up to me, offered a laughable contract. I like a woman who takes chances."

"Is that right?"

He smiled, the look not quite reaching his eyes. "Now it's your turn."

"My turn for what?"

He waved two fingers in his direction. "Something . . . anything you don't despise about me."

Was this a joke? "You're serious?"

"One thing, Gabi."

She thought about it, filed through a dozen things she hated and found one. "You have nice taste in flowers."

Now his smile moved higher. When it reached his eyes he looked younger. And for the first time since they'd met, she found herself relaxing in his presence.

For the rest of the evening, they talked about their daily routines. She showed him a list of houses and spoke of the things she liked and didn't like about each one.

He took in the information but didn't offer much in the way of advice. He asked that she give him a few days to find something suitable. If he questioned why she wanted a new house, he didn't ask her.

They ate their meal and finished with coffee.

"We're going to have to announce our marriage soon," he told her as he drove her back home.

"I'm going to call my family tomorrow."

"Let me know when that's done, and I'll plan the next move."

"What about your family . . . how are they going to take us?"

Hunter glanced at her before turning his attention back to the road. "My family isn't a part of my life."

She'd remembered something in his file about a brother . . . no mother, and a father who was alive. The details on where everyone was weren't something Sam had placed in the information given to Gabi.

"My brother won't take the news well," Gabi told him. "My mother will be livid."

"They know what you do for a living, right?"

"They do. But having me fall prey won't be expected. I'll do my best to convince them I wanted this. They will know it's temporary."

"As long as they can be trusted to keep that information to themselves."

"They will."

He pulled into her drive and she stopped him before he could walk her to the door. "This is awkward enough," she told him.

"All right. We'll speak tomorrow?"

She nodded. "I'll continue the house search, send you files on what I find."

She opened the door.

"Sleep well, Gabi."

A pleasantry sat on her lips, but she went with a parting better suited for the two of them. "Pull out in front of a bus for me."

He laughed as she closed the door and made her way inside.

First thing the next morning, a bouquet of flowers arrived. The note said simply, *The busses didn't cooperate. I'll try harder tomorrow.*

Chapter Eight

Gabi spoke with Meg first. Her sister-in-law worked with Sam as well . . . she knew the details of their work, and if there was someone who could buffer the information for her brother, it was his wife.

"I signed a contract," Gabi told her after they exchanged pleasantries and talked about the weather.

"What kind of contract?" Meg asked . . . then she barked, "No. You didn't."

"I did. We were married last week."

"What? Why? Oh, my God, your brother's going to shit." Leave it to Meg to blurt out the truth.

"It's just a contract, Meg. A year and a half. Val won't have to worry about taking care of me. The money is huge."

"Your brother doesn't give a crap about the money. You don't, either, so don't even try and pass that off as the reason you did this."

"Twenty-four million."

"Oh . . ." Meg hesitated.

"And a house."

"Really?"

Gabi was happy in her current home, but it sounded like Meg understood the bigger picture. "It's a year and a half. Not a big deal." There was no way Gabi was going to reveal any of the issues with insurance claims and offshore bank accounts.

"Who is it?"

"Who is what?"

Meg snorted into the phone. "The husband . . . you know, the guy you married?"

"Sorry. Hunter Blackwell. A friend of Blake's, actually." Well, maybe not a friend, but it sounded good and might ease some of the trouble Val was bound to make.

"I'd try and talk you out of it if you hadn't already done it," Meg said.

"Which is why I waited to call. I need to move on."

"OK . . . moving on doesn't mean getting married to a stranger. How about a date? Have you even been on one since . . ."

There was no reason for Meg to voice since when. They both understood the question.

"I don't want to date. I don't want that in my life, Meg. This is easier. People will think I'm normal and I can move on."

"Beg to differ with ya, Gabi . . . but it's perfectly normal for you to tell guys to bug off after what you've been through. But getting married instead of dating isn't exactly a sound act."

"There's nothing remotely romantic about our relationship. It's all business. Trust me."

"I have little choice, don't I?"

"It's my life."

Gabi heard Meg muffle the receiver of the phone. "Well, look who just walked in."

"Val?"

"Yeah."

Gabi closed her eyes. "OK. Wish me luck."

"All the luck isn't going to make this easy."

Valentino Masini was a self-made man, owned his own island with an exclusive resort he built from nothing.

The sound of Val's voice made the knot in her chest tighten. "The look on Margaret's face tells me there is trouble, what is it, *tesoro?*"

"No trouble . . ." Not if you removed the facts. She slowly delivered the information she needed to.

I signed a contract.

The marriage is temporary.

Yes, we've already gotten married.

No, I'm not crazy.

"I know you're not pleased, Val. Just try and understand I needed to do this."

Her brother's silence sliced through her.

"What is this man's name?" Val's question was cold.

"Hunter Blackwell."

Her brother's voice softened to tell her he loved her. Then he cut the conversation short.

Meg took up the receiver and reported that Val had opened a bottle of whiskey. "I'll talk to him," Meg said.

"I really am OK," Gabi told her.

"We're just worried."

"I know. I'm sorry for that."

They said their good-byes and Gabi sent Hunter a text.

My family has been notified.

———

Gabi's text arrived at eight in the morning, Hunter spoke with the real estate agent during his lunch, and Tiffany was sitting in his office a hair after four thirty working on a guest list for a special announcement for later in the week. Thursday . . . a week from their actual wedding would be perfect. And then he was taking the weekend off.

"And what announcement is this?" Tiffany asked as she jotted down notes on his expectations of the event. "I didn't think the Adams agreement was solidified."

"It's not business," he told her. "It's personal."

Tiffany stared. "You don't hold personal events."

"I do now."

The portable phone in Tiffany's hand rang, she answered it. "Mr. Blackwell's office. Hold on." Tiffany dropped the phone. "A Mr. Masini to see you?"

Mister? Gabi's brother. "That didn't take long. Tell him to come up."

Tiffany told security and stood.

"We will need privacy, Tiffany. Please hold my calls."

Hunter didn't have a sister and couldn't imagine how he would react if he'd found out his had agreed to a marriage for money.

Not well, he decided.

Defuse and deflect. Assure her safety . . . smooth it over.

The man walking into his office could blow so much.

Valentino Masini wasn't a small man. He wore a suit, ruffled and worn after what must have been a lightning flight across the country. His dark eyes held a death stare that would intimidate most. Hunter found strength in the other man's gaze and held it.

Tiffany quietly walked out of the room, leaving the two of them staring at each other.

"Mr. Masini." Hunter didn't offer a handshake.

"Why Gabriella?"

Just business, much like his sister.

Hunter dropped his hand. "She said yes."

"Gabi would never do this willingly."

Maybe the brother knew more than most.

"I assure you, she did."

"Your assurance means nothing." Valentino took two more steps into the office, kept his voice deathly low. "She doesn't need your money, doesn't need your home, and doesn't trust men. Her agreeing to your contract is completely outside of her character."

"Perhaps you don't know your sister as well as you think."

Masini clutched his fists at his sides.

For a moment, they simply stared at each other. Hunter was about to assure the man that Gabi was safe with him, when his temporary brother-in-law delivered a threat Hunter hadn't seen coming.

"If you hurt her . . . one hair . . . I will kill you."

Kill? Not, *come after you . . . make you regret it . . .* but kill?

"Don't you have a new wife that would be disappointed if you landed in jail for murder?"

"My wife would be standing in line to finish the job should I fail," Masini told him. "And she's an excellent shot."

The hair on the back of Hunter's neck started to rise.

"You have a lot of nerve coming into my office and threatening me."

The other man looked as if he was ready to charge. "My sister may be an easy target, but I am not."

Hunter opened his mouth to counter and heard voices beyond his office door.

Gabi sailed into the room, her eyes brushing over his before they landed on her brother. Her hands were in the air, her voice on fire. "What are you doing here?" she yelled.

Tiffany stood back, eyes wide.

"Did you really think I wouldn't come?" Masini yelled back.

"What's done is done, Val." Gabi glanced around the room and switched languages so fast it took Hunter a minute to realize she had. She said something to her brother in a heated tone.

He yelled back, just as heated.

Hunter was lost. Italian wasn't a language he'd cared to learn. Perhaps it was time he hired a tutor.

He exchanged glances with Tiffany, who kept her distance but watched.

Gabi argued something and moved to Hunter's side of the room. That's when he realized her hair was down. Her hands flew, her hair flew . . . she wasn't happy her brother was there, but unlike the quietly angry woman she was with him, with her brother, she screamed and yelled. She was incredibly beautiful this way . . . unleashed.

She said something with the name Alonzo and Masini abruptly changed his tone.

Hunter didn't understand the words, but Masini's anger started to fade.

That's when Gabi lifted her left hand and placed her right one on Hunter's arm. "You're too late," she said in English. "We're already married."

Masini spit out one more string of Italian before running a hand through his hair.

The silence in the room was broken by Tiffany. "You're married?"

So much for keeping things quiet until Thursday. "That's all, Tiffany," Hunter said, dismissing her.

Gabi grasped the ends of her hair and pulled it over her shoulder. "Go home, Val. Live your life and let me live mine."

Val shook a hand in the air. "One hair, Blackwell. One hair." Before taking his leave, Val pulled his sister into a desperate hug and all the anger seemed to simmer away. Well, between the two of them, in any event. Masini shot daggers with his eyes, killing Hunter where he stood.

"I love you, *tesoro*. You know where to find me."

Then he left.

Gabi collapsed in his office chair and her shoulders folded in. For a few seconds, Hunter thought he had a crying woman on his hands . . . then he realized she wasn't weeping . . . she was laughing.

He leaned against his desk and felt a chuckle deep in his gut. "That was very entertaining."

She started laughing harder, and it was impossible to sit there without feeling it grow and erupt inside him.

"He threatened my life," Hunter told her.

Gabi hiccupped, wiped tears from her eyes.

Hunter laughed. "It wasn't funny."

She was doubled over now, finding the humor for the both of them.

He walked to the private bathroom in his office and brought her some tissues. She thanked him, wiped her face, and continued to laugh.

"If my mother . . ." She started to laugh again. "My mother shows up, you might want to duck."

"What, she'll throw a chair at me?"

"Let's hope that's all."

Hunter watched as Gabi took hold of her laughter. She was radiant in her designer jeans and button-up shirt. The loose hair flowing over her shoulders looked like silk. No wonder her brother was so protective of her. He must have had his hands full watching over her all her life. The men must have flocked, like ducks to a pond.

"Do you always fight like that?"

"In Italian?"

"That and the yelling."

Gabi shrugged. "It *was* a fight. He shouldn't have come. Though it warms my heart that he cared enough to do so."

Hunter shook his head. "I'll never completely understand women."

"I would hope not. Where would be the mystery in life if we understood the opposite sex completely?"

"Mystery should be about the prize in the cereal box, not a question as to what weapon your family is going to come at me with."

That had Gabi laughing again. "Well if you'd just jump in front of a bus, we wouldn't have these concerns, now would we?"

She made him smile again as she stood to leave. "I ditched the real estate agent. Probably should get back to the search."

"I'll walk you out."

"That isn't necess—"

"By now most, if not all of my office staff, has heard of our marriage. Letting you leave alone not only speaks of trouble, it will suggest the rumors are wrong. We're married, and it's time to practice some of your acting skills."

She offered a short nod, and to her credit didn't flinch when he placed a hand to her back and walked her out of his office.

Tiffany lowered the phone and stood as they walked by.

Hunter didn't spare a glance, where Gabi offered a smile and silently walked beside him.

It was close to five, but it didn't seem any of the staff left even a minute early. Hunter ignored the looks and continued to the elevators.

"Everyone is staring," Gabi whispered close to his ear.

"They're all trying to figure out who you are. Hold your head up."

She stiffened her spine and walked into the elevator. They were silent beside the other passengers as they slowly made their way to the ground floor of the building.

Still eyes lingered, he felt them, knew Gabi did, too.

He noticed his car parked with the emergency lights flashing. The Aston suited her . . . elegant, classy.

"Mr. Blackwell." The doorman moved to the car. "I was about to call your office."

"No need, Benny. I assume you've met." Hunter looked between Gabi and the doorman to the office.

"Not really. I ran in," Gabi told him.

Hunter moved closer to the woman at his side and smiled. "Well then, Benny, this is Gabriella Blackwell, my wife."

Surprise took over the irritated look on Benny's face.

"Feel free to have the valet take care of the car in the future."

Benny nodded. "Yes, sir."

Hunter walked Gabi around to the driver's side and opened the door.

When she attempted to move around him, he blocked her path. "Try not to jump," he whispered.

"Excuse me?"

Using the hand lingering on her back, he pulled her close and lowered his lips to hers.

Shock registered in her eyes. She couldn't back away, the car was there to stop her, but she didn't push.

He kept his hold loose, didn't want to scare her.

Her full lips were soft, the scent of her skin and the exotic floral aroma of her hair were something he'd think about long after she left.

"Relax, Gabi."

Hunter felt her effort. Watched as her dark lashes fluttered closed.

He placed a hand to the side of her face and tilted her head back. Her lips parted enough for a brief, intoxicating taste.

The tight rein of control Hunter always had on his emotions, his desires, started to unwind. He pulled away, almost as abruptly as he'd begun their kiss.

Their eyes locked.

Gabi sucked in her bottom lip.

Hunter ran his thumb over her chin, coaxing her lips apart. "I'll call."

Her throat constricted with a swallow, and she slid out of his arms and into the car.

Hunter moved to the curb and watched her pull away.

———

"Was it awful?" Meg asked over the phone.

Gabi called her the minute she pulled into the parking lot of the real estate agent's office.

"I'm just happy Hunter doesn't understand Italian. Val threatened bodily harm with a half a dozen weapons."

"He'll calm down. He's worried."

"I know. But for my sake, make him go home. The last thing I need is him hovering over me."

"I've already booked his flight. He'll be back here tomorrow."

"Good. Thank you."

Gabi lowered the visor and looked in the mirror. The smudge of her lipstick reminded her of Hunter's unexpected kiss.

"Can I ask you something?" Meg asked.

"Of course."

"Why now . . . why Hunter Blackwell?"

"I told you . . . the offer was—"

"Too good to pass up, I know. But there have been many clients that have come along that had reputations ten times better than Blackwell's."

Gabi ran a finger under her lip and paused. "Alonzo had a better public reputation than Blackwell. At least with Hunter I know he's in this for his own personal gain. He's using me with my full knowledge. There's nothing clandestine or silent about the man, and for some strange reason that comforts me." As the words left her lips, Gabi realized how true they were. For better or worse, she knew where she stood with Hunter.

He was using her, and she in turn would walk away a rich, and more importantly, free, woman.

"It's not going to take long for word to spread. From what I've learned about Blackwell, he's one of the most eligible bachelors in this decade. There's going to be a lot of ticked-off women out there."

"He's not eligible anymore."

"It won't stop the gold diggers from calling. Watch your back."

Gabi hadn't really thought about the women in Hunter's life. Not for a minute did she believe that he'd taken himself off the marital block to simply end the pursuit of unwanted women. "I will."

"I should go. Your mother has been in the kitchen cooking since you called this morning. At this rate, I'll be gaining ten pounds before the end of the week. What is up with her feeding her emotions?"

"It's an Italian thing."

"Great. It's going to be a fat thing. Once you're settled in your new wifely role, you better invite your mom to visit."

"I don't know about—"

"Do you want her chucking pasta at your new husband in front of his employees? Because she's already made threats."

The image of Hunter covered in marinara sauce made her grin.

"Give us a couple of weeks."

"I'm booking flights."

Gabi grumbled and said her good-byes.

Two weeks to set up house and learn to be civil enough in a room with Hunter to convince her mother the man she'd married wasn't going to hurt her.

———

Next to his morning coffee, Andrew set a tabloid on top of the *New York Times*. The caption said it all. *Billionaire Playboy Off the Market.*

One grainy photo was of him walking into the complex that housed his current LA residence; the other was of Gabi on the phone standing outside of the real estate office. The only solidifying factor to the magazine was the blown-up image of Gabi's left hand. Too bad someone didn't manage a money shot of their kiss. He'd like to see the expression on her face through a lens. Bewildered . . . just as he'd been by his own reaction. He'd risked bodily injury touching her, and yet she hadn't pushed him into oncoming traffic, nor had she connected her knee with more sensitive parts of his anatomy. He wouldn't say that she kissed him back, but there was something there. Something very unexpected by the both of them.

The click of a tongue brought Hunter's attention around the room.

Andrew held a pot of coffee and waited for Hunter to sit back so he could pour.

Instead of moving away, Andrew stood over him. "Any pressing news your valet needs to know?"

Hunter sipped his coffee and smiled over his cup.

"Yes, actually. We're going to be moving soon."

Andrew lifted an eyebrow and waited.

"To a house."

"Is that right?"

"Hmm . . ." he took another sip and placed the tabloid aside. "I need you to change a name on the registry."

"What name would that be?"

"Gabriella Blackwell."

"Long-lost family member?" Andrew asked, knowing full well there were no such entities out there.

"New family member. The tabloids have it right, Andrew. I married Miss Masini last week."

Andrew blinked and uttered, "In the old movies, the butlers and maids knew everything that happened in a household, yet here I stand in the dark."

Hunter picked up his coffee and folded the paper under his arm. "You're going to like her. Sassy with a hot temper." The image of her fighting with her brother brought a smile to his lips. "And beautiful."

"Beauty doesn't go far with an old man."

Hunter tapped the edge of the paper on Andrew's shoulder. "Good thing I'm not old."

Andrew's eyes followed him as he exited the room.

Fish in a bowl, cells under a microscope . . . and Hunter as a married man had many things in common.

———

He ignored most of the looks and peered past the distant cameras as he walked into his LA office.

Tiffany was the only one brave enough to say anything. "The phone hasn't stopped ringing since I walked in. Should I call a news conference?"

"On Thursday."

Tiffany pulled another message from her pile. "Travis O'Riley asked that you call him."

"OK."

Tiffany handed him a message from her pile. "A Mrs. Masini called, said if you knew what was best for you . . . and I'm quoting here . . . 'You best call your mother-in-law at your earliest convenience.'"

There was no doubt about it; Tiffany was getting a kick out of delivering *that* message.

"Anything else?"

"One more thing . . . there's a Blake Harrison sitting in your office waiting for you."

Hunter's gaze moved to the closed office doors and he handed the messages back to Tiffany. "Hold my calls."

"And if your wife calls?"

He lifted a finger in the air. "Except hers."

Instead of a snarky remark or a look to match, Tiffany delivered something much more menacing . . . approval.

Without words, Tiffany returned to her desk, and Hunter moved into his office.

"Your Grace."

Blake Harrison wore a perfectly fitted suit, half a smile, and sleep deprivation under his eyes.

"I'll break you of that title one of these days."

"You can try, but I happen to like boasting my acquaintance with a duke."

They shook hands and Hunter circled his desk. "Coffee?"

"Your secretary already took care of that."

Instead of pretending this was a scheduled meeting, Hunter took his seat. "To what do I owe the pleasure of your company?"

"I'm here for Sam. She's preoccupied or she'd be here herself."

The memory of Gabi saying something about Sam's ill sister swam in his head. "How is your sister-in-law?"

"Not well. Which is why I'm here."

Hunter sat back and waited. Blake wasn't one to circle a bush, and thankfully, that hadn't changed. "What can I help you with?"

Blake unbuttoned his jacket and sat in the chair opposite Hunter. "I'm going to paraphrase Sam's words . . . but let me see if I can make this clear. *I've taught Gabriella better. Go find out what the hell that man did to get her to marry him.*" Blake's voice raised an octave when he repeated his wife's words.

He should have seen the question coming. Instead of revealing the truth, Hunter told his old friend something they both knew as truth. "Everyone has a price."

Blake frowned as he sucked in a tired breath. "Not Gabi. She's been through too much to have a price. Everyone who knows her knows that."

For the first time since he'd crawled into the back of the limousine . . . the moment he started the blackmailing of his wife, a knot of uncertainty took a solid hold in his stomach.

"I made her an offer, Blake. She took it."

Hunter knew, without a doubt, Blake didn't buy his explanation.

"You know, Hunter . . . I'm a few years older than you. You've managed to amass a fortune in less time than I, but with age . . . and perhaps a handful of years with a good woman, I'd like to offer you some free advice."

Hunter couldn't remember a time when another man had approached him in such a manner. He kept silent and listened.

"Karma," he began. "She's one rightful bitch. If you wiggled your way into marriage with Gabi in less than honorable terms, that shit's going to bite you in the ass. Not only does Gabi have a strong and powerful pool of friends, there's no possible way anyone who knows her is going to let her go through hell a second time."

Hunter felt an unfamiliar roll of cold sweat down his back.

"You have no idea, do you?" Blake asked.

"I know she's a widow."

Blake offered a sad smile. "Oh, Hunter . . ." He stood and stuck out his hand.

The handshake was out of place, but Hunter accepted it anyway.

"Next time you merge with a new acquisition . . . do your homework."

That sweat was starting to cool his skin.

Blake pushed away from the chair and turned to leave. "Do yourself a favor," he said. "Ask your *wife* who put the bullets in her late husband."

Oh, shit.

"Are we good?" Hunter asked . . . not quite sure why it mattered.

Blake turned and shrugged. "My wife takes personal responsibility for every marriage her company sets up. What's important to her is important to me. With Gabi, it's personal. Not simply because she's an employee." Blake leveled his eyes and paused. "Don't hurt her, and we'll be fine."

Hunter sucked in a deep breath while Blake left his office.

Chapter Nine

The mature trees thickened as they drove up into the Bel Air Estates.

"We will find you the perfect home today." At sixty-three years old and with over twenty years of selling real estate to the wealthy, Josie Fortier spoke with conviction.

"I hope you're right. The news vans in my current neighborhood are earning dirty looks from my neighbors."

Josie drove farther up the hillside and continued en route to the first of three homes they had scheduled to see that morning. "The neighbors here are much more accustomed to dealing with the press. It proves that private gates are necessary."

Gabi relented. "I suppose you're right about that."

"Everything I'm showing you today is gated. Each home has a separate guest house."

While Josie spoke of bedrooms, bathrooms, and square footage, Gabi's thoughts drifted to the taste of Hunter Blackwell. The frustrating bastard that he was had jolted something she thought was dead inside her.

The last thing Gabi wanted was to feel anything but anger and hatred toward her husband.

Desire wasn't on the menu.

Not now . . . not ever.

She shook the memory of his lips on hers and tried to pay attention to Josie's description of the home they were approaching. The double gates opened to reveal a tree-lined drive. The manicured landscape surrounding the drive added a sense of privacy the previous homes they'd looked at didn't have.

"You're sitting on a smidgen over two acres. Lots of room between you and your neighbors. Much more appropriate for your husband's needs."

"Excuse me?" Hearing Josie speak of Hunter was a strange twist.

Josie parked her car in the circular drive. "When Mr. Blackwell called me yesterday, he suggested more land."

And why would he call Gabi's real estate agent? Wasn't this her decision?

As the two of them exited the car, a sleek graphite gray Maserati pulled in behind them. Gabi wondered, briefly, if it was the current owner of the home. Then the now familiar frame of Hunter pushed out of the sports car, sunglasses perched on the bridge of his nose. His strong jaw and not-quite-perfect hair had the hair on Gabi's arms standing high.

Josie offered a brilliant smile and moved to join Hunter. "Mr. Blackwell. I'm glad you could join us."

"My schedule opened up," Hunter told them.

Gabi attempted to look away as Hunter shook hands with the real estate agent before narrowing the distance between the two of them. He stepped into her personal space as if he'd done so on a regular basis and leaned down to brush his lips to Gabi's cheek. "Smile," he whispered.

She did, and then chastised herself for following his demands so easily. "You didn't tell me you were coming," she said loud enough for Josie to hear.

"Work became impossible once the media leaked our marriage."

"You didn't tell me you were married to Hunter Blackwell," Josie said with a laugh and a slight pat to Gabi's arm.

"We . . . we were waiting to announce the union."

Josie unlocked the front door and started spouting off the home's qualities while Hunter and Gabi took several paces back.

Gabi leaned close and lowered her voice. "What are you doing here?"

He removed his sunglasses and tucked them inside his jacket. "Expediting our search."

"Expediting? We haven't been married a week."

"The sooner we move in together, the better," he whispered. Instead of letting her hold back to grumble quietly, Hunter placed a hand to the small of her back and moved the both of them closer to their tour guide.

"There are five bedrooms, six bathrooms in the main house, two bedrooms, one and a half baths in the guest quarters."

They walked through a foyer that held a double staircase to the second floor. The home was sparsely furnished, indicating the owners didn't live there.

White walls and marble covered most of the vertical and horizontal surfaces. They stepped into the kitchen, the same cool feeling keeping Gabi from seeing the qualities Josie was touting.

The great room moved into a formal dining room and Gabi found herself frowning.

"You don't care for it," Hunter said at her side.

She shook her head. "Too cold, too modern." Though it wasn't modern in the *hard edge and contrasting colors* kind of way.

Josie overheard her. "With furniture the space will warm up."

Hunter moved farther into the dining room and glanced out the window to the yard beyond. "I don't think so."

"You'll love the upstairs," Josie continued.

"I don't think so, Ms. Fortier. Let's continue to the next home!" Hunter's exclamation point was accented by his purposeful strides across the room and the gentle nudge of his hand.

He guided Gabi to his car and opened the passenger door. "We'll follow you," he told Josie, leaving her little option but to slide behind the wheel of her car and drive away.

"That was rude," Gabi pointed out when they took the position behind Josie's car.

"Why?"

"We could have at least looked at the upstairs."

"To serve what purpose? You didn't like it."

"We still could have taken the time to let Josie show us the rest of it."

"I don't like wasting my time."

Gabi turned her gaze out the window. "I don't remember inviting you to join us."

"I'll be living in the home for a year and a half, too, Gabi. I'd like to know what I'm spending my money on."

"Is that right? You didn't mention the need to approve the purchase of the new home during our negotiations."

"We didn't settle on an approximate price of a new home, either . . . but that doesn't mean we can't come to a quick resolution for our temporary home."

"Temporary for you, a little longer for me."

He glanced over the edge of his designer sunglasses and caught her eyes. "You choosing our home doesn't mean I'm giving you a month to find it."

Josie slowed and indicated a turn into another tree-lined drive; this one had the gates a little farther inside the property line.

"It won't take a month."

"It will if you let your agent show you crap."

They parked behind Josie and started over.

Instead of letting her emotions show on her face, Gabi pasted on a smile and made comments about the next two homes they visited. The colonial wasn't her style, the Spanish revival didn't hit the mark.

Hunter followed behind her during the tours and kept his desires to himself.

She didn't lie well, Hunter decided. Her plastic smile and overexaggerated praise for each property kept them in each house a little longer than needed.

Ms. Fortier would stop at some point and ask, "So you think this is the one?"

Gabi would hedge at that point with a complaint that the kitchen wasn't large enough or the outside space didn't flow with the inside.

The woman was stalling and Hunter knew it.

While the two of them walked around the guest house of the forth property, Hunter removed his cell phone and pulled up a list of homes Tiffany had sent him. He passed over several potential homes based on the things he'd heard Gabi say on their tours.

Hunter sent two listings to Ms. Fortier on a text message.

He noticed her remove her phone from her pocket and glance in his direction.

Hunter placed a finger in front of his lips and the real estate agent grinned.

Gabi joined him outside the front of the house and shrugged. "Looks like you wasted your time today after all."

"The day's not over."

"Josie said she had four listings to show me. This is the forth." Gabi's smug smile made him want her to eat her words.

Ms. Fortier locked the door behind her. "Looks like another opportunity is just around the corner. Do you have time for one . . . maybe two more, Mr. Blackwell?"

Gabi frowned.

Hunter smiled. "Of course."

Silence filled his car as they drove a short distance away. The ornate iron gates were set alongside ten-foot hedges and hundred-year-old trees. Interlocking pavers funneled them up a slight incline until the pavement spilled into a circular drive with a fountain in the center.

Gabi's tiny gasp had him watching her from behind his sunglasses.

He took a hunch and ran with it. Gabi's Italian heritage and years of living on her brother's resort island told him a few things about his wife.

Like with the other homes, Hunter stood back and observed.

Gabi ran her hand along the dark wood of the double front doors. The arched entry sat along a deep porch that looked to wrap around the entire house. One singular curving stairway sat at the far end of the large foyer. Dark wood and warm gold and tan walls looked like the cracking plaster in Rome but was a complete finish Hunter knew took at least ten layers to complete.

"Whoa." Gabi seemed to forget to hold her emotions aside as she gawked at the thirty-foot ceiling.

Unlike the other homes, this one had furnishings staged to sell the house. Perfectly matched sofas filled the huge living room, oversize candles sat on the hearth of a fireplace a small child could stand up in.

Ms. Fortier read from her phone and talked about the home's qualities, but from where Hunter stood, Gabi wasn't listening. She walked through the living room and into the kitchen. "Oh, my." She walked over to the professional stove and ran her delicate fingers over a faucet. "Do you know what this is?" she asked him.

"I don't cook."

"It's a pot filler. For pasta."

She opened the side-by-side Sub-Zero refrigerator. The light went on, displaying a case of bottled water . . . further evidence that the home wasn't occupied. Through the eat-in kitchen sat a dining room, a butler's pantry, and an open formal dining room. Several sets of double doors opened into a loggia that expanded the living space to twice the size of the inside space.

Gabi walked through the doors and muttered something about the fireplace and furnishings.

By the time they were upstairs and into the master bedroom, Hunter knew she'd found the right house. Like a child in a candy store, she giggled when she saw the size of the tub and shower. Iron accents and rustic colors were obviously Gabi's personal taste. The upstairs balcony looked down on the yard, the pool . . . the massive space below.

When they moved back downstairs, Ms. Fortier opened doors and poked around the spaces they'd yet to explore.

"You like it," Hunter said close to her ear.

"It's . . . it's too much."

He grinned and turned when Ms. Fortier called them over. "You have to see this."

Gabi had a spring in her step as they followed the real estate agent down a narrow stairway. The brick walls were darker than any of the other spaces but suited the home perfectly.

"What Italian home is complete without a wine cellar?" Ms. Fortier said.

They stopped at the bottom of the stairway and Gabi lost her smile before stumbling back. Hunter reached out and held her elbow.

She was cold, stone cold.

"Gabi?"

She shivered and closed her eyes. "I'm OK."

No, she wasn't. Hunter looked around the beautiful space, saw bottles of wine, empty racks for more. "Let's get you back upstairs."

The fact that she didn't pull away when he wrapped his arm around her waist and guided her back upstairs told him the wine cellar had sparked some kind of bad memory.

She was silent as he sat her on the nearest sofa and asked that Ms. Fortier find her a glass of water.

"Give us a minute," Hunter told the real estate agent once she returned with the water.

Ms. Fortier stepped outside, leaving them alone.

He sat on the wooden coffee table and waited for Gabi to stop trembling before he spoke. "Are you OK now?"

She sipped the water, her hand still shaking. "Yeah." Gabi laid the back of her hand to her forehead. "I didn't expect that."

"The wine cellar?"

"No. My reaction to it."

He hadn't expected it, either. "I guess we can mark this house off our list."

She offered a quick shake of her head. "No. The house is lovely. Perfect, really."

"You nearly passed out a minute ago by walking into a basement."

She attempted a smile and Hunter felt her squeeze his hand. It was then he noticed that he held hers. Gabi must have realized it, too, and pulled away.

"It's one room in a big house. I don't have to go into it."

He leaned forward, elbows on his knees, and asked, "Why the strong reaction, Gabi?"

Her gaze met his, her forced smile faded. "It's not important."

Which translated meant *none of your business.*

Hunter took the water from her hand, set it aside. He had a year and a half to discover her secrets. Something told him it wouldn't take that long.

Gabi swayed when she stood, reached out to steady herself on his arm, then promptly let go. "Thank you," she said. "For not prying."

"I want to," he told her.

"I know."

Ms. Fortier walked into the room, concern on her face. "Shall we move on?"

Gabi looked around the room, her eyes fell on him. "What are they asking for this house?"

There was shock in Ms. Fortier's voice when she spoke. "Eighteen point four."

Gabi's head snapped toward the other woman. "Million?"

"Yes."

"Didn't I say less than ten?"

"It doesn't matter." Hunter stepped between them. "Write up an offer."

"Hunter!" Gabi called behind him.

"The house is perfect, you said yourself. I'll bolt the cellar door. What do you think about the furnishings?" He shifted the conversation as if the purchase of the home was a foregone conclusion.

Gabi closed the space between them and tugged on his arm to get his attention. "You're being impulsive."

"I'm being practical. Buying furniture takes time."

"I'm not talking about the furniture. I'm talking about the house. Eighteen point four million dollars is—"

"*My* standard of living," he said, his gaze firm. "Just like *we* agreed upon."

Gabi glanced between Ms. Fortier and Hunter. "Fine."

"Wonderful," Ms. Fortier said.

Gabi leaned close. "I was trying to save you some money."

"If I wanted to save money, I wouldn't have gotten married."

"I want to pick out my own furniture!"

Hunter met her eyes . . . added a slow smile. "Fine."

Chapter Ten

"It's not possible to come and go without an audience," Gabi voiced her complaint to Gwen over tea. "Escrow won't close for two weeks, *if* everything goes as Hunter planned." Gabi held the curtain back and found a media camera swinging her way. Many of the news vans had grown bored and moved on, but a few of the entertainment television and magazine reporters settled in for the long haul.

Gwen lifted her regal chin and sipped. "You can always move in with him now."

She let the curtain drop, cutting out the images of reporters and cameras. "No. I want mutual ground. Moving in with him would give him the upper hand."

"How do you see that?"

Gabi shrugged. "I just do. Moving into a home neither of us has occupied feels safer." At least in her head.

Gwen's easy smile waned. "You don't feel safe with him?"

"I don't know him. It's that simple."

She carefully set her tea aside. "Yet you married him. You have to know that none of us believe you did so willingly."

"None of us?" Gabi knew the intervention was coming. She'd received daily calls from every Alliance team member and a few previous brides who were close personal friends of Sam and Blake.

"We can start with your brother and Meg."

"I'm aware of how Val feels. He's being the protective brother."

"It's more than that. Michael called Karen and asked if the rumors were true."

Michael was this side of Hollywood royalty and a former "husband" that Alliance had arranged. He and Meg had been visiting Val's resort when everything went to hell with Alonzo.

Gwen kept talking. "Then there is Neil and Rick. The two of them have had their knickers in a knot ever since you announced the contract."

Gabi unfolded from the chair and stood. She hated the wobble in her legs and did her best to steady herself. "I don't think I have to tell you that your husband is suspicious by nature. And Rick is probably following Judy's lead on this. I know she and Meg have been talking."

Gwen followed her into the kitchen and leaned against the counter.

"You can call it suspicion, but I will call it deductive reasoning. Since you've lived in California you haven't so much as gone to a nightclub or dinner without the company of a woman."

Gabi opened her mouth to argue and Gwen stopped her. "If I'm not mistaken, the only charity event you attempted to attend alone was the one where pictures of you and Hunter emerged. Correct me if I'm wrong."

"I've not been a recluse."

"Close. Dangerously close and you know it. Marriage, even the arranged kind with a prenuptial contract, doesn't make sense, Gabriella. You have friends . . . people who can help if you'd trust us."

Gabi couldn't take the worry on Gwen's face. Facing the sink, she proceeded to wash the cup in her hand. The emotional part of her wanted to confide in the other woman . . . but the smart and thinking part . . . that section of her decided now was not the time discuss a billionaire's blackmail. Without looking at Gwen, she attempted to stretch the truth.

"He's an attractive man." Which wasn't a lie. "While his proposal and financial offer were unorthodox, I must admit having a man at my mercy wasn't an awful position to be in."

"What are you saying? Hunter Blackwell is therapy?"

"Perhaps." She rinsed the cup and set it on a towel to dry before turning. "I realized the path I set since Alonzo hasn't been healthy. Hunter offered me an opportunity to break the cycle. He will be a safe companion for a few months, then we can go our separate ways and perhaps I'll be able to find trust in men again."

Gwen moved beside her, set her cup inside the sink. "I want to believe you."

Gabi met the other woman's gaze. "Then do."

A knock on the door interrupted the moment.

A floral delivery van sat in the driveway, the media cameras were poised and ready.

Gabi opened the door to the face of a bewildered teen. "Mrs. Blackwell?"

That was going to take some time to get used to. "Yes."

He handed her what looked like a dozen roses . . . velvet red. "Can you sign here?"

She did. "Let me get a tip."

"It's all taken care of. Have a nice day."

"How lovely," Gwen said behind her.

Gabi set the flowers next to those Hunter had sent her earlier in the week. Each bouquet was different . . . from tropical ensembles to lilies . . . the roses were a new direction.

The card held simple instructions. *Formal dress, seven tonight. H.B.*

Gwen glanced over her shoulder. "The flowers are a nice touch."

"For the cameras, I'm sure."

Gwen gathered her purse and kissed Gabi's cheek. "It appears you have a date with your husband."

"Does that sound as strange to your ears as it does mine?"

Gwen laughed and placed a hand on her arm. "Do be careful."

"I am. And please, if the masses begin to talk, remind everyone that I thought I loved a man who nearly killed me and I managed to survive. Hunter needed a wife and I'm filling a role. There are no emotions involved and no one is trying to end my life."

"If you truly believe that, then do me a favor," Gwen said. "Try and enjoy yourself." Her hand reached up and patted the side of her face. "The lines of worry etch across your beautiful eyes, making it very difficult to believe you're not scared out of your mind."

Gabi brought both hands to her face, forced the muscles under her fingertips to relax. "The sooner your temporary husband knows your past, the easier it will be for him to set you at ease. Without the knowledge, he's bound to stumble upon a panic button and leave you running."

The image of the wine cellar was proof of that. But confiding in Hunter wasn't an option.

She'd have to tiptoe through the minefield Alonzo had left in his wake. She'd done a good job for nearly a year and a half.

What was another eighteen months?

Charles had to double-park the limo outside of her Tarzana home. Gabi felt her pulse rise when the driver walked her to the car.

The media swarmed. "Mrs. Blackwell . . . a moment of your time?"

"Is it true you're pregnant with Hunter Blackwell's child?"

The questions kept coming. She answered none of them as she slid into the backseat.

Hunter wasn't inside, which surprised her.

It didn't take long for Charles to pull away, or long for the media to jump in their cars and follow.

"A year and a half of this," she mumbled to herself.

On the other hand, the stretch limo wasn't an awful way of traveling. It beat the sweaty palms and worry she was going to run into someone while driving Hunter's James Bond car. She should probably tell him she wasn't proficient behind the wheel.

She supposed the conversation would come up when he saw the tiny dent in the bumper. A dent she managed while avoiding a cameraman and hitting the neighbor's garbage can. Which, again, wasn't really her fault. If the paparazzo wasn't there, it wouldn't have happened.

Gabi found the button that lowered the glass between her and the driver. "Are they still following us?" she asked, unable to tell with the darkened windows in the back.

"'Fraid so, Mrs. Blackwell."

She looked out the back window and saw several sets of lights. "Are we picking Hunter up?"

Charles maneuvered the large car around the corner and onto the freeway. "He asked that I deliver you to his residence."

She glanced at the fitted full-length gown complete with spaghetti straps that held the dress in place, and high heels that would be better off walking into a concert hall than a penthouse suite. Then again, she'd never seen Hunter's home, the home she refused outright.

She sat back to enjoy the drive and realized she'd be alone with Hunter once they arrived on Melrose. And if escrow closed in two weeks as planned, they'd be alone together often.

Her nerves began a slow dance down her spine and to the tips of her fingers where she tapped them against the seat.

"Would you care for music, Mrs. Blackwell?"

"Yes—No, I . . ." This wasn't a good sign. "Tell me, Charles, how is it *you* always seem to be available to be my driver?"

She met the man's eyes through the rearview mirror. His pleasant, unthreatening smile helped.

"Mr. Blackwell requested my service. Said he wanted to know who was driving his wife around."

"Oh . . ." she wasn't sure what to make of that.

"He said that trusting your drivers was important to the both of you. I really appreciate your endorsement."

She was about to tell him that she hadn't gone out of her way to endorse him but realized that wouldn't come out right. "Did he say anything else?"

"Just asked me to watch out for you."

"Spy?"

"Oh, no, nothing like that. More like, he knows you're a beautiful woman and are married to one of the richest men in the States. You never know who might lurk, ya know?"

That didn't sit well. Her face must have shown her concern. Charles instantly jumped to put her at ease. "Before I took this job, I trained in firearms and hand-to-hand self-defense. You're safe with me, Mrs. Blackwell."

His conviction made up for his size.

She really needed to get over her paranoia. Maybe it was time to see her counselor again. It had been six months and she'd not felt the need. But since she said "I do," that need seeped back in.

Six blocks and four red lights from the complex Hunter lived in, Charles used his hands-free phone and called ahead. "Two minutes," he said.

If Gabi was worried about the paparazzi getting too close, she needn't have. Not only was Hunter standing at the curb when Charles pulled in, but beside him were two men twice his size, their hands loose at their sides while they all but dared the media to shove in too close.

Hunter opened the door and extended a hand.

He wore a tux. Crisp black, clean white shirt, and a tie that was a little askew. His hair was mussed a little in the front, as if he'd run a nervous hand in it prior to her arrival.

Gabi placed one leg out of the limo and felt his eyes find her bare skin under the slit of her dress. She placed her hand in his and let him lift her from the low car.

When she stood her full height, nearly meeting his gray eyes in her four-inch heels, she realized he hadn't let her hand go. Instead, he lifted it to his lips and kissed her knuckles.

Flashes exploded around them.

Of course . . . the media was close enough to grab pictures, but not close enough to touch.

"You're stunning," he said under his breath.

With a tug, she removed her hand from his and placed it on his tie. Once it sat perfectly, she smiled.

"Mr. Blackwell . . . one picture."

"Some of us have to make a living," another voice called.

Gabi noticed Charles move behind them and waved his hands in the air as if to remind the media to keep a distance.

"I have kids to feed, Mrs. Blackwell . . . help a guy out?"

Hunter started to pull her away and she held firm. The need to feed the kids was probably a line, but Gabi didn't think there would be any harm in smiling for a few shots.

Hunter nodded toward the building and Gabi pulled his hand closer.

A ghost of a smile met his lips and did a dangerous twist to her gut. Understanding of her desires had him moving close and placing a hand around her waist. That dangerous twist did a double flip. Instead of thinking about it, she turned toward the man with kids and a huge lens and smiled.

Hunter turned her toward the media on the other side of the bodyguards and tugged her closer still. She felt the full length of the man, from shoulder to hip, and for the first time in more months than she could remember, she didn't shiver. Even though the night was cool and she hadn't bothered placing a wrap over her shoulders, she was warm.

His lips moved close to her ear. "I hear the hungry kid thing once a week."

"Kids get hungry every day."

He laughed, putting her at ease, and walked her out of the media lights.

One of the bodyguards stayed in the lobby, while the other rode up the elevator with them.

"Do you mind telling me what we're doing tonight? Seems to me playing dress-up for an evening at home is a little overkill." Gabi kept her eyes on the double doors, counting the floors as the elevator made a rapid climb to the top.

"A small reception. Mainly business associates and a few key media personalities to spread the word."

She glanced at him briefly, realized he was staring. "You could have said as much."

"You don't like surprises?"

"Not particularly."

"Hmm . . ." he glanced at the rising numbers. "I'll remember that."

The bell dinged.

"Ready?"

Like she had a choice. She placed her arm through his and plastered on a smile as the doors opened.

Small reception?

Perhaps Hunter didn't understand the definition of the word small.

Women dressed to the nines, men in tuxes . . . it looked like a wedding reception, only she wasn't wearing white. Would she have, had she known?

No, the gold sequins was close enough. Besides, the man was made of gold and there would be those who called her a gold digger, so why not run with it?

Two things hit her at once . . . she knew no one in the room. Not one soul outside of Hunter . . . and roses. The same red velvet roses he'd sent earlier in the day sat in every possible horizontal space in the room. It wasn't a splash of color, it was a tsunami of fragrance and texture.

Hunter twisted away and returned with one single stem. "For you."

He was too good-looking, too full of testosterone . . . too much. She glanced at the flowers again and couldn't help but smile like a fool. "Who knew you had a pink side."

His laugh caught the attention of everyone within earshot.

"Only you would dare say such a thing."

She'd say more than that if they didn't have an audience.

A pianist's music filled the space as they walked into the room, his arm around her.

An older man approached instantly, as did a waiter with a tray of drinks.

"Mrs. Blackwell . . . can I take your purse?"

She glanced at Hunter, who nodded. "This is Andrew, Gabi. He works for us personally. You'll get to know him very well."

He had a soft, reassuring smile.

"You can trust him," Hunter whispered in her ear.

"The pleasure is mine," Andrew said with a slight dip to his head.

She handed him her purse and he walked away.

Hunter removed two glasses of champagne from the tray and handed her one.

A strange panic washed over her, she tried to push it aside but couldn't.

Instead of saying a thing, she handed him her glass and took his. Her world settled as he sent her a puzzled look. She knew he had a thousand questions from that simple move, but as luck had it, there wasn't time to ask or explain.

"Blackwell . . . is this her?"

"Frank Adams . . . I'd like you to meet my lovely bride, Gabriella Blackwell."

Gabi found her hand pulled into the meaty one of Frank Adams. His accent was pure Texas, his flirty wink comical in the room full of sophistication. He wore a tux and a Stetson. It made her smile.

"My Melissa is going to be terribly disappointed," Frank said with a lift of the eyebrow. "Then again, I assume there will be plenty of crying women when they hear you're all snatched up, Blackwell."

Gabi stood back and watched as Hunter engaged in a conversation with the outlandish Texan before moving away.

She leaned in. "I can't tell if that was friendly or not."

His lips nearly brushed her ear when he spoke. "I already told you I have no friends."

Gabi made a sweep of the room with her eyes. "Then who are all these people?"

"Colleagues, enemies . . . acquaintances."

From the far side of the room, she saw Andrew standing to the side, watching them. "And Andrew?"

"Well . . ."

So there was someone Hunter deemed a friend.

She didn't have time to think on that before Hunter introduced her to the next group. "They work in my New York office," Hunter offered as they walked away.

Gabi calculated the names into memory, moved to the next.

There were employees, partners in different professions . . . all of them eyed her with a mix of speculation and envy. Well . . . from the women, in any event.

"And you remember Tiffany."

"Of course," Gabi said, smiling into the weary eyes of Hunter's personal secretary.

"Maybe now that Mr. Blackwell has a wife, you can make sure his suits are pressed and the flowers are ordered."

Hunter shot his secretary a look that made Gabi cringe.

"Or not," Tiffany said before moving away.

Hunter took the untouched champagne from Gabi's hand and set it on a nearby tray.

"Senator Fillmore . . . I'd like you to meet my wife, Gabriella."

A face she recognized. "We've met," she managed as she extended her hand.

"We have?" the senator said.

"Yes, last year. I was a guest of Carter and Eliza Billings at the Hollywood fundraiser." Carter was the former governor of California and was taking a political break for a couple of years while he and his wife adjusted to parenthood. Truth was, Carter was destined for bigger things than the governor seat, and everyone knew it. Eliza . . . well, she and Sam were the best of friends.

"How is it I don't remember you?"

"There were over a thousand people at the event," Gabi reminded him.

The silver-haired senator shook his head. "I won't forget a second time."

Hunter didn't give her time to linger and moved them to another set of guests.

After a dozen more introductions, Gabi was ready for a break. She leaned close and whispered. "Restroom?"

"Down the hall, double doors to the master suite."

For the first time in over an hour and a half, she left Hunter's side.

The noise of the room started to fade as she made her way to the private, off-limits side of the home. She pushed through the closed doors and leaned against them, absorbing the quiet.

The lights turned on with her movement in the room. Soft light filled the wall behind the massive king-size bed. A dark gray coverlet draped over the mattress and the simple artwork of New York and Los Angeles skylines in black and white were the only pieces on the wall. The drapes hadn't been drawn, giving the room a slight chill. Drawn to the sight, Gabi moved to the floor-to-ceiling windows to soak in the view.

So this is where Hunter Blackwell sleeps.

She knew he had a residence in New York as well . . . one with a view most likely more magical than the one in front of her now. She wondered, briefly, if she'd ever see it.

Cityscape had its place. The single world, one without a family . . . a life . . . a pet.

Yet even as those thoughts filled her head, she realized that she'd been living in a suburban home without any of those things . . . and no view to speak of.

She'd always wanted a puppy as a child and never had one. After her father had passed, she'd stopped asking. Then again, she was a young teen and Val had taken over as man of the house. Her mother wouldn't stand for an animal, and then Gabi simply forgot about it.

The image of the house she and Hunter were purchasing surfaced. Maybe she could have a dog after all. An animal to depend on her. Something to come home to.

The gray slate floors and marble counter of the en suite bathroom were masculine but not deprived of texture. A simple flowering orchid sat in the center of two sinks . . . a shaver plugged into an outlet by one of the sinks. Without realizing she did so, Gabi opened a drawer, saw the usual suspects inside. Toothbrush, mouthwash . . . things of that nature. The next drawer housed an open box of condoms.

She had a strong desire to count them, then decided against it.

Instead of lingering in Hunter's space, she moved through the room and glanced at his bed once.

Well, maybe twice.

The presence on the other side of the double doors made her catch her breath. "Andrew."

"Sorry to startle you. Just wanted to ensure your privacy." The man stood back, giving her all the space she needed.

Lord, she could use a drink. "Can you show me the kitchen, Andrew?"

"It's a bit hectic in there right now."

She thought of the mass of caterers that were serving drinks and hors d'oeuvres. "I'd like to think I'm *not* a guest."

"Of course."

Andrew pivoted, and Gabi followed.

The kitchen was as sleek and modern as the rest of the home. A cook's kitchen put to work with an event such as this.

"I think they're fine. Murray wouldn't have sent them if they weren't servable!"

There was one woman, and one man, in solid white. The chefs.

And an obvious power struggle.

In Gabi's experience, one too many chefs in the kitchen always created problems.

Unlike her brother's island, the employees in this atmosphere weren't ones she needed to concern herself with for the long run.

The click of her heels sounded on the hard surface of the marble floors as she made her way to the trays of shrimp the two chefs argued over.

The servers noticed her first, then the two in white.

"What is the problem?" Gabi asked.

"No problem. The guests are out—"

Gabi cut the woman off. Her dyed blonde hair was pulled back in such a severe fashion she would never need Botox.

"I'm *not* a guest." Gabi moved to the tray in question and lifted one shrimp to her nose, touched the surface of the shellfish, and promptly turned to an open trash receptacle and emptied the tray.

The blonde gasped, the servers halted their movements.

"Did any of that go out?"

The second chef snapped his fingers and called out to a server, in Spanish, to retrieve the waiter who had just left the kitchen.

"Those were perfectly fine," the blonde managed.

"Is that so?" Gabi lifted a nearby tray and waved it under the blonde's nose. "Dig in."

The woman held her ground . . . didn't reach for the food.

"You can leave." Gabi dismissed her with a flick of the wrist.

"Excuse me?"

"Leave. Get into your car and leave." Gabi turned to the second chef. "How much of the order did the shrimp account for?"

"An eighth."

Gabi looked at the other trays, made a deduction. "Half the portion of skewers to keep the trays full." She found the eyes of a nearby waiter. "Tell the beverage servers to keep the glasses of the guests filled." Gabi turned to the remaining chef. "I assume the alcohol quota is twice what was called for?"

"Yes," he managed with a swallow.

"I'm in charge here," the blonde, who hadn't left, said in protest.

"The one paying the bill is in charge. Thank you for your service, but your insight on bad seafood is astounding. And I don't mean that in a good way. Please don't make me call security."

With an exasperated breath, the woman turned on her heel and left.

Without thought, Gabi moved to the refrigerator and found a bottle of champagne chilling. She removed a towel from the counter and proceeded to pop the cork. Boxes of flute glasses sat alongside one of the counters. She removed two and filled them.

She handed one to the remaining chef. "What's your name?"

"Hector." He wiped his hands on his apron and took the sparkling wine.

"You're doing a superb job, Hector." Gabi winked and lifted the wine to her lips.

It was savory, wonderful.

Untainted.

She drained the glass and poured a second before leaving the kitchen.

Andrew fell in step behind her as she walked back into Hunter Blackwell's world.

Chapter Eleven

His hand came down full force, the laptop bounced, as did the fully loaded Glock 40 sitting beside it. "What do you mean my money isn't touchable?"

"I'm sorry, Señor Diaz, the passwords have changed and locked us out. I have a second man working on it."

Diaz tapped his finger on the grip of his gun, seriously considered shooting the messenger. He hated the scrawny cokehead standing in front of him, but Raul knew his way around computers better than any of his other men.

"Who changed the password?"

"That I don't know. Only you and I have access to the account."

Diaz circled the trigger of his weapon, his eyes bored into Raul.

He lifted the gun and Raul had the good sense to back up, hands in the air. "I didn't do it. Why would I come to you if I did?"

Raul would have scurried away in the dead of night if he'd compromised any of Diaz's money, but watching the man fry a few brain cells as he attempted to talk his way out of death was worth the entertainment.

"Picano is dead. If you want to avoid his fate, you'll have an answer for me in twenty-four hours."

"But—"

Diaz pulled the lever back and loaded the chamber.

"Twenty-four hours. I'll have an answer in twenty-four hours."

Diaz waved the gun, dismissing the mule.

The thick Colombian heat had sweat rolling down Diaz's back. He lifted his drink to his lips, finished it. He dragged the computer close, clicked onto a different account, this one much farther away.

When the computer-generated warning *Denied Access. Misspelled Password* flashed, he locked his teeth together and slowly tried again.

Access Denied!

Without thought, Diaz unloaded a round into the computer.

The server who had been en route with a replenishing drink screamed, dropped the tray, and stood in paralyzed fear.

Diaz pushed back, the chair falling behind him. "Clean this up," he hollered before moving into the comfort of his air-conditioned refuge deep in the Colombian jungle.

—————

Hunter's wife emerged from the door of his kitchen with a lift to her lips. O'Riley stopped her and the two of them engaged in a conversation. When she tilted the champagne to her mouth, Hunter realized it was the first time he'd actually seen her drink something other than coffee, tea, or water. The memory of her switching his wine with hers when they first entered the room made him question why.

Did she have a problem with drinking? In his experience, those who didn't drink at their age weren't able to handle it.

O'Riley said something that made her laugh, and an unexpected snap of jealousy hit him.

Hunter excused himself and wove his way to Gabi's side.

"Is that right?" he heard Gabi say to O'Riley.

"Is what right?" Hunter slid a proprietary hand across the dipping back of Gabi's gown and let it rest on her hip.

She attempted to place room between them, but Hunter kept his fingers firm, not letting her go.

"Travis was just telling me that your absence in the New York office has your employees jumping whenever they see you."

"Well, *Travis*." He emphasized the other man's name, pissed that Gabi was using it. "I haven't noticed *you* jumping."

"I jump . . . I just hide it better than most."

Travis knew that flirting with Hunter's wife would result in more than a hop in the air. He'd be jumping into an unemployment line if he wasn't careful.

"I'll be sure and watch for that, *Mr.* O'Riley."

Travis lifted a brow, his smile waned.

Hunter leaned close to Gabi's ear. "I'd like to address the crowd for a toast."

"If you'll excuse us, Travis," Gabi said as Hunter pulled her away. "That was abrupt," she said so only he could hear.

"Flirting with an employee isn't wise."

She laughed. "Talking and flirting are worlds apart, Hunter."

Gabi passed a waiter and motioned him over. "Mr. Blackwell is proposing a toast. Have the champagne available for the guests."

"Yes, Mrs. Blackwell."

Hunter guided her to where the pianist played and watched Gabi motion the performer to pull the piece to a close.

Sitting back, Hunter noticed the servers—all of them— exchange their food trays for those filled with sparkling wine.

Though he hadn't researched Gabi's ability to be the perfect hostess, she obviously understood her way around a social event.

A waiter stopped before them, and instead of picking a flute for his wife, he offered her first choice.

She lifted two, handed him one.

His guests slowly stopped talking and turned their attention toward them.

It didn't take long for the low muttering of the crowd to dim, and the attention of his guests fell on him.

When Gabi edged back to give Hunter the spotlight, he reached out to keep her close.

She smiled and looked over the room.

"Thank you all for coming on such short notice," Hunter began. "After meeting my beautiful bride, I'm sure you can understand my need to keep her away from just about everyone in the room so I could encourage her to say yes."

A low level of laughter, and probably more secret nods than he'd prefer, commenced.

"I hope you embrace her as you have me."

He turned, made a point of capturing her eyes for his next words. "To Gabriella Blackwell, who has taken on the challenge of making me a better man."

A wicked smile met her lips. "I don't believe those words were in our vows."

Those who heard her laughed.

"To Gabi." He lifted his glass, set it against hers, and drank.

She was still smiling when he took her glass from her hand and set them both on the baby grand.

Someone in the room graciously started a ring of their glass, and within seconds there was a universal sound that every wedding reception understood.

Gabi's gaze fell to the floor, but the smile on her lips held when Hunter moved into her personal space. He set his hand to the side of her face and looked into the depths of her dark gaze. He saw acceptance there instead of fear . . . he took that as encouragement and lowered his lips.

Unlike their first kiss, on a street corner for the purpose of exposure, this one . . . while for exposure, was softer. Her lips parted, inviting . . . and God help him, he wanted to explore.

She moaned when he pulled away, and did the unexpected. Gabi pulled his lapel and forced a second kiss, bringing laughter to those watching. Her kiss was brief, and when she moved away, she ran a finger over his lips, removing the evidence of her presence.

He caught her eyes, and for a brief moment . . . the space of two breaths . . . neither of them blinked. Something, he wasn't sure what, shifted inside her, and she lifted her lips in a soft smile that wasn't forced . . . wasn't fake.

Hunter lost his breath, knew he grew a special shade of pale.

Gabi laid her hand to his arm.

"Mrs. Blackwell," one of the servers called while the guests resumed their previous conversations.

She turned, offered the waiter an ear. "Yes?"

"A little issue . . . in the kitchen."

She nodded. "I'll be back."

"Fine." He could use a minute alone . . . time to collect his thoughts.

He watched his wife . . . his temporary wife, he reminded himself . . . walk away, and in her place, Andrew stood.

"I'm not sure what I expected," Andrew said in a whisper. "But it wasn't her."

Hunter had disengaged . . . tapped out . . .

He hadn't said a word, or lent a hand to her, since she'd pulled him into an unexpected kiss.

The crowd in his home thinned, and eventually the only ones standing were Tiffany and a few select employees of Hunter's LA office.

Gabi meandered around, directing the staff as they cleaned and set the room to rights. The kitchen slowly became something respective of a bachelor pad.

Gabi walked out of the kitchen in time to see the last of Hunter's guests leave.

"I'll be back Tuesday," he told his secretary, "but out again on Wednesday."

Tiffany tipped a hand in the air, her eyes a tad glossed over from the free-flowing champagne. "Gotcha covered."

Hunter peered closer. "Someone driving you home?"

She waved a finger in the air and said, "Have that covered, too." She giggled, which seemed to surprise Hunter. Tiffany glanced over his shoulder and smiled at Gabi. "Good luck."

Then the slightly intoxicated personal secretary wobbled on a two-inch heel and stumbled out the door.

OK, maybe slightly was an understatement.

Once the door closed, Gabi called behind her, "Andrew?"

"Yes, Mrs. Blackwell?"

"Can you make sure Tiffany has a ride . . . that she doesn't get in her own car?"

"I'll call the desk."

"Thank you."

She went ahead and slipped off her heels. It wasn't quite eleven, but the night had taken a beating on her feet. With her shoes in her hand, she lifted the floor-length dress and made her way to the leather couch.

She dropped the shoes by the sofa and moved to what remained of the bar. "Marilyn, right?"

"Yes, ma'am."

"Thank you. You were great tonight." If there was one thing being the sister of a successful restaurateur had taught her, it was to be grateful for every efficient staff member.

"My pleasure."

Gabi took leave to pour a final glass of champagne for the evening. She'd refrained most of the night and looked forward to relaxing.

From the corner of her eye, Gabi noticed Hunter removing his jacket and tugging on his bow tie.

Hector and the remaining staff members emerged from the kitchen. "We're all cleaned up in there," the chef said.

"Are you married?" Gabi asked, feeling safe to ask with the evidence of said relationship sitting on the chef's ring finger.

"I am."

Gabi turned to the remaining bottles of champagne and took one of the many dozen roses in the room and handed them both to the chef. "For your wife. Thank you for ensuring our guests weren't ill."

Hector offered a full-watt smile, glanced behind her, then back. "Thank you, Mrs. Blackwell. Please call on us whenever you need a caterer."

"I'll do that."

Once the last staff member had left, and only Andrew and Hunter remained, Gabi collapsed into the sofa.

"Miss Tiffany was escorted home. Her car is in the garage," Andrew announced. "Unless you need me, I'll retire," he said.

Gabi glanced at her distant husband. "Good night," Hunter said.

"Thank you, Andrew." Gabi said.

With a slight tip of his head, Andrew offered a smile and left the room.

Hunter moved behind his bar and poured a splash of something stronger than champagne.

Without words, he stood beside the massive window overlooking LA. The tension in his body radiated.

"Are you going to tell me what I did wrong or be ticked all night?"

Instead of answering, he took a long drink and continued to stare out the window.

"Everyone loves you."

She lowered her glass to her lap. "Wasn't that the point of tonight? Introduce me . . . have your colleagues support my place in your life?"

He finished his drink.

Not a good sign.

She set her unfinished wine to the side and stood. "I'll call a car to take me home."

"No!"

She jumped.

"We just announced you as my wife. You leaving here tonight isn't possible."

The cold walls of the modern space started to close in. Hunter must have realized how he sounded and pulled back.

"Good God, Gabriella, I'm not going to attack you. Sit."

The couch became a better option than hitting the floor.

"I have a spare room," he told her. "You can sleep there. Tomorrow we're leaving for the weekend."

Her heart started a rapid ascent and her breathing quickened. "Leaving?" She stood again, her head spun.

"A weekend away. A honeymoon. We need to—"

On some level she knew Hunter was still talking, but Gabi's head soared to a completely different time . . . different place.

"A weekend away . . . I need to make up to you all the time I've been

away." Alonzo stood beside her, his smile genuine. "I want to reconnect with my fiancé."

She kissed him knowing the staff wasn't anywhere close and he wouldn't object.

Her stomach twisted and an all too familiar rush washed over her, hot . . . needy. "More . . . please."

Gabi felt the pinch of her skin. Felt the drug take hold . . . and she hit the ground.

———

Hunter dropped the glass in his hand, jumped over the table, and still only managed to catch Gabi a few inches before she hit the floor.

"Gabi?"

She was out. Her eyes rolled back, her face pale.

"Andrew?"

He lifted her onto the couch, careful with her head. "Andrew!" he yelled.

Half dressed, Andrew rushed into the room. "What happened?"

"Cold washcloth."

Andrew fled to fill his request.

He was an ass . . . he'd scared her with a few words. The strong woman he'd seen traversing the room all night couldn't possibly be the same one passed out in his arms.

Hunter felt three shades of awful.

Andrew emerged, thrust a cold washcloth into his hands.

Hunter ran it over Gabi's forehead. "C'mon . . . wake up."

They both hovered over her.

Andrew started to squirm. "Should I call nine one one?"

Hunter placed his fingers to her throat, felt a steady, albeit rapid, pulse and shook his head.

"Gabi? Wake up." He leaned his head close to hers, felt her breath on his cheek. "Please."

He was a breath away from telling Andrew to call when she started to stir.

Hunter dropped his forehead to hers. All the energy he'd placed in his anger diffused.

Her eyes fluttered open, but the blank look beyond her eyes told Hunter she was still lost.

The moment fear entered her gaze, Hunter drew his frame back but kept his hands on her shoulders to keep her from jumping again. "Are you OK?"

Her nose flared as she attempted to draw in a deep breath. Gabi looked beyond him to Andrew and blinked. "What happened?"

"You passed out."

Her lower lip started to tremble, she kept looking between the two of them as if uncertain what had happened. Her voice wavered. "Can I get a glass of water?"

Andrew didn't hesitate.

Hunter softly stroked her bare shoulders and waited for her color to return. When Andrew returned, Hunter helped her sit. She took the water and closed her eyes when she drank it.

"Thank you," she managed.

"Can I get you anything, Mrs. Blackwell?"

"No, Andrew. I'm s-sorry to worry you."

Hunter ignored the look of concern on Andrew's face as he disappeared around the corner.

Gabi set the glass aside and attempted a smile.

"Are you sure you're all right?"

She shook her head. "No. No, I'm not." She pushed away from him and his hand fell from her shoulder. "I won't go anywhere alone with you, Hunter. Not yet, anyway."

All this was because she feared being alone with him? "I gave you my word I wouldn't hurt you."

"I want to believe you."

"Then do."

"It's not that simple. My head tells me that lightning won't strike twice, but there's no guarantee." She was shaking again and Hunter had a strong desire to pull her into his arms.

"What lightning is that? What did he do to you?"

Doubt filled her face. "I can't . . . I'm sorry."

"Stop apologizing, Gabi. We're in this for the next year and a half. How am I going to know what words to be careful of using if you don't tell me what happened?"

The words were there . . . hanging between them. Her dark eyes searched his.

"Why did you need to get married?"

So this was how it was going to go. Give to get.

He offered a crumb. "My brother has resurfaced."

Confusion marred her brow.

"My twin. Word is he's posing as me." *Again . . .*

"So I'm a built-in alibi?"

Hunter shook his head . . . not willing to give more without a few answers from her. "What did he do to you, Gabi?"

She paused, swallowed hard. "He used me. Shred my dignity."

Not happy with her ambiguous answer, he asked, "How?"

"He pretended to love me and used my brother's island to traffic drugs." Her face lost color again.

"And he hurt you." It wasn't a question.

She nodded and looked away. There was more to her story . . . but he didn't push.

He took a chance and gathered her hands into his. "I'm not him, Gabi. Arguably, I am using you . . . but you know the score, and in the end, we will use each other. I don't trust easily, either. My brother is only part of why I needed a bride."

"What else?"

It was Hunter's turn to divert the conversation. "Are you ready to tell me the whole story behind your late husband?"

She winced.

That's what he thought. "We both have our secrets. Maybe in time we can share them. For now, I need you to trust that I won't hurt you. I won't let anyone else harm you, either."

"I still can't leave with you."

His mind scrambled. "What if you picked where? I need the world to know we're married. If we don't escape for even a few days, there will be some who guess the truth."

Her eyes traveled to the ceiling as if it held the answers. "I haven't been home more than overnight since . . ." She struggled for words. "Since Alonzo's death."

"Your brother's island?"

"Yes."

Jaw dropping, he said, "You want me to willingly go to your brother's world? The man threatened my life."

For the first time since she fainted, Gabi offered a tiny smile.

Hunter's blood warmed.

"Only if you hurt me. And since you're not going to do that, you don't have to worry."

He was still holding her hands when she squeezed them.

"The Florida Keys?"

She nodded.

How bad could it be? "OK."

Chapter Twelve

Somewhere over Texas, enjoying his second midflight drink . . . there was no way in hell he was doing the Keys completely sober . . . Hunter stretched his feet out in front of him and interrupted Gabi as she thumbed through the pages of a book.

"I'm growing on you," he said as if they were in the middle of a conversation.

She glanced over without lifting her head, then returned her eyes to the book. "Don't flatter yourself."

"You haven't told me to jump in front of a bus for at least twenty-four hours."

A ghost of a smile appeared and quickly fell away.

"I can't exactly wish your pilot to plunge to the earth while I'm on the plane, now can I?"

"You didn't poison my breakfast." Hunter emerged from his morning shower to the scent of food cooking in his kitchen. Considering neither he nor Andrew could fry an egg, it was amazing to find Gabi dishing up oatmeal pancakes and scrambled eggs for the three of them.

She flipped a page. "I'm rather fond of Andrew. Nice man. Not sure what crime he committed to be working for you."

"I'm growing on you," he declared again.

She grunted, kept reading.

"You kissed me."

She dropped her hands holding the book and gave him her complete attention. "Your ego is monstrous."

He shrugged. "True, but you did willingly place your lips on mine."

"It was the wine." She picked her book back up, shifted in her seat.

"You had one glass the entire night."

"Your guests expected it. I delivered. Get over yourself, Hunter. On my brother's island, no one will expect anything."

Gabi had explained the privacy of Sapore di Amore. Cell phones weren't allowed, though Hunter had no intention of turning his over. The island was the Vegas of the Florida Keys. What happened on Sapore stayed on Sapore. The exclusivity of the guest list and the screening that went into every guest assured privacy so that playboys could play . . . and wives could cheat. According to Gabi, about half the guests were there for private trysts, and the other half simply wanted privacy. No paparazzi, and celebrities avoided fans bothering them for pictures every second of their stay.

"And I had two glasses." Gabi's declaration brought Hunter back into their conversation.

He thought of her odd reaction to him handing her the champagne and had to ask. "Why the switch of the glasses?"

The muscles on her arms tightened. "I don't know what you're talking about."

"Yes, you do."

She didn't answer . . . instead she asked a question. "Why do you hate your brother?"

"I don't hate Noah."

"His name is Noah? Noah and Hunter . . . interesting."

Their names had always been the oxymoron of his life. "Why the switch of the glasses, Gabi?"

She dipped her head into her book and hesitated.

"He slipped drugs into my wine."

Holy hell. She didn't have to elaborate on who *he* was. "That's sick."

She turned the page much too quickly.

"That's an insult to those who are ill. He knew what he was doing." She muttered something in Italian, shook her head.

One step forward, Hunter mused. He asked a direct question, gave one answer in return. Maybe they could make it a year and a half after all.

She flipped a page. "Remind me to show you where to cliff dive on the island."

It was his turn to grin. "Shark-infested waters?"

She smiled, offered a noncommittal shrug. "Never know."

Gabi had only been on the island for Val and Meg's wedding. She couldn't stomach more. Her therapist told her it was completely normal to associate the island with the man who betrayed her. Most of their time together was on Sapore.

During Gabi's previous visit, she asked to stay in a bungalow. Not willing to walk into the private rooms she called hers, the rooms she shared with *him*.

It killed her that Alonzo had taken away her home. The safe place she should always feel free to return to was destroyed by a dead man. Maybe, just maybe, this time would be different.

But as Hunter's pilot called back into the cabin, asking them to take their seats and prepare to land, Gabi felt her palms sweat. How did palms sweat anyway? There weren't any glands in them to speak of.

Hunter moved from the plush full-size couch he'd been lounging on most of the flight to the seat beside her. He gathered her hand and squeezed. As much as she wanted to shake him off, she couldn't. And for some reason that brought a wave of emotion over her.

"When was the last time you were here?" he asked.

"Early spring. When my brother married."

He looked over her to the sea below.

"You spent time here with *him*, didn't you?"

She offered a nod, felt words clogging in her throat.

Hunter was alone in his thoughts for a moment. "Do you believe in ghosts?"

"Anything is possible," she told him.

The plane started its descent, her ears popped. Would Alonzo's spirit be on the island . . . along with her memories?

"I'm not one to give up control in my life, Gabriella. But I want you to know, here, on this island, if you need me to do anything for you, I will."

She knew his declaration was rare. She squeezed his hand.

"Maybe not the cliff dive . . . but other than that."

Laughter bubbled, she couldn't help it. "You said *anything*."

"I might have you taste all my food before I eat it."

"Happy to. Val's chef is beyond this world."

"I look forward to it. I couldn't tell you the last time I took a vacation."

"Too busy moving your money around the Monopoly board?"

"More like the game of Risk."

Hunter's personal flight attendant walked toward them. "We're clear to land, Mr. Blackwell."

The plane bounced, then glided along the pavement. Hunter's distraction took away the anxiety that rested in her bones since they'd taken off.

She stood and eased the lines in her pants with the palms of her hands.

Hunter waited, patiently. She fisted her clutch in her hands, knew the staff would deliver their luggage at some point.

The flight attendant opened the hatch, bringing in a wave of moist Caribbean heat.

The pilot walked through the narrow door from the cockpit. "I hope your flight was enjoyable," he told them.

"Perfect," Gabi told him.

Hunter lifted his hand. "Wait on my earlier request."

The pilot offered a nod and stood back as they exited the plane.

Most days, the Florida Keys held cloudy skies, hot with the occasional sprinkle, but today was pleasantly clear, giving the air a little less humidity than Gabi expected.

Hunter hesitated at the door, made a show of looking out. "Doesn't look like anyone is carrying a rifle."

Gabi clasped his hand and dragged him out of his world and into hers.

Val stood between her mother and Meg. His back was rod straight, his suit perfectly pressed. Meg offered an enthusiastic wave, her sundress blowing behind her, her short blonde locks hardly contained by the clip in her hair.

Her mother watched, first with watchful eyes on Hunter that seemed to travel slowly between them and then back. Those narrow eyes filled and a smile emerged.

With open arms, Gabi let loose Hunter's hand and ran into the embrace of her mother. "I've missed you," Gabi said in Italian.

"You're too thin," her mother said with little malice.

Val stood to the side, his eyes never leaving Hunter, while Meg moved in for the next hug.

"Hey, you!"

"Look at this tan. You look amazing."

"Good food, great se—"

Gabi's mother clicked her tongue before Meg could say the word *sex*, and they both started to laugh. "Grandbabies, Simona . . . grandbabies."

"Stop seeing that doctor and taking those little pink pills . . . then you can talk about your sex life."

Gabi wondered if Hunter was getting any of their conversation.

She turned, found him in a staring contest with her brother.

Gabi broke it off, pushing herself between their lines of sight. "No kiss for your sister?"

Val blinked her way, his face softened. "I'm pleased you're here, even with that bastard." His words were in Italian.

"He's not that bad," she found herself defending in their first language.

Val grumbled.

"Welcome to Sapore di Amore, Mr. Blackwell." Meg was quick with the agreeable conversation.

"Hunter, I'd like you to meet my mother, Simona Masini."

"I feel as if I know you after our conversation on the phone."

Phone? What? "You two have talked?"

Hunter offered a grin. "We came to an understanding."

She attempted to gain her mother's attention and failed.

"I see where Gabi acquired her thoughtful eyes."

Another man might say . . . good looks . . . beauty . . . no. Hunter went with the eyes. The one feature she and her mother shared without a shadow of a doubt.

Val stepped in, obviously uncomfortable. "I'm sure my sister has informed you of the rules of the island." He lifted his hand, palm up. "Your phone, Blackwell."

Gabi wasn't sure how this was going to go. One alpha male to the other.

"I'm here for Gabi," Hunter said. "Nothing else."

Val kept his hand extended.

Gabi turned to her temporary husband. "Trust needs to be earned. Please."

His gaze shifted.

He fished his phone out of the inside pocket of his suit and handed it over. "If the names Tiffany or Bridget flash, I need to know."

Meg huffed.

"His secretaries," Gabi found herself defending him a second time.

That seemed to relieve Meg's posture.

"Fair enough." Her brother pocketed the phone and glanced toward the plane.

"I assume you've made provisions for your pilot and staff in Miami?"

"I have." Hunter stood closer. "I'd like you to consider them staying here."

"That's out of the question." Val's firm response was short of aggressive.

Gabi felt the power play and couldn't help but question Hunter's intentions.

Hunter pushed his shoulders back and all amusement left his lips.

The move was powerful, and the reason many men cowered in his presence. "The ghosts of Gabi's past are here, Mr. Masini. If at any time during our stay she needs to flee, I'm going to help her do so without delay. We can both agree that having my pilot and plane here would expedite that."

Val clearly wasn't expecting that answer.

The thought of pushing Hunter off the cliff, which actually didn't house sharks . . . drifted.

Val held firm. "I'll have my helicopter and pilot here on standby."

Hunter offered a slight nod. "I'll send my staff on, then."

A breath escaped.

"I hope you like pasta, Mr. Blackwell," Gabi's mother said as she led them away from the island tarmac.

"Please, call me Hunter."

"We're still a long way from first names." Gabi's mother dismissed him with a wave.

Chapter Thirteen

The mental scoreboard in Hunter's head was plunged toward the murky depths of hell.

Valentino hated him. His dark, watchful gaze and short tone didn't need definition.

Margaret . . . or Meg, as Gabi referred to her sister-in-law, was close to impossible to read. From her words and watchful gaze, Hunter knew she'd be happy to see him gone.

And Gabi's mom . . . forget it. The woman told him, repeatedly, that he wasn't good enough for her daughter. *You don't speak Italian. What's wrong with you? Why go through all the effort to marry my daughter and not know her language? Call me Mrs. Masini . . . first names are for friends and family . . . and right now, you're neither.*

Hunter's head swam with the woman's insults.

For one brief moment, he wanted to remind the lady about his net worth . . . but knew she didn't give a crap about his bank balance.

Gabi . . . Gabi was the woman's concern.

The strange twist was Gabriella herself. She let her family deliver their verbal punches for a few hits, and then diverted the conversation.

Gabi didn't deny, nor did she agree . . . she listened and diverted.

He might be able to eat while on the island after all.

They'd taken residence in the special guest villa beside Val's main residence. Gabi had suggested they have their own space. At first, he thought maybe she was saving him from a twenty-four-hour inquisition of her family . . . but as it stood, he realized Gabi assured she wouldn't have to take the room she'd shared with her ex.

He barely noticed the ocean views before he strode into the villa and began setting his things inside the bathroom he'd be sharing with his wife.

He hesitated as he plugged in his electric shaver.

Wife.

How had he managed to move through life without acquiring one of those?

With a sigh, he shook his head, looked past the title, and remembered what Gabi was.

An acquisition to suit his needs for a short duration of time.

Dark, lush hair . . . soulful eyes that displayed more emotion than she'd ever know . . . wit and courage he hadn't expected . . . a body he'd coveted more than any bible verse he'd ever read.

An acquisition, he reminded himself.

Temporary.

"Sorry to interrupt."

Gabi stood on the other side of the door to the adjoining bathroom, a pair of high heels in her hands. "Dinner is at six. Did you want to shower first?"

Translation: *I want to shower and you're in the bathroom.*

"You go ahead."

A genuine smile reached her eyes. "Dinner is causal. You brought casual . . . right?"

"It's a tropical island. I didn't bring a suitcase full of suits."

Those dark eyes followed him as he exited the bathroom and she shut the door.

When the water turned on, he imagined his naked wife . . . Gabi . . .

Yeah, he should probably think of something else.

He reached into the side pocket of his jacket, and then patted his back pockets . . . oh, yeah . . . his cell phone was sitting in a hotel vault, or worse, Gabi's brother was searching his contacts . . . perhaps messages . . .

He tapped his fingers against his thigh.

His phone had a password, he reminded himself.

Hard to hack through a password.

Or was it?

The water from the shower turned off, and his brain raced from cell phones to skin.

They had four nights on the island. Four.

He'd been in more hostile environments than this . . . four days wasn't that long.

"The shower's yours," Gabi called from the other side of the villa. She'd taken the larger of the two rooms. The bathroom had two doors, one to the room she occupied and the other to the rest of the apartment suite.

He stepped into the bathroom. The steam raced against his skin, as did the scent of the floral soap Gabi used.

The door to her room was cracked, and he caught a glimpse of her wrapped in a large bath towel as she padded around her suite.

Bare shoulders and bare knees shouldn't make every part of his anatomy tighten . . . but they did.

Feeling like a peeping pervert, he silently closed the door and shed his clothing.

Cold showers and a warm climate.

Four days, he reminded himself. How hard could that be?

———

Holy hell . . . four days?

She emerged from her room in simple spaghetti-strapped silk that flowed over her curves and made then damn near invisible. They weren't.

Gabi's hair was tossed into what appeared to be a mess on the top of her head, which he knew many women paid close to two hundred bucks to have done for them. Her makeup was minimal . . . a little gloss, a touch at her eyes. She didn't need it.

"Do I have something on my face?" she asked when she caught him staring.

He considered diverting his obvious gawking, then decided against it.

"You're stunning."

The hand she'd brought to her face to wipe fictitious dirt away fell to her side.

And Gabriella Masini Blackwell blushed.

Before she could say a thing, he added, "This island has relaxed you already and we've only been here two hours."

She looked at her feet, then out the massive glass doors that disappeared when opened. "It's hard to take in that view and not feel your heartbeat slow."

Only his sped . . . from his vantage point, in any event.

Hunter shoved one hand into the linen pocket of his pants and took a step toward her. He offered his arm.

Instead of taking it, she lifted her dark eyes to his. "We don't have to pretend affection here," she reminded him.

That burned.

"You can't be stabbing me in the back when you're at my side," he told her. "And right now, you're the only person on this island who tells me to my face to jump off a cliff."

A soft grin started to lift her lips. "You need assurance no one will push you to a splattering death?"

He winced. "I'll stay clear of sharp edges."

He nudged his elbow her way a second time.

She took it.

"I like him."

Meg stood beside her mother-in-law and observed the newly-weds as Gabi introduced Hunter to one of the chefs who cornered them as they walked into the dining room.

"How do you know if you like him? You just met him," Meg said.

"First impressions are important. Gabriella walked off his plane with a smile on her face. One I haven't seen in some time."

"That could be all Gabi and not Hunter." Meg and Simona stood in front of their table, neither taking their seats. "Val can't stand the man."

Simona offered a snort.

Neither of them voiced what they both knew. Val had liked Alonzo, a fact that still haunted him.

The couple broke away from the chef and headed toward them.

Meg glanced around, wondered what was keeping Val. He'd been on the way down to the dining room when she'd agreed to walk Simona over.

The resort's main dining room was lush with tropical floral arrangements and white linen. Several guests were already well into their meals, and many others were coming in for a formal meal.

Meg and Val took a few meals a week in the main dining room. Simona insisted on torturing—or teaching, as the older woman put it—Meg to cook.

If there was one thing Meg wasn't, it was a cook. She managed pasta for fear of an untimely death at the hands of her mother-in-law. The relentless woman never eased up on Meg's ability to cook a proper Italian meal.

The only good news in the forced education narrowed down to the bottle of wine she polished off with every pasta-from-scratch lesson.

Gabi kissed her mother when they arrived at the table. "It's like I never left."

"Then come home," Simona suggested.

Gabi glanced up at Hunter, then back to her mother. "Not yet, Mama."

Simona grunted, the sound so familiar Meg found herself laughing. She patted the space beside her. "You're sitting here, Mr. Blackwell. Gabi, on my other side."

An amused grin fell over Hunter's face as he pulled out chairs.

"I'm going to see what's keeping Val," Meg told them as she excused herself.

She found him lingering outside the doors of the dining room greeting some of the guests. The act wasn't new, but his timing was off. Val was, above all things, prompt.

The same worry she'd seen etched between his eyes when he heard of his sister's marriage was tattooed there again.

She slid her arm around his waist and wiggled into the brief conversation he was having.

Val kept his tone even and wrapped an arm over her shoulders. "I'm delighted you've enjoyed your stay."

"We're already planning our return trip, Mr. Masini."

All pleasantries aside, the older couple moved inside.

"Everyone is seated," Meg whispered.

He grumbled . . . not the grunt of his mother, but close.

"I don't like him, *cara*. How am I going to manage to eat with him at my table?"

She squeezed the hand holding his waist. "One bite at a time. C'mon. Your mom already separated the two of them. And I'll sit next to Hunter to help buffer."

Val kissed the top of her head and took her hand as they walked toward their party.

Hunter stood briefly when Val pulled out Meg's chair. The gesture was normally reserved for those over the age of fifty . . . or from lands well beyond the shores of the Florida Keys. Meg noticed an appreciative glance from Simona. Even Gabi glanced at her temporary husband and managed a glimpse of a smile.

"I haven't had time to truly settle, Val, but from what I can see, you have a spectacular island here."

The compliment, freely given by every guest, wasn't accepted as easily from Hunter Blackwell.

"It serves its purpose."

Meg placed a hand under the table to Val's knee. The man was a ball of tension. His jaw twitched, his eyes kept in line with Hunter without so much as a single blink.

Meg diverted the conversation. "Tell me what's going on back in California," she said to Gabi.

"It's quiet . . . well, except for Jordan's condition."

Meg knew Sam's sister wasn't healthy.

"How's Sam doing?"

"I haven't seen much of her," Gabi told her. "We've spoken a few times. Eliza has been by her side more than not."

They discussed Sam's sister and broke the tension between the men, but didn't manage to lighten the mood at the table.

The waiter arrived with two bottles of wine. Val proceeded to sample the wine and wave his hand in agreement. "I've heard you're breaking into the oil business, Blackwell."

Hunter lifted the glass recently poured. "I am. Pipelines, actually."

"With the country investing so much in solar, isn't oil a risk?" Meg asked.

Val didn't give Hunter time to answer. "Not really, Margaret. There's plenty of oil here, just a lack of infrastructure to deliver it to refinery plants."

"Do you invest?" Hunter asked.

Val shrugged, but Meg noticed her husband's thoughtful gaze.

"We're eating, Valentino. Business can wait." Simona turned her direction toward Hunter. "Tell me about your mother."

Hunter swallowed half his glass of wine in one gulp. "I'd rather talk about oil."

For the first time since Hunter's arrival, Val chuckled.

Simona offered a disapproving scowl but didn't pull Hunter back into a discussion about his family after Gabi quickly changed the subject.

Later, once Hunter and Gabi both pleaded exhaustion after traveling and a busy week, Meg sat on the balcony veranda of their private home on the island.

Meg stretched out on a double lounge, arms above her head, when Val emerged from inside.

The sea lapped up on the shore, and the temperature, even in mid-November, was mild enough to lounge outside without more than a nightgown and a bathrobe.

Meg patted the space beside her, inviting her husband.

He'd shrugged out of his jacket and tie. Still the starched shirt was there, but opened enough to display the sexy edge of a chiseled chest.

With a heavy sigh, he tucked her into the safety of his arms. She didn't wait long to say what they were both thinking.

"You're starting to like him."

He grunted . . . just like his mom, and Meg had to stop from laughing out loud.

"He didn't want to speak of his family."

Meg shrugged. "Have you met mine? Not exactly mention-worthy."

Val kissed the top of her head. "I don't want to like him, *bella*."

"He's attentive to Gabi. The second she started to yawn, he made excuses."

"To get her alone."

Meg shook her head and watched the slow speed of the moon dance over the cloudless sky. "If he wanted her alone, he wouldn't have brought her here. Besides, there's nothing going on between them." *Not yet anyway.*

"How can you tell?"

"Your sister is much more transparent than you give her credit for. And Hunter was way too tense for a man who's getting lucky."

Val groaned again.

This time Meg did giggle.

"Why must you make me think of my sister and sex?"

"She's a grown woman, Val. Chances are, the last experience she had was with that asshole, Alonzo. Pity that!"

Meg noticed Val's eyes squeezed tight.

She placed a hand on his chest and kneaded the muscles under her fingertips.

"I don't want to like the man. He's bullied my sister into marriage. I know it."

Yeah, Meg thought the same thing. "Still, he's clueless."

"He's a billionaire on his own accord. No family money to speak of."

"Still clueless. If he wasn't, he wouldn't have brought her here. She's safe here, even if she doesn't feel it yet. If Hunter Blackwell truly meant to harm your sister, this is the last place he would have taken her for a fake honeymoon."

"Unless she left him no choice."

Meg lifted her knee over Val's stretched-out leg and inched it north. "If that's the case, then you need to give your sister credit. Blackwell is out of his league here." Meg inched her fingers under Val's shirt and rubbed the skin she found. "Enough about your sister and her husband."

Meg caught Val's grunt with her lips and made him forget about everything but the two of them.

———

Remington stood in the center of Miami International, plane ticket in his hand. The phone rang and rang . . . finally, he heard Blackwell's voice.

A recording.

Fuck.

He waited for the beep. "Columbia sucks this time of year. I expect severance pay for this shit. Checking out account number one. Will hit account number two soon."

He hesitated, then smiled. "Italy sounds good. Better call me soon if you don't want me there. It's your dime."

Remington hung up, smiled.

He loved his job.

Chapter Fourteen

The calm waters held no break to speak of, so Gabi swam a good half a mile from shore before turning on to her back to float.

The water was nourishment for her skin. The tang of salt water in her eyes, on her tongue was the taste of home.

She missed it.

Her family's interference and constant questioning the night before had kept a smile on her face all evening and even into her dreams.

The sun was still low on the horizon when she'd left the villa after the first decent night's sleep since she'd agreed to marry. Her husband was still sound asleep in his room.

She let the quiet waters lull her as she floated. The pull of the sea inched her closer to shore.

Water filled her ears, masking the sound around her.

The sound of a gasp and several strong strokes against the water splashed, bringing her relaxed position in the water to high alert.

She heard her name.

Hunter swam her way, his arms and chest bare. Only when he was on her did his stunned expression alarm her.

"What happened?"

His hand gripped her arm, tight. "Are you? Damn . . . you were still. I called your name."

Gabi kicked her feet, keeping herself afloat. "You thought . . . ?"

His grip tightened. "You didn't respond."

She moved her free hand to the one holding her. "I enjoy a morning swim." She looked around them. "Besides, the sharks aren't on this side of the island," she teased.

"That's not funny, Gabi."

He was worried. Really alarmed.

"I've spent many years of my life in these waters, Hunter. I'm fine."

"I saw you floating."

She grinned. "And you came out here to rescue me."

Hunter managed to stay afloat and cover his eyes with his hands. "You're killing me, lady."

"You try to be such a tough guy. In control of everything."

He shook his head, offered a glare. "I thought you were shark meat out here."

She laughed, kicked her feet. "Shark-infested island waters aren't a selling point to my brother's guests."

For a moment, they swam in place and stared at each other.

The clear water made her realize that Hunter had jumped in with only boxer shorts. On the shore, she noticed clothing carelessly heaped into a pile.

"Are you a good swimmer?" she asked.

"I manage."

She started to move. "Last one to shore cooks breakfast." She ducked under the water and came up to hear him sputter.

"I don't coo—" He gave chase, not letting the words finish.

Halfway to shore, he'd caught up, his arms stronger, his strokes taking the water and using it to propel him forward.

Still, her home-court advantage helped keep her in the race, but Hunter managed to crawl up on the white sandy shore before she did.

He sat with his arms resting on his knees, his lungs sucking in air.

The gentle waves brought her on shore with some grace. She felt Hunter's eyes watching her as she pulled herself from the water. The bikini hadn't had much use since she'd left her brother's island. The fact that the strips of material didn't hug her curves as well as they once had was a testimony to the weight she'd lost. Putting it back on hadn't been a priority.

Instead of dwelling on the condition of her frame, she sat next to Hunter and let the white sand take up residence on her skin. "Next time I get a two second head start," she told him.

"Five," he countered. His sharp gaze dipped to her chest and lingered.

She couldn't help the fidget. When was the last time someone other than a doctor looked at her in as little as a bikini?

"What would you cook me . . . if you'd lost?"

He turned his attention away from her chest and back to her eyes. "Crepes . . . maybe a Belgian waffle."

It was Gabi's turn to stare. His straight face and stoic delivery of menu choices had her stunned.

"Crepes?" Even she had no real idea how to manage crepes.

A ghost of a smile started at one corner of his lips and spread. For the first time since she'd met the man, that grin found his eyes.

"If only you could see the shock in your eyes," he said.

"Crepes?"

He bust. A larger-than-life laugh erupted.

She closed her eyes and envisioned Val's room service menu.

Gabi swept her hand along the sand, sending a plume of dust his way.

"Hey." He shot sand her way in retaliation.

"Can you cook anything for yourself?"

"Does coffee count?"

She rolled her eyes. Don't get mad, she told herself . . . get even. "If you want to get on my mother's good side, plead ignorance in the kitchen. She's a sucker for a helpless man in the kitchen."

"Offering tips on making your family happy?"

She leaned back on her elbows, mirroring his stance. "We're in this for eighteen months. Might as well find some peace."

"Hmmm."

She tilted her head toward the sun. "Besides . . . I miss the island."

She caught him looking at her through the corner of his eyes. He diverted his gaze to the ocean.

"I couldn't tell you the last time I sat in the sand."

"Hard to sand sit when you're playing millionaire."

He laughed.

"Sorry, billionaire." It was hard to wrap her head around his net worth. Money had never been a primary need in her life . . . but then again, she'd always had it. She'd read his portfolio . . . knew he'd made the majority of his worth on his own.

"One more zero."

"Two more. I crunched the numbers myself."

Hunter rolled onto his side, caught the side of his face in a sandy hand, and stared with amusement on his lips. "What numbers were those?"

"We can start with the Carlton takeover. The most profitable project to date." The soft grin on his face slid. "Sam suggested I dig a little deeper into that one. Seems there was much more to Blackwell Enterprises' merger with Carlton Ammunitions than what sat on the surface."

His eyes drifted to the sand, where she noticed him drawing circles with his nearly dry fingers.

"I was fresh out of college when we merged with Carlton."

"Merged and then imploded."

"I didn't implode."

No, he halted sales of ammunition to many retail chains, and then manufactured and sold, nearly exclusively, to the government. Carlton held the majority of stock in the company to domestic sales. Only the government needed ammo. And the company took contracts from the US of A, and domestic sales hit an all-time millennium bottom. Within two years, Blackwell bought out Carlton completely.

"Carlton knew the risk. He didn't wager using his brain."

"If not his brain . . . what?" She honestly wanted to know. From the outside, it appeared Hunter knew the government contracts were coming and pounced on Carlton when sales were low.

"He never wagered on the people losing their desire to own weapons. By the time the people made a run for ammo . . . there wasn't anything available for them to buy."

"Because of your contracts with the government." It made sense now.

"Blackwell isn't the only ammunition manufacturer."

His defensive tone made her pause. "No. I suppose you're not."

He frowned, kept drawing circles. Some took the shape of bullets.

"Do you sell to offshore buyers?"

He shrugged. "I'm not in daily contact with Blackwell/Carlton Ammunitions."

Translation . . . yes.

"Doesn't that bother you?"

He set his hand in the sand and caught her gaze. "Does your brother offer a vacation destination exclusively to Americans? Italians?"

Her jaw dropped, and she promptly closed it.

"It's business, Gabi. Toyota sells to America, McDonalds sells in India."

"We're not talking cars and burgers. We're talking bullets."

"If the country is an ally, what's the problem?"

Alonzo popped into her head. As much as she'd love to forget the man, she couldn't. "An ally today can be an enemy tomorrow."

He paused, waited for her to look his way. "I don't know the future of our world affairs any more than you do."

That was fair . . . she supposed. "You still managed the merger right as the political winds shifted."

"I read the papers. Carlton didn't. Sue me."

"You rolled your millions like dice on a craps table. Pulled out of real estate months before the crash. You took less than a five percent hit with the stock market crash."

He smiled. "Four point—"

"Six two . . . I know." Down to the penny, she thought. "You were up two point eight in eleven months. While everyone else was trying to keep their companies from capsizing, you thrived." She'd be impressed if she didn't wonder how. The numbers were there. What she couldn't find was all the backing behind them. Many folders were simple headings of names of countries and companies in languages she didn't know.

Her mind shifted, thinking in numbers. "You have offshore accounts." It wasn't a question.

"I have a branch in London."

"Not London." She waved in his direction, her head ticking. "Of course. That would make sense." Money converted from more than two currencies lost weight by the time it met the US. Yeah, the government wanted its share. But how much could Blackwell hide before Uncle Sam caught on?

Too bad Gabi hadn't followed this train of thought before meeting with Hunter the first time. Then again, what did it matter? He still had something on her.

She'd be better off working on her own offshore accounts. The ones she knew very little about instead of the ones Hunter had.

"What makes sense?" he asked.

She settled her eyes on him . . . daring him to call her on what she was about to say.

"Your numbers don't mesh, Hunter. I know it, you know it."

His hand stopped playing in the sand. His eyes didn't leave hers. "My accounts are legit."

Gabi pointed to her chest. "We all have one thing we're good at, Hunter. Numbers are my thing. Yours aren't right. Yeah, you're worth more than most people can count. But there are discrepancies." Discrepancies that would feed villages.

"My company has many legs. I wouldn't doubt there are a few thousand—"

She laughed. Couldn't help the burst of noise from her throat. "Don't insult me."

His relaxed pose on the beach shifted to a sitting position, arms resting on his knees. "How are numbers your thing?"

The question struck her as odd.

"They just are." That and languages. Well, not many languages, but she was working on expanding her foreign tongue.

"How is it I don't know this about you?"

"There are many things you don't know about me," she told him.

His eyes moved down her body, making her realize she wore next to nothing. He derailed her thoughts with only a look.

Gabi closed her eyes and tried to keep her hands at her sides and not cover her bare midsection.

"My numbers don't balance and this is why Alliance rejected me?"

"Alliance has many levels one must pass. Everyone has financial secrets. That isn't a complete deterrent."

"It's one. You believe my financial balance isn't zero."

"It's way far from zero. But again. Whose isn't?"

Hunter glared now. "What else?"

"There are foreign meetings . . . men from questionable backgrounds."

He nodded, as if her words meant nothing.

"And then there is the jerk factor."

A lift to his lip was slow in coming. "The jerk factor?"

"Arrogant. Egotistical. Jerk . . . I think Meg would classify you as an asshole."

"Meg?"

"She may not live in California, but she still works with and for Alliance."

Hunter grinned as if she'd just complimented him. "I'm an arrogant asshole whose billion-dollar company has divisions where the numbers don't balance."

When he said it like that, it sounded trite. "You blackmailed me," she reminded him.

He glanced around the empty beach. He lowered his voice. "I suppose there are things we both regret from our past."

She wasn't sure what to make of that.

"Yet here we are. Married, both of us uneasy about the other."

"I don't believe you'll kill me in my sleep," he told her.

She grinned.

"You don't wear orange . . . remember?" he asked, a smirk playing on his lips.

"Orange *is* the new black."

Gabi and Meg sat with their heads together, their ears tuned into the noise drifting from the kitchen.

"That's not right. Do it again."

"I'm not a cook, Mrs. Masini," Hunter said for the umpteenth time in the last half an hour.

When Gabi had peeked into her mother's space, flour covered the entire counter and half the floor. A telltale sign that pasta was in progress. Or at least a mix of flour and eggs. There was no guarantee anyone would be eating anything at this rate.

"Crack the egg *gently*."

When Gabi's mom groaned, Meg started to giggle. "I wish I had a camera set up in there." Meg stretched her neck in an attempt to see inside the mess.

"Do it again."

Meg nudged Gabi's arm. "How long are you going to let that continue?"

Gabi sat back, crossed her legs. "I have nowhere I need to be."

"No, no, no." Simona lowered her tone. "Pretend the egg is a fragile woman, not a twist top on a beer."

Gabi and Meg held their breath and waited . . .

"Better. Now, three more eggs."

Silence.

Sigh.

Silence.

"Damn it!" Hunter's patience had to be at an end.

Gabi pushed off the couch. "Distract my mother."

"You're going to rescue him?" Meg asked.

"I did throw him in the dark waters of my mother's kitchen. I think he's learned his lesson."

The two of them entered the kitchen at the same time. Meg instantly started to laugh.

Hunter stood over the sink, his hands dripping with raw eggs and flour.

Gabi's mother was scooping a mound of flour off the counter.

Hunter snapped his eyes to Gabi, causing her to step back. "Maybe I should—"

"Help?" her mother offered. "This husband of yours is useless."

Meg pushed around Hunter, patted his arm with understood sympathy.

Meg moved to Simona's side and nudged her away. "How about a break?"

Simona looked between the two women. "Don't you do it for him, Gabriella. He needs to learn."

"Yes, Mama. Why don't you rest?" Gabi pushed the open bottle of wine in her mother's direction before Meg led her out of the kitchen.

Gabi and Hunter were still until they heard the door to the outside patio open and close.

Hunter's shoulders slumped. "Your mother is the kitchen Nazi."

It felt good to laugh.

Hunter wasn't amused. "You set me up."

Gabi tossed her hands in the air. "Guilty. Serves you right for pretending to be able to cook crepes." She found a clean apron and tied it around her waist.

Hunter made to remove his and she stopped him. "Not so fast, Wall Street. I told my mother I would help you . . . not do it for you."

"I don't cook."

She stepped close and turned on the faucet to wash her hands. "Stop whining." She wasn't sure exactly where her confidence came from . . . maybe it was the mass of flour that covered the front of Hunter's apron and most of his shirt. Maybe the smudge on his cheek, the lock of hair drifting into his eyes . . . or maybe seeing him completely out of his element empowered her.

He untied his apron.

She snapped a finger in his direction. "Put that back on."

"Oh, God . . . the kitchen Nazi's spawn."

"I can call my mother back in."

"You're pushing me, Gabi."

She shrugged. "What are you going to do, divorce me?"

He moaned.

"Exactly. Besides . . ." she found a clean, empty bowl, "my mother won't let up until you master a few steps."

His eyes followed her as she completed the mountain of flour and punched a fist-size crater in the center for the raw eggs.

"Let me guess." She picked up an egg with one hand. "My mother showed you like this." With a gentle crack, Gabi opened the shell and slid the egg into the flour with one hand and a tiny flourish of her wrist.

Hunter sighed. "You make it look easy."

She smiled, moved close to his side, and handed over an egg. "Use two hands and crack it into the bowl. That way you don't ruin what you've started if the shell decides it wants to be part of our dinner."

He hit the side of the bowl too hard, the egg spilled on the counter, the shell in the bowl. "I look like a fool."

"You look like you're trying too hard."

She rinsed the bowl, retrieved another egg. "Place your hands over mine."

Hunter moved closer, the heat of his body seeping between them. *Maybe this isn't a good idea.*

Digging for the confidence that was there a moment ago, she attempted to ignore Hunter's large shoulders and spicy scent. When his hands covered hers, dwarfing them instantly, she shuddered.

Crack the egg.

"Slow and easy," she told him.

His hands where a whisper above hers while she cracked and separated the shell from the yolk.

Hunter didn't pull away when she moved to release the shell and dump the perfect egg into the flour.

Attempting to ignore his silent presence, and refusing to look into his face, she handed him an egg.

She placed her hands over his.

Gabi wasn't sure if Hunter hummed in concentration or something else. The something else was what kept her from looking directly at him.

"Slowly," she cautioned when he lifted his hands to crack the egg.

The break was clean.

"That wasn't hard, was it?" she asked, glancing at him as she removed her hands from his.

The anger and frustration that had been there moments before was replaced with something much more dangerous. Her heart kicked hard in her chest, reminding her of forbidden feelings. Dangerous desire.

His full lips parted, capturing her attention.

She caught herself staring. The silence in the room an open invitation for more than cooking.

Neither of them moved forward or away. Maybe it was kitchen chemistry . . . or a combination of nerves, but there was no mistaking the mutual attraction. Unwanted and completely forbidden attraction, but desire nonetheless.

"What are we doing, Gabi?" Hunter's question was just above a whisper.

She blinked, pulling her eyes away from his parted lips. "Cooking." She put space between them, nearly knocking over the bowl with the eggs inside.

They mixed with their hands and slowly turned the flour and eggs into dough. The air between them sparked with current.

Hunter played with his section, his eyes on her hands.

"We will never eat if you can't concentrate," she told him.

His hand stopped hers from pushing the heel of her palm into the dough. "I think we should talk about what's going on here."

She swallowed. "We're cooking."

"Gabi, look at me."

She shook her head, taking the coward's way out. If she noticed the lock of hair falling into his eyes a second time, she might have to push it back in place.

"Gabriella?" The smooth texture of his voice was like chocolate on her tongue.

His sticky hand tucked under her chin and forced her to meet his gaze.

He stepped closer, his frame molding to hers and pressing her back against the counter.

She couldn't breathe.

His thumb traced her bottom lip. "This is a bad idea," he mumbled her thoughts.

She nodded. "Very poor choice." Her hands gripped the side of the counter to keep from touching him.

Hunter sucked in a deep breath. "You smell like flowers."

"I'll change my shampoo."

He started to dip his head and she kept talking. "Something musky, so you won't notice me."

"I don't think that's going to work."

He was close enough to catch the scent of mint on his breath. "I don't even like you." One of her legs lifted and rubbed against one of his.

"I don't trust you." His hand moved from her lip to the side of her neck.

"You blackmailed me."

"You tricked me into cooking with your mother."

She smiled. "The two hardly compare."

Instead of dropping his lips to hers, he detoured to the side of her neck and kept talking, his breath brushing her skin. "Have you met your mother?"

"That's sill—"

His lips found her neck.

She moaned and closed her eyes. *Such a deliciously bad idea.*

Her head fell back, giving him room to do whatever he wanted.

"Well, well." Meg's voice filled the silent kitchen.

Gabi froze.

Hunter's hand on her neck tightened.

"Your mom is on her way back in. Guess it's a good thing I came in to warn you."

Heat swept up Gabi's throat. "It's not how it looks," she managed.

Meg simply laughed and left the room.

Chapter Fifteen

Comfort food and wine . . . lots and lots of wine.

What the hell was he doing? The last thing he needed was to seduce his wife. Had he forgotten the terms of her contract? The part where a child conceived between them would cost him half of everything he'd worked for?

Gabi sat across from him at the dinner table, picking at the food on her plate. Food they'd managed to make together under the watchful eye of the kitchen Nazi.

Meg kept a knowing smile on her face; Val appeared mildly irritated with the tension in the room. It was still midday, a strange time for a large meal, but Hunter ate anyway. The eating had more to do with the fact he'd actually cooked the food, and less to do with hunger. If anyone had told him he'd be cooking pasta from scratch at any time in his life, he would have wagered a six-figure sum against them.

Who knew?

Meg pushed her plate aside. "Not bad for your first attempt."

My only attempt.

One look at his mother-in-law and Hunter kept his words to himself.

"I don't think I'll be applying for a chef position anytime soon," he said instead.

The first smile from Val flashed on the other man's face.

"Well," Mrs. Masini pushed away from the table. "I need a nap."

When she stood, Hunter moved to help her. Her wrinkled and spotted hand patted his.

"Thank you for teaching me something new," he told her. "But let's not do it again anytime soon."

It wasn't a real smile . . . more a smirk. "I'm not a young woman. My patience only holds for one lesson a month."

Good thing she lived an entire country away.

"Gabriella," Mrs. Masini said. "Walk me to my room."

Gabi moved to her mother's side and took her arm. She offered a coy glance over her shoulder before walking away.

Instead of burning under the microscope of Meg and Val, he said, "I'd like to make a few calls."

"All the phones on the island are operable."

Hunter was certain they were . . . and traceable, too. "My contacts are in my phone."

Val stood, retrieved his jacket. "You can use my office."

They walked into the heat of the Keys. Hunter followed Val to a golf cart, the only form of transportation on the island.

"You survived my mother. I have to give you points for that, Blackwell. I didn't think you'd follow through."

They turned up a two-lane road to the main building on the island. The three-story structure held Val's office, rooms designed to hold staff that needed to sleep on the island. The long verandas swept around the building with massive windows that opened to a dining room and kitchens. The resort's swimming pools and spa were a hedge and greenbelt away. A nightclub and separate gathering halls completed the lower portions of the building. "Your mother didn't leave me much of a choice."

Val nodded. "She has her ways."

"Stubborn, much like your sister."

Val pulled to a stop and turned toward him. "It runs in the family."

"We have that in common, then. Once my mind is set on something, I seldom let down until I have it in my fingers."

"Like my sister." Val's observation couldn't be closer to the truth.

"My relationship with Gabi isn't the same."

There was a tick in Val's eye. "The last man I allowed to court my sister nearly killed her. You'll have to forgive my need to protect her."

Killed her? Wait . . . "Picano?"

"A man I trusted. A man we all trusted."

"Even your mother?"

Val looked away. "My mother never liked him." Val muttered something in Italian. "I don't think she cares for you, either."

Hunter wasn't so sure. He caught Simona close to a grin at least twice when he destroyed her kitchen. "Did Picano ever cook with your mother?"

"Lord no. She wouldn't have bothered."

Interesting . . . yet she did with him.

Hunter moved to leave the golf cart, Val stopped him. "Has Gabriella told you about Picano?"

All the answers felt as if they were only a question away. So why was he hesitating?

"Not everything."

Val opened his mouth and Hunter cut him off.

"She will tell me when she's ready. For the first time in a long time, I will wait for her to reveal the truth."

Val regarded him in silence. "You surprise me, Blackwell."

Hunter pushed out of the cart. "It probably won't last." He thought of the question Blake had asked him and decided one question could be asked without learning too much about Gabi's past. "Who shot him?"

Val hesitated.

"Never mind." What if it was Gabi? He shouldn't have asked. "I'll wait for Gabi to tell me."

"I don't think Gabi knows. She wasn't there when it happened."

Now he was confused. He thought . . .

"I, however, was."

"You shot him?"

Val shook his head. "If only I had a gun in my hand. No . . . I didn't have the pleasure. Between the Coast Guard, Neil, Rick, and my wife, there wasn't much left for me to take out."

Meg . . . Val's snarky blonde wife?

"I see you have more questions than answers."

He did. "I've said this before, but I'm going to repeat myself. I won't hurt her, Valentino. You have my word."

Val shoved his hands in his pockets, the tick in his eye gone. "I'm holding you to that," he said.

Hunter offered a nod and followed Val to his office.

When he was alone, he checked his messages. First was Tiffany. She muttered something about liking his wife and wondering if she still had a job on Monday. Hunter couldn't remember another time when a secretary had drunk too much at a cocktail party and spoken out of turn. Tiffany was a rare find. The second message was Andrew's. "You received a message . . . one you were expecting."

Damn. Not good.

The third message was from Remington. As the man rambled about Colombia and Italy, Hunter held his head in his hand. He needed to divert his PI from finding any personal facts about Gabi and concentrate on her offshore accounts. Any trust he was building with his temporary wife would be shattered in one phone call if she knew he was paying someone to learn about her past. For some strange reason, he wanted her trust.

Wanted to trust her.

He dialed Remington first and met with a voice mailbox. With caution, he stepped out onto Val's veranda and looked below. Once Hunter was assured of his privacy, he kept his message short. "It's Blackwell. I need you to drop what you're doing. I need to find out who Picano dealt with in Columbia. Someone accessed those accounts, I need to know who. Same with Italy. If you come across Gabriella's name anywhere else, contact me immediately."

He sent a text to Tiffany, said he'd see her on Monday.

Andrew picked up on the first ring.

"How is Florida?" Andrew asked.

"Warm, sticky . . . beautiful. Tell me."

Andrew sighed.

Hunter knew, before Andrew opened his mouth to confirm, what he was going to say.

"The paternity test is positive."

———

"Oh, Luuucy . . . you have some 'splaining to do." Meg's singsong voice called Gabi outside once her mother finished her interrogation.

There was no way out of this conversation, though Gabi had to try. "Can we ignore what you walked in on?"

Meg shook her head. "Hell to the no! I want details, lady . . . lots of details."

Gabi glanced up the stairs and motioned toward the outside. "How about a walk?"

"Good idea. Your mother is trying to make me fat. Pasta in the afternoon? Who does that?"

"We're Italian, we do."

They walked out to the shore and both left their shoes close to the entrance of Meg and Val's private villa.

"I thought this was a name-only marriage," Meg started in.

"It is. I don't even like the man."

Meg lifted her eyebrows.

"Well, most of the time."

"His body was molded to yours and it didn't look like you were pushing him away."

"He's a very attractive man," Gabi defended.

"Mmm-hmm."

She thought of his breath on her neck with a sigh. "Extremely attractive."

"There are plenty of attractive men out there, Gabi. Why Hunter?"

Gabi pulled her hair back to keep the wind from tossing it in her face. "He's convenient."

Meg laughed. "So is the taxi driver. You haven't so much as blinked at the men that have come on to you since . . ."

It was sweet of Meg to avoid saying his name. "Since Alonzo."

"Yeah."

They walked in silence a little longer.

"Can I ask you something?" Meg asked. "About Alonzo?"

He was *the man who shall never be spoken of* . . . or had been since his death. Hearing his name so many times in the last month had the opposite effect it had in those early days. It was easier, she realized, now that Hunter was there to annoy and distract her.

"I suppose."

"If you don't want to answer, I'll understand."

"I won't fall apart with a question," said Gabi.

"How were things . . . you know, sexually . . . between the two of you?"

It had been a long time since she'd thought about intimacy. Even with Hunter recharging her hormones, she hadn't once thought of her time in Alonzo's bed.

"Well . . . before." She shook her head.

Meg placed a hand on her arm briefly as they walked down the empty beach.

"It was satisfying."

"Satisfying?"

It was hard to remember any of their time together as being something other than a lie. She'd told herself that their sex life was off because of his deception.

"Are we talking *prime rib* satisfying, or *bologna sandwich fill the stomach* satisfying?"

Gabi looked out over the ocean, tried to remember. "I have to admit I was always a little hungry . . . after."

Meg looped her arm through Gabi's. "That's so wrong."

"I know . . . I can see that now."

They dodged the water climbing up on the shore.

"What about with Hunter?"

"Oh, we haven't. I mean . . . what you saw in the kitchen . . . we haven't." How was it possible as a grown woman she had such a hard time talking about sex?

"What I saw in the kitchen looked really hot."

Gabi felt the blush reach her cheeks. "It was," came her breathy reply.

Meg laughed.

"I don't want to compare, but did the big asshole ever make you feel like Hunter did today?"

Her answer was swift. "No. Absolutely nothing alike."

"Hmm . . ."

"It can't happen," Gabi voiced the caution running in her head since she parted Hunter's company.

"Why not? He's obviously into you. You're stuck in this marriage for a year and a half? Meaningless hot sex is better than supposed meaningful wet-noodle sex."

"There shouldn't be sex of any kind. I'm not the woman who has meaningless sex."

"Have you ever tried? Seems Val kept you sheltered most of your life."

"True," Gabi managed. "But I've had more opportunities than Val is aware of. I simply didn't act on them."

Meg pinched her lips together, her expression amused. "How did that work out for you?"

"What are you suggesting, Margaret . . . that I sleep with my husband to scratch an itch?"

Meg shrugged with a nod. "You said he was attractive. My guess is all the parts work."

Gabi gave a playful shove and had Meg dancing at the water's edge.

"I can't trust him."

Meg's smile fell. "You think he'll hurt you?"

"No. Not physically. I don't get that from him at all."

"So emotionally?"

Gabi couldn't put a finger on what her thoughts were. "How does someone have sex with someone they don't like?"

"Men do it all the time."

"I don't have the plumbing to qualify as a man."

It was Meg's turn to push her. "You know what I mean. Listen, I'm not suggesting you ignore your head. But don't be afraid to follow a smoking hot distraction. You know he's not telling you he cares to get you in bed. You're already married. There's a deadline to your relationship that might give you exactly what you need to find your sexual self. It doesn't sound like Alonzo helped with that at all."

"And I trusted him," she mused.

"If it helps at all . . . I like Hunter. Yeah, he's hard around the edges, and I wouldn't have passed him as a client for Alliance, but he's enduring all of us rather well. And considering how much that man is worth, I don't think he'd have to pretend at all if he didn't want to."

"He cooked dinner."

Meg once again linked arms with Gabi as they turned back toward the villa.

"I don't think I'll ever get the image of him with all that flour covering him out of my head," Gabi said.

"It's not the flour that's bringing that blush to your face. It was his attempt to be your personal spandex that's heating you up."

Chapter Sixteen

Remington hoped the leads in Columbia would dry up quickly. Unfortunately, they didn't. Now he was on day three in the hot, humid urban jungle, leaning against the crumbling side of a building that called itself a bank. It wasn't the bank where Picano's account was set up, but inside was a slightly shady teller whose tongue wagged with every fifty-dollar bill Remington flashed. It helped to have Blackwell's never-ending wallet.

Juan emerged from the broken-down building and searched the busy street. Before his eyes found Remington, another man, this one skinny and skittish, intersected. Remington let the smoke from his cigarette drift to the sky and lifted the newspaper in his hands to observe for a little longer. Juan had said he had a friend at the Picano branch who would meet with the two of them. He had a few hundred-dollar bills on him, and a few more in the hotel room tucked behind the toilet. From the lack of cleanliness, they wouldn't be discovered there until the next millennium.

The two men shook hands and held what appeared to be an amicable conversation. Within a couple of minutes, Juan was once again scanning the street. The answer to who might be behind the activity out of the Picano account was only a few questions away. Problem was, in Columbia, it was impossible to determine who to trust.

Remington trusted no one.

He tucked the paper under his arm, tossed the butt of his smoke to the ground, and wove through traffic, pedestrians, and a few stray dogs roaming the street. A child, no older than three, pushed against his leg, his grubby little fingers out for anything Remington might spare. He pushed past the kid without a sideways glance. If he so much as offered a quarter, the kid would multiply like a fucking gremlin in water. Attracting attention was not on Remington's list.

"There you are," Juan said, his lips pulled back in a grin. "Señor Remington . . . my friend, Raul, the one I told you about."

Remington lifted a chin, offered a hand. "You speak English?"

Raul placed a sweaty hand in his, nodded as if a bobble doll had taken over his scrawny frame. "It's the international language, isn't it?"

Remington removed his hand as soon as possible. From the way Raul shifted on his feet, he was either seconds away from a heart attack driven from fear or was in need of a hit.

"Columbian bankers need to speak English." Juan nudged his friend. "Right, amigo?"

"*Sí, sí.*"

Remington nodded toward an outside diner down the street. He'd already scoped out the area, knew of two escape routes if he needed to vacate his newfound friends' company in a hurry.

The three of them stepped into the shade of the patio; Remington took a seat with the wall to his back, an out to his right, his amigos on his left. A waitress was on them the second they sat down. Not risking anything, he ordered a bottle of beer, waited for the three of them to be left alone.

Raul ran a hand under his nose before he spoke. "Juan tells me you're looking for someone."

"Could be someone, or several someones. You tell me."

Juan rolled his fingers together; Raul kept his eyes moving around the restaurant.

"Who wants to know?"

"Maybe I do."

Raul scooted forward, his eyes blinking. "Information isn't free, señor."

The waitress returned with three beers and disappeared.

"You have information for me?"

Raul rubbed his upper lip again. Yeah, the man was dipping into some of Columbia's finest . . . or perhaps cheapest. Hard to tell watching from the outside.

"If you have money . . . I have information."

Remington removed two fifty-dollar bills from his pocket, made sure the man saw the hundreds packed behind them. "I need a name."

"If I told you Picano is using the account?"

Remington lifted his hand holding the money away. "Don't fuck with me, Raul. Picano is dead."

Raul kicked back in his chair. "What about Mrs. Picano?"

Remington stood. The man was looking for quick money. He didn't know shit.

Juan stood, along with Raul. "Wait, wait . . . I can get—"

"You can get the fuck out of my way. I don't deal with people who waste my time, cokehead."

"But . . ."

Remington nudged the other man out of the way and left the two bankers behind.

Back at square one. He pushed through the kids that circled him, bumping into him with their hands out. He shoved his hand into his pocket, fisted the change there, and tossed it several feet away. Like a flock of birds to crumbs, the children scattered to pick up what they could as he jogged across the street and disappeared.

He hustled up the filthy steps of the hotel and into his room. He shoved everything into the duffel bag and retrieved the cash behind the john. He patted his right back pocket, in search of his phone.

He froze, checked his left pocket . . . front pockets.

"Son of a bitch."

Hunter wasn't sure who was avoiding who. Both he and Gabi all but jumped on the opportunity to spend time in the nightclub instead of retiring in their private villa.

He didn't trust himself.

Even with his head in a hundred different places, the one place it wanted to be was buried in his wife.

A dangerous thing, that.

For the both of them.

Across the room, Gabi danced with her brother. The two of them laughed and smiled . . . obviously caring for the other. Hunter couldn't blame the man for being such a hard-ass. If he'd had a younger sister who had said yes to a temporary marriage, he didn't think he would sit by and watch silently.

Meg slid up beside him. "You don't seem the wallflower type," she told him.

He allowed his eyes to leave Gabi.

"Just watching."

"They look good."

He nodded.

"I haven't seen Gabi dance since before Alonzo died. Even at our wedding, she did what she had to, but she wasn't happy about it."

He couldn't help but wonder why Meg was opening up.

"I never liked the man."

"And why are you telling me this?"

She sipped her drink. "I'm not sure."

He ran his fingers over the condensation on his glass. "Let me guess, your next words are a warning that if I hurt her I'll have to answer to you."

Meg lifted her eyebrows. "I thought about it. But no. I won't have a chance."

"Too many people in line in front of you."

"Exactly."

They both watched their spouses on the dance floor for a minute before he lifted his hand, palm up. "Dance?"

Women loved to dance. It was something Hunter learned about them early on. The music was upbeat enough to engage in a few twists and enough movement to avoid a lot of body contact. Still, he felt Val's eyes on him as he led Meg through a few moves.

When the music changed, this time slowing down, Val tapped his shoulder and they switched partners.

The tropical scent of Gabi's hair hit him first.

When her hand gripped his, her other reaching up on his shoulder, it took every ounce of power to avoid molding his body to hers.

After a few tentative steps, she leaned in close. "You're a good dancer," she told him.

He moved them around with style. "I dated a theater major in college. I had to learn or get left behind."

Gabi smiled. "And how long did you date Miss Actress?"

"Two months."

Her hand reached around his back. The feel of her fingers flexing on his shoulder distracted him enough to where he missed a step, but quickly recovered.

"Two months is hardly dating . . . more like a fling."

"It was college."

"But you kept that style of dating most your life."

He glanced down, narrowed his eyes. "Part of your background check?"

"I stopped searching for names after I reached thirty."

"Thirty? The tabloids stretch the truth."

"So there weren't thirty?"

He'd never counted. And even he knew that counting past dates while dancing with another woman . . . his wife . . . wasn't smart.

"Nowhere close to thirty."

She laughed. "I'll pull my notes and we can compare."

He distracted her with a few quick circles, pushing her out of his arms and back in. Fred Astaire would applaud.

People around them offered a little more room. He glanced at Val and Meg. "Well it's official. Everyone in your immediate family has threatened to take care of me if I hurt you."

Gabi pulled in a breath before dropping her forehead on his chest. "I should apologize."

"They don't know how strong you are."

"I'm not that strong." Her voice was low, nearly impossible to hear over the music.

He held her a little tighter after that.

The song ended, the pace picked up, and Hunter led her off the dance floor. At some point he realized he hadn't let her hand go. Jesus, when was the last time he held a woman's hand?

Meg interrupted their silence. "We're headed in," she told them.

Gabi released Hunter's hand and hugged her sister-in-law.

"I can't believe you're leaving tomorrow. We didn't have enough time."

"I'm an airplane away," Gabi reminded her.

"Yeah. Let me know when escrow closes. I'll help you furniture shop."

Val offered a laugh. "I hope that wallet is as deep as you say it is, Hunter."

It's part of the deal, he wanted to say, but didn't. "I think I have it."

Gabi kissed both her brother's cheeks and watched Val and Meg walk out of the nightclub.

With the two of them now alone, he felt his pulse pick up. Nerves? Really? Since when?

"Do you want to go? Another drink?"

Gabi glanced at the bar, wrinkled her nose. "It's late."

He offered his arm and she took it.

The fragrant scents of the island, along with the ocean, mixed with the warm night air. Music drifted from the nightclub until they wound past the main building and down a path to their villa.

"Your brother has built something really special here," he said.

She sighed. "After our father died, he was driven to take care of us. It wasn't an option for the resort to fail."

Hunter understood that . . . the drive, the determination to move forward, conquer the next hill.

"Has he ever considered expanding . . . different locations?"

Her hand loosened on his arm as they walked. "At one point he talked about it. Then . . ."

Her words caught in her throat. A universal sign that he was treading in Alonzo waters.

The outside veranda of their private villa faced the ocean. The moon wasn't full, but the sky was clear, letting the reflection dance off the waters like brilliant diamonds of the clearest cut. Instead of stuffing themselves inside, Hunter pulled out a lounge chair and encouraged her to sit. As much as he wanted to take her inside and start up where they left off in the kitchen earlier that day, he knew acting on that now would be a colossal mistake.

With feet stretched out before him, he toed off his shoes and leaned back once he knew Gabi had done the same.

He could see her mind turning . . . memories of Alonzo? Worry about what was happening between them? Hell, he had no idea what was going on inside him. For all the planning, he hadn't expected to give a crap about her as a person. Yet much like everyone around her, Gabi demanded attention, and protection. She did it by nature . . . not practiced skill.

"You stiffen when you think of him," he told her.

He heard her take a deep breath.

"Earlier today, your brother and I had a little talk."

"Oh, no."

"No," he said quickly. "As much as it was against every cell in my body, I didn't ask your brother to elaborate."

He heard her relief with her exhale.

"I have a confession to make," he said.

"Do I even want to ask?"

"Probably not. But the way I see it . . . we're in this for a while. For better or for worse as they say . . . I'd just assume to avoid land mines if that's at all possible." Some secrets he wasn't quite ready to reveal, but others . . .

"Well don't stop now. It can't be called a confession without an admission of a crime."

He watched the gentle waves on the ocean. "I hired a private investigator to learn everything he could about you. "

She stilled. "I hoped you wouldn't follow through on that threat."

"I'm a man of action, not threats."

"So you already know my secrets." Her voice was tight.

He shook his head. "No. Not the personal stuff. My investigator was working on the personal stuff until this weekend." That afternoon . . . but Hunter didn't think his confession needed that minor detail.

"What is he working on now?"

The rest of his confession wasn't an admission of any guilt, and the words flowed. "I promised to work toward removing your name from Picano . . . from the bank accounts. He's working on determining who is behind the offshore money."

When his words met with silence, he ventured a glance and found Gabi staring. Her eyes softened, her smile easy and inviting.

Genuine.

She opened her lips to say something, then closed them.

"What?"

She hesitated. "Why? Why remove your investigator away from the information you seek?"

The answer came in one word. *Trust.* He wanted her to trust him. Only revealing that now . . . this early in their contract gave her too much power. If she knew he wanted her trust, she could pull out now and where would he be? No . . . as much as it killed him, he left that word out of his explanation. "You'll tell me when you're ready."

He heard her legs shifting on the lounge.

"You're impossible to place a finger on . . . you know that?"

He felt a smile on his lips. "I try."

"See . . . I don't believe that. I think it's natural. Like a God given-right born unto only you."

"I'm like everyone else . . . just a little more driven to get what I want."

"Even if you have to blackmail to get it."

He winced. "It sounds so ugly when you say it that way."

She laughed. "It *is* ugly."

He shrugged. He wouldn't change it . . . and in light of the past week, didn't think he did the wrong thing.

The conversation waned until he thought maybe they had exhausted all their words for the night.

"He was a manipulative bastard."

Hunter practiced the fine art of silence.

And the gates opened.

"Our chance meeting, which I learned later wasn't so chance, happened on the mainland. A fundraiser my brother and I were a part of. He was attentive and Val liked him. I liked him."

Hunter heard the hurt in her voice.

"I was sheltered . . . as Meg has pointed out . . . living on this island. Not that I cared. But when Alonzo landed in my life I was more than ready to explore shores other than these."

Hunter knew the story ended badly, and searched for words to keep her talking. "So you did."

"I did. He would sail to the island, bring crates of quality wine as a gift to my brother. Val didn't need the wine, but the guests seemed to enjoy it."

The pieces of the puzzle in his head started to fall into place.

"He was supposedly setting up our future home in the vineyards of the California coast. His land in Italy was already prosperous . . . or so I thought, so when he suggested we start our life together in the States, I couldn't be happier. I'd spent time in Italy, but the thought of being that far away from my family didn't sit well."

"Let me guess, Alonzo banked on that." He was watching her now . . . the play of emotions on her face . . . the drop in her voice when she spoke of herself.

"I was such an easy target. It wasn't until Margaret and Michael arrived on the island that everything came unraveled."

There was a name Hunter had yet to hear. "Michael?"

"Michael Wolfe . . . the movie star."

For the first time in the conversation, Hunter was stunned. "What do Meg and Michael Wolfe have in common?"

"Meg is best friends with Judy. Michael is Judy's brother."

He tried to catch up, and just went with the names and hoped he could connect the dots later.

"So Michael and Meg were here on vacation and Meg ended up with your brother?"

Gabi was smiling now . . . some of the earlier tension having left her body. "Meg was here checking out the privacy of the island for clients of Alliance."

"Ohhh . . . got it." That made sense. "So Meg and Michael hit the island . . . then what?"

"Michael knows a lot about wine."

"So he heard of Picano's wine?"

"No. The opposite. And when Alonzo figured out Michael was on to his misleading label, Alonzo made their stay here very difficult," Gabi said.

"Misleading label?" Hunter was lost.

"Alonzo may have owned the land in Italy, that did in fact grow grapes, but he didn't make wine. He used his supposed status as a winemaker to smuggle drugs."

"Ohh . . ." He followed along with relative ease. "He smuggled the drugs with the wine he brought onto the island."

Gabi was silent for a few moments. "I could have destroyed everything my brother built here with my fiancé's deceit."

"I doubt you knew anything about the drugs."

"Still my fault."

The desire to reach for her was huge.

She'd all but curled up onto herself as she spoke, giving no indication that she needed comfort.

"What happened next?" They'd yet to get to the personal stuff . . . the part that shattered the woman in front of him.

Gabi hugged her bent knees, her gaze fixated on the ocean. "While Meg and Michael accompanied Val to Italy . . . in search of the truth, I was oblivious. *He* took me away for a short weekend . . . a vacation off the coast on his yacht." She shivered and her skin grew pale. She swallowed, and continued. "I grew up on these waters . . . well, maybe not grew up, but certainly never found myself sick on them."

Hunter felt his hand clenching the arm of the chair.

"From the minute I stepped on the ship, I wasn't right. We ate, drank . . ." her nervous laugh left him cold. "I slept. Woke to aspirin . . ." She laughed again and Hunter's back teeth ground together.

"He told me it was for my headache." Her eyes were a hard stare on the water. "Everything blurred."

Hunter was sitting on the edge of the lounge chair, his knees bumping her chair. He wanted to touch her, but didn't. He waited for the words to tell him the worst of it. Knew the story was going to get worse.

"The morning we married, I was lucid. Well . . . blurry, but I can't say I didn't know what I was doing." She blinked in his direction for a moment, then looked away. "It would be easier if I knew he forced the marriage certificate." She rested her head on her knees. "Let's get married, he said. Today . . . now . . . he talked about romance. I said yes." She sighed. "I said yes."

Hunter found his tongue. "You loved him."

She shook her head. "I thought I loved him."

The waves crashed a few times . . .

"I remember bits from there. A meal . . . the stateroom. The nausea. I thought I was sick. After, the doctors told me the drugs he slipped into my wine . . . my water . . . was triple the prescribed amount."

Hunter couldn't help his hand that found her ankle. It was a comfort that she didn't back away.

"I'm sorry."

She shook her head, a tear fell from her eye. "He didn't stop with pills."

Hunter's nose flared and his skin grew ice-cold.

"Alonzo smuggled heroin. I have a memory of his captain sliding a needle into me."

Holy fuck. Hunter had to force the hand on her ankle to relax or risk breaking her delicate bones.

She looked into the star-filled sky. "They found me floating alone in a dingy in the middle of the ocean. I don't remember how I'd gotten there, or how long I was bobbing in the sea. I remember a helicopter, then nothing until I woke in the ICU in Miami. I'd learned what he'd done to me, and why . . . he heard that my brother and Meg were on to him, so he forced his hand . . . used me . . ."

"Jesus." No wonder everyone he'd met that knew Gabi threatened to kill him if he harmed her. Hell, he wouldn't hesitate after hearing that story.

Hunter removed his jacket and took a chance.

He slid into the space beside Gabi and covered the two of them. The need to tell her everything, every reason he needed her as a wife, sat on his lips.

He couldn't. The risk of her walking way, and him letting her, was too great.

"It's a good thing he's already dead," he said a long time later.

She'd snuggled into his chest and finally settled into slow, easy breaths.

"Oh?"

"Yeah . . . I don't look good in orange, either."

Chapter Seventeen

They were cruising somewhere between 27,000 and 30,000 feet. The open book in Gabi's lap sat unread. She and Hunter had fallen asleep under an open sky. Sometime later, he'd lifted her into his arms and carried her to her room. The connecting door to their bedrooms was left open, giving her space, but not closing her off. It was probably one of the sweetest things anyone had ever done for her.

What surprised her more was a lack of dreams . . . of memories. Whenever she spent time talking about her tragic past, dreams plagued her for nights after.

Instead, she dreamed of Hunter covered in flour.

Hunter's breath on her neck.

Hunter on the dance floor.

He had left the villa before she rose and showered for their return trip home. He'd kept their conversation polite, if not cold. The heat generated in her mother's kitchen was a distant memory.

She shouldn't be surprised. The image of her with a needle in her arm sickened her as well.

Gabi gave up on the language textbook and stood.

"Can I get you something, Mrs. Blackwell?" The flight attendant appeared from a niche around the corner with a smile.

"I have it, thank you."

She disappeared again, leaving Gabi to fend for herself. She wasn't hungry but needed to do something with her hands, so she proceeded to fill a glass with ice . . . a splash of vodka. Maybe she could sleep?

The ruffling of Hunter's paper caught her attention.

He was watching her, his expression as unreadable as it had been that morning.

Telling him what had happened to her felt right the night before. Now she regretted it. The distance between them had narrowed on the island and was destined to spread like the Grand Canyon now.

Hunter shook his head and looked away. "I'm leaving tomorrow night for New York. I'll be there until Saturday."

She wasn't sure what to say. A week ago, she would have applauded. Today it felt like rejection. "Oh."

"I need you to join me in Dallas Saturday for dinner with the Adams."

She sipped the vodka, wish she'd poured more into the glass.

"All right."

"I'll have the jet ready for you Saturday morning. I'll meet you at the Hyatt." He sounded like he was talking to Andrew.

"Should I make a reservation?"

"Tiffany will take care of it."

Wonderful. She finished her drink, poured a second.

"What are you doing, Gabi?"

She didn't meet his eyes as she lifted her glass in the air in salute. "Enjoying a cocktail. Would you like one?" She turned and opened the cupboard that housed the crystal glasses with a little too much force. The glassware rattled as she tossed ice into his glass.

She hadn't seen him approach and only stopped when his hand covered hers.

She snapped back as if burned.

He stepped back. "You're upset."

"No," she said. "I'm pissed. At myself." The worst kind of anger.

"Why?"

She abandoned his glass and fisted hers as she put a few feet between them.

"I should have never told you about Alonzo."

"Why?"

All her nervous energy kept her from sitting. She swirled the ice inside her drink and looked into it as if it held the right words. "Because I'd rather endure your hate . . . your passion, than your cold tolerance or pity."

"Cold tolerance?" his voice rose. "I'm trying to give you space."

"You're disgusted with the facts. Don't try and tell me any differently. I've seen the look before." In the mirror, for months after Alonzo had died.

He ran a hand through his hair. "You're right. I am disgusted."

She cringed. Wanted to cry.

"With a dead man. With myself."

"With me."

"No!" he yelled.

"Then why are you being so cold?"

Gabi's hand went still, her eyes followed him as he attempted to move.

"I don't know what else to do."

"You seemed to know last night."

He stopped pacing, looked at her over his shoulder.

Some of her anger faded in his look of distress.

"Damn it, Gabi, don't look at me like that."

"Like what?"

"Like you trust me."

Did she trust him? Maybe a little more than when they'd met.

"You can't trust me. I will fuck up. I always do."

Now it was her turn to feel pity . . . pity for him.

"Hunter—"

He lifted a hand in the air, cutting off her words. "Last night while you slept, I laid there trying to figure out a way to release you."

Instead of the elation she would have expected, a stronger sense of denial swam up her spine.

"Then the cold son of a bitch I am clicked in. I can't let you go . . . not now . . . not yet."

She set her drink down, crossed her arms over her chest. "So you decided to treat me like baggage instead."

His gray eyes held hers. "I know how to handle baggage. I don't know how to handle you."

She stepped forward and poked two fingers into his chest. "Well let me give you a tip, Wall Street. You don't let me open up to you, especially after my mother's kitchen, and then wake today acting like nothing happened."

She dug her nail in a little harder.

He captured her hand and squeezed. "Your mother's kitchen is exactly why I'm being the bastard that I am now."

She tried to pull away, failed.

"Your image of me is different now. I get it. It's hard to see past a needle once you've envisioned it."

"What?"

Insecurity was thick on her tongue. Alonzo had taken pictures of her. Those nasty pictures that he sent to Val flashed in her mind. "I don't blame you." She tugged her hand again.

"Blame? You think my need to touch you is gone because of what that bastard did to you?"

She didn't meet his eyes.

He tugged her hand closer and turned her into the closed door of the bedroom suite. He was on her in a breath.

His hard body molding itself to hers, his growing erection pressing firm on her belly. Long fingers let loose her hand and wove onto her neck. And then his lips were in the exact place they'd been before Meg had interrupted them. Insecurity flew away like the wind blowing past the plane at over three hundred miles an hour.

Hunter's lips were hot, open as he dragged his teeth along her neck.

Gabi slumped against the door.

She felt Hunter's free hand run down her waist and hip.

"Does this feel like a man who doesn't desire you? A man hung up on your past?" he whispered, his warm breath against her ear.

He shifted her hips closer, the hard edge of him pressing her into submission.

"No."

He nipped at her chin, the side of her lips. "Never think for a minute I don't want you . . . just like this."

She reached around his waist, tried to get closer.

He groaned, his breathing heavy. "You're not ready for me."

Gabi was fairly certain she was. The scent of her desire mixed with his.

"You hated me last week," he said against her cheek. "You'll hate me again next."

She started to shake her head.

"Yes. You will." He took some of his weight off of her, but didn't completely let go. "Hating me I can handle. Hating yourself for letting me inside of you . . . I don't think I can live with that."

His rejection still stung, even if he made sense.

Instead of the hot kiss she expected . . . wanted more than air, he kissed her forehead and walked away.

—————

True to his word, he stayed away from his wife for nearly an entire week. He did, however, find a reason to call her every day. *Is escrow going as planned? Have the media let up? Do you know where to go to catch my plane for Dallas?*

She saw through all of it. By Friday, she sent him a text . . . Escrow is closing next week, probably Thursday. I only hit one tabloid today. You're in two. The car will be here at eight to take me to the airport . . . and before you ask, the weather is fine.

As he read her text, he smiled.

Another blinked in before he could respond. The flowers are beautiful.

Her local florist knew his credit card number by heart.

He tapped his fingers on his desk, searching for a reason to hear her voice.

She picked up on the first ring. "Couldn't stop yourself, could you?" There was laughter in her voice.

"This is important." He leaned back in his chair, stared out over the New York skyline.

"I'm waiting."

"What are you wearing?"

"Excuse me?"

He laughed, caught his own slip. "In Dallas?"

"I was thinking yoga pants and a sport bra . . . you?"

He squeezed his eyes shut. The image of her in spandex shot straight to his balls. "That might work."

"A dress, Hunter. I'm wearing a dress."

"What color?"

"What is it with you and women's fashion? Going to take on Bloomingdales? Macy's?"

"I don't think the world of fashion could handle me."

She laughed, the sound warmed him more than it should. He was playing a dangerous game but couldn't seem to stop himself.

"I was thinking black. Or red . . . red is a power color, and since you're going into a business relationship with the Adams, I thought a power color would be appropriate."

Damn, that was smart. He remembered early on in his acquiring years he'd listened to a media consultant say nearly the same thing.

"Did your brother teach you that?"

Her short laugh told him otherwise. "*I* taught *him*. He's taken the power suit to a new level, but I spent countless hours explaining the need to dress like you're already the boss."

"Wear black."

"And if I want to wear red?" she huffed.

Once again, he was reminded that she wasn't his employee. "Please."

"It kills you to say that . . . doesn't it?"

"Years off my life."

"Well, if that was your *important* question . . . I need to go."

"Hot date?"

"You found me out, Hunter. I'm cheating on you already."

She was teasing, so why did the hair on his neck stand on end? "What's his name?"

"Dale," she offered without hesitation.

Silence.

"Blooming*dale*. Seems I'm in need of a new black dress."

"I'll get you for that."

"No, I'll get you. I'm using your credit card."

As she should, he mused.

"Drive safe," he told her.

"Jump off a building," she replied.

Hunter hung up with a smile on his lips.

He turned to drop his cell into the cradle on his desk to charge when it rang. Thinking it was her, he answered laughing. "Couldn't stop yourself, could you?"

There was a moment of silence, then a sound that resembled a fax machine tone. He glanced at the screen, noticed the call came from Remington.

Hunter listened for a few seconds of continuous hum and squeals, then hung up.

He attempted to call Remington back and was met with the same tones assaulting his ears.

Without thought, Hunter disconnected the call.

Chapter Eighteen

She'd arrived at the Dallas/Fort Worth airport to a long limousine that drove her to the hotel. She'd had a stopover in the airport a time or two in the past but had never visited the city. It was greener and much flatter than she expected. Overall the city was easy on the eyes. Wide streets compared to the mainland of Florida that she'd spent time in . . . and certainly more spread out than the Los Angeles area.

Seeing as it was Texas, she half expected to see cowboys on horseback, guns mounted on their hips.

There were plenty of Stetsons, and boots . . . but not a horse to be seen . . . well, outside of the few fields they'd passed before landing.

The two-bedroom penthouse suite at the Dallas Hyatt held a second floor. A second floor in a hotel. Gabi tried not to be impressed and failed.

Hunter had yet to arrive, but he was already there.

Flowers, yellow roses, adorned the table in the center of the dining area in the suite. A card to the side had her name. She leaned against a chair as she opened the note from Hunter. "I thought the state flower of Texas was the yellow rose. I guess I didn't pay enough attention in my geography class. Bluebonnets are a little harder to cut and place in a vase. I hope these will do."

She leaned down to take in the fragrant blooms.

Hunter was wooing her. She felt him slipping a little deeper with every passing bud.

"They're just flowers, Gabi. Don't forget that."

Still, it was more than that.

She knew it . . .

He knew it.

She went ahead and took the upstairs bedroom. Her dress didn't have to suffer baggage claim and didn't need to visit an iron. After unloading a couple of days worth of clothing . . . more than she needed, she moved back into the main living room and opened the massive blinds.

A vibrant city sat below, cars traversed the highways . . . people scrambled to make their deadlines.

She watched in silence.

How had she gotten here? The penthouse suite in a Dallas hotel waiting on her billionaire husband . . . a man in name only.

Well, maybe not *only.*

He'd flirted with her on the phone, albeit under the cloak of necessity.

Still, she wasn't so far outside the mating game to not recognize when a man was trying *not* to sound interested.

The constant barrage of flowers and phone calls were the most unexpected part of Hunter's pursuit. The fact he pursued her at all was shocking. Why bother? They were married and stuck for a little while at least.

Yes, it would be easier for both of them if they could find a comfortable wave to ride.

If someone had told her she'd be eagerly waiting his arrival and wondering how he would greet her when he did show up two weeks ago, she'd have argued. As it was, she wanted to see him. Wanted to sit back and witness his interaction with his business partners. She'd been too caught up the night they'd announced their marriage to notice much about how he spoke with his colleagues.

Would he be arrogant? Confident? Demanding?

Yes, she decided. All of the above. How else could a man his age be as successful as he was?

Perhaps his need of a wife was there to soften some of his edges . . . or at least give the appearance to others that he had a smoother side to his personality.

If his need for a wife were that simple, she'd know about it already. No, Hunter needed her in his life for something bigger. But what?

She'd thought about the *what* for the better part of the week.

It killed her not to hire her own private investigator to find out.

He'd trusted her to tell him her secrets, and she would hold off and wait for him to reveal his.

The sound of the lock in the door disengaging with a beep caught her attention.

He wore a suit, the cut perfect on his broad shoulders.

Their gazes caught.

The bellhop moved around him. "Would you like this upstairs, Mr. Blackwell?"

His eyes still hadn't left her. "No. Here is fine." On autopilot, Hunter removed his wallet, fished out a bill, and handed it over.

"Anything I can do for you, Mr. Blackwell . . . anything at all."

Hunter waved him off. "Thank you."

The door closed behind him, leaving them alone.

Gabi noticed Hunter flex his hands a couple of times. His feet didn't move.

"Do you have any idea what you gave that man?"

He shook his head.

She chuckled. "It's impolite to stare, Hunter."

He took a few steps in her direction, much like a leopard would stalk its prey.

Gabi moved so the window wasn't at her back. Not that she was trying to escape . . . or so she told herself.

"Where is the yoga outfit?" he asked.

With a straight face, she managed, "Tucked in my suitcase."

He growled, nose flared.

She traveled around the table, the six chairs . . . dividing herself from him as he followed.

"The flowers are lovely."

He didn't change his course . . . or his gaze.

Gabi pulled herself to a stop and let him advance. The hair on her arms stood on end, her mouth went dry.

"Hunter? What are you—"

He ended the space between them in two steps, his arms pulling her flush with his body, his nose in her hair.

"Thank you," he said, making no move to do anything more than hold her.

"For what?"

"For not changing your scent."

The loss for words was huge.

He held her, rested his head close to hers.

As greetings went . . . this one didn't suck.

She broke the silence a few moments later. "I see you didn't throw yourself off a high rise."

His shoulders folded in with laughter. "Such a messy ending."

"Bad for the image?"

"Hmmm . . ."

He took her head in his hands, and for a brief moment, she thought he'd kiss her.

He didn't.

"I missed you more than I should," he confessed.

"You called every day."

"Wasn't enough."

His thumb traced her lower lip before he released a long-suffering breath and moved away.

The slow, simmering onset of sexual frustration started to burn. It shouldn't, she cautioned herself. Hunter was showing restraint, and she should follow his lead.

No matter how difficult that proved.

———

Gabi loosened a strand of hair from the messy bun on top of her head and added a little curl.

She went with a little heavier makeup, stuck with a scarlet red lipstick . . . something she was thankful she could pull off.

The knit dress had a turtleneck collar and half sleeves. It hugged her curves, stopping a couple of inches above her knee. The garter belt and fishnet stockings were a last-minute decision. Probably a foolish one that wouldn't be seen by anyone but her.

As she fastened the last clasp and ran her hand over the edges, she admitted, if only to herself, that she hoped Hunter would discover the sexy addition to her outfit. As much as she loved frustrating the man, she could live on the sexual waves penetrating their every conversation. Pushing him, making him forget his own name, was a power she'd never had with a man before.

She liked it.

A lot!

With one last glance in the mirror, she turned off the light and made her way out of the suite.

Hunter turned away from the picture windows as if in slow

motion. Instead of a tie, he wore a slim-fitting knit shirt that sat high on his neck. Over that, he wore a jet black jacket. If she didn't know better, she'd swear they had coordinated their outfits. His slacks matched the jacket, his shoes the perfect shade of black to blend. The man really knew how to dress. Casual, confident . . . the billionaire he was.

She took her time walking down the stairs, felt his eyes following her.

Speechless. Gabi liked this side of Hunter much better than the conniving bastard who'd all but forced her signature on their marriage certificate.

"I half expected you to wear red."

She stopped at the bottom of the stairs and let him approach.

"I considered it."

He offered a ghost of a smile as he rounded the furniture separating them. He picked up a box sitting on a side table and held it out.

"What is this?"

"Open it," he told her, that ghost smile still lingering.

His fingers brushed hers as she took the obvious jewelry box from his hands.

The hair on her arms prickled and her fingers trembled as she lifted the lid. Sitting on crushed black velvet was a pair of drop ruby earrings. The pear-shaped stones were the size of her little fingernail, a long length of tiny white diamonds set in what looked like white gold made them sparkle in the limited light.

"Oh, my . . . Hunter . . ."

"A splash of power."

She met his gaze and felt the edges of her heart crack.

"You shouldn't have," she told him. And before he could reply, she said, "But I'm happy you did."

"Wear them for me?"

She grinned. "I think they'll look better on me than in the box."

A mirror sat above the foyer table. She removed the simple gold loop earrings she'd put on and replaced them with the gems.

Their weight was a testimony to the carat of the stones. When she attached the second one she gave her head a tiny shake. They found the light and sparkled.

Hunter slid up from behind her and caught her reflection in the mirror. He brushed one of the earrings with the backs of his fingers.

She stood perfectly still and watched the wonder of emotions pass over his face. "You're beautiful, Gabriella."

The tilt of her head wasn't voluntary.

A hint of his frame brushed hers from behind and sparked.

"I don't deserve you," he whispered.

The request to be set free sat on her lips unspoken. The truth was, she hadn't felt this alive since . . . since ever. Being set free now would mean an absence of the emotions inside her. Moving from day to day had been her life since she left Florida.

Perhaps it was time to start living again.

She lifted a hand to the side of his face. "Thank you."

They stood staring at each other through the mirror.

"We should go," he said without moving. "Before I blow off the Adams account and destroy every self-made pact I made about you."

"Self-made pact?" she asked with a giggle.

His lips came dangerously close to her neck before pulling away with a growl.

He grasped her hand and pulled her toward the door. "We're leaving . . . now."

The upscale restaurant sat in the heart of Dallas and was frequented by celebrities, the rich . . . and the up-and-coming entrepreneurs who wanted to make an impression. Money in Dallas was a lot like it was on the West Coast. The people in this town didn't care if you just made your millions or if Daddy left them to you. If anything, a self-made man held a hair more clout.

Hunter led Gabi to the bar to await their dinner companions. Heads turned their way as more than one man took notice of his wife. During the drive to the restaurant, he'd kept his distance from her in the back of the limousine. He now made sure some part of their bodies were touching. It was his way of making sure any man watching understood she was with him.

Hunter wasn't sure where the jealousy stemmed from. He couldn't claim a time he'd given any thought to another man's eyes on his date.

It was the ring, he decided. Gabi wore his ring, and somehow that deemed him capable of jealousy, demanded it even. That was the bullshit he fed his head in order to ward off anything deeper.

They found a high-top table and Hunter tucked her into a chair. "What do you want?"

"Dry martini . . . two olives."

He stepped away and captured the bartender's attention. While he waited for their drinks, he kept an eye on his wife.

She sat with her back rod-straight. The earrings dangled over her slim neck and glistened with every shake of her head. Her full breasts hugged the inside of her dress, which slimmed to her waist. He let his gaze fall and noticed her tapping her foot to the music. He really didn't deserve her. He meant the words he'd uttered in the hotel room. The thought of letting her go was a double-edged claymore ready to decapitate him. He should be isolating himself, emotionally, from her.

Yet he'd thought about nothing *but* her since he'd left LA. He thought the distance would ease the fire inside him. Instead, it blew a steady puff of air and forced that flame to life.

The bartender tapped his arm. Hunter tossed a bill on the bar and grasped the drinks. By the time he turned around, someone had approached Gabi and was leaning over the table.

Hunter wove through the people crowding the bar and interrupted the stranger midsentence.

"I could most certainly quench your—"

Hunter wasn't sure what the Texan was suggesting he quench, but Hunter set the drinks down and did something he never did . . . he wrapped an arm over Gabi's shoulders and glared.

"Well." The other man stood as tall as his boots would let him and smiled. "Looks like you do have a man attached to that ring."

"I tried to tell you," Gabi said as she shifted into Hunter's side.

The infatuated man held out his hand, and in order to avoid a scene, Hunter had no choice but to grasp it.

"You're a very lucky man," the Texan said. He let go and sent Gabi a wink before wandering off.

Beside him, Gabi started to silently laugh.

"What was that?" Hunter asked.

"A bar hookup that failed," she told him.

Hunter stared after the retreating back of the man hitting on his wife.

Her tapping hand brought his attention back. "You're growling."

He stopped. When he brought her back into focus, she was laughing.

"You're enjoying this entirely too much."

"More than you can possibly know." She lifted her drink and clicked her glass to his. "You know what they say about payback," she teased.

He was growling again.

Chapter Nineteen

Every once in a while, Gabi would catch Hunter watching her as they sat across from Frank and Minnie Adams. His gaze would capture her hand on the stem of her martini glass and linger.

She stroked it a few extra times until Hunter gently kicked her under the table.

Oh, the power . . . who knew she'd be so invigorated with it?

The older Texan couple were everything Gabi pictured as a happy pair entering the second stage of adult life. Their only child, Melissa, was grown, and from what Gabi could surmise, trying to find her place in Daddy's company.

They were ordering coffee, deciding on a froufrou dessert to share, when Mr. Adams broached the subject of business.

"I like you, Blackwell," Mr. Adams said as he leaned over the table. "Even though you're ruthless and according to my lawyers, can't be trusted—"

"Frank!" Minnie nudged her husband.

"They say you're going to take over my company and bankrupt

the oil production portion and dedicate all your devotion to new pipelines."

Hunter sat beside her and listened, his eyes focused on the man in front of him.

"Pipelines are the future."

"Without oil . . . what is the worth of the pipeline?" Frank opposed.

Hunter sat back. "Every oilman in Texas . . . in the US would need to go through Adams/Blackwell pipelines in order to deliver their crude. We'll make money on every barrel manufactured regardless of whose land it stems from."

"Monopolies are frowned upon."

"We won't be a monopoly for long. We'll be the trendsetters." Hunter sat forward. "Consider the phone in your pocket. The first cellular concepts were nothing more than ham radios . . . devices used in war and eighteen-wheelers. Eventually Motorola expanded the concept, and within a decade, others emerged . . . then came analog, digital . . . Bell held the monopoly . . . but not forever. US pipelines are the future in US oil, Adams. We both know it."

"It's risky."

"Life is risky."

Frank sat back and Gabi soaked in her husband at work.

"I want another ten percent," Frank said.

"I'm putting up the capital."

Frank shrugged. "You need me or you wouldn't be sitting here. I need to protect my family. If I give you controlling interest, there is nothing keeping you from kicking me and my people to the Gulf. I want a merger, Blackwell . . . not an acquisition."

Under the table, Gabi noticed Hunter fisting his hand and relaxing it. This was obviously *not* his plan.

Unable to help herself, Gabi interjected, "What are you willing to do for that extra ten percent, Frank?"

He offered a placating smile. One that irked her, but she didn't call him on it.

She met Frank's eyes and held them until he flinched.

"I have connections here in Texas, other oilmen who can be persuaded to hook up early on . . . lay down the infrastructure to deliver to the main pipe."

"You've already told me that," Hunter reminded him.

"I know politicians . . ."

"So do I." Hunter glared.

Gabi let her thoughts run. "I would think pipelines . . . along with production, is the perfect plan for the future of our country. My guess is Carter would back a solid direction to remove our demand on foreign oil. And if I'm not mistaken, Carter has an uncle who's in the Senate." She was musing out loud, and captured the attention of all those at the table.

"What are you rambling about?" Frank asked.

Gabi directed her attention to Hunter. "Samantha is great friends with Carter and Eliza Billings. He recently left the governor's seat in California. Word on the Republican block is he might be running for the White House in six years."

"Might and could? Words that don't mean anything to me," Frank managed.

Hunter sat forward again. "The point my wife is making, Frank, is simple. You know people . . . we know people . . . the difference is I have the capital to push this forward and start buying the land and all the rights. My reach is farther than yours."

"Without me you have nothing."

With a game face, Hunter said, "Without you . . . it will take longer."

The table went silent.

"I need to protect my family," Frank finally said.

Hunter sat back, inched closer to Gabi, and placed a hand on the back of her seat. "I understand that. Ten percent is steep. We can have our lawyers renegotiate the numbers until we're both happy."

Was this one of the reasons Hunter needed a wife? Was the ploy of understanding family his only goal?

If it was . . . how much money was the pipeline worth?

The question would wait.

The waiter was refilling their coffee when Hunter removed his phone from the inside pocket of his jacket and glanced at the screen.

The agreeable expression on his face fell, and within five minutes he was wrapping up their time together.

"I will have my team call yours on Monday," Hunter told Frank as he signaled the waiter.

"In a hurry all of a sudden?" Frank asked.

Yeah, something on the phone had pulled him far from Dallas.

When Hunter hesitated, Gabi lifted her napkin from her lap and laid her hand on top of his. With a practiced smile, she leaned in. "Forgive us. We are still newlyweds and Hunter has had to spend the week in New York while I've been stuck in LA."

Minnie nudged her husband and offered a knowing grin. "You two go along then. We'll take care of the bill."

Hunter was already removing his credit card and handing it over.

While they waited for the credit to go through, Minnie asked. "How did you two meet?"

Hunter turned to her.

"At Starbucks," Gabi said.

"Really? What are the chances of that?"

Hunter lifted her hand and kissed her fingers. "Really high, if you drink coffee."

Hunter's head was buzzing with an approaching headache. He and Gabi rode in relative silence since leaving the restaurant. There were so many conversations he needed to have with her . . . none of which needed to begin in the back of a limousine.

"Where are you?" Gabi asked.

Good question. "Want the truth?"

"Do you even have to ask?"

He took a fortifying breath. "Somewhere between truth and redemption and purgatory and hell."

"That's quite a long road."

As if on cue, the car pulled to a stop in front of their hotel and his multitude of confessions had to wait.

The two of them demanded attention as he guided her through the hotel lobby and into the elevator. Those eyes often turned into the flash of a camera after he stayed in a hotel for more than two nights. It wouldn't be long until the media would follow Gabi everywhere she went. Especially once the news broke.

Gabi paused inside the door and removed her shoes.

Hunter went straight to the bar. "Want something?"

Gabi walked toward him, her shoes dangling from her fingers. "I don't know . . . do I?"

He went ahead and poured her a vodka before shrugging off his jacket and sitting at one end of the sofa.

She followed his actions, dropped her shoes beside a chair, and sat. She tucked her feet under her and waited.

Where the hell was his tongue? He couldn't wait any longer. The collision course in his life, the one that drove him to rapidly acquire a wife, was on him. More than that . . . the woman waiting patiently for him to open up was doing something inside him that he hadn't expected.

He didn't deserve her trust, her respect, but he was hell-bent on earning it.

"Tell me about your truth and redemption," she said when he remained silent.

"I can't do that without feeding purgatory and hell."

"You have to start somewhere. Why not start with what caught your attention during dinner."

He removed the phone from the jacket he'd carelessly tossed on the back of the couch, brought up the picture, and handed it to Gabi.

She leaned forward and took his phone. "Unless this was taken yesterday, I don't see the problem."

Gabi handed him back the phone.

"It was taken three months ago at a studio party. Her name is Sheila Watson."

"You two look cozy."

Hunter glanced at the image again, saw things Gabi didn't.

"Looks can be deceiving. I'm not entirely sure how that picture was taken, but one thing is for sure, it was taken on purpose. Just like the others."

"Others?"

He found the e-mail hidden in a folder and pulled up a handful of pictures that had started to arrive shortly after he'd met Sheila. Hunter once again handed her the phone and told her to scroll.

As Gabi looked at the many pictures, some more suggestive than others, her face was blank. "How long was your affair?"

The question alone was why he'd embarked on his dance to hell in the first place. "We didn't have an affair. That isn't me."

Gabi lifted the phone closer and opened the pictures wider.

"My brother, Noah."

"The one you don't get along with."

"Understatement, but yes." Hunter swirled the ice in his glass, took a drink.

"Wow, you two really look exactly alike."

"Our looks aren't the only thing my brother is banking on. You see, he had an affair with Sheila."

Gabi gasped. "Oh, no . . . posing as you?"

"No. Not that I know of. No, I'm sure Sheila knew exactly who she was sleeping with and why. The picture at the studio event was me. It was the first time I'd met the woman. Everyone at the event knew I was there. There is no disputing our acquaintance. To make things even sweeter, she showed up in my New York office pleading a need to see me. She was much too pushy and needy for my taste. Flattery from someone's attraction dissipates quickly when you believe they're unbalanced."

"Do you think her motivation in invading your work was just attraction?" Gabi asked.

"No. It was by design. She wanted people to see us together."

"For what purpose?"

"Blackmail." He finished his drink. "Ironic when I think about what I had to do to destroy her goals."

Gabi sat a little taller. "This is where I come in."

He unfolded from the couch and brought the decanter of whiskey to his glass. "I wasn't lying when I first told you I needed a wife to ward off the number of women claiming I'd promised them marriage."

"I'm sure that's true, but sincerely doubt marriage was your only solution to that problem."

He offered a half-ass smile from across the coffee table. "Except some were determined to make a killing on their accusations. You see, Sheila had a child nine months ago. My twin brother's child. I don't know what came first, the child or the plan. Doesn't really matter."

"Oh, no."

Hunter could see the light in Gabi's eyes spark.

"Sheila manages a few pictures of the two of us at the party . . . makes a surprise appearance in my office, corners me during a lunch meeting. Then a note arrives from Noah. *Congratulations, Daddy.* Words no man ever wants to hear and yet every one of us deserves to at least once in our lives. But not from a woman they've never touched."

The confession hung between them for a few seconds before Gabi asked, "Your need for a wife was so she wouldn't blackmail you into marriage?"

He hated the irony. "In part . . . but she never would have managed. Having a contractual wife certainly removed *that* from her plans."

"How is it she can pin this child on you if it's not yours anyway?"

"DNA. Noah and I are identical in every way genetically. I received word last week that the paternity test proved me to be the father."

"It proved one of the two of you to be the father," Gabi corrected. "Surely someone with your wealth and influence can find a way to dispute this woman's claim."

His eyes collided with Gabi's.

The forced smile she held slowly melted. "Unless you don't want that." Her jaw dropped.

"My hell will be Noah's purgatory. How dare he use a child as leverage for money." The early memories of his brother's deception to claim something of his that wasn't, flooded him. Yeah, they'd used the identical twin thing in unison in primary school . . . by the time they were halfway through high school, their mother had completely disappeared, their father was easily persuaded to follow whatever financial path Noah thought he should. What Blackwell Senior didn't realize, or if he did, didn't care about, was Noah's self-serving nature. Avoiding responsibility and pretending to be someone he wasn't was Noah's gift. Another gift . . . he pleased everyone he met. There wasn't a soul who would say he was a bad guy. He reserved his nasty side for Hunter.

There'd been many times in the past Noah had come along asking for a little money to hold him over . . . finance a "brilliant idea." It was easy to hand over money when you had it. Eventually, however, Hunter knew he wasn't doing the right thing.

He stopped being his brother's bank and subsequent doormat and shut him out. Less than three months later Noah had opened a line of credit using Hunter's name . . . drained over a hundred grand before Hunter learned of his brother's deception. After, Hunter stopped all communication, and his bookkeepers kept a close eye on all credit inquiries.

Hunter's reward for tough love . . . a child he didn't father. Payback is a bitch.

Gabi lifted a hand to her lips and spoke through it. "You're going to keep the child."

"A move neither of them are expecting."

Gabi dropped her hand in her lap, her jaw tightened. "This isn't a game of chess. We're talking about a child, Hunter."

The hair on his neck stood on end. "A child being used as a pawn by his own parents. What kind of life will he have? My mother forced my father into marriage with her pregnancy. She left the first time in third grade, only to return and play the back-and-forth game until high school. My brother knows I won't support him, so he's devised a plan to support his child. Only Noah thinks I'm going to do it by handing him money to avoid being the child's father." He couldn't sit any longer and crossed to the windows and the lights of the city below. He never spoke of his mother. Most people thought she was dead. To him, she was. After Noah's game, his brother would be dead to him, too.

"I'm sorry."

"I don't want your sympathy."

"Well that's too bad. Abandonment from a parent isn't easy at any age. My father died and I still felt cheated. If he had chosen to leave and never returned, it'd be an unfathomable betrayal. What I don't understand is why you didn't tell me all of this before now."

"Before our marriage?"

"Yes."

"Would you have believed me?" He glanced at her over his shoulder.

With a small shake of the head, she said, "No. Probably not."

"Then you have your answer." The lack of friends and loyalty kept him from opening up and expecting people to do the right thing. He returned his stare to the skyline.

"You're a very impatient man . . . do you know that?"

"I don't like to waste time."

"Which makes you impulsive, makes you force marriage on unsuspecting women."

How could he respond to that? Luckily, she continued talking and kept him from having to.

"Do you have any idea how you're going to bring this child into your life? What it takes to be a father?"

Up until Gabriella had landed in his life, he'd thought of nothing but that. "No more than any man who's been told they have a child."

"You're really going to do this. Take on your brother's child as your own."

"Hayden doesn't deserve a life with parents that only had him to make money off his DNA. I'm not delusional, I know it won't be easy."

"And you're willing . . ."

The image, the one he had of the boy, swam in his head. Hunter turned to look at Gabi. She was sitting forward in her chair, her feet planted on the floor as if she were ready to bolt from the room. "He isn't yet ten months old. The babysitter, day care . . . whatever you wanna call it, doesn't differ much from an orphanage. Sheila retrieves him on occasion, but she's been spending most of her time with Noah, and Noah isn't father material. He can't care for himself, let alone another human being."

"So how do I fit into this picture?"

"I have a team of lawyers, as well as private investigators, working on deeming Sheila incompetent as a parent. As a stable, married man, it's not only easy to avoid Sheila claiming I agreed to marry her, but the court will use the evidence, and my current stable state, to grant me custody. My guess is, she will vacate the scene with a little money and time."

"And if she doesn't?"

Hunter was betting she would. "I'll cross that road when I come to it."

"And Noah?" she asked.

"He will get nothing. If I caved to any of his demands now, what is to stop him from doing it again?"

"Nothing."

"Exactly."

"Do you have a picture . . . of Hayden?"

Hunter removed his wallet from his pocket as Gabi walked toward him.

A mop of dark hair sat on top of a chubby face, the child's fist was in his mouth, drool ran down his chin.

Gabi lifted her hand to the picture and placed a fingertip to the image. "He's adorable."

Yeah . . . the thought hit Hunter the first time he'd seen the kid. "Innocent."

On a sigh, Hunter returned the picture to his wallet and tucked it into his pocket.

"What am I going to do with you?" Gabi whispered.

Hunter looked into her eyes, saw a hint of moisture hiding behind the dark depths of them.

"You'd be wise to keep your distance."

Instead of distance, she closed the minimal space between them and placed a hand on his chest. "One minute you're impersonating the greatest bastard out there . . . the next you're rescuing babies from bad parents."

"I'm not a hero, Gabi. Nowhere close."

"No," she agreed. "You're not a saint. Your tactics are ruthless, tasteless, and seemingly without conscience. You're impatient, greedy, and egotistical."

He frowned.

"You're cynical, downright nasty—"

He placed a hand to his chest. "You're killing me."

"I'm not done!" She batted his hand away from his chest and smiled. "You're driven, which isn't a bad thing. You're influential and a little brilliant. I mean, c'mon . . . how many men at thirty-six make the Forbes billionaire bachelor list without family money?"

Some of his frown lifted.

"You fear honesty, but who doesn't? It's hard to reveal truths about yourself when you don't know if the person you're talking to is going to use it against you. It's hard to trust when your own twin is screwing you over."

He lifted a hand to her shoulder and held on. "I'm not—"

"I'm *not* finished."

He sighed with a smile.

"You're sexy, and the women in your life would have been fools to not try and capture whatever attention they could from you."

Yeah, he was working out the muscles in his face with his grin.

"You've probably broken hearts from LA to New York to Europe. God help you if more than one woman arrives with a child in their hands that you can't avoid."

"I've always been safe."

Gabi placed a finger over his lips, silencing him.

"And while you're impatient with many mergers and acquisitions . . . and marriages . . . you've shown amazing restraint with your nephew and your wife." She paused, her smile faded. "And that . . . Hunter Hayden Blackwell . . . is what is placing your feet on the road to hero."

His hand gripped her shoulder. The trust in her eyes too powerful for words. "My restraint for you is a tightly strung string on a violin. One stroke and it's going to snap."

Her delicate fingers rode up his chest and wove around his neck. "God, I hope so." She brought his head closer to hers, and kissed him.

The Stradivarius shattered.

Chapter Twenty

He was stunned, Gabi felt it in his kiss.

His hesitation lasted only a fraction of a second before he wrapped her into his strong arms and threw his weight into the meeting of their lips. So many sensations hit her at once. He tasted like whiskey, smelled like sin, and kissed her like a devil guaranteed to break her heart. There was no letting go, however. After lying dormant for so long, having a man as powerful as Hunter Blackwell devouring her wasn't something she wanted to resist.

Not any longer.

She opened to the swipe of his tongue and lifted on her tiptoes to taste. There were no careful, languishing movements . . . both of them were much too anxious to feel the next zip of pleasure. Hunter ran a hand down the length of her back and back up to catch in her hair.

He released her lips to say, "Let this down. I want to see you with it down."

She opened her eyes to see his hooded gaze.

With both hands, she released the clip and comb holding her hair. It cascaded over her shoulders in a wave.

Hunter growled and pushed both hands into it, his eyes focused on his own hands as they ran through the silky length. With both hands holding her face, he finally met her eyes. "I've never wanted a woman the way I want you."

She didn't have time to respond, not that she knew what to say after his confession. He dragged his lips across hers in what felt like desperation.

When Gabi let one hand fall to his hip, the other to his ass, Hunter pressed her against the massive window and gathered her hands in his. He lifted them above her head and leaned into her, from shoulder to knee. It was as if he was controlling his own ability to slow this down by keeping her from touching him.

It was frustrating, and erotic.

Though they were both still fully clothed, the extent of his desire pressed low on her belly, close, but not close enough.

Hunter continued kissing her, hot, urgent kisses that left her utterly breathless.

With her hands inoperable, Gabi ran one leg up his.

He tore his lips away. "If you keep touching me, I'm going to make love to you right here, with all of Dallas watching."

She swiveled her head and attempted to catch the lights behind her. She wasn't quite ready for that leap into exhibitionism. "Then I suggest we find a proper bed."

One of his hands loosened on hers and his free palm held her cheek. "Are you sure, Gabriella?"

Is there any question?

He was giving her an out . . . an out she no longer wanted.

"Your bed, or mine?" she asked with a smile.

One minute she was bound to the window, the next she was in his arms. "Mine's closer."

He tossed back the down comforter and laid her on the white sheets.

Gabi welcomed him back into her arms and continued the kiss he'd kept from her for over a week.

The weight of him, his strength, made her dizzy. Or maybe it was the lack of air. Gabi lifted her chin, forcing his attention to her neck.

She tugged his shirt from his slacks. Removing his shirt wasn't possible without space between them. And right at that moment Hunter was using the tip of his tongue to explore the space behind her ear.

When her fingertips met with skin, she let her nails drag.

Hunter lost his concentration and moaned.

With her lips close to his ear, she whispered, "I love when you lose control."

"Grrr."

She giggled, let her fingers slip into his pants.

His sought out the bottom of her dress. The feel of his fingers riding over the edge of her stockings made her smile.

He froze, and half lifted from her heated frame. He gathered the edge of her dress and lifted it higher on her thigh.

She knew the moment his eyes feasted on her garter. "Christ, Gabi. What are you wearing?"

"If you have to ask . . ." she let her words fade as she took in his reaction to the lingerie.

He ran a hand under the clasp, left it in place, and continued to explore her. "You're like Christmas."

Heated from his touch, his words, his eyes, she said, "It's time to remove some of the wrapping."

She sat up and reached behind her back. The zipper of her dress wasn't an easy catch, so Hunter took over.

She heard the gentle slide, felt his fingers lightly brush her skin as cool air met her flesh. Sitting still, she didn't fidget when Hunter took his time removing the dress from her shoulders.

Only when the dress pooled around her waist did Hunter stop staring and lean forward to touch. He lingered on her shoulder, trailed his lips to the tops of her breasts, still bound in her black lace bra. He was attempting to remove her dress, and she tugged at his shirt. They both met the floor at the same time.

Gabi knew Hunter filled out a suit, but under was the real view. A view she'd thought a lot about since she'd first seen it on the beach on her brother's island.

With the liberty to touch, she did. Everything about the man was confident and strong.

Hunter left the bed for the two seconds it took to shed his pants. He tossed his wallet on the nightstand and returned in only his boxers.

He ran his hands over her breasts, cupped them before moving to the back to unclasp her bra. "Christmas and birthdays," he mumbled as he tossed her clothing away.

Her breasts were heavy in need of his touch.

She didn't have to ask. Hunter replaced his hands with his mouth. Had she ever felt so completely ready to accept a man into her body? Was there a time she felt this cherished?

Cherished was probably the wrong word, but it was the only one that continued to scroll in her head. Hunter was making love to her . . . not simply trying to get inside. Pushing away any doubt of his intentions, she leaned back against the pillows and drowned in the feel of him.

He took his time, until she was raw and squirming. He'd yet to touch her most needy parts, and they screamed for his attention. He moved down her waist, kissed the edge of her hip.

When she lifted her hips, she heard him laugh.

"Now it's me who's dying," she told him.

He lifted one of her legs until it was bent at the knee, and he knelt between them.

The first clasp snapped, catching her by surprise. The second was expected.

He rolled the stocking down and turned to her other leg. Once they were both gone, he led his fingers on a slow dance up her calves, her thigh, and stared everywhere he touched. When she was certain he was going to relieve some of the monstrous tension in her body, his hands bypassed her core, took the edge of the garter, and pulled it off.

Her breath caught when he removed the final layer. She'd never been this exposed to a man, but instead of feeling embarrassed, the word *treasured* popped in her head. "Please," she mumbled.

Hunter's eyes shot to hers with such lust . . . such passion, her heart skipped in her chest. "I don't deserve you."

It frightened her to think he'd stop. "You've taken me this far, Hunter. It would be cruel to leave me like—"

With his eyes locked to hers, he let his hands find the top edge of her inner thighs. "I passed turning back before we entered the room, Gabriella."

He lowered his head. The first touch was with the swipe of his tongue.

Gabi cried out, clenching the sheets with her fists.

He didn't need to be told where to touch, what to taste . . . he was simply there, completely consumed with her in two breaths. "Oh, Hunter."

It had been so long . . . too damn long. The strings on her violin were drawing tight too quickly. Her hips lifted from the bed and she shattered.

Literal stars shot as her orgasm ran over her.

Hunter didn't ease away, he shifted, his boxers found the rest of the clothing on the floor, and Gabi heard the tearing of a wrapper.

She captured his hand as he rolled the condom on, smiled. The impressive anatomy with his clothing on was just as extraordinary without it.

She opened herself up to him. Wrapped her arms around his neck. The feel of him nudging her had her smiling.

"Last chance, Gabi."

"I thought we passed turning back," she said with a grin.

He growled, tilted her hips, and offered a sample. "You're right." He gave her everything. "We did."

Yes.

He filled her, every empty space was now branded with his scent, his touch.

Hunter pulled her into his arms, his lips once again took possession of hers, and he slowly started to move. Gabi's buildup was slower this time. And Hunter didn't rush.

He muttered about her beauty, said more than once he didn't deserve her, told her how amazing she felt.

Their pace sped up until kissing wasn't possible and all their attention was on the spot they were so intimately joined.

Her nails pulled him closer, the edge of completion only a hair out of reach. Just when she thought she was going to lose it, Hunter whispered, "Come for me."

She did. And the feeling rolled and rolled, then shot past both of them.

Hunter soon followed with a growl she was all too familiar with.

Remington hadn't slept on the plane, and the sun in Rome was entirely too bright.

He exited the airport and found his way to the taxi station, grateful to be out of Colombia. The place had eyes, and he couldn't help but wonder who, exactly, had been watching him. Other than the kids lifting his phone, he hadn't been mugged or even propositioned.

The only promising lead on the Picano accounts was the two so-called bankers. After he left them, Remington's information dried up.

Once he was settled in a cheap motel . . . or what would be equivalent to an American dive, Remington dialed Blackwell. It was the middle of the night in the States, so when voice mail picked up, he relayed the important details. "Ahhh, Rome. Such a big city. Colombia was a bust. If I knew better, I'd swear whoever had their hands in that account had a reach far outside those boarders. Lips were closed up tighter than my first wife. Anyway, my cell is back on, same number. If you tried to call earlier . . . sucks to be you. Damn kids," he muttered. "I'm posing as your hot tamale's personal agent. Vouch for me. These Italians aren't as quick to talk, which leaves me wondering how far I'm going to get. I might need to pull in another set of ears . . . or someone who speaks the damn language." Remington caught a yawn and kicked off his shoes. "Don't bother calling for at least six hours. I won't answer."

He pushed from the bed and closed the blinds. "Have I told you how much I love traveling on your dime?"

He hung up.

He would be up by dusk and ready to find the contact he'd made before he boarded the plane. Then, after a decent night's sleep, he'd be at the bank in the morning.

As the city around him woke, Remington did his best to drown out the noise and the light. He hit the bed and instantly felt his body sinking. His last thought before he fell asleep was, *I need to have something tomorrow or Blackwell's wallet is going to shut.*

Sleep first . . . information later.

Hunter woke with a start. His head swiveled to the side.

Gabi was still there. Her hair splayed on the pillow, her eyes closed, and her lips slightly parted as she slept.

They'd just complicated everything.

He couldn't bring himself to care. It was still dark, the clock on the table said it was after three in the morning.

Gabi shifted in her sleep, and Hunter reached around her waist and moved closer. Only when his head rested on the same pillow as hers and her floral scent met his nose did he let himself relax.

He'd heard people talk about mind-blowing sex . . . rock-the-universe orgasms . . . and yeah, he'd had his share of encounters that he thought were defined in those terms.

He'd been wrong.

Maybe it was the conquest itself. The reality that the woman sleeping in his arms had told him that under no terms would she let him touch her.

Maybe it was Gabi.

Maybe unadulterated lust poisoned his brain.

He started to doze and Gabi wiggled one of her legs between his.

His body responded to her slight touch. Hunter considered taking her . . . again . . . then decided a wide-awake lover would prove better than one half-asleep. The sun would rise in a few hours.

He could wait.

Chapter Twenty-One

Hunter sat across from a bathrobe-clad Gabi as they sipped tea and enjoyed room service.

She'd been just as passionate in the morning as she had been the night before. If she was having second thoughts on what had happened, there wasn't any sign of it in her voice, or her actions.

And since when did he want to talk about sex after he'd had it?

Since he woke up, apparently.

"Is it me?" Gabi asked as she spooned a forkful of scrambled eggs into her mouth, "Or are these eggs magnificent?" She licked her lips, the tip chasing a tiny speck of egg inside.

"Watching you eat them . . . that might be classified as magnificent."

She tilted her head and gave him a slightly embarrassed smile. "I'm starving. I haven't been awake and active that long at night since . . ." She lowered her fork and studied the ceiling. "I don't think I ever have."

God she was good for his ego. She'd also just opened the door to the conversation that had been on his mind since he showered. "Any second thoughts . . . on last night?"

Her eyes met his. "Probably. They just haven't made themselves known yet."

An honest answer.

"What about you?" she asked, forking more eggs into her mouth.

"I'm more concerned about you. You were adamantly opposed to intimacy."

She lowered her fork and leaned back in the chair. "I didn't know you. I probably still don't. Not completely, in any event."

"Couples that have been married for twenty years learn secrets about the other."

Gabi wiped her mouth with the napkin in her lap before she spoke. "I've learned a lot more about Hunter Blackwell in the past month than I ever thought possible. Intimacy, however, has been something I've feared . . . I think you can understand why."

He leaned across the table and placed his hand over hers.

"I'm not afraid of you," she said. "I probably should be."

That hurt, but he had to own her statement. "You probably should be," he agreed.

She actually grinned with his words. "Thank you for not ignoring the elephant in the room."

"You're my wife," he reminded her. "You're not someone I can ignore."

She removed her hand from under his and continued eating. "Would you? If we'd just met . . . no marriage contract . . . no drama? Would you ignore me after last night?"

"And this morning?"

Her fork hesitated and her cheeks turned pink.

"And this morning," she repeated.

"Another woman? Maybe. I didn't get my reputation by speculation alone."

She seemed to respect his answer, so he continued, "Gabriella Blackwell demands something more. And it isn't simply the last name . . . though I think we can both say neither of us have embarked on a sexual affair with our spouse."

"That sounds so strange."

"Do you have another way of putting it?"

She continued to chew as he shrugged. "Affair sounds better than a one-night stand. And is that what we're doing?"

He lifted his coffee cup, brought it to his lips, and muttered. "One night? I don't think so. I can't say I know what the hell I'm doing."

She gave up on her breakfast, dropped her napkin on her plate.

"I don't either," she told him. "But I do think we need to cover a few rules."

There she was . . . the woman who stormed into his office with a contract only a fool would sign.

Color Hunter a fool. "What kind of rules?"

"We both have issues with trust . . . yes?"

"Yeah . . . I suppose."

"So honesty above all things. I'll start. When I put the clause in our contract about affairs, it was more to push your buttons than me caring if you slept around. But as long as you and I are . . ." her gaze drifted to the closed door behind him.

"Intimate?"

"Yes. As long as we're intimate, monogamy isn't something I want to live without."

He swallowed. He hadn't agreed to that kind of relationship since high school . . . and that was for what? Two weeks? Then again, he hadn't thought of another woman since he'd met and encountered the force named Gabriella.

"And if either of us feels the itch with someone else, we're honest about it," she said.

The thought of her with another man left him colder than he liked. "I can agree to that."

She kept her eye on his. "No matter how it might hurt the other person."

"I promised I wouldn't hurt you." But could he keep that if someone else came along? God, he was such an asshole.

"That promise was physical. It's up to me to protect my heart, Hunter. That isn't your job. Yeah, it would hurt if you were to tell me, *last night was great, but let's not do it again*, but that's better than pretending attraction when there isn't any."

He couldn't help it. He laughed. "*Great* isn't a word I'd use, and *let's not* isn't even in my vocabulary."

"So we agree. Monogamy and honesty . . . even if it hurts."

"And one more thing," he added. "Our contract still stands. Eighteen months."

"Seventeen months, two days."

"Did I miss a couple of weeks?"

"Our contract was signed before we said *I do*. You really should read the fine print, Wall Street." It made him happy to see her smiling.

"Fair enough." He lifted his hand across the table as if he was talking with his lawyer. "Should we shake on it?"

Instead of extending her hand, Gabi stood and removed the belt on the bathrobe.

The sight of her body . . . all of it, unclothed and standing in the middle of a hotel room in Dallas, had his mouth completely dry.

"I have a better idea," she said as she started toward the stairs.

It took a minute for his brain to register, but when it did, he growled and gave chase.

———

Escrow closed the following Friday, and on Saturday, Samantha's sister, Jordan, went into respiratory arrest and was on life support.

Instead of moving into her new home, Gabi was keeping pace with all the current and past members of Alliance in an effort to support Samantha and Blake.

"Is there anything I can do?" Hunter asked her over the phone when she called to tell him there wouldn't be any moving vans over the weekend.

"It's round-the-clock coffee in the waiting room. Unless you love the smell of antiseptic and something I can't identify."

They'd spent the majority of the week apart.

Dallas would never look the same. They debated separate rooms in the new house . . .

Then Wednesday came . . . and dinner . . . and the back of the limo. But Gabi was working hard to push that memory from her head as she spoke with Hunter now. "I'm sure you have some packing to do."

"I have people for that," he said. "Besides, I'm not moving anything from the condo, so my packing is limited to suits."

He was keeping his place in the city, a decision made before Dallas. BD . . . an acronym Gabi kept thinking.

"So you're bored and need somewhere to go . . . and the hospital is it?"

"Bored? I don't know what that word means."

She felt a smile on her face. Around her, hospital staff walked in and out of the locked doors of the ICU. The lobby was filled with familiar faces. Gwen sat next to a former Alliance employee, Karen Gardner. Karen had worked with Samantha's sister early on and was taking this latest turn in Jordan's health to heart. It didn't help that Karen had recently learned she was pregnant with her first child and emotions ran high.

"If you're not bored . . . what are you doing?"

"Multitasking."

There was nothing laughable going on around her, yet she found herself giggling. "What does a billionaire do when multitasking?" she asked.

"This billionaire is trying to figure out how to hire a nanny without tipping off the world of my intentions while simultaneously guiding two private detectives in different parts of the world."

"When do you think Hayden will come?"

"A month . . . maybe two. Hard to tell. I have a child and family lawyer and her team working it. If my PI can document neglect, we'll get him sooner. Emergency case could be in a week. Who knows?"

"Want my advice?" she asked.

"Bring it."

"Skip the nanny search. We'll deal with that when we get him. Between the two of us, we'll manage."

Hunter hesitated. "I work every day. I can't dump this on you."

"You're not dumping, I'm volunteering. Once we have him, we can begin Operation Nanny Search. Besides, I don't want some beautiful, young blonde in my home tempting my husband." She was only half teasing.

"I don't know . . ."

"Hunter, please. Concentrate on your detective. You have two on this?"

"No, only one. The other one is on you."

The smile on her face fell.

"On finding the name behind the trafficking of money through your accounts," he said quickly.

"Don't scare me like that," she scolded.

"Seems all the secrets are on the table . . . unless you're hiding something."

Gabi took another look around to ensure no one was listening. "My skeletal closets are empty, Hunter."

"Good to know."

"Your PI doesn't need to worry about any more trafficking. I put a stop to that."

"You what?"

"The night you cornered me with the information I found both accounts. It only took me a few tries to figure out Alonzo's passwords. He never was that clever about numbers. When I backed out of the accounts, I changed them."

"Oh, Gabi . . . no. You didn't." Distress laced Hunter's voice.

"Yes, I did. I don't want someone going around using my name on an account with that kind of money in it. Freezing the accounts until I could hire someone to find the person behind them seemed the best course of action."

"No, no, no, no . . ."

She turned toward the wall, lowered her voice. "What?"

"Think about it. Whoever has their hands on that money can no longer access it. That's gonna piss someone off."

The smugness of a moment ago was gone now. "I didn't consider that."

"I'm switching gears . . . you need a bodyguard until we have this sorted out."

"That's ridiculous, Hunter. I do not need a bodyguard." Her words were louder this time, and several heads swiveled toward hers.

Gwen ended her conversation with Karen and started toward Gabi.

"We'll talk about this later."

"There's nothing to talk about," Hunter said.

Gwen stopped right in front of her, eyes sharp. "A bodyguard?"

Gabi lowered her cell phone from her ear. "It's nothing, Gwen. Hunter's being overprotective."

Gwen placed her hands on her hips and glared. "I've found that when a man as rich as Hunter thinks you need a bodyguard . . . you need a bodyguard. Tell him I'll have Neil give him a call."

Gabi placed her hand over the receiver of her phone. "I don't need—"

With one swift movement, Gwen snatched the phone from her hand and put it to her ear. "Hi Hunter, it's Gwen. Yes, it's been a long time. Right, one of my brother's weddings . . ." Gwen laughed and then kept talking. "Listen, about a bodyguard, my husband heads up Blake's security . . . yes, that's right, Neil . . . brilliant. So glad you remember. I look forward to it. Anytime."

Gwen lifted her chin, handed the phone back, and walked away.

"Happy now?" Gabi asked Hunter once she lifted the phone to hear ear again.

"Very. One less thing to research. I'm going to come by and pick you up."

"Enough. I'm not a child." And she was getting a little more than slightly irritated with everyone *handling* her.

"Maybe I just want to see you."

He was lying, but the words were sweet. "Why haven't you jumped in front of a bus yet?" she asked.

He started to laugh. "There's my girl. You need to eat. I'll pick you up at five in the lobby."

"If you don't get hit by a bus first." There was no bite in her voice.

"I'll try. If not, I'll see you at five."

"Fine, but nothing fancy. I'm not dressed for fancy."

After disconnecting the call, Gabi returned to the waiting room couch and an internal interrogation.

"So," Gwen started, "what's this about needing a bodyguard?"

Chapter Twenty-Two

It was ten minutes before five, and the hospital walls had started to close in. Stepping into the cool fresh air outside to wait for Hunter appealed on a very high level.

It was already dusk, but a recent dusting of rain left the air crisp and moist. Gabi pulled up to the side of the building and leaned against it. After hours of sitting, drinking tea, and attempting to cheer up her boss and friend, she was in need of a break. Hospitals, ICUs, and patients on ventilators were triggers for too many bad memories. She hadn't realized the stress on her shoulders until she noticed Hunter walking toward her.

He was dressed more casually than she'd ever seen him. Jeans and a jacket . . . and running shoes? Maybe it was his multitasking outfit.

She pushed off the side of the building to greet him. "You didn't have to park."

He stopped short and silently stared.

She moved closer, thinking he would greet her with a kiss. "What? Did your tongue step in front of the bus?"

A complete look of confusion crossed his face and Gabi felt her smile fall.

"You must be her."

"What?"

"Hunter's wife."

Gabi stepped back. In an instant, she realized her mistake. Dear Lord, they looked exactly the same. "Oh."

"You're more beautiful than the pictures in the magazines," Noah said . . . the inflection in his voice mimicked her husband.

A charming smile, one Gabi had seen a few times on Hunter's face since Dallas, put her on edge more than she expected.

"I thought you were Hunter."

Noah was quick to laugh. "We get that a lot."

Gabi made sure there was plenty of space between them. "I've heard a lot about you."

That charming smile didn't fall, but something shifted in his eyes. "Nothing good, I'm sure. My brother has an interesting grasp on reality."

There was no proper reply, so Gabi kept silent.

He stuck his hand out in front of him. "Noah Blackwell."

Nice controlling move . . .

Gabi looked at his hand but made no movement to close the distance to shake it.

"You'll have to excuse me, Mr. Blackwell. In the space of one minute you've insulted my husband, and in turn, me. What are you doing here?"

He slowly lowered his arm, his smile becoming much more sinister. "What did he tell you?"

This was not a game she wanted to play. She glanced out into the circular drive of the hospital, fully expecting to witness someone with a camera nearby. If they were out there, they hid well.

"I'm not the evil twin, Gabriella."

Her head snapped to his. "I don't believe I've given you leave to use my first name."

"I see he's already poisoned you. He does have a way of manipulating everyone around him to get what he wants."

"Why are you still standing here? Whatever goal you've set out to accomplish is not going to happen."

Noah Blackwell sat back on his heels and smiled again. "I have a feeling our paths will cross again. It's been a pleasure, Mrs. Blackwell."

She didn't look at him as he passed by her and into the hospital.

Two minutes later, Hunter pulled his car into the drop-off.

Casual slacks . . . but not jeans . . . and his button-up shirt and dinner jacket brought relief. He stepped out of the car to greet her and she stepped into his embrace and sighed.

"It's good to see you," she said.

"Well, if I thought dinner was going to start like this, I would have come earlier."

She started to shake.

"Gabi?" Hunter pulled out of her hug and studied her. "What's wrong?"

She looked behind her. "I-I just met your brother."

Hunter's hand squeezed her shoulders, his face turned to stone. "You what?"

"Here . . . he stepped into the hospital less than three minutes ago."

His gaze moved beyond her, then back. "Did he hurt you?"

"No . . . just said a few things. I thought he was you at first."

"Wait here." Hunter ran toward the door.

"Don't do anything stupid," she yelled after him.

If Hunter heard her, he didn't indicate it.

Gabi stood beside the open door of Hunter's Maserati, the engine still humming as it idled in the drive.

Hunter disappeared behind the sliding doors of the hospital, leaving her staring after him. She held on to the top of the car with the passenger door opened and tried her best attempt at appearing patient.

With all the fidgeting she was trying to control, Gabi was fairly certain any cameras pointing on the outside of the hospital painted her as a woman standing by the getaway car.

Hunter emerged from the doors several minutes later. Gabi did a mental check . . . he was wearing slacks, not jeans.

She sighed.

"Did you see him?"

He shook his head. "He doesn't stick around for long."

There was a car behind them, pinned because of a small bus that had sandwiched them in. The driver tapped his horn. Hunter held the passenger door while Gabi slipped inside.

"Are you OK?"

"Shaking . . . which is stupid, he didn't do anything. I think it was the shock of realizing a half a second too late that he wasn't you. I almost kissed him."

Hunter gripped the steering wheel with both hands. "But you didn't."

Gabi wrapped her arms around her stomach. "No." She really wasn't feeling well. The car hit a buckle in the road and her head started to spin.

"What did he say?" They stopped at the red light and Hunter glanced her way.

"That he wasn't the evil twin. I told him he was wasting his time talking to me."

"But he knew who you were."

"Yes. Said he recognized me from the paper . . . or something like that." The light turned green and Hunter kept driving. "What game do you think he's playing?"

"The same one he's been playing since our teens. Undermine, discredit, and deceive."

"Wouldn't it be easier if the man followed in your footsteps and earned his own living?" Gabi asked.

Hunter actually laughed. "Not when someone else can do all the hard stuff and he can sweep in and take." Thirty minutes later, they were sitting in a quiet booth in a tiny, informal steakhouse.

"You look like you could use a drink," Hunter told her.

"I don't think—"

The waiter stepped up and Hunter ordered them wine.

He waited until after their wine arrived before asking for every detail of her encounter with Noah.

When their brief meeting had been recited, she sipped her wine, thankful Hunter insisted on it.

"His presence wasn't an accident. This is what he does. He shows up in the places I'm going to be . . . makes nice with those around me, and sprinkles doubt about my resolve to keep my distance from him. A master manipulator must first gain the trust of those he's sinking his claws in. Now that you've seen him once, he will be around again. I'd bet money on it."

"How would he know I was there? Or do you think he was trying to find you?"

"If he wanted to find me, all he would have to do is show up at the office. He could have followed you, got wind via the media. He was after something else." He sat back in thought. "His drive-by makes it clear why you need a bodyguard."

She opened her mouth to argue.

Hunter cut her off. "It's already in motion, Gabi. I spoke with Neil before picking you up. He will have a team at the new house to wire tomorrow, a personal bodyguard will meet us at the hospital when we go back."

"Oh, Hunter."

"You're a smart woman. You know I'm right about this."

The thought of mistaking Noah for her husband a second time . . . alone . . . made her pause. "Fine. You're right."

Hunter lifted both eyebrows. "Did that hurt?"

"Saying you're right?"

He chuckled. "Yeah."

She tapped her chest. "A little. Right here."

Hunter leaned forward and took her hand in his. "God, you're beautiful."

"Smooth talker."

"Is it working?" He kissed the back of her hand.

Yeah . . . her stomach had settled and she was no longer shaking. "Well," she started, "I haven't told you to jump in front of a bus for at least an hour."

The funeral took place a week to the day after Jordan passed away. The minister spoke of happier times, of the lives Jordan had touched and the love one sister had for the other.

Gabi looked around the church at the multitude of the Harrisons' friends. She knew that many of the couples were together because of Samantha's service. Alliance was born in an attempt to make the money Sam needed to care for her sister. In a way, Jordan was partially responsible for the marriages surrounding her.

For that, Gabi kept a smile in her heart for the young woman whose life touched so many.

Family and close friends took up the front of the church. There were politicians, businessmen, members of parliament who flew in from London to show their respect. Toward the back of the church sat dozens of caregivers who had taken care of Jordan over the years.

From the care home she'd lived in before Sam and Blake married to the private care nurses who were round the clock in the Harrison home, the venue was filled.

When the procession moved to the graveside, the numbers thinned . . . and then again when they finished at a reception at the Harrisons' Malibu estate.

Gabi took the role of coordinating staff, keeping the kitchen moving, the servers working. With so many dignitaries in attendance, there was an equal amount of bodyguards and security staff. To make matters worse, the three different service attendants wore wires to their ears, but instead of sidearms, they held cocktail trays.

Gabi made it a mission that no one bothered Samantha with anything. Being far removed from an emotional connection with the deceased made it easier for her to act as ambassador to the event.

The house appeared to swell with people. Just when Gabi thought they were at capacity, more arrived.

Cooper, the man assigned as her bodyguard for the day, tried his best to blend into the background. He sucked at blending.

"What are you doing in the kitchen?" The question came from the doorway. Gwen stood with a hand on her hip. "You don't need to do this."

Gabi glanced in her direction and then back to the tray in front of her. "These are ready, Alice, thank you." The server lifted the tray over her shoulder and into the fray.

"You're ignoring me."

"I'm Italian . . . I ignore what I don't want to hear."

Gwen laughed. "Well I'm English, and I'm calling you on it. Hunter asked me to pry you from the kitchen."

Gabi couldn't help the smile on her face. Hunter continued to surprise her. Not only had he put most of his life on hold in the past week, but he selflessly offered more of his time and attention to her network of friends and family.

"I like to keep busy; he should know that about me by now."

The staff buzzed around the room like a well-oiled machine.

"He does know you by now. And how is that?" Gabi grabbed a toothpick full of Gouda as the server passed and tossed it in her mouth. "I thought you two were an Alliance union."

"We are." There wasn't any heat in her words. "Most of the time."

Gwen lifted a very English brow. "Most of the time?"

Just then, Meg and Judy walked into the kitchen . . . the staff continued to work around them. "There you are . . . Hunter's looking for you," Meg said.

Gabi rolled her eyes.

"She's in here," Gwen said. "Telling me how she and Hunter are an Alliance union *most of the time.*"

Meg nudged Judy with a knowing smile. "Told you."

"Most of the time? What exactly does that mean?" Meg asked . . . as if she didn't know.

With a kitchen full of hired staff, Gabi turned toward them and placed her hands on her hips. "It means I'm not a saint," she confessed with heat in her face.

Judy and Meg started to laugh and Gwen caught on.

"So what does this mean?" Judy asked.

Meg shoved her friend again. "It means they're having sex."

Gabi shushed her and Gwen laughed.

Thankfully, the staff dipped their heads and pretended they weren't listening.

"Oh, for crying out loud . . . I'm intimate with my husband. What a crime."

All three women simply stared.

Gabi shook her head, left the kitchen, and found herself straight into the chest of the man in question. "Oh, thank God." She looked up into his face and sprang back. "Noah." Her skin crawled.

"Mrs. Blackwell."

"What are you doing here?"

Cooper exited the kitchen, on his heels the three teasing women. Gabi took a massive step back.

Noah wore a suit, one similar to that of her husband. But the way he held his shoulders . . . the cut of his hair, and more to the point, the way her looked at her, was completely off.

She shuddered.

"We found her," Judy said in Noah's direction.

Gwen stopped laughing first.

Gabi didn't offer an explanation. "What are you doing here?"

Noah looked beyond her. "Gwen, it's been a long time."

"Noah?"

Judy and Meg grew silent.

Gabi stood back as Noah greeted Gwen as if she were a long-lost friend. It stood to reason that if Hunter knew Blake, perhaps his brother knew him and his sister as well.

When Gwen hugged Noah, something in Gabi's stomach turned sour. Hunter's words rang in her head, *This is what he does. He shows up in the places I'm going to be . . . makes nice with those around me, and sprinkles doubt about my resolve on keep my distance from him.*

Gabi waved Cooper to her side. "Find Hunter."

Cooper frowned but moved to fill her request.

She said nothing as Gwen introduced Meg and Judy to Noah. Once she uttered the word twin, understanding filled the eyes of her friends.

Gabi wanted to quiz the man further on his presence, but Gwen seemed to think his attendance was acceptable, so she let it go.

Hunter pushed through the crowd and eased his pace only when he saw the people around her. His eyes shot to his brother and all conversation around them dried up like water in the desert.

"Oh, my." Gabi couldn't tell who blew out a breath, but she understood the desire. Seeing them close together was a shock to the system.

Neither man placed his hand out for the other.

Noah stood smiling . . . like a cat with a secret, and Hunter held tight control of his emotions.

"What are you doing here?"

"Paying my respects, brother."

"Pay them . . . then leave." Hunter's deadly tone drew prickles all over Gabi's skin.

Noah continued to smile as he broke eye contact with his brother and offered a nod to those who could hear him. Then he stared directly at Gabi. "A pleasure to see you again."

Gabi grabbed Hunter's arm to keep him in place as Noah turned and walked away.

"What the hell was that about?" Meg asked.

Gabi didn't answer as she moved in front of Hunter's gaze. "Hey."

He finally looked at her.

He didn't smile.

"He's trying to get under your skin. Don't let him win." Gabi set her hand on his chest and felt his tight breath finally release.

Hunter captured her cheek in the palm of his hand and kissed her gently . . . briefly. "Thank you."

"For what?" she whispered.

"For keeping me from killing him. I owe you."

She laughed and leaned closer.

"Well," Meg said loud enough for everyone to hear. "Seems I have more questions . . . and only a few answers."

Instead of facing her friends, Gabi slipped a hand around Hunter's waist as they walked away.

Chapter Twenty-Three

"That goes in the kitchen." Gabi waved her hand in the direction of the door.

"It says bedroom," Meg argued.

"I lied. When I was packing I mixed up the boxes . . . placed a heart on the box." She rolled her eyes. "Doesn't matter, it goes in the kitchen."

Meg lifted the box a second time and started back down the stairs. "I'm really thankful that most of the Tarzana household didn't belong to you."

Gabi grinned as she unpacked a box of bathroom essentials.

In a few minutes, Meg was back at her side. "We have some serious shopping to do in order to get this place looking like a home."

Gabi glanced into the bedroom sans an actual bed. With everything exploding around them, furniture shopping didn't make the list of things to do.

"So?" Meg motioned toward the empty bedroom. "Where is Hunter going to sleep?"

They hadn't been together in days. Between his schedule and hers, there was very little time for phone calls and a simple text.

"It better be in here with me," she said under her breath.

Meg nudged her.

Gabi shoved her back. "I really shouldn't care about him as much as I do."

"I'm trying to see the bad, Gabi . . . I really am."

She shook off her thoughts and continued to fill the cubbies of the en suite bathroom with useless crap that might be better off in the trash. "He's a good man . . . just doesn't always know the right way to get what he wants without hurting people."

Meg held still and stared. "Has he hurt you?"

Scared her . . . in the beginning. It didn't take long for her to see under the facade that encompassed her husband. Even then there were flowers . . . playful banter between them that was only half meant in the space of a week. "It took me less than twenty-four hours to see the vital differences between Hunter and Alonzo."

Meg hopped up onto the counter. "What was that? Other than the obvious hot factor."

"Hunter is gorgeous."

"Not as amazing as your brother . . . but that's weird for you. Tell me what you see as different, other than the physical."

Gabi cocked her head. "You sound like a counselor."

"I'm sure I do. I just wanna know what you see. Then I'll tell you what I see."

Gabi went ahead and took a place on the counter next to Meg. "He's driven. You can say Alonzo was driven, but I never knew the reason for his drive until it was too late. God . . ." Gabi lowered her head and shook it. "I shouldn't be comparing the two of them."

Meg placed a hand on her leg. "It's OK. You were in love with Alonzo—"

Gabi shook her head. "No. I wanted to love Alonzo. I thought he was something he wasn't. After I knew his secrets, I wanted nothing to do with the man. I know Hunter's secrets . . . what drives him . . ."

"And your feelings toward Hunter are . . . ?"

She couldn't solidify them . . . not with words. Not yet. "Do you know why he needed to get married?"

Meg shook her head.

Gabi popped off the counter and grabbed Meg's hand. She led her into a room across the hall from the master suite. "I'm thinking blue walls . . . dark blue with stars on the ceiling . . ."

"I'm not following you."

Gabi tilted her head toward the ceiling and smiled. "His name is Hayden. Not even a year old and already in the middle of family drama."

Meg sucked in a breath. "Hunter has a son?"

Gabi wasn't sure how much she should say. The house was wired with sound . . . the monitors already recording their movements.

"Let's just say . . ." Gabi started, "Hunter's need to marry wasn't as selfish as I first believed."

Meg moved about the empty room, her head deep in thought. "A family is a huge step."

"Sometimes family just happens. Look at you and me. I love my brother but always wished for a sister. And here you are."

"Do you even want kids?"

Gabi ran her hand along the window ledge. "My biological clock, as they say, has been ticking for some time. Before Hunter, I'd given up on relationships altogether and pushed booties and bottles from my head."

"Women have babies without active fathers all the time."

Gabi met Meg's gaze. "I know that. My father passed away when I was in my teens, leaving Val to step into his role. What if I'd decided to have a child on my own and something happened to me?" She shook off the empty thought of a child growing up without any parent. "I couldn't take that risk."

"You have us."

"I know. With Hayden falling into our lives, Hunter and I will both determine very soon if we're parent material." The thought should scare her, but for a reason she couldn't say, it didn't.

Meg stopped moving and hugged her. "Tell me the whole story, when no one is listening," she whispered.

Gabi nodded.

When Meg stood back, her eyes were dusty with tears. "Val and I . . . we . . . I think I might be pregnant."

Gabi's jaw dropped. The hair on her arms stood on end and every happy cell in her body sang. "You think?"

Meg shrugged. "I'm meeting Judy later with the pee stick. Seems wrong without Val here . . . but."

Gabi shrieked like a teenager laying claim to the star quarterback on the football team. She hugged Meg too hard. "I'm so happy."

"I don't know yet."

She waved her off. "A woman knows."

Meg laughed. "You sound like your mother."

"My mother knows. She knows everything. Oh, Margaret . . . I'm so happy for you."

"Your mom has been eyeing me lately."

Gabi hugged her again. "When is Judy coming over? We need to celebrate."

"It might be a false alarm."

Yeah . . . it could be. Gabi didn't believe it was.

"Italy was a bust." Remington sat across from Hunter in a bistro in Hollywood. "The owners of the vineyards surrounding the property that still belongs to your wife had nothing to say about the property owners. Other than nasty things that I couldn't completely translate, the general feel was one of disdain. As for Picano's family . . . there is a mother who refuses to acknowledge that she had a son and a grandfather who was just as mortified that anyone asked about him. A younger sister, however, seemed to know she had a brother once . . . a rich one. But from what I could tell, she knew nothing about money in any account."

"How could you tell they didn't know about the money?" Hunter asked.

"No connections. Picano cut family ties early on. The only one who even cared I was asking around was the sister. If I had to guess, Picano still had a relationship with her at his death. But she was a college student when he died. She's in debt to the tune of forty grand . . . a drop in the hat of what is in her brother's account. If she had access, my guess is she wouldn't have the debt."

Hunter agreed. "So no family involvement."

"Exactly."

"Which leaves those he was dealing drugs with."

Remington shook his head. "Dealing . . . no . . . smuggling. Different ball game. The amount of drugs this douche bag was shoveling proved he was working directly with the main guy. Whoever this guy is."

"I need a name," Hunter told him.

"Don't we all. The guy they caught alive, Steven Leger, slipped and fell on a knife in prison before he made trial. Picano's onboard staff were just as lucky with their short lives. Whomever Picano was smuggling with didn't take prisoners."

The chill in the room dropped to subtemperatures. *No prisoners* . . . he had arms that reached into the prison system and took out his enemies. How easy a target would Gabi be if this man wanted her dead?

"I need to step up Gabi's security," he muttered to himself.

"What's that?" Remington asked.

"Nothing . . . listen, we need to find this man from a different angle. Drug smugglers from this part of the world are rich, right? Most of them are part of known cartels. We look into the players and reference those who dealt with people like Picano—"

Remington lifted both hands in the air and shook his head. "You don't pay me enough, Blackwell. As it was, I felt eyes on me the entire time I traversed that forsaken country. I don't need a target on my back by peeking into a multitude of drug runners. I'd tap into all those politicians you're becoming so chummy with. Chances are someone in your circle knows a name or two."

"Isn't that what I pay you for?"

He shrugged. "Your friends won't talk to me. I can tap into security files, but that wouldn't be legal." Remington lifted a mocking brow. "You're not suggesting I do that, are you?"

Hunter wouldn't direct the man to an illegal act . . . not with his words, in any event. "Would I ask that of you?"

Remington's smirk said it all.

Even if Remington had a name, Hunter would need to use his connections to keep the drug smuggler away from his home. The thought of reversing the passwords that locked him out crossed Hunter's mind. Chances were, however, Mr. Smuggler would avoid touching the money to prevent a trace. Or worse, look for deeper pockets and silence money. The last thing Hunter's reputation needed right now was that of a man who gave in to blackmail.

Hunter pushed from his desk and stood. "I need dirt on Sheila Watson." He pulled a notepad off his desk and scribbled the address he had for the mother of Noah's son. "I have someone working on current habits, what I need is her past. And keep an ear out for Picano's partners."

Remington tucked the note in his pocket and offered a mock salute. "You're the boss."

Once Hunter was alone in his office, he lifted the phone and called his new security.

"MacBain." Neil answered the phone with his name.

"It's Blackwell. I want another set of eyes on Gabi."

There was silence on the other end of the line.

"Did you hear me?"

"Why?"

"I think she needs it."

"You know, Blackwell. I've been doing this a long time. I'm sure you have enemies, but if you think there is *one* in particular we should be looking out for, I need to know who they are."

Hunter felt a headache coming on. "I don't have a name, Neil."

"Tell me what you're afraid of."

"It's not about me."

More silence.

"It's Gabi's ex."

"He's dead."

"Yeah, but whoever he worked with isn't."

"Wait . . . is there an actual threat? What aren't you telling me?" Neil asked.

Hunter hadn't told Neil about the bank accounts and drug smugglers when they set up Gabi's security. "A hunch. One I have to listen to."

Crickets filled the line for the third time. Finally, Neil gave an ultimatum. "We can do this one of two ways. You start talking now . . . or I put my very persistent wife on Gabi's doorstep until we have answers."

Hunter shook off his frustration with Neil's tenacity before he opened his mouth. "I found two offshore accounts . . ."

By the time he was finished delivering the information, Neil's silence was like talking to a rock, and Hunter became increasingly uneasy.

"Why didn't you tell me this sooner?" Neil asked.

"I wanted to deal with this myself. I've found the more people that know the details of my life, the more tabloid exposure I find myself explaining. I can deal with me, it's Gabi I'm worried about. She doesn't need the grief of her past haunting her."

"Doesn't sound like she has a choice. I'll put another man on her while I make a few calls. I'm also going to put a tracking device on her car."

"It's in the shop."

Neil's short laugh made Hunter pause.

"Why am I not surprised."

"She backed into a pole," he found himself explaining.

"Yeah, I'm sure she did. It's better this way. I'll have one of my guys following and one behind the wheel. A personal driver doesn't attract attention like a bodyguard. And the less questions the tabloids will ask."

"Good."

"Then I'll make a few phone calls. My friend in the Coast Guard might have a name to attach to Picano's."

Hunter wasn't expecting that. "A name is all I need."

Neil huffed. "You need more than a name . . . and you need to start putting some trust in those around you."

"Trust is earned."

"Agreed. One thing you can count on, when it comes to Gabi, or any of the women in our circle of friends, we will *all* step up."

"I'll keep that in mind."

"Good." Neil disconnected the call and Hunter found himself staring out the window of his office.

They'd owned the house for over three weeks but were embarking on their first night in it. The kitchen and the bedroom were the main priority, at least according to Gabi. The rest of the house could take shape over time.

With Meg safely tucked into a plane flying back home, Gabi felt some of the weight of responsibility lifted. She hated the relief that trickled in after Jordan's passing. The guilt was easier when she noticed Samantha returning to her normal self. Gabi knew it would take time, but the end was simply too difficult for everyone . . . especially Jordan.

The one thing that stuck with Gabi long after the service was over and the house was clean . . . the Harrisons' extended family, their friends, and those that Gabi now considered her friends were some of the most genuine people she'd ever met. They stuck with Samantha and Blake, took care of them and their two children . . . did everything so they didn't have to. Having grown up with only her brother and mother most of her life, Gabi was humbled by the friendships she'd managed in her short time in California.

She checked the baked ziti one last time and opened a bottle of cabernet to breathe while she waited for Hunter to come home.

The alarm system in the home told her the gate allowing cars in had been opened. She took a moment to light the candles on the kitchen counter. The kitchen and dining room tables were on order . . . the living room furniture was nothing more than several pictures on her phone that she couldn't decide between. The house had a den . . . and Gabi decided Hunter was on his own for that space. She'd never furnished a bedroom, let alone an entire house. Having a blank checkbook and tastes that ranged from island simple to elegant Italian castles, Gabi was torn.

The sound of Hunter's dress shoes against the wood floor announced his arrival.

"What is that wonderful smell?"

She blew out the match as Hunter rounded the corner of the kitchen, flowers in one hand, his jacket in the other.

Gabi leaned a hip against the counter and smiled.

Hunter stopped before he entered the kitchen. "Hi, honey . . . I'm home."

The laughter that erupted wasn't expected.

"I couldn't stop myself," he said.

She kept giggling. "I see the busses missed their mark again."

Now he laughed as he walked into the middle of the kitchen, tossed his jacket and the flowers on the counter, and captured her around the waist. This was all they'd really managed over the past few weeks . . . a kiss. Yet each one was charged and full. Each one kept her up at night.

When Hunter drew his lips away, he hummed. "Hi."

"Hi." She smoothed back a lock of hair from his forehead.

"This is a first."

"What is?"

"Walking into the front door of *my* home and finding a beautiful woman cooking."

"Our home," she corrected. "And good." She pushed away. "Maybe tomorrow I won't ask that a bus take my blackmailing husband out."

Hunter placed a mocking hand to his chest. "I'm touched."

Gabi lifted a brow. "Not yet."

His smirk dropped and something a whole lot sexier took its place.

She turned on her heel and made a show of checking the ziti in the oven.

Hunter grabbed her from behind, turned her around so fast she couldn't think, and pinned her against the counter. He robbed her of coherent thought as he tested the endurance of her molars with his tongue. Out of control, Hunter was a force. One she loved to unleash.

Something soft hit the floor and Hunter's arms were molding her body to his. The buzzer on the oven didn't break their connection. It had been too long, and they were both hungry.

She slapped the oven, cracked it open before Hunter dragged her away from her dinner.

Halfway up the stairs, he stopped trying to kiss her, leaned over, and tossed her over his shoulder.

A little breathless, and laughing more than she ever had, he tossed her on the bed and pounced.

She welcomed him into her arms, curled her legs around him, and rolled until she was straddling his hips.

His hands traveled inside her shirt and played with the edges of her bra.

Gabi tugged on his tie without releasing the knot as Hunter rid her of her blouse.

She pulled the tie from over his head and slid it over hers.

He growled. "That tie is forever branded." He used it to pull her close as he kissed her senseless.

He was hard.

And she was hungry.

Her bra found the floor, his shirt . . . until only the tie remained. "I need to be inside you, Gabi."

"Please." She reached for a box of condoms she'd bought and placed under his pillow. "Let's burn through these."

Hunter's smile filled his gray eyes, his laughter echoed in the nearly empty room. Then he was there, filling her, completing her.

Seemed every time they'd managed to make love since Dallas, her resolve to stay distant became nothing more than a memory. In Hunter's arms she was alive, loneliness left her alone, and passion took its place.

When he'd rocked her universe, twice . . . Gabi wasn't hungry at all.

———

Later, the candles were glowing along with the fire Hunter had started in the master bedroom. She wore his shirt, his tie, and he donned boxers while they enjoyed her slightly dry ziti and a lovely bottle of wine.

"A kitchen and a bedroom . . . it's all we need." Hunter shoved another forkful of pasta into his mouth.

"You could be on to something there."

He leaned forward and ran his finger along her lip before licking the sauce away.

"House parties would be easier without a mess of furniture."

"True, but where would people sit?"

"Bring your own lawn chair?"

Gabi imagined the massive living room filled with wicker and plastic. "I don't think that will work."

He took another bite. "This is so good."

"It's dry."

"It's perfect."

"It would have been perfect if we'd eaten it an hour ago."

Hunter wiggled his eyebrows.

Gabi shook her head and tried not to blush.

"We need to make a decision on the furniture," Gabi insisted.

He broke off a piece of bread before popping it into his mouth. "What's the hurry?"

"Child Protective Services."

He stopped chewing and stared.

"I've been doing some research. As much as you need to find Hayden's mother unfit, Child Protective Services is going to use that same microscope on us. A furnished and safe home is only the beginning."

Hunter leaned back, unconcerned. "Furniture doesn't determine a decent home."

"Neither does money. Statistically, the mother is often given custody even when the scale dips in the father's favor, which means we need to dip that scale deep."

"I have the deeper pockets."

"Possession is nine-tenths of the law. Hayden is in his biological mother's custody."

"A biological father has rights."

Gabi picked at her food while she talked. "Your case for full custody is stronger if she's unfit and you're a saint. That's why we needed to get married, right?"

"I'm not a saint."

Gabi stopped chewing and stared. "Thank you for the clarification that this woman doesn't need. Point being, you're too rich to leave loose unsaintly ends, and she's too self-centered to think you're going to petition for custody. There's only one factor I don't think either of us has considered."

Hunter pushed his empty plate away. "What's that?"

"Noah. He could swoop in and claim Hayden as his. Once he realizes this isn't going the way he wants it."

"I hadn't considered that."

"The man suddenly starts appearing wherever we are? He has to be on to something."

"He's pushing my buttons. Trying to look like the upstanding guy and me the unreasonable ass. Not much has changed since we were kids."

"Didn't your parents ever clue in to the truth?"

"We were lumped into the same person most of the time. By the time Noah showed his real drive, my father was clued out, my mother was gone . . . and I was determined to live life differently. I'd always been one of two."

"A lot of people would want that."

"Not when one of the two is a complete emotional opposite. You'd think identical twins would have the same personality. We don't. I had the drive to become self-made, he had the drive to let someone else do everything for him. Worse, he thinks I owe him simply because of our DNA. I never have understood that mindset."

"When do you think you'll be prepared to petition the court for custody?"

"I'm looking for a couple more nails and then we can move. Two weeks . . . maybe."

"Before Christmas?"

"Christmas?" His eyes were wide.

"Yeah, you know . . . that big holiday at the end of December?"

"I know what Christmas is . . . I just haven't thought about it."

Neither had she . . . not until earlier in the day when she noticed lights going up around the city. "What do you normally do for the holidays?"

He shrugged. "Company Christmas party . . . a few *I can't get out of* events."

"I mean on Christmas. Without family . . ."

When he didn't have a quick reply, she felt instant remorse for asking the question. "I'm sorry I asked."

Hunter shook his head. "Christmas is a holiday for close friends and family . . . both of which you know I don't have. I don't accept invitations from my associates. I keep my employees at a distance."

"What about your father? Is he so awful?"

Hunter rolled off the bed, took their plates with him. "He's a hermit. A shell of a man he once was. Ten minutes in the room with the man is about all I can take." He placed their plates on a cardboard box that hadn't yet been unpacked and proceeded to stoke the fire.

"Your father was once a successful businessman, right?"

"He was. He didn't get rich, but he managed. My mother thought he was better off than he was. Insisted on fancy schools . . . which is where I met Blake."

"And Gwen."

"Blake didn't let any of us around his sister. He was known to break the noses of her dates. Noah took an interest, and that's about the time I ducked out of their lives. Last thing I wanted was Blake mistaking him for me."

"How is it I didn't know this?"

"Noah backed off quickly. Our mother left and took most of my father's money with her. I saw an instant decline in my father's will to move forward. Noah took our dad's depression and worked it to get whatever he wanted."

"And you held up the pieces."

"I wouldn't say that. I made my own way. I'd been accepted into the colleges I wanted. I moved, learned after three semesters that I didn't need a degree to run a successful business."

"Wait . . . I saw a degree in your portfolio."

"Honorary. They hand them out like candy if you write a big enough check."

"That's crazy. So you dropped out of college and set the world on fire . . . burning bridges along the way."

"Making money, not friends, was my goal."

"Mission accomplished."

He moved back to the bed and sat. "Christmas was my sacrifice."

She fought the frown on her face. The ache in her chest for those missed holidays tightened. "I guess we'll simply have to make this year all the better."

Hunter reached out and played with a lock of her hair. "If you want to spend it with your family—"

She caught his hand. "I don't know where we will spend Christmas . . . but I don't see any reason why we can't be together."

"Unless I screw up between now and then."

"Then don't screw up."

"I'm not sure that's possible."

"Try."

Chapter Twenty-Four

Hunter sat across from Frank Adams and his squad of lawyers. Travis and Hunter's team sat beside him. The meeting was a formality. In truth, the contracts could be signed with each of them in their respective states. But they agreed face-to-face was better. Hunter hedged on the final agreement, giving Frank a larger cut and enough say in the oil sections to prevent a hostile takeover . . . which had been part of the long-term plan. So long as Frank didn't bankrupt Hunter's efforts, they could comingle.

He couldn't help but wonder if marriage had made him soft. He wouldn't have agreed to a larger cut a year ago.

"Are we ready to do this?" Frank asked.

"My t's are crossed if yours are." Hunter reached out a hand and Travis placed a pen into it.

His lawyer opened each page, told Hunter where to initial and sign before turning the document over to Frank. The signing took thirty minutes to complete before both of them stood and shook hands over the table.

"I hope you have time for a liquid lunch," Frank proposed.

Hunter agreed with a nod. "One martini. I told Gabi I'd be home for dinner."

"Has you trained already, does she?"

"You've met my wife, Frank. It's not a hardship."

Frank patted him on the back as they left the lawyers and associates in the conference room.

"I'm surprised," Frank said over his martini. "Minnie insisted you'd give a little more, and I was convinced you were stuck on the original offer."

"I was stuck on the original offer," Hunter admitted. "I even considered pulling the deal."

"What stopped you?"

He'd asked himself that question a lot. The answer was simple. "Marriage." And family . . . Hayden, a figure who had yet to make his way into his life. "I want to work smarter, Frank. This merger, if managed properly, is going to make us very wealthy men."

"You're already wealthy."

Hunter offered half a smile. "Can you ever have enough?"

Frank sucked back his drink, waved to the bartender for another. "I don't know. I'll tell you when I get there."

"We don't have to make a decision now, but I'd like to open offices here. A location dedicated solely to this project."

"You're considering relocating?" Frank asked.

"No. I'll oversee my operation from LA. I'd place a point man, one I trust, on this end. There's going to be a lot of activity in the beginning . . . probably for the next five to ten years. Flying back and forth—"

"You don't have to explain. I have a wife. Just wait until you and Gabi have a child. Complicates everything."

"I'm sure it does."

"I like the idea, Hunter. Let me know what I can do here."

"I will."

The entire living room was filled with the fresh scent of pine. Two guys hoisted the tree into the middle of the room and awaited Gabi's instruction. She only had half a day to complete her task. Christmas was still two and a half weeks away, but Mrs. Claus was busy with a house full of elves.

A crew was unloading her selections for dining room, living room, two guest bedrooms, the remainder of the master suite, and the beginnings of a nursery. People scrambled in every direction. On top of the furniture, Gabi insisted that Christmas arrive early. She'd hired a professional decorator, one Samantha had used in the past. There had to be a dozen college-aged kids working like the crew at the White House.

"Mrs. Blackwell?"

Felicia ran the crew of decorators, and called for her attention. "Is this where you want the tree?"

The twenty-foot Douglas fir was still miles from scraping the ceiling. "Mind the fireplace. I don't want to burn the place down before we have a chance to host our first party."

Felicia directed those holding the tree to move the tree closer to the window.

Gabi turned to the sound of her name. "Yes, Andrew?"

"You need to sign off on the bedroom delivery."

She followed him into the hall, while one of the many workers wiggled around her, lamp in hand. The first guest room was set, sans the final touches. Bags of delivered bedding sat in a heap in the corner. The bed was set, tables . . . the flat screen was fixed to the wall, and an attendant from the electronic department making sure it was operable.

Gabi ran her hand over the iron bed with a smile. "It's perfect."

She signed the papers shoved in front of her and the delivery crew moved to the next room.

"I'm almost done here, Mrs. Blackwell. Where is the next one going?"

Gabi pointed toward the retreating crew. "Just follow them."

The twentysomething kid winked and continued to wire the television.

Cooper caught her as she entered the dining room. Three smaller pine trees were in the corner, all in varied sizes. Two college kids were placing lights and giggling. "Neil is on the phone. He wants to speak with you."

Gabi rolled her eyes but took her security guard's phone from his hand. "Yes, Neil?"

"My last count was twenty-six breaches in security running around the house."

"I have a crew of five more arriving any minute to climb on ladders and set up the outside lights, too."

"Gabi. This isn't a joke."

"It's one day, Neil. One day with so many people running around there is no possible way I'm going to be harmed. Cooper is right here, Solomon is outside watching everyone as they come and go."

"Twenty-six to two."

The lights on the smaller trees were plugged in. "Oh, those are lovely. Thanks, girls."

"Gabi?"

"Mostly college kids, Neil. Happy for the temporary work. I'm fine."

"Mrs. Blackwell?"

Gabi swiveled toward her name. "I gotta go." She handed the phone back to Cooper and went back to the job at hand. "Andrew, can you be sure and bring out a tub of bottled water? Maybe we should have the deli send over some sandwiches."

Andrew turned away, phone in hand.

Now that the tree was in the right position, the living room furniture was being bumped through the mess of people and set in place. "More to the right."

The men shuffling the furniture didn't argue, merely moved it and sat back, waiting for her direction.

"Mrs. Blackwell?" The heavy accent of one of the deliverymen called her name.

"Yes?" She looked up at him.

"We have garland in the truck. For the doorway, maybe?"

Gabi glanced at Felicia, who offered an enthusiastic nod. "Sounds good to me."

"Lunch will be here in forty minutes."

"You're a doll, Andrew," Gabi told him.

The older man crossed his arms over his chest. "He's going to love this."

Another set of lights was going up over the fireplace. "Everyone deserves Christmas."

Two hours later Andrew flagged her down as she made beds. "His flight just left Dallas."

"We have four hours."

"I'd shoot for three. Get everyone out of here and a little time to clean up."

Gabi left the room, clapping her hands. "We only have three hours, folks. Let's get this done."

She stepped outside to check the progress on the lights and let the rest of the crew know about the deadline.

The tree deliverymen were finishing the placement of the garland. Not the best job, but it looked like Felicia was close by to nip and tuck bows and lights into the spray.

"It's nice, yes?"

"Yes." She didn't have time to debate, simply moved on. "Solomon will make sure you're taken care of."

"The security guard, señora?"

She caught Solomon talking with one of the men working on the outside lights. "Him." She pointed.

"Right, security."

"Thanks again," she said before moving to the next eruption.

In two and a half hours, Felicia and her crew were cleaning each room as they exited it. The house took on an elegant holiday appearance with silver and white blanketing the formal dining room. Silver, white, and splashes of burgundy emptied into the living room. Garlands mixed with lights laced the banister of the stairway. The tree glittered with glass bulbs, crystal ornaments, and two sets of lights . . . one clear, the other red. Garlands and bows and a five-foot Saint Nick welcomed those at the front door.

Gabi signed off the lighting crew, delighted with their work. "I can't wait for the sun to retire for the night."

"My people will call you in a few days to schedule the day to take it all down after the first."

"Perfect."

Solomon followed the lighting crew out to pick Hunter up from the airport.

Andrew met the caterer at the gate and brought in the special dinner Gabi had ordered for their private celebration.

Felicia and the remainder of her crew exited the house at exactly three hours from the time Gabi said they needed to finish.

Gabi kissed the woman's cheek. "I couldn't have done it without you."

"It was crazy in there for a while. But I think it turned out pretty spectacular."

"It jumps off the pages of a magazine."

"Enjoy your holiday, Mrs. Blackwell."

One by one, the trucks and vans left the property. The outside lights were starting to glow as the sun started to fade.

The three left standing took in the outside of the house. The shrubs twinkled, the eaves took on larger bulbs, mainly clear, but a splash of red adorned the columns, reminding Gabi of a candy cane. There was just enough color to add fun to the elegant feel of the decorations.

"Pizza and beer in the guest house," Andrew called to Cooper.

"I'll take you up on the pizza once Hunter arrives."

"Thank you, guys. I know that was nuts. But just look at this." Cooper winked. "Looks good, Mrs. B."

Diaz despised the States. Too many eyes, too many ears. Not enough guns.

Raul walked into the sparsely furnished home one block over from the Blackwells'.

"Well?"

Raul pointed both index fingers in the air and walked over to the computer. "We're all set."

The cocky attitude, Diaz could do without . . . problem was, Raul was good at what he did when he wasn't strung out. Seemed he'd been off the shit for a couple of weeks . . . or at least cutting down.

The computer fired up and audio feeds buzzed through the speakers.

Normally, Diaz wouldn't have traveled all the way to California to retrieve his money. Hit men were good for something. When he'd learned how deep Mrs. Picano's pockets had become, however, he made an adjustment in his plans.

"One video feed smack in the middle of the living room, audio everywhere else."

The computer was a grid of boxes. Raul's fingers flew over the computer, pointing, clicking, typing in a command. The video feed came to life in living color.

A tall, slender woman waltzed into the frame and walked right past. "Is that her?"

"Yep, Mrs. Blackwell."

Diaz lifted an eyebrow. He had to give credit to a dead man. Alonzo lucked out with that one before he managed to get dead.

Raul pulled up an audio feed deeper in the house. The sound of running water met their ears.

"The house is completely wired. Massive security system. She has two bodyguards and the butler lives in the guest house."

Diaz didn't think it would be easy.

"Did you clean up your loose ends?"

Raul pointed his damn index fingers at him again and winked. "Now we just have to wait."

Great . . . Diaz wasn't a patient man.

———

Hunter had his head buried in an e-mail on his open laptop when Solomon slowed the car at the gate. He looked up briefly, returned to the mail, then snapped his eyes back out the window.

The hair on his arms stood up, and an unexpected chill took the form of a tsunami over his skin. "Whoa."

Solomon watched him through the rearview mirror.

He absently closed the computer and moved it off his lap as Solomon brought the car to a stop.

In a daze, Hunter slid from the backseat and gawked.

He hardly recognized the house, lights exploded everywhere with tasteful design and elegance. "Gabi," he whispered.

The giddy excitement normally reserved for children grew as he approached the front door.

He stepped into the foyer, smiled at the Santa that greeted him. A high table that hadn't been there when he left warmed the space. The crackle of a fire and the scent of pine met the visual feast as he rounded the corner to the great room. Christmas had arrived.

He ran his hand over the back of the sofa Gabi had chosen. The closer he moved toward the tree, the better it smelled. There were even wrapped gifts under it. How had she done so much in so little time? Twisting his head around the feat of creating a home where it was only walls and empty space hours before was impossible.

"Do you like it?" Gabi's musical voice interrupted his thoughts.

Dressed in a soft white silk jumpsuit, Gabi watched him from across the room.

"You did all this?"

She tilted her head. "Me and a small army. I wanted to surprise you."

"Goal obtained." He turned to the tree again. "It's real."

"Of course."

He caught the dark orbs of her eyes and crooked his finger in her direction. "Come here."

When she was close enough to touch, he placed a hand on the side of her face. "It's the nicest thing anyone has ever done for me."

"It's just a tree."

"It's so much more. You know it . . . I know it."

She leaned into his palm and he kissed her. Gabi softened, parted her lips, and let him pull her closer.

He broke the kiss and leaned his forehead against hers. "I don't deserve you."

Gabi tugged on his hand. "C'mon. I have more to show you."

The master suite was complete. Bedside tables, a plush chaise for two by the fireplace. Potted plants filled empty space. Gabi pulled him into several rooms, all of them completely furnished. She muttered about art for the walls, suggested a trip to Italy to find the right pieces. The last stop, however, was the best. The smell of fresh paint told him more had been done to the last room than the others.

A fresh white coat of paint wrapped around the wainscoting with a light blue topping. The ceiling had fluffy clouds. A crib sat center with a dangling moon and star mobile just waiting for tiny, eager eyes. A changing table, a dresser, and a gliding chair with a large stuffed bear sat to the side.

Not only had Gabi embraced the idea of Hayden being a part of their life . . . she'd taken it to a very real level.

"Say something," she told him.

"I don't know what to say."

She came up from behind him and wrapped her arms around his waist. "Every child should reach for the sky."

He glanced up, felt emotion threatening his dry eyes. "This morning," he started. "This house was real estate. Tonight it's a home."

Chapter Twenty-Five

Meg sat at her computer and waited for the Internet video feed to go through.

Sam answered with a practiced smile. "Hello, Meg."

There was a sense of relief when Meg noticed a lack of circles under her friend's eyes. "You look good."

"We're doing all right."

They talked briefly about the kids, about some of the aftermath of Jordan's passing. News of Meg's pregnancy had spread quickly. "I'm happy for you both."

"You should see my mother-in-law . . . she's going crazy already."

Sam pulled at her mop of red hair and flicked something on her right. "So what's this about a potential client?"

It was good getting back into business and away from personal drama. "She's thirty-four, owns a big chunk of Manhattan, and wants to piss off her ex with a hot younger man."

Sam's smile grew into a full-blown laugh. They exchanged information, made notes, and a plan to help "rich in the city" find a spouse.

"This is exactly what I need right now," Sam said when they finished. "A challenge."

"I thought so, too." Meg leaned back in her chair. "Do you have another minute?"

"Sure, what's up?"

"It's about Hunter."

Sam groaned. "I feel like I dropped the ball on that one."

"I saw the notes in the file. It didn't sound like you approved him as a client at all."

"I didn't. I was wrapped up when he came to us, told Gabi to take the interview and make a final decision. I never thought she'd approve him, let alone marry the man."

That's what Meg thought. "If it's any consolation, I haven't seen Gabi this happy since I met her."

Sam looked at her through squinted eyes. "Really?"

Meg nodded. "The man has an edge, but I like him. Even Val is coming around."

"Blake said he's unpredictable and savage when it comes to getting what he wants."

"Criminal?"

"I didn't find anything to put him behind bars."

"He's too rich to leave a trace," Meg mused.

"True. He does seem to have Gabi's safety at heart. Neil has set up quite the system at their new place, two personal bodyguards."

"What?" Bodyguards? This was news.

Sam snapped her lips shut. "I thought you knew."

"Knew what? Why does Gabi need a bodyguard?"

Sam placed both hands in the air. "I hate gossip."

"Well you can't stop now." Meg sat forward, watched for any telling signs on Sam's face.

"Apparently her late husband set up two very large accounts in the name of Mrs. Gabriella Picano. One was actively being used, the other mildly dormant. I'm not sure how she found out about them, but she changed the passwords and locked out whoever was using them. According to Neil, Hunter thinks she's painted a target on her back. And before you ask, no, there hasn't been a threat."

"Why would Alonzo do that?"

"Who knows? Maybe he thought if there was big money in her name, she was a part of the smuggling . . . keep her silent if he'd survived."

"So who is behind the money going in and out?"

"No idea. Neil told us that Hunter has investigators on it."

New worry for her sister-in-law surfaced. "If it's drug money, she could be set up, end up in jail."

"Someone would have to know about it and want to hold that over her."

"Blackmail."

The two of them were lost in their own thoughts for a minute . . . then caught each other's eyes through the monitor.

"Blackmail her into let's say . . . marriage?"

"You don't think—" Sam cut her own words off. "Oh, no."

Meg hated where her thoughts went. "It makes sense. Damn it. I really want to like the man."

Sam was twisting her hair now. "But why? What was the big friggin' hurry for Hunter to marry? Why would he blackmail a stranger into marriage in the first place?"

"The baby. Which is the most unselfish thing I've heard of."

It was Sam's turn to stare. "Baby? What baby?"

Shit, the cat was out of the crib and crawling up the walls now.

Shopping . . . nothing like a little retail therapy to pass the time. Gabi walked through the department store, felt the eyes of Solomon on her back. He kept his distance but was always close by. She probably wouldn't notice if she were shopping with a friend, but Gwen was watching over her sick toddler and Judy was at work. Bugging Sam wasn't an option.

She'd always found her brother difficult to buy for, but with a baby on the way, the daddy door was open and filling her head with ideas for Christmas gifts.

Unable to stop herself, Gabi wandered into the baby department and found a tiny pair of socks and a plush rattle for her unborn niece or nephew. Her gaze traveled to a pair of denim overalls. She turned away. Clothes shopping for Hayden would have to wait. A teddy bear, however, was in order.

She shifted the bags in her hands as she exited the store in search of a tie with baby bottles or some such nonsense on it.

Gabi glanced over her shoulder, saw Solomon close by. When she turned around, she stopped short.

Dark eyes bored into her as the woman slowly approached. Sheila Watson was much more beautiful in person than in her pictures. A little shorter than Gabi, more curves, but nothing remotely close to overweight.

The other woman let her eyes draw a slow line up and down Gabi's frame. Instead of shying away, she held her ground and waited to see what the other woman was going to do.

Gabi skirted her eyes around Sheila and landed on the chubby cheeks and sleeping frame tucked into a stroller. Gabi's breath caught in her throat, and her hands ached to touch Hunter's nephew. Sheila's words snapped Gabi's attention back to the woman. "You know who I am?"

Gabi kept silent and waited.

"He promised to marry me, you know."

"Is that right?"

Sheila lifted her chin, or maybe it was her nose. "He'll use you, like he did me . . . then throw you away."

That was the original plan.

"My question is . . . are you as cold as he is?"

Gabi attempted to keep all emotion from her face and forced her eyes from returning to the baby.

Sheila's jaw tightened. "He owes me. He owes our son." The anger in Sheila's eyes dimmed quicker than a light switch. "If you have one decent bone in your body, you'll convince him to take care of his son."

A thousand different retorts died on Gabi's lips. She bit her lip. Anything she said could tip the woman off to Hunter's intentions.

Gabi noted Sheila's hand gripping the strap of her purse, the baby at her side all but forgotten as the other woman stepped toward her. Shoppers funneled around them, annoyed with their stationary presence in the middle of the mall.

Sheila's hard stare returned and she inched away from Hayden, moved closer to Gabi.

Too close.

"You look like the perfect cold bitch to his bastard."

There it was . . . the unstable part that Hunter talked about.

Gabi pivoted but didn't turn her back on the other woman. "If you'll excuse me."

The welcome voice of Solomon interrupted them. "Mrs. Blackwell?"

Sheila placed a smile on her face that hadn't been there before. "Already have a toy?"

Gabi moved to Solomon's side. "I'm ready to leave."

He placed himself between the two women and nudged her toward the door.

"We're not done," Sheila called after her.

Gabi didn't respond but felt the woman's anger as they walked away.

"Who was that?" Solomon asked as they walked into the parking lot.

"Someone who can't be trusted. If she approaches me again, please step in."

He ran his hands through his hair, looked behind them, and walked faster.

Once they were in the car, Gabi sucked in a deep breath. "Take me to Hunter's office."

"You got it, Mrs. B."

Half a mile away from the mall, Solomon said, "I should have jumped in sooner. I failed you."

"She could have been a friend. I doubt many assailants are pushing around babies. You had no way of knowing."

"It won't happen again."

Gabi tried to put the man at ease. "Don't worry about it."

Tiffany ushered Gabi into Hunter's office without an announcement. Solomon stayed behind by Tiffany's desk.

Hunter's face lit up when she walked into the office. He kept the phone to his ear but waved her over to his side. "That's right. I really don't care how you deal with it, just deal."

Hunter stood as she approached and wedged herself between his desk and his chair. His hand found her waist and squeezed.

"I don't have time right now," Hunter said to whomever he was talking to. "Something important just showed up on my desk."

Gabi felt the tension placed by Sheila drift away.

"Right . . . do it." Hunter reached around her and hung up the phone before nuzzling her neck. "If it isn't Mrs. Claus. What did I do right to have you visiting me here?"

Gabi leaned her head back, liked the feel of his lips on her neck . . . distracting as it was. "It's not for pleasure, I'm sorry to say."

He stopped kissing her neck and looked into her eyes. "What's wrong?"

Was she so transparent?

"I met Sheila."

The hand holding her waist tightened, his face darkened. "When? Where?"

"The mall, thirty minutes ago."

Hunter set her up on his desk and gripped her knees as she told him about the encounter. "Where the hell was Solomon?"

"Right there. I didn't call out to him . . . he had no way of knowing she was a threat."

"That's not an excuse."

"Yes it is. Having a bodyguard glued to my side is unnecessary and uncomfortable. She was sizing me up, not assaulting me."

"Once we have Hayden, that might change."

The memory of Hayden's tiny face, pouty lips parted in his sleep, placed a soft smile on her face. "I saw him."

Hunter paused. "Hayden?"

She nodded. "He's beautiful, Hunter. He was sleeping in the stroller. I didn't get more than a glimpse before Sheila started in on the ugly."

"It's the ugly I'm worried about," Hunter said.

Gabi agreed. "Which is why we need to be slow and methodical about this. The woman wasn't right. Pulling Hayden away if she can still manage partial custody would be tragic."

"She isn't expecting me to petition for custody. She's expecting a payoff."

"Makes me wonder what kind of crazy is going to happen when Hayden is removed as a bargaining chip."

"The kind of crazy that requires a bodyguard . . . or two . . . or three." He looked worried.

The phone on his desk buzzed.

He dropped his hand on the intercom. "Yes, Tiffany."

"Sorry to interrupt, but there's an Officer Delgado on the phone."

"Did he say what this was regarding?"

"Something about a missing person report."

Gabi shifted as Hunter brought the call to the speaker on his phone. "This is Hunter Blackwell."

"Mr. Blackwell . . . thank you for taking a minute to talk to me."

Hunter shrugged and looked at her. "I find when the police call, not talking to them isn't an option."

Delgado offered a short laugh. "True. I'm an investigator with LAPD. We had a missing persons report filed this afternoon on an electrician that was at your residence yesterday and wanted to ask you a few questions."

Gabi sat taller. "Who?" she asked.

"I'm sorry?"

"My wife coordinated the staff at the house yesterday. She's here in my office with me now and I have you on speaker."

"OK . . . good. Mrs. Blackwell?"

"This is her . . . who is missing?"

"Name is Mark Collins."

The name sounded familiar. "There were over thirty people at the house yesterday, officer . . . you'll have to forgive me."

"He wired your televisions—"

"Oh, yes! Right. Nice boy . . . he's missing?"

"He phoned in to his employer that he'd completed your job and was returning the work truck but never showed up."

"I'm not sure how I can help. He left in the rush with many others. I couldn't even tell you exactly what time."

"Anything you can tell us will help. I'd like the names of those at your house yesterday, too."

Gabi didn't know where to begin.

Hunter laid a hand on her thigh. "We will come up with a list and get back to you."

"Time is our enemy, Mr. Blackwell."

"My decorator will have a list of the kids, and the name of the tree lot . . . the men who set up the lights outside. All those numbers are at home, Officer."

"As soon as you can get them, Mrs. Blackwell . . . the better."

"Of course."

Hunter took Delgado's number and hung up.

"What do you think that's all about?" Gabi asked.

"Couldn't tell you. What do you remember about him?"

"Kid . . . twenty-three, maybe. Some of the college girls were flirting with him. Felicia kept snapping her fingers, telling them to get on with their work and hook up later." She felt a little smile. "You think that's what he did? Skipped out on work, hooked up with someone?"

"Possible. What do you want me to do?"

She waved him off, stepped around his desk, and grabbed her purse. "Nothing. I'll gather the numbers and call Officer Delgado back."

"I can be home in twenty minutes if you need me."

She paused at the door with a smile.

Andrew met her at the house, phone numbers in hand. Hunter was, above all things, efficient. Once she contacted Delgado and gave him the numbers he needed, she glanced at the other messages Andrew had taken for her for the day.

Meg called. Call her back.

Meg picked up on the second ring. "Hey, Mama," Gabi teased.

There was no hello . . . no how do you do . . . just a quick and to-the-point question. "Hunter blackmailed you, didn't he?"

Chapter Twenty-Six

Hunter clicked out of the video conference call with a huge sigh of relief. Travis had found the man embezzling his funds and was working with a team of undercover detectives to catch the man in the act. Hunter was about to give in and ask his wife for her savant help on his accounts, see if Gabi could narrow down the location of the missing funds tighter than his team had managed. Looked like now all he had to do was deliver the good news.

He was turning off his computer when Tiffany stacked yet one more unexpected interruption in his day, fifteen minutes before she was due to leave the office. "Sorry for—"

"Save it."

Tiffany stepped to a paneled wall and opened a hidden door that housed a flat-screen television. "PR called, asked what you wanted to do about this."

Hunter stood and waited for Tiffany to turn on the set and bring up the recorded feed someone on their team had captured.

The image of Gabi standing beside Sheila in what looked like a sworn enemy stance filled the top right of the screen. The reporter captioned the image with one statement. "The mistress and wife meet."

The media had been a thorn for years. Now Gabi was feeling their claws.

The reporter went on . . . "Join us at seven for the exclusive interview with the day care worker who claims to be caring for Hunter Blackwell's illegitimate son. Mr. Blackwell recently and quite unexpectedly married a Florida socialite . . ." The reporter continued to spew his tease for the evening segment.

Tiffany clicked off the set and waited.

"I need Ben Lipton on the phone. Tell PR *no comment* until I say otherwise."

Tiffany hesitated, then put her feet in motion.

By the time he was off the phone with his private lawyer, Remington had left a message on his cell and his secretary in the New York office asked for his instructions.

On his way home, he stopped by the florist.

Gabi met him at the door with a smirk. "Flowers? How cliché."

"You saw the news."

She took the red and white roses from his hands and led a path to the kitchen. "Everyone saw the news. The phone hasn't stopped ringing since I returned from your office."

He studied her movements as she found a vase and filled it with water. He searched for any uncertainty in her actions and found none.

"Flowers from a cheating husband makes you look guilty," she told him.

"And if anyone asks, the day Hayden became public knowledge I bought my wife flowers and came home early."

"It's after six."

"Early for me," he corrected himself. He shrugged out of his jacket and laid it on the back of a chair.

She picked the tiny sealed card from the floral spray and pointed it in his direction. "Good thing you're taking me out for dinner."

"I am?"

"You are. Meeting the mother of your son is exhausting," she teased as she pulled at the edge of the envelope. Gabi's teasing smile fell when she opened the check. "What's this?"

He leaned a hip against the counter. "One million for every affair, alleged or proven."

Her eyes narrowed and didn't let his go. "I should cash this just to spite you."

"A deal is a deal."

———

"How many eyes do you have on him?" Gabi lay beside Hunter, her knee draped over his, her hand on his chest drawing circles.

"You're asking about another man after that?"

She smacked his chest. "Hayden. How many eyes do you have on *him*?"

"My extended eyes are on Sheila and Noah."

Gabi leaned up on her elbow and her gaze went cold.

Before he could utter a word, she leaned her naked body over his and fumbled with the phone on the side table. She shoved the phone into his face. "All eyes on Hayden."

"Wha—"

"The entire free world was told, by the media, that you have a son. You want the free world to believe he's yours . . . would you let your son have less protection than your wife?"

He sat up in the bed, as did Gabi. The sheet pooled around her waist, leaving a picture of beauty he had to ignore. "I have private investigators on Sheila and Noah . . . not bodyguards."

Gabi placed a hand on her naked hip as she straightened her shoulders. "Why do you have bodyguards watching over me?"

"Someone out there could . . ." His words trailed off as the point she was trying to make drove home. "Shit."

He tossed the sheet from his spent frame and shoved off the bed as he dialed. His head was so bent on the taking, he'd completely disregarded the target.

"MacBain."

"I know it's late," Hunter told Neil as he made his way to his office. "I need eyes on . . ." the moment of decision was on him.

"On who?" It was late, but Neil's voice was solid.

Hunter clicked on his computer. "My son."

Silence.

"The news had the truth for once?"

Something told Hunter that eventually Neil and those who knew Gabi would know the truth. Instead of a flat-out lie, he stated what he needed. "Hayden is the innocent one here. I want eyes on him, Neil. I'm here with Gabi and can send Solomon or Connor."

Hunter gave the address he had, the name of the day care, and the two private investigators working the case so Neil's men didn't mistake them for someone else.

By the time he was off the phone, Gabi stood in the doorway, arms crossed over the black flowing robe covering her bare shoulders. "You need me," she told him.

Her words and stance were flippant.

The reality of her statement, anything but.

The difference between defense and offense is really about the placement of the players on the board. Only for Gabi, her life went from defending her position to taking what she wanted overnight.

Hunter met with his lawyers first thing in the morning and Gabi met with hers.

Lori ushered her into the office, offered tea and a smile. "Looks like we missed an angle in your contract with Blackwell," she said before Gabi could explain anything.

"Hayden wasn't expected."

Lori relaxed in her high-back chair. "Something tells me Blackwell knew all about his little bundle before he offered you a contract."

"No doubt about it. But that's not why I'm here."

"Oh?"

Gabi opened the folder she'd brought in and held it over Lori's desk. "Everything I say in here is confidential . . . right?"

From the drop of Lori's jaw, she wasn't expecting the question. "Completely."

Gabi handed her the papers. Lori glanced through the pile as Gabi spoke. "My late husband was a drug smuggler."

From the expression on Lori's face, this wasn't new information. She'd been Samantha's lawyer for some time, and if Gabi had to guess, some of the less public information was old news to the attorney.

"You already knew that."

Lori shrugged.

"What you don't know . . . what few know is . . . I killed him."

Lori snapped her eyes to Gabi's "He died in the hospital."

"I pulled the plug."

The attorney released a sigh. "Telling the doctors to take him off life support isn't the same as killing him."

"Not according to the life insurance company that paid out after Alonzo's death."

Lori flipped through the papers until she found the forms regarding the payout.

"That's a big payout."

"I cashed the check and then promptly gave the money to a multitude of drug prevention programs. If you look at the fine print in the policy, if my hand was in any way responsible for the death of my spouse, including removing him from life support without a court order, the policy was voided."

"Only you cashed the check."

"You see my problem."

Lori pulled out a legal pad and scribbled a note to herself. "Insurance fraud is a bigger deal than holding up a liquor store and shooting the clerk these days. Big companies are making examples out of anyone caught. We're going to have to proceed with caution."

Gabi hated the fear in her gut. "Had I known about the clause I would never have cashed the check."

"Do you have the money to pay it back?"

Gabi removed the check Hunter had given her the night before and handed it to Lori.

The attorney laughed. "That's a lot of zeros."

"I think Hunter is good for them."

Lori paper clipped the check to the file and closed it.

"There's a couple other things I'm dealing with that you might need to know about."

Lori held out her hand. "Another file?"

Gabi shook her head as she leaned over the desk and flipped the pad around. She wrote down the two bank names and account numbers in question. "The first is a bank in Colombia. The second in Italy. Both have my name on them. Well, Gabriella Picano." Gabi went on to explain the details she could provide. Limited that they were.

"You have no idea who dipped into them?"

"No. The one in Italy had money going in, barely anything coming out. The Colombian one had a steady stream coming and going."

"Laundering."

"Probably. When I found out about them, I changed the access numbers and they've been silent ever sense."

Lori cringed. "Do I even want to know how much is in these accounts?"

"A lot more than that personal check."

"This complicates everything. If the insurance company finds out about the foreign money—"

"It's not mine."

"They don't know that." Lori turned to the computer on her desk and started typing. "This is going to take some time."

Gabi thought presenting this information was the right direction and would leave her with a sense of accomplishment at the end of the day. She was wrong. "I can't go to jail."

"I don't *think* it will come to that."

There was safety in that. "We have to be as quiet as possible about this while we fix it."

Lori was writing a note again. "*That* I can't promise. When was the last time someone as high profile as you are was accused of fraud and it didn't make the evening news?"

"I'm not high profile."

Lori burst out laughing. "You're married to one of the richest and most influential men in the world. You're *so* high profile half the people out there will want to see you in jail out of jealousy, the other will assume you're guilty and hiding other crimes that will land you in prison eventually." Lori took her attention back to the computer and clicked a few buttons. The printer behind her desk sprang to life. "This would have been easier to fight if you weren't married to Blackwell. A widowed socialite done wrong by her dead husband is a lot more sympathetic than the wife of a billionaire."

Gabi went cold. "Do you think Hunter knew that?"

Lori raised a brow. "Did he know about the insurance policy . . . the accounts?"

Gabi didn't answer and Lori shook her head. "Hunter didn't get where he is by stupid luck."

Even if he had known . . . things had changed.

Hadn't they?

"He's not as selfish as it seems."

Lori scoffed.

"No, really," Gabi defended him. "He's with his lawyers right now working on the immediate removal of Hayden from his mother's custody."

"Taking a child from his mother. Sounds noble." The sarcasm was rich on Lori's tongue.

"The woman is crazy."

Lori tilted her head and stared. "Let me paint this picture a little more clearly. Blackwell wanted a wife to demonstrate to the court what a stable married man he was . . . and he's working hard to find fault with the child's mother to gain full custody."

"She wants money. She doesn't care about the baby."

"Is that what she told you . . . or him?"

Gabi opened her mouth. Closed it. Then muttered, "I trust him."

Lori pointed directly at her. "That's your first mistake."

"You don't know him." There was a little less defense in Gabi's tone.

"No, you're right, I don't know him. But I know his type. He's rich, arrogant, and will stop at nothing to get what he wants. Men like him bend the law, bribe the law . . . seduce it even, to reach their goals. You went into this contract cold and detached, Gabi. I suggest you find that woman and bring her back if you want to walk away a whole person. Don't let Blackwell do to you what Picano did."

"That's not possible."

"Are you sure about that?"

Gabi stared at her lawyer and knew the woman gave sound advice.

Not that Gabi wanted to hear it.

Back inside the car, Solomon reached inside the glove compartment and removed a small box. "Neil had this made," he told her. "And he wants you to wear it at all times."

She opened the lid and found a locket on a silver chain. "Why would Neil be buying me jewelry?"

Solomon laughed as he pulled out into traffic. "It's a GPS device. As much as one of us will be glued at your side, there are times, like today, where you'll be out of our sight. I meant to give it to you earlier. Sitting in the lobby reminded me that you didn't have it on."

She placed it over her head and looked at the simple design. Fiddling with the latch didn't result in opening it.

"It doesn't open."

"Oh." Overkill. From bodyguards to lockets.

"It's merely a tracking device, right? It doesn't record what I'm saying?"

Solomon offered a shake of his head. "Nope. Just GPS. It's waterproof, too. So you can shower with it."

With a shrug, Gabi tucked the locket under her shirt and focused on the passing landscape and the barrage of people surrounding them . . . people who weren't wearing tracking devices or traveling with an armed bodyguard at their side.

The morning visit to his office was met with a subpoena from Sheila requesting Hayden's child support. Seems the woman was moving forward faster than Hunter could run.

274

Hunter sat across from Ben Lipton and his team of family law attorneys.

"She has to consent to a paternity test," Ben told him.

Hunter already had one. Underpaid staff in the clinic Sheila was taking Hayden to had no problem supplying saliva for a little money.

"The test will prove I'm the father," he told them. "Your job is to use the information I give you to obtain my complete and exclusive custody."

"As I told you before, she has to be unfit to care for her son. Your stability and proof positive that Hayden is your son will only grant you partial custody. Child support will be inevitable."

"The woman wants a payout, not the title of mother."

The lawyers glanced at each other. "She will appoint a paternity testing doctor, and we'll have ours. That will buy us forty-eight hours to find something on her that's unfit."

"You have the reports from my investigators."

"An antidepressant isn't a smoking gun. And she hasn't seen a doctor for anything psychological in five years. She might not provide well for Hayden, but she does have him with adults when she's not by his side."

"Incompetent adults."

"Which makes *them* liable, *not* her," Ben told him.

The attorney on Ben's left sat forward. "She's not expecting you to take her son. She might come back fighting."

"She's only in this for the money. Dangle a check, she'll take it."

Ben crossed his arms over his chest. "How can you be so sure?"

Hunter knew the lawyers were obligated to keep his secrets. So he gave them what they needed. "Because Hayden isn't my biological son. I never slept with Sheila Watson . . . my brother did."

A collective sigh went through the room.

"And if your brother seeks custody?"

"He can try. Once Sheila proves I'm the father, and I confirm it, Noah will have nothing to support his claim. If he tries, I'm sure you men can make his case disappear."

A few nods were knocked back and forth.

Hunter stood to leave. "Call me with the doctor we're using. Gabriella and I will be here on Friday for the hearing."

"If I can push the court that quickly," Ben said.

Hunter offered a cold stare.

Ben lifted his hands. "I'll make it happen."

"That's better. Good day, counselors."

Before he left the room, he heard someone whisper, "And I thought Christmas with my family sucked."

Chapter Twenty-Seven

Gabi sat on the sofa, her legs curled up under her as the twinkling of Christmas lights added a glow to the room.

Lori's words had haunted her all day.

Was she making the same mistakes? Was she trusting the wrong man? If Hunter was capable of bribing the law, seducing it . . . was he doing the same to her? All his mutterings of not being good enough for her infused her with power in their relationship. Was it false power? Was his seduction of her an extension of getting what he wanted?

He wanted Hayden . . .

Or maybe he just wanted to stick it to his brother.

Lori's other words . . . the ones not spoken bothered her, too. What if Hayden really was Hunter's son? Perhaps the woman in the mall was fighting for the rights of her son.

Gabi hated the doubt running like a crazy person in her head.

The alarm on the gate sounded, signaling Hunter's return. She saw the lights of the car, heard the front door open and close. His footsteps hesitated when he entered the room.

"Gabi?"

She didn't answer, just picked at the fringe of the throw pillow in her lap.

He approached slowly until he was standing close enough to take in the scent of his skin. The scent that had seduced her from the first day they met.

He knelt down until he was eye level with her. "What happened?"

"I visited my lawyer today . . . you remember Lori Cumberland."

"How could I ever forget Ms. Cumberland?" he asked with a half smile.

Gabi didn't smile back. "I told her about the insurance policy, about the international accounts."

Hunter lost his smile and sat in the chair to her side. "I told you I'd take care of that."

Gabi lifted her chin. "I didn't see a need to wait."

"Now's not the time."

"That's similar to what she said." Gabi kept her eyes glued to Hunter's. "Did you know how difficult it was going to be to clear my name *after* I became your wife?"

There wasn't an ounce of emotion on his face.

Something inside her died. "Jesus." She tossed the pillow from her lap and stood.

Hunter jumped to his feet and grabbed her arm, keeping her from fleeing the room. "I didn't know you, Gabi."

"And you were willing to use the information you had to blackmail me, knowing damn well I could still end up in jail for something I didn't do."

He moved closer and she pulled from his grasp. "You won't go to jail. I'll see to it."

"How are you going to do that, Hunter?"

"We'll pay the insurance company back."

"It's not that simple. You knew that long before you showed up in the back of my limousine."

His jaw grew tight. "Yes. I knew that."

"When were you going to start working on clearing my name?"

He looked past her. "Once I gained custody of Hayden. We'll clear your name then."

She colored herself all kinds of fool. "Once you have what you're in this for."

"None of that was hidden from you," he told her.

"And nothing has changed. With everything between us . . . nothing has changed. You get Hayden and I end up in jail."

He looked at her then, anger close to the surface of his stance. "You really believe that?"

"I don't know what to believe, Hunter."

He took two swift steps and reached for the back of her head. His kiss was hard, demanding . . . just like the man. Damn her for responding even in her anger. She desperately wanted to believe in him, but she couldn't.

Not blindly.

Never again.

She pulled away and brought a hand to her lips before she turned and fled the room.

His tie hung loose around his neck, ice cooled the bourbon in his glass. The lights of the Christmas tree, the only one he'd had since he was a kid, filled the room.

Gabi had finally stopped crying.

Every tear was a knife in his side, every sob . . . and he had nothing to offer as support. He didn't trust himself to go to her, tell her she was wrong about him. When in fact, she wasn't.

When he'd first learned of the insurance fraud and the foreign account, he assumed she was guilty of more than trusting the wrong person. A beautiful, artful woman batting her lashes to get what she wanted in life. He blackmailed her before he knew her.

Even when he learned more, he still kept himself slightly detached.

Get Hayden.

Deny his brother of everything.

Then Gabi struck again, where he never expected.

The Christmas tree mocked him.

"There you are." Andrew walked in the room, took in the half-empty decanter of bourbon, and frowned. "Busy?"

"Not now, Andrew."

Andrew sat, uninvited.

"I mean it."

"Fire me."

"You're fired."

Andrew simply laughed. "When are you going to slow your personal life down and think before you act?"

Hunter didn't comment, merely studied the ice melting in his glass as Andrew went on.

"You're brilliant in business. You turn blades of grass into dollar bills; always capture the flag before the opposing team. Something tells me, however, that on your report card in school, it stated, *does not play well with others.*"

"Why are you still sitting here?"

"Because I'm the only one who will. If you don't start exercising patience, you're going to be one lonely, bitter, albeit rich, old man. Sound like someone you know?"

"I'm not my father."

"I'm thinking of a tree and an apple right about now. Funny thing about clichés, they are all true."

Hunter finished the rest of his drink and set the glass aside.

"You have a unique opportunity with a woman who has a heart the size of Texas. You're about to bring a child into your home who is going to need more than a bitter old man raising him. You have the world a snap away and you're blowing it."

Hunter fixed his eyes on the only person in his life willing to talk to him this way. "I blew it before I began."

"Then you need to do what every other red-blooded man out there does. Find some damn duct tape and fix it." Andrew took to his feet and started to leave the room.

Hunter stopped him.

"Why do you care if I fix anything?"

Andrew looked around the room. "I want the solo title of bitter old man."

Hunter smiled at that.

"And the tree is a nice touch."

He walked out of the room, leaving his wisdom behind.

———

"So Blackwell wants to be a daddy . . . how perfect." Diaz tapped the table in thought. Of all the useless information he'd obtained by listening to the Blackwell's conversations, this one would pay off.

"This is going to be easier than I thought, eh, Raul?" Diaz snapped his fingers. "I need those pictures."

"Pictures, what pictures?"

"Picano sent you pictures before he ended up dead. Blackmail-worthy pictures. I think a few were of his wife."

Raul shrugged and twisted back to the computer.

Diaz had to give the dead guy credit. He covered his tracks when it came to Gabriella. Marry her, put the money in her name, make her look as guilty as he was . . . have dirt on her . . . string her up. Had the man lived, he would have walked far enough to run until the law couldn't find him.

Damn shame he ended up with a chest full of lead.

Screws up anyone's day.

It took Raul a good hour to find and hack into the images.

Diaz flipped through the pictures, held the one with Gabriella Blackwell holding her arm out for a hit. Nothing better than an image of Blackwell's wife banging up caught on film. "Perfecto." There were others . . . but the most damning was the one of an imperfect socialite in the throes of a drug-induced high. The picture was worth a few million if Blackwell wanted to keep it from the judge deciding his eligibility to hold sole custody of his son. Diaz nodded Raul's way. "Now I need you to find the life insurance company Picano used. I need his policy number, a name of an agent . . . everything."

Raul sniffed, shot both index fingers in the air, and started typing.

Later, Diaz pulled his cigar from his lips, sucked in the smoke, and blew it out slowly. He had everything he needed, and soon he'd have Hunter Blackwell's balls in his hand. The man had a couple of important decisions in front of him.

His son . . . his wife . . . or his money.

———

Gabi didn't know which room Hunter slept in, but it wasn't hers. She woke the next morning with bloodshot eyes and a headache to kill all others. She'd managed to come to a conclusion somewhere around two in the morning.

The bed she made was her own. She'd chosen Alonzo and all his false advertising. She'd decided to marry Hunter instead of bringing her troubles to the doorstep of her family. She'd consciously and quite willingly begun a physical relationship with her temporary husband. The emotional attachment wasn't something she had expected, but somewhere between fall and winter, her heart started to crack and Hunter took hold.

He said he couldn't be trusted and didn't deserve her. He freely admitted he was using her, and yet she'd hoped that something had changed inside him as it had her.

How had Lori put it? To come out of this marriage whole, she'd have to find the cold and detached part of her that had entered into it.

Only as she showered and attempted to hide the circles under her eyes, the image in the mirror was of a broken woman, not a cold one.

She squared her shoulders and added one layer at a time. Moisturizer, something to block the circles . . . a layer of armor disguised as foundation. A blush of confidence she was going to have to fake until it felt natural. Her eyes, the best asset she had, were going to have to pop today. An uplifting swirl of liner and a thick coat of mascara were equivalent to a clown painting on a smile. The dark plum lipstick completed her cosmetic arsenal. She piled her hair on her head with a teasing strand or two lying on her neck.

Hunter liked it down . . .

She'd wear it up.

Gabi stepped into the walk-in closet and dropped her robe. Every inch of clothing had a job other than what the tailor intended. Her underclothing made her smile; even more when she knew Hunter would like them but never see them.

The sexual part of *them* was over.

The knit top hugged her breasts and slimmed over her waist before sitting low on her hips. The silk pants felt like a layer of soft skin, and the three-inch heels offered the right amount of sex appeal she desired.

The entire routine took an hour of her morning and reminded her of how strong she was. No more tears.

No more trust.

No more mistakes.

She moved into the kitchen to find Andrew sitting with a morning paper. He jumped to his feet when she walked in. "Good morning, Mrs. Blackwell."

The need to remind Andrew to call her by her first name stuck in the back of her throat. *Cold and detached.*

"Good morning, Andrew."

"I've made coffee, or would you prefer tea?"

"Coffee's fine."

He was around the counter and pulling a cup from a cupboard before she could stop him.

She accepted the cup and took a sip before muttering her thanks.

"Hunter asked me to tell you that he'd gone to the office."

She glanced at the clock on the wall. It was after nine. "Fine."

She heard footsteps and then the familiar call of her new name. "Mornin', Mrs. B."

"Good morning, Solomon."

He headed straight toward the coffeepot and hummed his approval as he gulped the brew.

"I've been perfecting my pancake skills, if you'd like some," Andrew said.

"I'm fine with this," she told him.

His smile flattened.

The sound of the buzzer of the gate interrupted the silence that followed.

Andrew answered and let in whoever rang.

Gabi sipped her coffee and contemplated her day, her life, as the men in the house regarded her in strained silence.

Andrew pulled her out of her thoughts after he opened the front door.

Gabi set her coffee aside and found the valet standing at the door, his hands behind his back.

A deliveryman, one with an armload of flowers, stood with a mocking grin. "Special delivery," he said as he thrust the bouquet into her arms.

Her nose flared, her eyes swelled with unshed emotion. "Who sent them?" As if she didn't know.

"A Mr. Blackwell."

She didn't trust too many coherent words to pass her lips. "Andrew," she lifted her free hand. "Can you—"

"I have it, Mrs. Blackwell."

Andrew dug into his pocket and tipped the man before shutting the door.

They were beautiful. Much like the ones Hunter had sent her the first time they'd met.

I can't do this again.

Gabi plucked the card from the flowers and enjoyed the fragrant blooms for the time it took to cross into the kitchen. Once there, she opened the door to the garbage receptacle, and dropped the flowers inside.

She knew, without a doubt, that every move she made would be reported to her husband.

As much as it killed her to throw away perfectly lovely flowers, it was the crossing to the fireplace and the strike of the match that gutted her.

She lit Hunter's note with a flame, watched it lick up the sides of the waxed paper before threatening to burn her skin. Then she tossed the card into the cold, dark fireplace unread. "Fool me once," she whispered to herself.

As the note evaporated into ash, so did Gabi's concern about the thoughts of others. "Solomon?"

"Ah, yes, Mrs. B?"

"I'm not a very good driver," she said in a monotone voice as she watched the rest of the note smolder and smoke.

"Yeah, I, ah . . . Neil mentioned something to that effect."

She turned away from the message that she'd never read and tried to smile.

Both men were staring at her as if she suddenly sprouted a tail.

"You're a good driver."

Solomon stood a little taller, added a half-ass smile. "I considered the NASCAR circuit before I joined the service."

A thought formed in her head.

"The Aston is back from the shop, right, Andrew?"

"It is . . ."

That solved that.

"How do you feel about offering a lesson in defensive driving?"

Solomon lifted a brow . . . blinked.

"We'll take my car."

Blink.

Blink.

"The Aston Martin?"

Gabi shrugged. "What's the worst thing that can happen?"

Chapter Twenty-Eight

He couldn't concentrate. All it took was one text sent to Hunter to blow his entire day. Andrew took a picture of the flowers he'd sent to Gabi in the trash and added the message: The card is in the fireplace, unread and smoldering.

The next message simply said, Duct Tape!!!

He needed to fix this. Admittedly, he had no idea how. All his life, money and power fixed his problems. With more money came more power and a quicker resolve. Andrew's words stuck in his head. *Slow down.* He needed to slow his personal life down or watch it spiral out of control. Flowers in the trash were a sign of an impending tornado.

He twisted his desk chair until he was staring out over the city. It was gray . . . not at all the Southern California weather he'd grown used to. It matched his mood, he supposed.

Gabi's, too, he guessed.

His goals were easily defined a few months ago, now they were mucked up with emotion and consequences. Having Gabi by his side, having his back with something as simple as decorating a nursery in support, was a priceless example of the depth of her heart. With all she'd been through, he'd think she'd be jaded and dead on the inside.

Her family and friends adored her, would think nothing of burying him if he harmed her. Even Andrew was squarely on her side of the swinging pendulum.

A conversation . . . flowers . . . these things weren't going to duct tape his relationship back together.

He wanted it back together.

He took in his colorless office and thought of the penthouse condo that held the same empty, quiet life. He wanted more.

And he wanted it with Gabi.

A plan began to form in his head.

A plan that meant slowing down his objectives and speeding up hers.

The cell phone in his suit jacket buzzed. He considered ignoring it before he pulled it from his pocket to check the caller.

Hope flared when he saw Gabi's name.

"Gabi," he whispered her name as his answer.

Silence met his ears.

He was close to begging. "Talk to me, Gabi."

He heard laughter . . . male laughter.

Hunter froze, looked at the screen again, saw Gabi's name.

"Who is this?"

"Mr. Blackwell . . . I'm your new best friend." The voice was deep, with a south of the boarder accent.

"Who is this? Where's my wife?"

"Ah, your caring wife is right where she's supposed to be . . . for now. That can change, my friend. I don't take kindly to people stealing my money. Makes my fingers itchy to take from others. You understand, no?"

"What are you talking about? Who are you?" Hunter leaned over and took his office phone off the hook.

"Ten million, Mr. Blackwell."

"Excuse me?"

The voice laughed. "Check your e-mail. Gabriella . . . beautiful woman your wife. She sent you a picture."

Hunter started clicking, found a message in his private inbox, and opened it.

His stomach twisted. Gabi, from what had to be during the darkest days of her life, looked like the shell of the woman he knew. Dark circles under her eyes, the white dress hanging on her thin shoulders . . . her arm extended with a needle hanging out.

"Who the fuck are you?"

"A man who will be ten million dollars richer very soon, eh? And so you know not to fuck with me . . . I will give you ten minutes to keep your wife alive."

Hunter gripped his desk and stood.

"Do I have your attention, Mr. Blackwell?"

"Yes," he gritted out between his teeth.

"Aston Martins have been known to blow up in those Bond films. You might encourage your driver to end his driving lesson to watch the fireworks from *outside* the car."

"What the—"

"I'll be in touch."

The line went dead.

His heart sped and the light inside him threatened to fade as he dialed his home number and yelled to the closed office door, "Tiffany?"

Andrew answered on the first ring. "Find some duct tape?"

"Put Solomon on the phone."

"He's not here."

Tiffany ran into the room.

"Where is he? Where's Gabi?" There was no mistaking the urgency in his voice.

Hunter glared at Tiffany. "Get Neil MacBain on the phone. Now!"

Tiffany fled the room as quickly as she entered.

"Driving around. Gabi wanted a driving lesson."

"In the Aston?"

"Yeah. What's going on, Hunter?"

Oh, God. "No time."

He hung up as Tiffany scurried back in. "Line two."

"Neil?"

"Talk to me."

"I just received a death threat for Gabi. I have nine minutes to get her and Solomon out of the Aston."

Fear kept Hunter's hands moving. The cell phone sat on his desk, he took a chance and redialed Gabi's number. It went to instant voice mail. He slammed his hand against the desk.

He heard Neil barking orders through the phone.

"Do you have him?"

"Not yet."

"Eight minutes, Neil."

———

It was a closed course, so why was Solomon gripping the side of the car with such intensity? Gabi let up on the gas and concentrated on avoiding the cones. She'd done rather well, when she kept the speed under thirty.

At fifty, things became a little dicey.

"You're oversteering," Solomon instructed her. "Relax your grip on the wheel and let the car balance itself out."

The car jerked in the opposite direction.

"Relax, don't let go."

"Oh . . ." Gabi took the next curve a little faster and attempted to *relax*.

The phone in her purse rang, and she glanced behind her.

"Don't even think about answering that."

She looked at him with a frown. "Well of course not."

Solomon swung his gaze out the window and gripped the door rail. "Watch it."

Several cones went down as she missed the next turn completely.

She straightened the car as Solomon's phone started to buzz. "Straighten her out and let's try again. You can't let phones and people distract you, Mrs. B., or you're going to end up getting hurt."

Gabi squared her shoulders and started again. They rounded the second turn for the umpteenth time. When Solomon's phone went off again, Gabi praised herself on ignoring the noise.

She didn't even look when Solomon answered his phone. "I'm a little busy right now," he told whoever called.

"What?"

Ease into the corner; let the wheel do the work.

Perfect. Not one cone off course.

"Oh, fuck."

Gabi wanted to look toward the passenger seat but thought Solomon was testing her resolve to avoid distractions.

She smiled and kept driving.

"Stop the car!"

The S curve was next. Gabi kept going.

"Stop the car!" This time Solomon grabbed the wheel.

Gabi hit the brake, hard.

As soon as the car rolled to a stop, Solomon hit the button of her seat belt. "Get out."

"What? What's—"

"Get out!" He reached over, opened the door, and pushed.

She couldn't move fast enough before Solomon was out of his side and dragging her from the car. He grasped her hand and ran. She had no choice but to move her feet or risk taking them both down.

"What's going on?" The words no sooner fell from her lips than noise, heat, and an unknown force pushed her off her feet.

Solomon tucked her into his side as the ground rushed to meet them. Her left arm took the brunt of her fall and pain shot through her.

She couldn't hear, but the flames coming from behind told her why.

Gabi shielded her eyes when the second explosion went off.

Solomon forced his face in front of hers, his lips were moving but all she heard was ringing.

The Aston blazed in flames.

Solomon placed a hand on her chin. His mouth moved in what she thought was a question. *Are you OK?*

She nodded even as she began to shake. *I can't hear.* She felt vibration in her throat but couldn't hear her own words.

Solomon pointed to his own ears and shook his head. He lifted his hand that still held his cell phone and said something into it before dropping it to his side.

One of the back tires blew and Gabi's entire body shook.

Her life could have ended today.

Solomon reached around her and held on.

She let him.

The closed driving course belonged to the police department, making them first on the scene. Gabi knew her hearing loss wasn't permanent when she heard the high pitch of the fire department sirens.

Dazed, she watched a dozen officials running around the otherwise empty lot. The orange cones close to the Aston melted in a surreal slow death. Someone lifted her arm and encased it in a bandage. She looked down, noticed blood for the first time. Adrenaline must have taken over, because she hadn't felt a thing after her first kiss with the ground.

Shock, she realized on a level outside her consciousness.

People around her were speaking, but she couldn't hear any of the softer sounds.

It wasn't until a paramedic attempted to get her to stand that the adrenaline left her system.

Pain shot in her arm, her knee, and her head was on fire.

The medics lifted her onto the gurney and laid her down.

Solomon shook off the men at his side and stayed close. Watching life, and feeling the pain begin a series of explosions inside her without all the sound that came with it, offered a twist in her conscious.

Movement to her left had her twisting her head.

Hunter . . . his crisp suit slightly ruffled . . . why she thought of the condition of his clothing wouldn't occur to her for hours, but his clothes stuck out. The frantic man under them, however, wasn't something she recognized.

He pushed through the police at the scene, pointed her way, and rushed to her side.

Sound was muffled, a mix of sirens and low-pitched bass that made it impossible to hear single words.

Hunter was talking to her, but she couldn't take in a single word.

He gripped her hand and turned his attention to the paramedic.

Hunter nodded a few times, then looked at her.

That's when she saw it.

Emotion . . . raw, unscripted.

Unshed tears sat behind his eyes, desperation filled his face.

He climbed into the ambulance with her, spoke to someone behind him. When the door closed and what she could hear was nothing but the screech of a noisy emergency vehicle, she closed her eyes.

Hunter squeezed her hand.

She squeezed back.

Apparently patience was something Hunter was going to learn in the course of a week. He arrived in time to sit beside Gabi on the way to the hospital, but he couldn't talk to her. The second she was unloaded from the back of the ambulance, the emergency room staff whisked her away.

Someone dragged him away to ask questions . . . most of which he couldn't answer. Allergies to medications, previous medical conditions?

He didn't know his wife at all.

It wasn't long before Neil and Gwen arrived. Shortly after, Samantha ran in. When Judy arrived, she was on the phone with Gabi's family.

Neil explained what he knew but didn't elaborate.

When one of the nurses called Hunter's name, he jumped. So did everyone else in their party.

She ushered them into a small room, where the women took a seat and the men stood. "You're wife is resting comfortably, Mr. Blackwell. The doctor medicated her and splinted her arm."

"Splinted her arm?" Samantha asked.

"A fracture. Nothing that won't heal in six weeks."

Hunter wasn't worried about her arm. "Can she hear anything yet?"

The nurse didn't commit. "Like the medics told you . . . the blast will affect her hearing for a few hours. She responds to loud sounds, but words might take a day to come back. Most of the time this is temporary. The man she was with—"

"Solomon?" Neil asked.

"Yes, his hearing is already returning."

Thank God. At least they could talk to him and learn something about what had happened. Not that Hunter needed that.

"When can I see her?" Hunter asked.

"I can take you back now. Two at a time. We're really busy and can't have the halls filled with people."

Hunter stood and Judy took the space beside him. "If I don't give Meg an update, she'll go crazy."

The nurse led the two of them through the busy halls of the ER and into a private room where Gabi lay.

Her eyes were closed, her arm hung in a sling. The monitors hooked to her buzzed with bleeps and dings. None of it made any sense. All that mattered was that the woman on the gurney was breathing

She opened her slightly glossy eyes and tried to smile.

"Oh, Gabi," Judy moved to the gurney first, placed her hand next to Gabi's. "Can you hear me?"

Gabi focused for a minute, then muttered, "Can't hear you." She lifted a white board someone in the ER had given her and pointed to it.

Judy lifted it, scribbled the question *How do you feel?* and then turned it toward Gabi.

"Like garbage," he heard Gabi say.

Gabi laid her hand over Judy's before she could write another question. "Tell Val I'm fine." The words were almost a whisper this time . . . evidence that Gabi couldn't hear her own voice.

Judy looked at Hunter. "Does she look fine to you?"

No. She looked tired, injured, drugged. "There isn't anything Val can do, even once they get here. Put the man at ease. Tell him what the nurse told us. Broken arm, temporary hearing loss."

"What if it isn't temporary?"

Hunter's nose flared. "There still isn't anything Val can do. Give the man something to hope for."

Judy nodded and wrote a note. *Calling your brother. Love you.*

Gabi tried to smile before closing her eyes.

Judy left the room and Hunter moved to the chair beside the gurney and sat while Gabi slept.

He slowed down . . . to the beats of her heart on the monitor . . . Hunter paused his life.

Every once in a while a loud noise would present itself outside the door of her room, and he felt her jolt. Proof she was hearing something even as she slept.

The phone in his pocket buzzed, rocking him out of his thoughts. He answered when he saw Remington's number. "I don't have time for you right now."

Silence.

Hunter waited, and then bit his lip.

"Get my message?" The Hispanic voice filled the call.

You're a dead man sat on his lips. Practicing the patience life was teaching him. Hunter said, "Yes."

"No cops, Mr. Blackwell."

"Questions will be asked."

"Questions you can divert. Ten million . . . cash."

"Not possible."

"Shall I blow up a day care, Mr. Blackwell?"

Hunter now knew what it felt like to have his balls in a vise. "When?"

"I'll be in touch."

Chapter Twenty-Nine

Pause . . . Pause everything.

Easier said than done.

Random car explosions had a way of attracting police attention. Fortunately, or perhaps unfortunately, Gabi wasn't able to communicate with the authorities. The amount of friends that exploded on the scene was ridiculous. And to sweeten the pot, the media had parked themselves outside the hospital doors in search of a story.

Hunter looked around the lobby of acquaintances and found one set of stoic eyes. He waved Neil over and suggested they find a quiet, private place to talk.

"The police are asking questions," Neil told him once they were alone.

"The caller said no police." Hunter ran a hand on the back side of his neck.

"Tell me exactly what he said."

Hunter rephrased the first conversation on the phone, and then told Neil about the second. "Both times, the phone calls came in from phone numbers I recognized. First was Gabi's cell, then a colleague."

"So our guy has hacking skills."

"How can he do that?"

"Same way someone sends e-mails about Viagra to you using Grandma's e-mail address. All you need is a contact list."

Hadn't Remington said that his phone had been jacked in Columbia? "Fuck."

"He had a thick Hispanic accent."

Neil scowled. "Like, say, a Colombian drug lord?"

Hunter came to the same conclusion. "Have you heard from your people in Florida?"

"I have the name Diaz. No description. From what I'm told, he has all his dirty work done for him. His drug operation is well-oiled, and if anyone on his route is caught, they end up dead. Looks like he has ties to the prison system in Colombia, as well as Florida and Texas. He's been quiet since Picano's last shipment ended up in the bottom of the ocean."

Hunter shook his head. "I deal with corporate sharks, Neil. This is out of my league."

"Lucky for you, I'm not out of mine. I'll have my cyber team work on the cell phone calls. You need to convince Gabi to accept a house arrest until we solve this. We can protect her there."

"The car was in our garage this morning."

"Didn't you tell me it was in the shop last week?"

He'd forgotten that.

Neil moved on. "I'll check on that. Most likely our guy used that opportunity."

"How did he know there was an opportunity to take?"

"He's watching you. Watching Gabi."

Hunter found himself looking around.

"What about Hayden?"

"It's easier to protect him in your home."

"I don't have custody yet. If I mention any of this to the mother, she'll run to the wrong people, painting a target on both of them."

"Is there someone you can trust to make them disappear?"

Holy hell.

He was so screwed.

They released her from the hospital the next day. Gabi's hearing returned and the only indication that she'd escaped near death was a broken arm and a scraped shin. Val had called her first thing in the morning to express his concern and offer her safe haven on his island. Thankfully, Neil and Gwen had convinced her brother and the rest of the family to stay away. She spoke to her brother in Italian, doing her best to keep any possible ears eavesdropping from understanding her words.

"I want you home, Gabi."

"And invite this on your doorstep? I don't think so. I made this bed."

She heard her brother grunt. "If you weren't married to this man, none of this would have happened."

"Or I could be dead. Please, Val, don't make this harder than it is. I will call you every day."

"And text me every night."

"Fine. Please try not to worry."

They spoke for a few minutes before Val finally relented and hung up.

A new car drove Gabi home. There was a car that followed with more security than any one woman should ever need. She couldn't imagine the secret service providing this kind of detail.

Andrew met her at the door with a hesitant smile. "So happy you're home, Mrs. Blackwell."

"Thank you, Andrew." She looked around the living room, where nothing had changed. Hunter wasn't there.

He'd left her side during her conversation with Val without a commitment of his return. Gwen had whispered in her ear, once her hearing had returned, that Hunter and Neil were working closely together. She'd also told Gabi that a mandatory house arrest was in order to keep her protected.

Seemed life had been slapping her in the face enough for Gabi to heed her friend's words.

Refusing more than a couple of Motrin for the pain in her arm, Gabi moved slower than she'd have liked. As easy as it would have been to find her bed, literally, and lie in it, she opened up her computer and ran it through several security checks. She wasn't big on social media and didn't have to worry about eyes there. But there were a few online accounts that she dropped into and changed all her passwords.

She called and canceled her cell phone service, found another carrier, and ordered a phone to be delivered with a new number. She logged into the foreign accounts, determined nothing in them had changed, and backed out. Gabi systematically went through a list of the items she needed to replace from her missing purse. Crazy how when it blew up, everything slowed down. Credit cards . . . driver's license.

When it was all done, Gabi pushed away from the desk and moved into the kitchen.

Andrew and Solomon stopped talking when she entered the room.

"This is going to get uncomfortable in one day if you don't stop doing that," she told them both.

"Sorry, Mrs. B."

She crossed to the pantry and looked inside. "I need to go to the store," she said.

"Uhm . . . Mr. B. suggested we stay here."

She knew that. "Let me rephrase. I need groceries from the market. We can order them to be delivered, ask a stranger to show up, or someone can go for me."

As it turned out, they ordered the food and Andrew went with a security guard to retrieve it.

One-handed baking wasn't ideal, but it kept her from wondering where the hell Hunter had been gone to all day.

She had questions.

Questions only he could answer.

When she pulled the last of the cookies from the oven, the guard at the gate informed her that the police were requesting a conversation with her.

Solomon was on the phone before the team of officers were let into the house.

Connor led the police into the house and stood at the door. Both men wore uniforms with every possible toy needed tucked in their belts. One kept his side to Connor while the other scanned the room as he entered. She approached the two men and told them her name.

"Thank you for speaking with us, Mrs. Blackwell. I'm Officer Delgado. We spoke on the phone last week."

"Yes, about the missing boy."

"Right."

"I hope you found him."

The policed exchanged glances. "We did. Unfortunately he was deceased."

Gabi felt her jaw drop. "Oh, no . . . what happened?"

"We're treating it as a homicide. He was found inside his burned-out work van in the desert past Lancaster."

"That's awful."

"His family is devastated."

"I can't imagine. What can I do for you? I already told you what I know."

Officer Delgado looked at Solomon, who had just entered the room, and Connor, who was at the door. His eyes traveled over Andrew before returning to Gabi. "Didn't your car blow up yesterday?"

Her face went blank.

Solomon moved to her side. "The car was in the shop last week."

Delgado took a tiny step back. "You're Mrs. Blackwell's bodyguard?"

Solomon offered a nod.

"And who are you?" the second officer asked Connor.

"Security," Connor said.

"And the man at the gate?"

Gabi stepped in. "My husband is a very wealthy man. We can't be too careful."

"I find it interesting that you have a house full of security shortly after your own life was recently spared and another was taken. I also find that dots in a line eventually connect."

"I don't know what happened to that boy, Officer."

"But you know something—"

Solomon stepped between the officer and Gabi. "This meeting is over, Officer. Connor will show you out."

"We only want to talk to you, Mrs. Blackwell. No one is accusing you of anything."

Was that what was happening? Suddenly the presence of the cops was anything but comfortable.

"Are you arresting *anyone*?" Solomon asked.

Delgado met Solomon's gaze and turned to leave. "We'll be in touch."

Gabi waited until after the officers left before turning to Solomon. "What the hell was that all about?"

"I don't know."

She glared. "That man was right. My car blowing up . . . the missing boy who was last seen in this house . . . those odds are too good to ignore. They're connected, aren't they?"

"This is the first I'm hearing of the kid, Mrs. B."

She remembered the young man's smiling face as he wired one of the televisions, envisioned him flirting with the girls. "There were a lot of people in the house that day. They could be in danger."

"We don't know that."

"We can't rule it out. Holding back information might result in someone else getting hurt . . . or worse." She twisted toward Andrew. "Where is Hunter?" It was the first time she'd asked.

"I don't know."

Well that's convenient. She lifted the phone and dialed Hunter's office.

Tiffany apologized, said he wasn't there . . . asked about her well-being.

No, Tiffany didn't know where Hunter was. He asked for her to clear his calendar for the rest of the week.

Gabi hung up and dialed his cell.

Voice mail picked up.

"I don't know where you are, and wouldn't care if the police hadn't just left our house. I need answers, Hunter. If I don't get them soon, I'm going to the police myself and telling them everything I know."

No sooner than the space of time it took to hang up the phone, it was ringing again.

"It's Neil."

Gabi glanced at the hidden camera she knew Neil and his team monitored. "Where's Hunter?"

"I can't tell you that, Gabi. Going to the police could be suicide."

"A boy is dead."

She heard him sigh. "Tell me what you know about him. What exactly was he doing at the house?"

"He wired the televisions, connected the cables . . . stuff like that. I think he helped a few of the girls with hanging some of the higher Christmas lights."

"Anything about him seem odd?"

"There was a massive crew that day. Nothing felt off." She paused. "Except the tree delivery guys. They weren't off so much as overly helpful."

"Tree delivery?" Neil cussed under his breath. "I'm sending over a team."

"You already have a team here," she said in protest.

"A different team. No more talk about going to the police, Gabi. You have to trust me on this."

"If someone else ends up dead—"

"We will find them. Put Solomon on the phone."

Frustrated, she shoved the phone into Solomon's hand and left the room.

———

Hunter pulled into his father's drive in a Jeep he'd picked up from the dealer before noon. If anyone was following him, they would have targeted the Town Car he had one of the security guards jump in the back of. It was all very cloak-and-dagger, but he didn't trust anyone.

Wearing jeans—something he did on such a rare occasion that he had to hunt for an unopened box that had been sent from the high-rise condo he recently slept in—Hunter glanced around the secluded home of his father.

Tucked into the far suburbs of the Santa Clarita Valley, his father's property wasn't gated or secure in any way.

No one cared to notice.

There was a pickup in the drive, one Hunter had bought his dad a few years back. Beside it, a tiny sports car five years past its prime.

He pulled the key out of the ignition and lifted the collar on his jacket. Hiding under sunglasses and a baseball cap, Hunter jogged up the steps to his father's home and didn't bother to knock.

Hunter knew for a fact that a maid showed up every week to clean the place. Gardeners took care of the yard, and if the maid found the cupboards bare, she ordered groceries that were delivered.

Hunter might not care to spend time with his father, but he made sure the man had the basics.

He shed his cap and sunglasses the moment he closed the door. He pushed past the familiar hall and up the few short steps of the split-level home.

Standing in front of the sliding glass door was Noah, his back to him.

"I was starting to wonder if you were coming."

Hunter looked around the room. "Where's Dad?"

Noah didn't turn from his perch, simply nodded behind him. "In the den. Probably out cold."

Hunter tossed his keys, hat, and glasses on the table. He set the briefcase he brought with him down and left it.

He paused . . . as he'd been trying to do regardless of how difficult it felt.

How had he and his brother gotten to this point? How could they be as different as they were? Wasn't there a time when they enjoyed each other? Would have blackened the eye of the other guy just for saying the wrong thing to their sibling? High school . . . it all changed in those formative years, and there was no going back.

Hunter moved to the front window of the house and looked out. When he was confident no one had parked themselves outside the drive, he moved back into the dining area where his brother stood.

"I don't have a lot of time," Hunter told him.

Noah's laugh started out slow, then grew. "You never do, brother."

"This time it's not about me."

Noah turned then. When they were younger, looking at his identical twin was routine, now he found the image of an animated version of himself eerie. "Since when?"

Pause . . . patience.

"Why are you doing this?" If Hunter was ever going to get answers, it was now.

Noah looked down Hunter's frame. "Wearing a wire, Hunter?"

Hunter shrugged off his jacket and shed his shirt with one smooth scoop. "Do I need to take off my pants?"

Noah lifted an eyebrow. "Because I could," he said. "Because you stopped taking my calls."

"I cut you off! Something *he* needed to do years ago." Hunter flung his hand behind him to indicate their father.

"You think you're so much better than everyone. But you never saw this coming, did you?"

Hunter sucked in a slow breath. "No, I didn't." He glanced at the briefcase on the kitchen table. "How much?"

Noah ran a hand down his face and over his chin as he took in the case.

"What changed your mind?"

"Does it matter? You have what you want. Name your price, Noah."

Noah placed his hand on the briefcase and Hunter slapped his over his brother's.

Their eyes caught and didn't let go. "My conditions."

Noah eased his hand away.

"You leave here, retrieve Hayden, and meet my pilot."

Noah gripped the back of a dining chair. "And where are we going?"

"Someplace safe."

A flicker of humanity passed over his brother's face. Had Hunter not been watching, he would have missed it.

"Safe?"

Hunter's next words were slower than a turtle marching across the desert sand. "Your son's life has been threatened . . . all in an effort to get to me. You take this money and your son and you both disappear. I'll contact you when it's safe to move on with your life."

"And if I don't agree?"

"Then you take this, give it to Sheila . . . split it . . . burn it for all I care, but Hayden comes with me. Today."

To say Noah was stunned would have been an understatement. His jaw dropped, his eyes were tiny specks of confusion.

"You're willing to take *my* son?"

Hunter made sure he articulated every syllable of his next words. "Hayden is already mine. I'm a week away from taking permanent custody, and neither you, nor Sheila, will see one penny." It was a bluff. But Hunter had to try.

A weak smile started on Noah's lips. "Always impatient. I don't know how you managed to get so far in business when you show everyone your cards."

Hunter slammed his hand on the table, causing everything on it to jump.

"My wife's car was blown up yesterday, Noah. She escaped with her life by less than a minute. Someone out there with bigger balls than yours is willing to take out your son because you told the world he's mine. Either you leave with him, now, or I take him and keep him safe. Make your choice and make it now! I don't have any more time to fuck with you. Fair warning, Noah. If Hayden comes with me, he's mine. You'll never see him again."

Noah turned white.

Hunter looked at his watch. "I have a car coming in five minutes." He swept the car keys across the table until Noah had to catch them or watch them fall to the floor. "I have a bodyguard and a private investigator watching your son. Both are ready to take him on my call. What's it going to be, Daddy?"

Noise from behind him had Hunter turning around. "What's it going to be, Noah?"

Sherman Blackwell stood, scruffy faced and more than a little worn around the edges as he fixed his eyes on the two of them. How much of the conversation he'd heard, Hunter couldn't say . . . but from the look in the older man's eyes, it was enough to understand the severity of the situation.

Noah grasped the briefcase and opened it. Inside were stacks of hundreds . . . it paid to have business associates who owned casinos, where cash could be removed and IOUs given.

Noah took two stacks of bills, shoved them in his pocket, and closed the case. He tapped his hands alongside it and said, "For Sheila. I'll keep her with me until I hear from you. If I leave her here, there's no telling what she'll do."

With the briefcase in one hand, the keys to the Jeep in another, Noah stood.

"Go to John Wayne Airport. I'll call my people."

"Who's Neil?"

"Doesn't matter. I'll be in touch."

Noah hesitated as he passed their father, and then disappeared behind the door.

Sherman crossed the room, opened the fridge, and pulled a beer he didn't need from the box. "What's this about a wife?"

Chapter Thirty

Hunter finally pulled into the gates as the sun was setting.

Gabi was livid.

He stepped from the back of the car and opened his arms to all the activity. "What's going on?"

With one hand on her hip, and anger in her words, she told him the only reasonable thing she could. "Chaos! Chaos I'm dealing with alone because you're too busy to bother."

"I had something to take care of."

Gabi rolled her eyes and twisted away.

Neil and company had descended on her home like locusts. The garland around the door had been stripped away; the Christmas tree in the living room nearly decimated as they searched for God only knew what.

Neil . . . Lord only knew how Gwen put up with his quiet tight ass. The man offered nothing.

While a team looked over every strand of lights, every inch of garland . . . every decoration she'd had the staff place a few days before, Neil and a few others were inside poking in every nook and cranny of the house.

Before she could make it back inside, the man of the hour met them both out the front door.

"We found bugs that don't belong to us."

Gabi stood motionless.

Hunter wasn't. "Where?"

"Inside the TVs. Audio for the guest room, the master bedroom . . . video with audio in the living room."

The hair on Gabi's arms stood up. "Someone has been listening to us? Watching us?"

Hunter was livid. "How did this happen?"

"Sophisticated equipment placed inside the televisions. The technology isn't something I've seen before. My equipment didn't pick it up. And my stuff picks up an out of place ant."

Gabi grabbed Neil's thick arm. "Do you think the deceased boy placed the bugs?"

"I think it's a high probability. Obviously not for his gain since he ended up dead."

"Can you trace the feeds?" Hunter asked.

"The transponder looks Internet enabled."

"If we turn off our Internet, it will stop reporting feeds?"

"I'd need a lab to see if it holds its own hotspot."

"So whoever is listening . . . watching . . . could be anywhere in the world?" Gabi asked.

"But close enough to rig your car and know when you come and go. No, my gut says whoever did this is physically close."

Gabi pinched her eyes with her free hand. "What a nightmare."

"We've removed the bugs and are searching for more."

"Won't the police want to know about the bugs?"

"I'll tell them," Neil said as he turned away. "Eventually."

He moved back into the house, leaving Gabi and Hunter standing in the driveway.

"You should be resting," he told her.

"And you should be here. I realize this marriage is a complete farce, but you could at least *pretend* to care." She turned, not letting him reply. Instead of moving into the master bedroom full of bugs and men stripping the room, she detoured to the guest room that was void a television and slammed the door.

She flopped on the bed, instantly regretted the force with which she landed, and propped her broken arm on a pillow.

When her eyes started to leak, she told herself it was the pain in her arm causing it.

———

Hunter crossed the threshold behind Gabi. His feet faltered when he realized the magnitude of destruction Neil and his team had managed in search of bugs.

No wonder Gabi was so upset. She'd worked so hard to create a holiday on an empty canvas to have it all look like the Grinch showed up and took it all down.

Andrew met him in the living room. "These men are like bulls in a china shop."

"I can see that."

Hunter's nose caught his attention and had him twisting around.

Laying on the kitchen island were drying racks and platters filled with cookies and sweet breads. His mouth watered and he licked his lips.

One of Neil's workers swept a cookie from the counter and waved it in the air. "I'm addicted."

"What's all that?"

Andrew crossed to the kitchen and positioned a nutcracker that had been nudged out of place. "Seems Gabi bakes when she's upset."

"With one hand?" Hunter asked.

"She managed."

He'd forgotten to eat lunch and approached the mini bakery with a growling stomach. He picked up something that looked like a tiny glazed breadstick sprinkled with sesame seeds and popped it in his mouth. "Oh, my God," he muttered with a full mouth.

Someone behind him caught Andrew's attention. "Hey, watch that."

Andrew shot past him to keep one of the mini trees in the dining room from being toppled over.

Hunter's phone buzzed. He glanced at the screen to see a text message from Remington.

Cargo is airborne.

He placed his hands on the counter and slumped his head. His brother had done the right thing . . . well, he'd taken the money, but Hunter expected nothing less.

And Hayden was safe.

A strange empty space inside him opened up. He'd gotten used to the idea of a child in his life. Even if it wasn't his son, Hunter was ready. He'd never held the child, nor had he seen him outside of a photograph, but the loss wasn't mistakable. Hayden left a strange hole.

Neil's men started to funnel out of the main living quarters of the house and into the backyard.

Andrew was righting the mess they left.

Hunter shrugged out of his jacket and joined him.

They worked together in silence.

The living and dining rooms were set. A decent dent had been made out of Gabi's cooking before Neil's men wound up their equipment and left.

Andrew called for a dinner delivery and Neil hung back.

"Have you heard from our guy?" Neil asked.

Hunter shook his head.

"You will. He won't like his eyes and ears being taken away."

"Are you sure they're all gone?"

Neil offered one affirmative nod.

"What's the next step?"

"We wait."

The weight of the day started to pull Hunter down. "Like pawns on a chessboard."

"This guy isn't used to waiting. It won't be long."

Hunter was about to ask him what he meant when Rick popped his head into the room.

"We're all set downstairs."

"Downstairs?"

Neil turned away. "Follow me."

They twisted down the steps and into the wine cellar that had yet to be stocked with anything but dust.

In the center of the room was a desk and four monitors. A man Hunter didn't recognize sat with his back to them, a set of earphones on his head. He clicked a mouse, typed something in, and then realized they were standing there.

He pulled off the earphones and pushed the rolling chair away from the desk. "We're all set," he told Neil.

Hunter peered closer. The monitors were images sent from all parts of the house. Hallways, kitchen . . . living room. He saw the Christmas tree in full living color. The backyard was a set of shapes as if through some kind of night vision lens.

One of the security guards outside walked by a camera, and the lens followed him until he was out of the frame.

"Have you two met?" Neil asked Hunter as he pointed to the other man.

The other man extended a hand. "Dennis. I've been watching on the other side."

"And now he'll be watching from here."

Hunter didn't argue.

Dennis clicked a few buttons and the full-screen monitor switched to an office space . . . his downtown LA office space. "How the hell—"

"Floral delivery with a bug. Our bug."

Hunter turned his eyes to Rick. The man was all smiles and a wink. "Comes in handy, trust me."

"Is all this necessary?"

"Consider it DEFCON four. There's one man dead. Gabi and Solomon nearly ate it yesterday, and we have yet to figure out when and where the bomb found its way under the car. Someone is willing to kill for a chunk of money," Rick told him.

"I doubt he'll come here to get it."

"From the looks of the equipment we found, this guy isn't stupid. He's going to want leverage to ensure he gets the money he wants."

"Leverage?"

"Collateral," Rick said.

Hunter shivered. "You mean Gabi?"

"Or Hayden," Rick said.

"Hayden is taken care of."

It was Neil and Rick's turn to offer looks of confusion. "He's on a plane right now with his real parents. My brother will keep his head low until I tell him otherwise."

"One less potential hostage," Dennis said from the desk.

The word hostage wasn't one Hunter wanted to hear, even if he knew that's exactly what all this was about.

He pointed to a dark corner of one of the monitors. "What's that one?"

"Reserved for your cars." Dennis clicked, brought the image of the front seat of the town car, clicked again to view the front seat of his Maserati.

Lights from a car pulled into the frame of the front gate.

Dennis turned up the volume and they witnessed the surveillance together. Hunter didn't recognize the new guard at the gate, but he spoke with the driver of the car.

Looked like their dinner had arrived.

The guard didn't open the gate, simply paid for the meal through the bars, took the food, and thanked the delivery man before he took off.

Solomon retrieved the bags, said something about bringing the man back a plate, and then walked down the drive and into the house. Back inside, Andrew took plates from the cupboard.

Should I wake Mrs. B.? Solomon asked from the monitored image.

Andrew looked past the other man before Dennis cut off the audio feed.

"I try my best to disconnect any private conversations. Can't guarantee it," Dennis said.

"Privacy will have to wait," Hunter replied.

"I will click in and record every telephone call. It takes a few seconds to amplify the opposing conversation. If our guy calls, I need you to signal me and turn off any removable noise."

"Wave and turn down the TV. Got it."

Neil went on to point out that the bathrooms and walk-in closet weren't monitored.

"Looks like you have everything covered." And it did. It also helped to know that every man in the house, sans himself and Andrew, were armed. If this were to go on for any length of time, he'd rectify that, too.

Rick took his jacket off the back of the chair. "I'll be back in the morning." He nudged Dennis's arm before pointing to the screen. "Chinese food sounds good. Hope Judy's game."

He took the stairs two at a time as he left.

Hunter walked Neil out at a slower pace.

Neil placed a hand on the top of his car as he opened the door. "My wife is going to want a report on Gabi."

Hunter blew out a breath. "You've spent more time with her today than I have."

"I noticed."

He tucked his hands into his front pockets, leaned back, and studied his shoes. "Have you ever found yourself in a self-made hell and have no way of digging out without someone getting hurt?"

Neil cracked a smile. "I've been to war."

"I'd do it all differently if I could, Neil." *So differently.*

Neil's silence made Hunter look up.

"Would you take a bullet for her?"

"Yes!" There was no hesitation.

Neil extended his hand. "Barring any unexpected activity, I'll be here tomorrow."

Hunter slipped into the room as quietly as he could.

He tried to stay away, told himself she was better off alone than by his side. He couldn't stand the thought of Gabi thinking the worst of him.

She'd been crying before she fell asleep. Her eyes were swollen and black smudges lived under her eyes.

One look at the cast and he cringed.

He removed his shoes and moved to the bed. Fully clothed, he sat carefully before settling his back against the headboard, his feet on the bed. He lifted the pillow holding her arm and carefully placed them both on his lap.

He wanted to make this right. Wanted to make *them* right.

At this rate, Gabi was destined to walk out of his life just as quickly as she'd entered it. Only she was taking something with her that was more precious than money.

He felt like a thief when she shifted in her sleep and moved closer to his side. He didn't have a shred of decency as he relaxed into her unconscious presence. It was all borrowed time, time that would have to take him through a coming storm.

"I do care, Gabi," he whispered to her sleeping frame. "Please don't walk out of my life."

She sighed in her sleep and Hunter closed his eyes.

Chapter Thirty-One

The shrill alarm of the telephone brought Hunter to full awake in a second.

Beside him, Gabi jumped, then moaned.

"Shh," he said, trying to soothe her nerves.

He caught the call on the second ring.

"What are you doing in here?" Gabi said as she pushed away from him.

He lifted a hand as he scooted up the bed and lifted the phone to his ear. "Hello?"

The voice on the line was muffled, incomprehensible.

"Hunter!" Gabi was on her feet and glaring at him.

"Duuuude."

"Who is this?" he asked the caller on the phone while he turned on the bedside light.

"This is some craaazy shit."

"Remington?" The voice was slurred and sounded like it was coming from a mouth full of cotton.

"Blackwell. Are you here?"

Gabi was stewing beside the bed.

Hunter waved her off and placed a finger over his lips.

"Are you drunk?"

Remington started to laugh and then moaned. "Hurts, man. Dudes fucked me up."

"What the hell is going on? What are you talking about?"

"Two Mexican dudes. Big fists."

Hunter's head calculated the information Remington could reveal. "Did you tell them about Hayden?"

"They knew about . . . aww. Fuckers broke my nose."

The door to the room opened and Solomon stepped inside.

"Focus, Remington. What did they know about?"

"Hayden. Knew he was gone. Not the target."

Hunter did a double take at Gabi to assure himself she was still there.

"Don't do drugs, Blackwell. This is crazy."

"Drugs? Where are you, Remington?"

The PI muttered a few incoherent sentences.

Hunter placed his hand over the receiver. "Can we trace this?"

"We're working on it," Solomon said.

" . . . goddamn truth serum. I'm good with secrets. You know that, right, dude?"

The fact that Remington kept calling him dude was evidence enough to know that he was high on something.

"Are you at home, Remington?"

"No . . . feel sick."

Hunter leaned over and tugged on his shoes. "Where are you?"

All Hunter got was another muttering to not take drugs.

Dennis ran into the room with a piece of paper and thrust it into Solomon's hands. "Neil is already on his way."

Hunter looked down at the address and froze.

Gabi came up beside him, placed a hand on his arm. "Who is it?"

"My dad."

She bit her lip and shoved him. "Go."

Genuine concern filled her gaze.

He leaned over, kissed her hard, once, then said, "Don't leave the house."

She shoved him again. "Go."

"We'll take my car," Solomon said as they left the room together.

———

Gabi heard the gate open and close and turned her attention to the stranger in her kitchen.

"I'm Dennis."

"One of Neil's men?"

"Yeah." He nodded toward the back stairs. "I gotta get back to my post."

She'd seen men coming and going downstairs the day before, but hadn't asked why.

"I'll make coffee."

"That'd be great."

She offered a smile she didn't feel and one-handedly set the pot to brew.

She wasn't sure what had just happened. From the tragic expression on Hunter's face, his dad was in danger . . . hurt . . . or worse.

Gabi filled the coffeepot with water, dumped it into the machine, and proceeded to grind the beans. The buzz of the grinder stopped and the phone rang.

She jumped.

She looked around, realized she was alone, and saw Hunter's cell number light up the caller ID. "Hunter?"

The line was full of static.

"Is this Mrs. Blackwell?" The voice was female.

Her heart started to pound. "Yes."

"Yeah, uhm . . . there's been an accident. Corner of Bellagio and Sunset. Your husband, he . . . he handed me his phone."

Gabi dropped the coffee grounds in her hand. "Is he OK?"

"He's messed up pretty bad."

She started to shake. "Did someone call the paramedics?"

"I hear sirens. I gotta move my car."

The woman hung up and Gabi tossed the phone on the counter.

The keys to the cars sat in a bowl in the foyer table. She grabbed them and turned toward the door.

Dennis ran up the back stairs. "Wait."

"No time. There's been an accident. I've got to go . . ." She was already out the front door.

Dennis ran beside her and yelled for Connor, who stood at the gate.

Gabi opened the garage door and decided the Maserati would get her there quicker.

She opened the driver's door only to have Connor push in. "I'll drive."

She looked at her broken arm and relented.

He sped out of the drive and down the street, avoiding the cars as he went.

"They crashed on Sunset," Gabi told him.

Connor kept looking out his rearview mirror.

He rolled the stop sign and kept his foot on the accelerator. Thank God he was driving, because her entire body was shaking. Solomon and Hunter had sped off so fast, an accident could have been predicted. She clenched her free hand and sent a prayer that Hunter was OK.

They didn't need this . . . not with all the chaos infused in their life.

Traffic thickened the closer they got to Sunset. Connor made a few illegal moves, had cars honking as he passed them.

Gabi held on and craned her neck to peer ahead.

Connor's cell phone rang. She was shocked to see him pull it out and click into the call. "Yeah?"

The intersection was closing in fast.

Traffic flowed.

"Oh, shit."

Connor slammed on the brakes and swung the car around.

Gabi lunged forward, felt a vibration up her arm, under her cast.

"Where are you going?"

"It's a setup."

A car slowed in front of them.

Connor twisted the wheel and sped in the opposite lane of traffic.

"A setup? So there wasn't an accident?"

"No."

She didn't know whether to be relieved or frightened.

Connor kept looking in his rearview mirror until Gabi twisted around to see what he was looking at.

"Hang on."

He punched the accelerator as a car pulled into their lane.

The car behind them kissed the back bumper, pushing them into a full spin.

When they came to a stop, Gabi looked past the exploded air-bags and up into the lights of a car glaring at her through the driver's-side door.

Connor was pinned and she was dazed.

Someone yanked her door open. "Are you OK?"

She set her hand over Connor's. "Connor?"

He mumbled.

"We need an ambulance," Gabi said.

She looked again at the man at her door. He wore a suit, as if he were on his way to work. His dark fingers were holding on to her arm. "I've got you, Gabriella."

She focused on his face again. "Do I know you?"

That's when she felt the pinch and an all too familiar rush of heat move through the beat of her heart.

Her last thought, as the stranger helped her out of the car, was *not again*.

———

They were speeding through the valley toward the 101 when Solomon answered his phone. Hunter looked up from the list of contacts in his phone to find Solomon swerving to the off-ramp.

"What the—"

"Gabi and Connor just left the house."

Hunter dropped his phone. "What?"

"She got a call, someone told her you and I were in an accident."

"No." No, no, no . . . Gabi on the road with Connor . . . alone. "Hurry."

"I am." Solomon drifted through the light, took the on-ramp too fast, bottomed out the car twice before he made speed.

What felt like forever couldn't have been more than ten minutes, and he and Solomon were closing in on the street that turned up into the neighborhood of his new home.

A fire truck blocked the road, police cars were everywhere.

Hunter pushed out of the rolling car and ran.

The closer he came to the scene, the deeper the despair in his stomach.

The Maserati was a mangled mess of metal.

The fire department was preparing to rip the roof of the car away from the frame.

When others stood to the side to watch as if this were a spectator sport, Hunter ran into the scene in search of one person.

"Hey!" Someone called his way.

Hunter kept his feet moving.

The passenger door was open, the seat was empty.

Someone grabbed him and tried to hold him back. "This is my car!" he yelled at the uniformed man trying to hold him back. "Gabi?"

He ducked down to see Connor lying across the center of the car.

"Connor?"

"We need to clear this area."

Hunter twisted away and knelt by the car. "Connor?"

The man focused. "Setup."

"Where's Gabi?"

"W-L-H-six-four-nine."

"What?" Hunter was past the point of panic.

"W-L-H-six-four-nine." He kept repeating the letters and numbers until someone finally grabbed Hunter by his stomach and pulled him away.

He struggled out of the police hold. "My wife was in the car. Where is she?"

The cop kept a safe distance and looked around. "We didn't find a woman in the car."

Hunter spun in a circle. "Someone had to see something."

Solomon ran toward him.

Hunter grabbed him in a panic. "She's gone. Aww fuck, Solomon, he has her."

"We don't know that."

Hunter pushed away and started yelling toward the horde of lookie-loos. "Who saw what happened? Someone saw something." The crowd parted around him, fearful of the crazy man yelling at strangers.

Finally one of the police officers was able to corral him long enough to tell him what they knew.

Gabi . . . or a woman with a broken arm and dark hair, had stumbled out of the car on the arm of a well-dressed Hispanic man. Goatee, dark hair, tall. Looked like she was really messed up but able to walk . . . kind of. Four-door car, maybe gray, maybe silver. Honda, Acura, maybe an older Lexus. Hard to say.

They sped off toward Sunset.

No one followed.

Connor was pulled from the car, heavily concussed with an unknown amount of internal damage. As the paramedics pushed him into the back of the ambulance, Hunter motioned Solomon toward the emergency vehicle. "You should go."

"My priority is keeping you safe."

Hunter glared. "I could only hope the man would come after me and not the people I care about."

Solomon didn't budge.

Officer Delgado and his partner showed up as the police on scene were finishing their questions. "Ready to talk to us now, Blackwell?"

Solomon and Hunter exchanged looks.

"Connor might have recorded something on the dashboard camera."

Hunter looked at the cops, knew he didn't have any choices left. "Follow us."

Her arm no longer hurt, her foggy head was full of color and muffled noise. Gabi was vaguely aware of the two men holding her up and leading her into a house. They could be taking her to a ditch on the side of the road and she wouldn't care.

She remembered this. How could she have ever forgotten?

The rush, the heat . . . then the next to nothing. How much of this would she remember? She attempted to keep her eyes open and take in what was going on around her. A nagging voice in her head told her to stay aware, keep alert.

Another part told her to just feel. The floating and the power to forget everything would only last so long. Then the pain would return.

Unlike the crash she'd experienced at the hands of Alonzo, she knew this one would be harder.

Gabi wasn't sure how she'd managed to be slumped on the floor of a nearly empty living room, but the men who took her were kneeling beside her talking. "How much did you give her?"

"We have at least an hour."

The handsome one placed a hand on her cheek and slapped it. *Where's the pain?*

"You've caused me so much trouble, Mrs. Picano. If you'd left my money alone, none of this would have had to happen."

She closed her eyes, opened them when his palm slapped her again. "Not my money," she mumbled.

"No. It's mine."

His hand hadn't left her face as he stared at her.

"You can have it. I don't, don't . . . don't want it." *Sleepy.* She closed her eyes and heard the man switch languages.

She recognized the words but didn't process them.

Sleep was a much better option.

Chapter Thirty-Two

Andrew handed Hunter the phone as he walked in the door. "It's Neil."

"Gabi's missing," he told his friend.

"I know."

Hunter lifted the receiver to his ear. "Is my father alive?" he asked Neil without saying hello.

"He's not here. Your friend is banged up. Probably be able to sleep off most of it. Sounds like a couple of men ambushed him, knocked him around, and then jacked him on something that got him talking. He directed his attackers here, they slapped him with more drugs, then left. He remembers it being light when they jumped him."

"Last night?"

"Must be."

"So the men who have my dad could be the same ones that have Gabi."

Neil was silent for a moment. "Yes. We do have Gabi on GPS, Blackwell."

"What?" For the first time in an hour, hope flared. "You have what?"

"GPS . . . inside her necklace. It must have took a hit, because it's spotty, but Dennis is working with the data coming in."

He heard the police walking into the house and Solomon talking to them.

"The police are here."

Another long pause. "Tell them what they need to know. I have a couple of friends I'm calling within the department. Time is critical right now."

Hunter hated the thought of cooperating with the criminals, but Gabi's kidnapper had made it clear he didn't want the police involved. "He said no cops."

"That was before he publically kidnapped Gabi. He changed the rules, Blackwell."

Hunter's voice broke with his next words. "He has my wife, Neil."

"He needs her for the money, needs her to assure his own freedom. He won't kill her."

Hunter squeezed is eyes shut. Hearing his deepest fears said aloud gutted him.

Dennis walked into the living room, paused, then waved Hunter toward him. "I think I have her."

"What?" Hunter lowered the phone and followed Dennis downstairs.

The police were close behind.

One of the cops whistled as they walked into the wine cellar recently converted into the command post of surveillance.

Three of the monitors were full screens, all of them frozen. Dennis sat and started clicking as he spoke.

Hunter put the phone on speaker. "You hearing all this, Neil?"

"I am."

Dennis rolled the first screen.

Hunter watched as he saw Gabi jump into the passenger seat of the Maserati and Connor peel out of the garage.

They crashed on Sunset, Gabi had said.

Dennis pointed at the screen. "Notice how Connor is constantly looking out the back window?"

"He saw someone behind him," Delgado observed.

"Probably."

It appeared that Connor had racked up a dozen moving violations as they approached Sunset.

Hunter heard the phone ring on the recording.

"This is me calling him . . . letting him know that you and Solomon were fine and the call was a setup."

Gabi was tossed around when Connor swung the car around.

Hold on, were the last words before it appeared someone hit the car from behind. An explosion of white filled the frame.

"Airbags," Dennis said.

Hunter was relieved to hear Gabi's shaken voice call Connor's name.

Connor was muttering, but Hunter couldn't make out what he said. The camera was knocked out of place, not giving them a shot of Gabi's face, but Hunter saw her attempt to reach Connor with her broken arm. He could hear her breathing heavily as she called his name.

The door to the car opened and a male face filled the frame.

Dennis froze the frame, looked behind him to the cops. "That's our guy."

"Keep rolling," Hunter said.

The man in the frame used Gabi's name. Rolled his r's in a slow, seductive way.

Do I know you?

Her captor simply smiled.

They all heard Gabi offer a gasp and then a sigh.

When he lifted her from the car, she was limp.

"What did he do to her?"

"Chloroform, drugs . . . hard to tell," Dennis said matter-of-factly.

Hunter fisted his hands.

Dennis flipped to the next screen. "Here's the GPS. I'll run this with the video and you can see where the problem is, and possibly the location of Gabi."

His eyes darted back and forth between the video of the car footage and the blip on the map. The second the car crashed, the GPS blinked out. When Gabi was lifted from the car, it blipped again in the same location for ten seconds, then it went dark. When it blipped again, it was a quarter mile down Sunset. It was dark. On the other monitor, bystanders were poking their heads into the car telling Connor an ambulance was on the way.

"I'm going to fast-forward." Dennis pushed both videos forward.

Hunter heard his own voice frantically calling for Gabi.

"Wait, can you back that up?" Delgado asked.

Dennis pushed a button, only for Hunter to hear his plea again.

"Your driver is saying something."

Dennis rewound again, turned up the sound.

W-L-H-six-four-nine.

Delgado, Solomon, and Dennis all said, "License plate."

Delgado turned to his partner. "Run it."

The other cop turned away and spoke into his radio.

"This is about thirty minutes ago." Dennis showed the blip on the GPS. It glowed steady for a few seconds, then blinked off.

"And this was ten minutes ago."

"It's in the same spot."

Dennis offered a nod.

Hunter poked a finger on the screen. "Zoom in."

"Holy crap."

"That's two blocks over," Delgado said.

Hunter stood tall and turned for the stairs.

Delgado stopped him with his arm. "Where you going, Blackwell?"

"To save my wife."

"Slow down."

Hunter pulled out of his grip and glared.

"He's right, Mr. B. We don't know what we're walking into."

"Neil?" Hunter yelled to the phone.

No reply.

Dennis lifted the receiver. "Not here."

Delgado lifted both hands. "We'll bring in SWAT, hostage negotiators . . . we do this right and no one gets hurt."

"Don't forget your father. We don't know if he's in there," Solomon said.

Delgado stepped forward. "Your father?"

Dennis shrugged. "Hostage number two."

"Damn it." Delgado lifted a finger in front of Hunter's face. "No one goes anywhere. Don't make me arrest you, Blackwell." The cop turned and walked up the stairs.

Hunter's teeth started to ache with all the grinding they were doing. "Now what?"

Dennis offered half a smile and turned back to the monitors. The third one fired up. Another set of GPS blips moved on the screen. "Gabi?"

"Nope." He pointed to the red blip. "Neil." Pointed to the green blip. "Rick . . . probably." They were closing in on the neighborhood fast.

———

It will all go away if I keep my eyes closed.

She tried, but the need to crash into the real world sucker punched her.

With the light came the pain.

With a mouth full of cotton and her body in a cold sweat, Gabi attempted to focus.

A house. Yeah, she remembered a house.

Her captors left her propped up against a wall and an empty bookshelf.

She wasn't tied up, but her limbs were difficult to move anyway. All the windows were covered with thick drapes that barely let any light in.

"You're awake."

Gabi swung her head, quickly regretted it. He was tied up, arms behind his back, legs together with duct tape. Swollen eye and split lip. He'd put up a struggle, but he wasn't a young man, and from the condition of his clothes and appearance, didn't seem fit at all.

"Who are you?" she asked.

He attempted to smile, his good eye crinkled in a familiar way. "Sherman Blackwell."

"Oh." Hunter's father.

"And who are you?"

"Gabriella Blackwell."

"Ahh, the woman turning my son around."

She disregarded his words and pulled one of her legs close to her chest, then the other. She looked beyond the entry to the room. "Are they still here?"

Sherman nodded. "Other room. Walk in every ten minutes to see if you're awake."

"What time is it?"

Sherman rolled his eyes. "Left my Rolex at home."

"How long do you think I've been here?"

"An hour . . . maybe."

Gabi ran her good hand over her chest to rub out the ache. She looked down to see a nasty bruise from what she guessed was the seat belt of the car. Her fingers fell across the pendent on her neck.

She bit her lip before lifting the GPS device and kissing it.

Heavy footfalls came from the direction of what looked to be a hall. Gabi shoved the pendent under her shirt and tried to relax against the wall.

"Awake at last, señora."

She blinked several times. "Who are you?" The familiarity of his face scared her.

He lifted his pants before kneeling at her side. "I'm offended you don't know."

"We've met?"

"Not formally. I'm surprised your husband did not introduce us."

"You're a colleague of Hunter's?"

"Not that husband . . . your poor departed one. He and I were very close."

Her ears rang, reminding her of an old saying about how when your ears ring it was a sign of someone in the future walking over your grave. "Diaz," she whispered.

"I'm flattered. Too bad I can't let you live now that you've seen my face and know my name. It's not personal, Gabriella."

Her stomach twisted.

Diaz ran a finger under her chin. "Such a shame with one so beautiful. You understand, no?"

She pulled away from his fingers and he laughed.

"Why am I alive now?"

He kept laughing. "Beautiful but a fool, eh, old man?"

"Leave her alone," Gabi heard Sherman tell Diaz.

"Chivalry . . . how sweet. Unfounded in this circumstance, but a nice gesture." Diaz reached behind him and removed a gun from the waist of his pants.

Gabi tried not to breathe as Diaz ran it along her jaw. "Here are the rules, Gabriella. Do I have your attention?"

"Yes," she muttered.

"You scream, and I shoot him. He yells, and I shoot you. Equality is important in this decade, no?"

What a sick man.

"You understand my rules so far?"

She nodded once.

"Good. When I put the phone to your ear, you say exactly what I want you to say, or I shoot him." Diaz swung the gun toward Hunter's father.

"You're going to kill us anyway," Sherman said.

Diaz tapped the gun onto Gabi's chest, his finger hovering over the trigger.

"Yes, but slowly, or quickly?" Diaz moved the gun along Gabi's arm and rested at the crook. "Or maybe I'll show mercy and let you leave this life on a cloud." He leaned close, she felt his lips on her ear. "You'd like that . . . wouldn't you?"

She whimpered.

"Once they have a taste, they always want more."

With that, Diaz shifted on the balls of his feet and stood. He grabbed Gabi's good arm and hauled her to her feet. "Time for that phone call."

The media made it outside the house before the cavalry.

The phone rang long before any hostage negotiator was en route.

Hunter picked up the land line on the first ring. "Hello?"

"I told you no police, Blackwell."

Solomon rolled his fingers in the air. "Keep him talking," he whispered.

The police in the room quieted down.

"You kidnapped my wife in broad daylight. I didn't call the police."

"Nevertheless, you're going to make all of them leave. That manservant of yours, and your driver . . . they all leave. You have five minutes before I begin removing parts of your beautiful wife one by one."

"How do I know if Gabi's alive?"

"Say hello."

There was a muffle, then Hunter heard the sweetest thing ever. "Hello."

"Gabi?"

"Tell him you're OK." Diaz instructed every word out of Gabi's mouth.

"I'm OK, Hunter."

"God, Gabi. We'll get you out of there." He gripped the phone tight enough to break it.

Diaz laughed. "Now tell him you love him."

He heard the cry in her voice. "I love you, Hunter."

His heart cracked. "I love you, too."

Only his words fell on Diaz's ears. "Five minutes, Blackwell."

The line went dead.

Hunter twisted around the room. "Everyone out!"

Chapter Thirty-Three

As the five minutes Diaz gave Hunter to clear the house ticked on, Gabi's head slowly cleared from the fog. The fear she'd heard in Hunter's voice scared her. Was there a problem tracking her? Did he know where she was? Did the security team know?

She'd been in the house for over an hour, had no idea how much time had passed before arriving. Plenty of time for the team to track her. Why had they not intervened?

A cell phone lying on the table rang and Diaz answered in Spanish.

Gabi moved her eyes to the other side of the room, doing her level best to pretend she didn't understand one word.

The one-sided conversation proved easy to follow.

The police were exiting the Blackwell home, the media was pushed down the street.

Hunter was alone.

Diaz instructed the caller to stand by.

He picked up another phone and dialed.

"Very good, Mr. Blackwell. Now . . . when I give you the signal, I want you to take the money, climb over that back fence of yours, travel though your neighbor's yard to the other street, and continue north. I will call you when you need to drop the money."

Gabi hung on the next words.

"Oh, you'll know the signal. It will make the evening news."

She started to shake, told herself it was because of the fear in her veins. Her arm under her cast started to itch.

Diaz disconnected the call and turned his attention to the other line.

In Spanish, Diaz told the person on the phone to press the button and to return to the house where he could collect his money . . . and his heroin.

Gabi scratched the back of her neck.

With a wicked grin, Diaz winked at her. "Hold your ears."

"What?"

The house shook.

Gabi found herself ducking, expecting the house to topple.

Diaz disconnected the call and mumbled, "Stupid bastard. Never put your trust in the wrong person, Gabriella." He actually laughed. "Oh, that's right, you've already done that a few times."

Another man, this one thin and jumpy, moved into the room. "I'm ready to go."

Diaz waved him off.

The thinner man ran into the living room, and Gabi heard Sherman protesting.

She started to stand only to have Diaz point his gun in her direction. "We have to give your husband something for his money."

Gabi bit her lip and scratched the itch under her skin.

From the corner of her eye she saw that Sherman's feet were cut free, his hands still bound, as he was shoved at gunpoint out of her sight.

Hunter stood in the wine cellar and waited.

When the explosion rocked the house, he and Dennis both ducked. When he looked up, Dennis was checking the monitors. The cameras around the house were secure, a glow from the south told them the explosion wasn't far away, but it wasn't on the property.

"Guess that's my signal."

Dennis reached over and zipped up the jacket over the bulletproof vest and spoke into his phone. "Eagle is leaving the nest."

"Copy."

"Stay close to the edges of the road so you can duck and cover into a yard. If the guy is smart, he'll know you're armed. When he asks, remove the one from your back and toss it."

Hunter looked at the GPS screen, noted four dots. Two were on the house where Gabi sat. The other two were closer to them.

The police radio at Dennis's side sent a command.

"Go!"

Hunter took the stairs three at a time. He picked up the heavy duffel bag and started out the back door. He tossed the bag over the brick wall dividing the properties and followed it. The neighbors weren't home, and they didn't own dogs.

He'd take his blessings one at a time.

He hopped another fence and headed north. A quarter of a mile up the road, Hunter started to wonder if this was a decoy, or a setup of some sort.

When his phone rang, he answered without stopping.

"There's a Dumpster on your left."

"I see it."

"Drop my package inside."

Hunter turned in a circle. "Where's Gabi?"

"Safe. I assure you."

"Your assurance means shit."

"Look ahead. See that van?"

A white van with what looked like a pizza delivery logo on the side sat at the end of the street. The side door opened and Hunter peered closer. "Dad?" he whispered.

"A good con always has two options, eh, Blackwell? You're a businessman, you understand. Drop the money in the Dumpster and I leave your father behind."

"What about Gabi?"

"All in due time. Gabi will help me leave in one piece. You show me good faith, and I'll live by my word."

Hunter refrained from laughing.

A man held his father and shoved him until he yelled, "Fuck these men, Hunter."

Hunter ran to the other side of the street and tossed the duffel into the bin and stepped away.

"Good man."

His father was shoved from the van before it sped away. Hunter started to run toward his father.

Around the corner, a garbage truck turned onto the street.

As Hunter fell onto his father, the van that fled exploded. Hunter ducked his head and covered his father's.

When he looked up, the van was engulfed, his father was out cold . . . and the garbage truck disappeared ten million dollars richer.

———————

Gabi focused on the syringe that sat just beyond her reach on the table. She'd seen him draw up the heroin and knew it was enough to kill whoever came in contact with the needle.

Her death blow . . . the way she'd leave this world? The gun in Diaz's hand didn't scare her as much as that syringe. He shouted orders, waited to hear they'd been followed, then shouted more. He switched from Spanish to English, none the wiser that Gabi caught every word.

Gabi flinched when the house shook a second time.

The second explosion took place while Diaz was on the phone with his accomplice. In a cold response, Diaz shook his head and placed his phone into his pocket. "These kids just keep blowing up."

"You killed them?"

"Such a nasty word. I liberated them to their next destination. Death is simply a route to the next life." He shook the gun in her direction. "It's the fear of death that keeps men in line. When you don't fear it . . . that's when you make the most of this world . . . this life."

Gabi felt herself breathing heavily.

He was crazy, calculated . . . and smart.

Right at that moment, she felt just as crazy . . . just as calculated, and much smarter.

"Time to go, Mrs. Picano."

"Don't call me that," she told him.

Diaz paused. "Giving demands."

"It's Mrs. Blackwell."

He lifted one brow and grinned.

A shadow outside the drawn blinds of the kitchen caught her attention.

Diaz turned and Gabi reached across the table and palmed the syringe. Before Diaz turned back, a third explosion went off.

The smile on Diaz's face fell as he swung toward the noise, obviously not expecting it. He let out a stream of obscenities as he grabbed her arm and pulled her to her feet.

As her captor lifted the hand holding the gun toward her, Gabi stopped fearing death. With the arm in a cast, she swung against his weapon, watched it scatter across the room as it filled with smoke.

He twisted his body so hers shielded his.

She felt her air cutting off.

As Diaz backed them toward the door to what she assumed was a garage, Gabi removed the cap of the syringe without Diaz noticing.

Struggling to stay on her feet, Gabi lifted her hand as she was dragged back and each breath became an effort.

She went for his neck, prayed she didn't miss and hit hers.

Her thumb pressed the plunger the moment she heard him curse.

Diaz took two steps back, cursed her name as his hand fell, and they both stumbled to the floor.

Two darkly clothed men wearing some kind of breathing masks over their faces burst into the house with guns bigger than any she'd ever seen outside of a movie.

They hesitated when they saw her. She turned toward Diaz.

The syringe was still in his neck, she saw blood inside. His eyes were wide open, a sick smile forever on his face.

Her eyes drifted closed.

A mask was shoved over her nose and mouth, and someone tied a string around the back of her head as sirens sounded outside the house.

"Gotta go, babe." Someone patted her head and the two men left.

Hunter heard a third explosion in the direction of Gabi's GPS. He saw smoke as his father was waking up.

"You alive?" Hunter asked in a rush.

"I gotta stop drinking," Sherman said.

Hunter released a breath of relief. "I have to find Gabi."

"Go."

Hunter didn't have to be told twice. He ran toward the third explosion with a prayer on his lips.

When he hopped the fourth block wall of the day, Hunter vowed to hire a personal trainer to make this shit easier.

As he crossed the street before the explosion, Hunter noticed two fully masked, armed men running toward a dark van. One turned his way, offered a salute, and slammed the door before peeling away.

Hunter moved faster.

He burst through the door of the house that was filled with smoke as sirens assaulted his ears. He didn't get far before he found Gabi on the floor, a man at her side.

Someone pushed in beside him and helped drag her out of the house.

Hunter's lungs filled with smoke, causing him to cough.

The Good Samaritan started back into the house. Hunter stayed behind and held Gabi's head in his lap.

The unknown helper stumbled out coughing. "Dead . . . he's . . ."

Three squad cars rolled up, lights blaring.

He felt Gabi's hand touch his arm and she smiled through the mask.

Hunter released tears he didn't think he owned and dropped his head to hers.

Gabi refused the ride to the hospital, which prompted Hunter to request a house call from his personal physician.

With a few questions about the dead man in the house, and Gabi's and Sherman's accounts of who he was, the police allowed Hunter to take her home. She was still groggy as Hunter slipped her into a hot bath.

Mindful of her cast, he washed the day out of her hair and off her skin. He moved in silence, as if treasuring every moment. He worked in silence and she let him. With the help of a giant bath towel, he dried her off and brushed out her hair. Only when the doctor arrived did he leave the room.

Gabi pointed to her aches and pains, let the doctor know that her captor had definitely drugged her. She wanted to omit her knowledge of the drug, but there wasn't any mistaking the heroin that had ran in her veins. The doctor drew a few vials of blood and requested she go to the hospital should any of the lab results return with a failing grade.

Hunter met the doctor at the door. She overheard him asking the doctor about her health. Felt some satisfaction when he said she was probably fine. If anything pained her excessively in the morning, to report to him so they could run a few tests . . . take an X-ray or two.

She was drifting off to sleep in the comfort of her bed when she heard Hunter arguing.

"We have a few more questions and then we'll leave until tomorrow."

"Hasn't she been through enough?"

"No one is arguing that, Blackwell."

"It's OK, Hunter. I just want to get this over with," Gabi said from the bed.

Officer Delgado entered the room with Hunter.

Hunter helped Gabi sit up on the bed and tucked the covers around her.

"I'm sorry we have to do this, Mrs. Blackwell."

She closed her eyes. "Let's just do it."

"Tell me what you remember."

She started from the moment the car crashed. Paused briefly to ask about Connor. Hunter said at last check he was concussed with a few broken ribs, but he'd be back to normal in a few weeks.

Gabi replayed the moment when she knew she'd been drugged.

Hunter moved to the bed beside her and held her hand as she talked. "Then I met your dad."

"He's OK. At the hospital."

Gabi nodded and continued.

She talked about the gun, the threats. How Diaz had no intention of letting her go.

She replayed seeing someone outside the window and the house filling with smoke.

"I knew the syringe held a lethal dose. He told me it did. I couldn't fight him . . . it's all I had."

Officer Delgado wrote a note and looked up. "I can't imagine anyone faulting you for his death. You managed to keep your wits, and that couldn't have been easy."

Gabi rested her head on Hunter's shoulder.

"What happened next?"

"It was foggy. I couldn't breathe. Someone was there and a mask helped clear my lungs."

"Who was there?"

She shook her head. "I never saw a face. Black mask. Then Hunter was holding me outside."

"You have no idea who placed a mask on your face?"

"I'd just escaped death, Officer . . . knew my assailant was dead. I wasn't questioning my good luck and quizzing the man offering clean air."

"It was a man?"

"Or a bulky woman. I couldn't say for sure."

Delgado blew out a breath.

The officer stood and extended a card. "If you remember anything else."

Andrew and Delgado passed in the doorway.

"I brought soup."

———

Three days later Gabi and Hunter sat beside Lori and a team of lawyers, half Hunter's, half Samantha's, and the district attorney.

Every detail on who Diaz was, why he had targeted her . . . her bank accounts, and the insurance mistake she would gladly pay in full if the courts would allow it, was spelled out.

It helped that the media had painted her the unfortunate social-ite who had married a billionaire only to find herself kidnapped and held for ransom. There were three men dead and a few more recovering in hospitals . . . and Gabi sporting enough color on her face to make a supermodel happy.

In case the outcome wasn't what they wanted, Hunter and his PR team had prepared a press conference directly following the meeting with the DA.

As it turned out, Diaz had been a vicious player in the drug community who had taken a hit when the shipment Alonzo Picano was responsible for went missing. Diaz was quickly recovering when Gabi switched the accounts. All that said, the DA said they would have to launch a full investigation, but he didn't see any criminal charges being brought against her.

As for the insurance fraud, the DA held little jurisdiction, but would offer testimony on her behalf. With the return of the money, and the DA refusing to press charges, the chances of the insurance company getting anywhere was slim.

Gabi left the DA's office on Hunter's arm, their team claiming a holiday victory.

Instead of a press conference, the family and friends who'd gathered in her support followed them home.

There Andrew and a small team of people had prepared a pre-holiday feast.

Perhaps *bought* a preholiday feast was a better word. Not that Gabi cared. The thought was what counted.

"Why are we having a party today?" Hunter asked Blake when he noticed Samantha ushering children and a few nannies into a yet-to-be-furnished downstairs den.

"Appearances are important," Blake told him. "I don't really get it, but Sam insists."

Hunter smiled and moved beside Gabi as they walked around the room. They thanked Judy and Rick for their support, and Gabi noticed Hunter's predatory gaze when she hugged Judy's brother Michael. "Thank you for coming."

"If those sharks started picking on you, they would have had to deal with me."

Gabi turned to Hunter. "Have you two met?"

"I doubt there are many left who don't know who you are."

Gabi laughed. "Sucks being a movie star."

Michael winked and turned his attention to a man who approached with a glass of wine. Gabi introduced Ryder without an explanation as to who he was or why he was there. Hunter didn't ask, and she didn't offer more.

Carter Billings moved beside Neil and shook Hunter's hand. Gabi accepted a hug from Carter and a pat on the arm from Neil. "I feel I need to thank you," she told Neil.

He shrugged. "Not sure why."

Dressed in black, armed to the teeth . . .

She leaned in and kissed his cheek. "Thank you."

Neil tipped his beer back, offered one nod, and walked away.

"Such a chick magnet, that one," Carter muttered before walking away.

Gabi sipped on wine, thankful once again that she could enjoy it. She reacquainted Hunter with Zach and Karen.

At one point Meg pushed in and pulled Karen away.

Hunter leaned in and whispered, "You have a great group of friends."

She reflected on his observation. "Two years ago, I didn't have one friend to call mine."

Hunter didn't look convinced.

A scruffy voice said her name from behind her. "Sherman!" Gabi opened her uncasted arm to the man.

"I'm so glad you could make it."

"Doctor wanted to keep me for a few more days. Told him I had better places to be."

Gabi stood back as Hunter and his father squared off.

"Glad to see you vertical, Dad."

"It's a new look."

Hunter laughed.

"Been four days without a drink. First day didn't really count since that shit cut me off without asking, but I'm claiming it anyway."

Gabi's heart tugged a little when Hunter and his father embraced.

The sound of someone tapping a glass and making it ring made her turn around.

Val stood with a glass in his hand, a smile on his face. "I'd like to propose a toast."

Meg lifted her glass of what looked like sparkling cider and leaned into her husband.

Gabi's mother was already a couple of glasses into the wine. She didn't have far to go until "nap" time.

A few more people pushed into the circle and raised their glasses.

"I know we're all here for Gabi . . . to support her. But I also know my sister," Val said. "She's genuinely shy enough to avoid that attention. So this toast isn't only for her . . . it's for everyone. For friends. The kind that stick by you . . . support you whenever and wherever you need them."

Val lifted his glass and the room filled with the clicking of glasses.

Gabi took in the faces and the glasses.

Gwen was drinking milk . . .

Karen held cider like Meg. "Hey!"

"What?" Hunter asked.

Ignoring him, she narrowed her gaze toward Gwen. "Milk? You're drinking milk?"

Gwen glanced at her glass and closed her lips.

Eliza stopped sipping her champagne before she said, "Gwen's knocked up."

Meg squealed.

Sam giggled and sipped her wine. "Don't look at me. We're good, right, Blake?"

"Diapers and middle of the night food runs . . . I'm good," Blake said.

Gwen lifted her milk in the air. "Three months along."

Rick turned to Judy. "Time to step up to the plate, don't ya think, babe?"

Judy hit her husband and Meg spit out her drink.

Judy turned red. "Plus sign this morning. I wanted to wait to tell you."

Rick, who was all smiles, stumbled back. "Wait . . . what?"

Blake smacked Rick on the back. "It's about to become an unholy hormonal mess. I say we leave now, men. Come back in nine months."

There was another round of toasts . . .

The only ones feeling the buzz at the end of the night were a few good women, and a gaggle of men.

Chapter Thirty-Four

Ever since she'd returned from her brief captivity, Hunter had been by her side, offering his support. He tucked her into bed, spent time with her until she fell asleep. But when she woke, the space beside her was cold and empty.

The kitchen held the usual suspects. Solomon sat beside Andrew sipping coffee, a stack of pancakes were piled next to the stove.

"Mornin', Mrs. B."

Andrew jumped up and fixed her a plate. He'd gotten in the habit of not asking and simply serving since her return. She wasn't about to tell the man no, and he knew it.

She took a bite to appease the man. "You added cinnamon."

"I've been online researching recipes."

Gabi took a second bite and smiled. "Where's Hunter?"

The men did that looking thing she was getting used to . . . they looked at each other, said a thousand words without uttering one.

"Andrew?"

"He's a . . . at the uhm . . ." His stuttering had the pancake in her stomach turning to stone.

"Spit it out."

"The condo. He slept at the penthouse last night."

From the way the men were staring at her, waiting for her reaction, Gabi knew it wasn't a trip to his flat to retrieve his personal belongings.

"Oh." She pushed her plate away and stood.

Gabi took her coffee, grabbed a throw from the back of the couch as she made her way outside. She opened the French doors that spilled onto a deep, covered patio. A double chaise sat on one end and looked out over the backyard. The gray skies and moist drizzle matched her mood and offered the perfect quiet to reflect on her life.

At least now she knew where Hunter was spending his nights. She thought perhaps he'd taken to a guest room, but apparently that wasn't the case. He didn't need her any longer. Noah had paid off the mother of his child and had taken Hayden to a suburb of Boston. According to Hunter, his brother was looking for work in the city. What kind of work, he didn't know. But he hadn't asked for any money. Then a registered letter arrived with Hayden's official birth certificate. Noah's name was posted in the box under "father."

When Hunter had told her the story of how he convinced his brother to leave, she'd never been more proud of the man she'd married. She didn't doubt he was ready to take Hayden as his own son, but he was doing it for all the wrong reasons.

Still, when she passed through the unused nursery, a deep part of Gabi ached.

It was starting to look like she was going to be the childless aunt. The woman who couldn't marry the right man. Too bad she didn't care for cats. A house full of them would complete the cliché.

The coffee had gone cold, and despite the prickle of her skin, Gabi huddled under the blanket and watched the drops of rain fall from the sky.

"Hey."

She glanced up from her meditative state to see Hunter standing in the doorway. He wore a turtleneck sweater and dark pants. His casual *I'm not going to the office* look. Looking at him physically hurt.

"Hey."

He moved to the end of the lounge chair and sat. In his hand was an envelope that he nervously tapped on his thigh.

"Did you sleep well?"

They'd been reduced to small talk. "Can we please skip the niceties?"

His silence had her looking up. Hunter stared at the envelope in his hand.

"What is that?"

Instead of answering, he handed it to her.

She moved quickly, refusing to dwell and linger over what-ifs. Gabi removed the thick stack of official papers and unfolded them.

One word was all she needed to see.

"You filed for a divorce."

She didn't need to see any more and dropped the papers at her side.

He reached out and touched her foot.

She flinched.

His eyes met hers as he returned his hands to his lap. "It's not what I want."

"Last time I looked, the one who filed for a divorce is the one who wants it, Hunter."

"It's not what I *want* to do, it's what I *have* to do."

She bit her lip to keep it from trembling. "Mind explaining that? I've had a crazy week and playing on words is too much for me to process right now."

He paused. "I met this beautiful, intelligent, caring woman who flat-out turned me down. My overinflated ego was mortally wounded and what did I do? I blackmailed her. I found any and every speck of dirt I could dig up and used it to get what I wanted. Completely disregarding what it would do to her." Hunter's self-degradation was a new twist, not something Gabi enjoyed seeing even if all he said was true.

"My inner selfish bastard took complete advantage of the situation and I brought you into my bed. Then I nearly got you killed, not once, not twice, but three times, Gabi. All for what? Pride? Money?" He ran out of words and lowered his head.

Her head started to bob. "You're right . . . about all of it."

"I don't deserve you."

"Except about bringing me into your bed. My eyes were wide open then. Did you seduce me? Maybe. I'd like to think I share some of the credit for that time."

"I should have stayed away."

"I like to think I made that impossible."

A ghost of a smile passed over his lips. "I'm so sorry, Gabi. Sorry for forcing this marriage, for putting your life in danger." His eyes lingered on her cast. "For bringing you so much pain. Giving you what you've wanted since we met is the only thing left for me to do."

She picked up the divorce papers a second time. "You said this isn't what you want."

"It isn't," he said.

She looked at him and asked, "What do you want?"

"I want the impossible. I want to go back and do this over. I want to meet that beautiful, intelligent, caring woman again and slowly bring her into my world until she can't see hers without me in it. I want to treasure her every day of the week, every month of the year. I want her to know that because of her, I want to be a better man . . . the kind of man that deserves her. The kind of man she wants for all her tomorrows."

Moisture gathered behind his eyes as he spoke while hers spilled over.

This time when he placed a hand on her leg, she didn't pull away. "I want to hear her tell me she loves me because she does, not because she's forced to. I want to ask her to marry me, and stand before a minister or priest . . . a rabbi for all I care, and watch her walk down the aisle and freely join her life with mine."

"Hunter . . ."

He picked up the papers and dropped them again. "I know this is a backwards way to go, but divorcing you and trying again is the only way any of this can happen. I will forever question our life if we don't do this first." He scooted closer and placed a hand alongside her face. "I love you, Gabi. I know I don't deserve you right now, but I'm going to one day . . . God willing, you'll take me up on my promise for tomorrows."

Her heart kicked hard as she removed the space between them and placed her lips on his. He melted and drew her close. She opened to the invitation of his tongue and kissed him with her whole being. He loved her . . . wanted forever. And the knowledge of his feelings fueled her passion even higher.

"Take me inside, Hunter. Make love to me."

He rested his head on hers. "One last time before I move out?"

She shook her head. "I'll agree to the divorce, because your twisted view makes jumbled sense in my head. But you're not moving out."

"But—"

"Marriage is a two-way street, Hunter. Sometimes things go your way, sometimes they go mine."

"But—"

She placed a finger over his lips. "You want me to sign those papers?"

He nodded.

"Then it's my turn to blackmail you. I'll sign if you agree to stay. We can wait on all of the other parts, but leaving me alone in this house isn't an option."

He pushed away a strand of her hair. "OK, Gabi. Whatever you want."

"And one more thing . . ."

"Yes?"

"I love you, too."

Epilogue

Six and a half months later . . .

Picking a maid of honor was the easiest decision in Gabriella's life.

Samantha patted Gabi's back as she fastened the last pearl on her dress. "You're all in."

Gabi turned to the full-length mirror and gazed at her reflection. Pearls and lace . . . crystals and silk . . . the dress belonged on royalty.

Today Gabi felt royal.

"Hunter's going to have a hell of a time getting this off."

"He deserves it. Brat moved out the last two weeks. All the stress of a divorce and a wedding and he hasn't put out once."

Sam started to laugh and didn't stop until her eyes started to well up.

A knock on the door preceded a parade of maternity wear. Gwen and Karen were on borrowed time. The Harrison pack flew in with a private physician and a nurse. There was no telling if either of them would make it through the ceremony without going into labor. Meg was just as big, but a week away from her due date. Judy held last place with a month and a half to go. Being closer to Sam than Eliza, Sam was the easy choice of attendant to officially witness her vows to Hunter.

Gabi's mother pushed into the room, patting bellies as she went. She paused when she saw Gabi in front of the mirror. "You're the most beautiful bride," she said in Italian. "Your father would be so proud."

Gabi kissed her mother's cheeks. "Thanks, Mama."

"Let's not wait long. That husband of yours . . ." Simona stopped herself with a shake of her head. "That fiancé of yours is already pacing."

Gabi listened to her mother leave the room muttering about crazy daughters, divorces, and weddings.

"OK, ladies . . . do we have everything?" Sam asked.

Karen raised her hand, presented a tiny box. "Something old."

Gabi let out a long sigh. "Oh, you didn't have to."

"I didn't. It was your mom. She said she wore it when she married your father and wanted your marriage to be as happy as hers."

The box held a delicate comb to place in her hair. Sam kicked off her four-inch heels, stepped on top of a chair, and attached the clip.

Eliza handed the next box. "Something new . . . and before you ask, I didn't. It's from Hunter. He insisted, and everyone here is too damn tired to shop."

That had the women laughing and holding their bellies. The diamond tennis bracelet captured her breath.

"Well played, Hunter," she heard Meg say under her breath.

Judy handed the next gift. "Something borrowed. They're from me. I wore them on my second wedding day to Rick." The pearl drop earrings were perfect.

"This is why you said no jewelry with the dress," Gabi said to Sam.

"I'm sneaky that way."

"Something blue," Meg said. "For the record, I wanted to give you an early pregnancy test . . . blue for yes, pink for no . . . but I was vetoed."

"I'm not pregnant," Gabi said with a laugh.

"The day is young," Eliza pointed out.

The blue garter was perfect. Sam did the ceremonial placement while Gwen approached last.

"I always give the sixpence for the shoe."

A what?

Gwen dismissed her pending question with a look. "It's a British thing, just go with it."

Gabi placed the tiny coin in the bottom of her shoe with a giggle.

Music started to play outside and the women waddled toward the door.

Sam handed Gabi her bouquet and pulled a strand of hair from her perfectly messy bun. The kind of hairstyle Hunter couldn't resist.

Gabi looked through the open door to find her brother staring with an open mouth.

"I'll see you out there." Sam kissed her cheeks and left the two of them alone.

"My God, *tesoro* . . . Hunter is a lucky man."

She took her brother's hands in hers as he kissed her cheek. "This is what you want, Gabi? You're not married . . . you can walk away now and—"

She placed a finger over her brother's lips before resting her hand on his shoulder. "My life isn't complete without him. I want your blessing, Val. Completely."

"You have it. Papa would be proud."

Gabi glanced at the ceiling. "I like to think he's here."

Val kissed her fingers before offering his arm.

The island courtyard had been fashioned for a wedding. A string quartet started the march, and everyone stood and turned her way.

Gabi matched Hunter's stare, felt his excitement as much as her own as she approached. Dangerously handsome, Gabriella was self-ishly claiming him a second time.

Val placed her hand in Hunter's before taking his seat.

"You're stunning," he said once she was by his side.

"You say that to all the women you're about to marry."

He kissed her hand. "You sure this is what you want?"

She felt the eyes of everyone watching them . . . listening to their intimate conversation. "Well, since you refuse to step in front of a bus, and I'm not going to let any other woman have you, this looks like the best option."

They were both holding back laughter as the priest cleared his throat.

Blake tapped Hunter on the shoulder.

Hunter lifted a hand in the air. "One more thing."

He leaned in. "I love you," he whispered right before he kissed her.

They turned toward the priest.

"Ready now?" he asked.

They nodded together.

"Dearly beloved . . ."

Acknowledgments

The entire Weekday Bride Series has been a journey from page one of Sam and Blake's story in *Wife by Wednesday*. From rejection to the *New York Times*, *Wife by Wednesday* and all its amazing readers made me the luckiest romance writer in the world. For every person who helped me to this point . . . thank you!

For bloggers, such as Sara from Harlequin Junkies, to my street team filled with dedicated fans and readers who pimp better than any Sunset Strip "manager" out there . . . I can't thank you all enough.

I have to thank Crystal Posey, my personal assistant who keeps me sane in insane times. Not to mention your cover art ROCKS!

For Angel/Sandra – My critique partner. I say it in every acknowledgment, I mean it in every breath I take, thank you! You call me out when I'm being lazy in my writing, you make me want to please you . . . make me want to be a better writer.

Jane Dystel and everyone at Dystel and Goderich Literary Management. You are the cornerstone of agents. You set the bar, Jane. Your father must have been extremely proud to have you as his daughter. For me, I say your name with pride. Thank you for being a part of my world . . . in literature and in life.

For my Montlake team . . . time to shout out names. Kelli, my editor, who simply gets me. Susan, who makes the extra effort and works with whatever I throw at her . . . for Jessica who never misses a beat, even with those crazy-ass things on her desk . . . and Thom . . . with your long hair and magnetic smile . . . and your ability to set into action the tools I need to reach readers. For JoVon and Hai Yen and even Jeff Belle of Amazon Publishing who believed in me throughout this series. Thank you.

Now let me get back to Tiffany.

I dedicated this book to you for a couple of reasons. Yes, I lost the bet and had to use your name as a character . . . Tiffany Stone wasn't a name pulled out of a hat. Funny that I didn't know you had wicked typing skills until after I sent you that passage about my character . . .

Dedicating this book to you is karma at its best. I would never have met you had this series not taken off. And while I've only really gotten to know you well in the past couple of years . . . it reminds me of the last heroine in the Weekday Brides. Gabi might not have known these characters a few years ago, but they become significant now. As you have to me. Thank you for your friendship. It means more than you know.

Now . . . let's talk about some Holiday Brides . . . shall we?

Thank you readers . . . I'll be seeing you again . . .

Catherine

About the Author

Photo © 2012 Lindsey Meyer

New York Times bestselling author Catherine Bybee was raised in Washington State, but after graduating high school, she moved to Southern California in hopes of becoming a movie star. After growing bored with waiting tables, she returned to school and became a registered nurse, spending most of her career in urban emergency rooms. She now writes full-time and has penned the novels *Wife by Wednesday, Married by Monday, Fiancé by Friday, Single by Saturday, Taken by Tuesday*, and *Seduced by Sunday* in her Weekday Brides series and *Not Quite Dating, Not Quite Mine, Not Quite Enough*, and *Not Quite Forever* in her Not Quite series. Bybee lives with her family in Southern California.